Otherworldly
MAINE

EDITED BY NOREEN DOYLE

Cover painting: *Night into Day* (detail), © Greg Mort, watercolor, 2004
Used by permission of the artist.

ISBN 978-0-89272-746-9

Printed and bound at Versa Press, East Peoria, Illinois

5   4   3   2   1

Down East
BOOKS·MAGAZINE·ONLINE
www.downeast.com
Distributed to the trade by National Book Network

Library of Congress Cataloging in Publication Data:
Otherworldly Maine / edited by Noreen Doyle.
    p. cm.
  ISBN-13: 978-0-89272-746-9 (trade pbk. : alk. paper)
  1. American prose literature--Maine. 2. Science fiction, American. 3. Maine--
Social life and customs--Fiction. I. Doyle, Noreen.
  PS548.M2O84 2008
  810.9'9741--dc22
                              2008004693

For my mother, Adrienne Adams Doyle,
without whom I would never have passed
through that mysterious door into Maine.

CONTENTS

INTRODUCTION

I   Musings on Maine and the Roots
of Modern Science Fiction and Fantasy

by Noreen Doyle

"Every boy has his first book; I mean to say, one book among all
others which in early youth first fascinates his imagination, and
at once excites and satisfies the desires of his mind. To me this
first book was the 'Sketch-Book' of Washington Irving . . .
Whenever I open the pages of the 'Sketch-Book,' I open also
that mysterious door which leads back into the haunted chambers of youth."

—Henry Wadsworth Longfellow, 1859

Washington Irving was a New York writer, but what Longfellow glimpsed through that mysterious door of Irving's
prose was the haunted chambers of a youth Longfellow had
spent in Maine.

Of course, no Mainer looks only back toward the past. As much as we
cherish our heritage and traditions, our state motto is, after all, *Dirigo* ("I
Lead"). Take the case of Frank Andrew Munsey (1854–1925). Born in
Mercer, he became a frustrated telegraph office manager in Augusta who
wanted "the future . . . and with it the big world." After considering rail-
roads, steel, and banking, Munsey forged his future in publishing.

He emigrated from Augusta to New York City in 1882 with his editorial ideas in tow. Persevering through a series of financial crises, Munsey
founded a weekly paper that evolved into a monthly called *The Argosy*.
Starting in 1896, he printed it in magazine format on inexpensive wood-
pulp paper: through Yankee frugality, Munsey invented the pulp magazine.

Periodicals had been publishing science fiction, fantasy, and horror since long before Munsey arrived on the scene, but the real flowering of genre short fiction occurred within the pulps of the twentieth century. Although not "science fiction magazines" as such, *The Argosy* and Munsey's other periodicals did present readers with all manner of speculative fiction. Perhaps most famously, Edgar Rice Burroughs's Tarzan was born in Munsey's *All-Story*. Rival publications followed Munsey's lead into the pulp fiction market. Names of magazines and authors still well-known today debuted in the ensuing decades: *Weird Tales, Amazing Stories, Astounding, The Magazine of Fantasy and Science Fiction*; Ray Bradbury, Arthur C. Clark, Robert Heinlein, Philip K. Dick, and others. Science fiction's Golden Age and its giants emerged from the foundation of Munsey's economizing innovation.

These authors owed a sort of second-hand debt to yet another Mainer, novelist and critic John Neal (1793–1876). In 1829, Neal praised a book entitled *Al Aaraaf, Tamerlane and Minor Poems*. The young poet called Neal's review "the very first words of encouragement I ever remember to have heard." And so it was thanks to the Portland native that Edgar Allan Poe gained footing for his success—and the genre gained one of its most important founding fathers.

Although Neal himself is largely forgotten, his literary theory laid the groundwork for authors from Longfellow to Mark Twain and countless others besides. Neal's own novels and short fiction cannot be called fantasy, but they were highly Gothic and he clearly appreciated Poe's fantastical imagination. Neal advocated the use of American—especially New England—characters and settings to form the basis of a genuinely American literary tradition.

So Neal might have approved of the twenty-one speculative fiction writers assembled here, each one inspired by Maine and its people. (And Munsey might have published them, too, given the chance.) Both two-time Maine governor Edward Kent and the incomparable Missouri writer Mark Twain give us nineteenth-century views of future Maines, while Elizabeth Hand's Nebula Award-winning story and Daniel Hatch's tale afford us post-9/11 glimpses of days to come. Edgar Pangborn, whose first fiction appeared during the Golden Age, leads us deep into the primeval Maine forest. Maine's towering contribution to modern fiction, Stephen King, drives us down nearly forgotten (but unforgettable) back-woods roads. In Gardner Dozois's strange Skowhegan, Jack Chalker's interdimensional maritime ferry crossings, and other writers' lakes, woods, and towns, the reader will encounter just a few of Maine's many haunted chambers.

But first an account—a true account—by Henry David Thoreau will carry us over the threshold of that mysterious door:

II   Two Excerpts from "Ktaadn"

by Henry David Thoreau

Ktaadn, whose name is an Indian word signifying highest land, was first ascended by white men in 1804. It was visited by Professor J. W. Bailey of West Point in 1836; by Dr. Charles T. Jackson, the State Geologist, in 1837; and by two young men from Boston in 1845. All these have given accounts of their expeditions. Since I was there, two or three other parties have made the excursion, and told their stories. Besides these, very few, even among backwoodsmen and hunters, have ever climbed it, and it will be a long time before the tide of fashionable travel sets that way. The mountainous region of the State of Maine stretches from near the White Mountains, northeasterly one hundred and sixty miles, to the head of the Aroostook River, and is about sixty miles wide. The wild or unsettled portion is far more extensive. So that some hours only of travel in this direction will carry the curious to the verge of a primitive forest, more interesting, perhaps, on all accounts, than they would reach by going a thousand miles westward.

Perhaps I most fully realized that this was primeval, untamed, and forever untameable *Nature*, or whatever else men call it, while coming down this part of the mountain. We were passing over "Burnt Lands," burnt by lightning, perchance, though they showed no recent marks of fire, hardly so much as a charred stump, but looked rather like a natural pasture for the moose and deer, exceedingly wild and desolate, with occasional strips of timber crossing them, and low poplars springing up, and patches of blueberries here and there. I found myself traversing them familiarly, like some pasture run to waste, or partially reclaimed by man; but when I reflected what man, what brother or sister or kinsman of our race made it and claimed it, I expected the proprietor to rise up and dispute my passage. It is difficult to conceive of a region uninhabited by man. We habitually presume his presence and influence everywhere. And yet we have not seen pure Nature, unless we have seen her thus vast and dread and inhuman, though in the midst of cities. Nature was here something savage and awful, though beautiful. I looked with awe at the ground I trod on, to see what the Powers had made there, the form and fashion and material of their work. This was that Earth of which we have heard, made out of Chaos and Old Night. Here was no man's garden, but the unhandselled globe. It was not lawn, nor pasture, nor mead, nor woodland, nor lea, nor arable, nor waste-land. It was the fresh and natural surface of the planet Earth, as it was made for ever and ever,—to be the dwelling of man, we say,—so Nature made it, and man may use it if he can. Man was not to be associated with it. It was Matter, vast, terrific,—not his Mother Earth that we have heard of, not for him to tread on, or be buried in,—no, it were being too familiar even to let his bones lie there,—the home, this, of Necessity and Fate. There was there felt the presence of a force not bound to be kind to man. It was a place for heathenism and superstitious rites,—to be inhabited by men nearer of kin to the rocks and to wild animals than we.

We walked over it with a certain awe, stopping, from time to time, to pick the blueberries which grew there, and had a smart and spicy taste. Perchance where *our* wild pines stand, and leaves lie on their forest floor, in Concord, there were once reapers, and husbandmen planted grain; but here not even the surface had been scarred by man, but it was a specimen of what God saw fit to make this world. What is it to be admitted to a museum, to see a myriad of particular things, compared with being shown some star's surface, some hard matter in its home! I stand in awe of my body, this matter to which I am bound has become so strange to me. I fear not spirits, ghosts, of which I am one,—*that* my body might,—but I fear bodies, I tremble to meet them. What is this Titan that has possession of me? Talk of mysteries!—Think of our life in nature,—daily to be shown matter, to come in contact with it, — rocks, trees, wind on our cheeks! The *solid* earth! the *actual* world! the *common sense! Contact! Contact! Who* are we? *where* are we?

LONGTOOTH

Edgar Pangborn

M y word is good. How can I prove it? Born in Darkfield, wasn't I? Stayed away thirty more years after college, but when I returned I was still Ben Dane, one of the Darkfield Danes, Judge Marcus Dane's eldest. And they knew my word was good. My wife died and I sickened of all cities; then my bachelor brother Sam died, too, who'd lived all his life here in Darkfield, running his one-man law office over in Lohman—our nearest metropolis, population 6437. A fast coronary at fifty; I had loved him. Helen gone, then Sam—I wound up my unimportances and came home, inheriting Sam's housekeeper Adelaide Simmons, her grim stability and celestial cooking. Nostalgia for Maine is a serious matter, late in life: I had to yield. I expected a gradual drift into my childless old age playing correspondence chess, translating a few of the classics. I thought I could take for granted the continued respect of my neighbors. I say my word is good.

I will remember again the middle of March a few years ago, the snow skimming out of an afternoon sky as dry as the bottom of an old aluminum pot. Harp Ryder's back road had been plowed since the last snowfall; I supposed Bolt-Bucket could make the mile and a half in to his farm and out again before we got caught. Harp had asked me to get him a book if I was making a trip to Boston, any goddamn book that told about Eskimos, and I had one for him, De Poncins' *Kabloona*. I saw the midget devils of white running crazy down a huge slope of wind, and recalled hearing at the Darkfield News Bureau, otherwise Cleve's General Store, somebody mentioning a forecast of the worst blizzard in forty years. Joe Cleve, who won't permit a radio in the store because it pesters his ulcers, inquired of his Grand Inquisitor who dwells ten yards behind your right shoulder: "Why's it always got to be the worst in so-and-so many years, that going to help anybody?" The Bureau was still analyzing this difficult inquiry when I left, with my cigarettes and as much as I could remember of Adelaide's grocery list after leaving it on the dining table. It wasn't yet three when I turned in on Harp's back road, and a gust slammed at Bolt-Bucket like death with a shovel.

I tried to win momentum for the rise to the high ground, swerved to avoid an idiot rabbit and hit instead a patch of snow-hidden melt-and-freeze, skidding to a full stop from which nothing would extract us but a tow.

I was fifty-seven that year, my wind bad from too much smoking and my heart (I now know) no stronger than Sam's. I quit cursing—gradually, to avoid sudden actions—and tucked *Kabloona* under my parka. I would walk the remaining mile to Ryder's, stay just long enough to leave the book, say hello, and phone for a tow; then, since Harp never owned a car and never would, I could walk back and meet the truck.

If Leda Ryder knew how to drive, it didn't matter much after she married Harp. They farmed it, back in there, in almost the manner of Harp's ancestors in Jefferson's time. Harp did keep his two hundred laying hens by methods that were considered modern before the poor wretches got condemned to batteries, but his other enterprises came closer to antiquity. In his big kitchen garden he let one small patch of weeds fool themselves for an inch or two, so he'd have it to work at: they survived nowhere else. A few cows, a team, four acres for market crops, and a small dog, Droopy, whose grandmother had made it somehow with a dachshund. Droopy's only menace in obese old age was a wheezing bark. The Ryders must have grown nearly all vital necessities except chewing tobacco and once in a while a new dress for Leda. Harp could snub the twentieth century, and I doubt if Leda was consulted about it in spite of his obsessive devotion for her. She was almost thirty years younger and yes, he should not have married her. Other side up just as scratchy: she should not have married him, but she did.

Harp was a dinosaur perhaps, but I grew up with him, he a year the younger. We swam, fished, helled around together. And when I returned to Darkfield growing old, he was one of the few who acted glad to see me, so far as you can trust what you read in a face like a granite promontory. Maybe twice a week Harp Ryder smiled.

I pushed on up the ridge, and noticed a going-and-coming set of wide tire tracks already blurred with snow. That would be the egg truck I had passed a quarter-hour since on the main road. Whenever the west wind at my back lulled, I could swing around and enjoy one of my favorite prospects of birch and hemlock lowland. From Ryder's Ridge there's no sign of Darkfield two miles southwest except one church spire. On clear days you glimpse Bald Mountain and his two big brothers, more than twenty miles west of us.

The snow was thickening. It brought relief and pleasure to see the black shingles of Harp's barn and the roof of his Cape Codder. Foreshortened, so that it looked snug against the barn; actually house and barn were connected by a two-story shed fifteen feet wide and forty feet long—woodshed below, hen loft above. The Ryders' sunrise-facing bedroom window was set only three feet above the eaves of that shed roof. They truly went to bed with the chickens. I shouted, for Harp was about to close the big shed door. He held it for me. I ran, and the storm ran after me. The west wind was bouncing off the barn; eddies howled at us. The temperature had tumbled ten degrees since I left Darkfield. The thermometer by the shed door read fifteen degrees, and I knew I'd been a damn fool. As I helped Harp fight the shed door closed, I thought I heard Leda, crying.

A swift confused impression. The wind was exploring new ranges of passion, the big door squawked, and Harp was asking: "Ca' break down?" I do still think I heard Leda wail. If so, it ended as we got the door latched and Harp drew a newly fitted two-by-four bar across it. I couldn't understand that: the old latch was surely proof against any wind short of a hurricane.

"Bolt-Bucket never breaks down. Ought to get one, Harp—lots of company. All she did was go in the ditch."

"You might see her again come spring." His hens were scratching overhead, not yet scared by the storm. Harp's eyes were small gray glitters of trouble. "Ben, you figure a man's getting old at fifty-six?"

"No." My bones (getting old) ached for the warmth of his kitchen-dining-living-everything room, not for sad philosophy. "Use your phone, okay?"

"If the wires ain't down," he said, not moving, a man beaten on by other storms. "Them loafers didn't cut none of the overhand branches all summer. I told 'em of course, I told 'em how it would be...I meant, Ben, old enough to get dumb fancies?" My face may have told him I thought he was brooding about himself with a young wife. He frowned, annoyed that I hadn't taken his meaning. "I meant, *seeing* things. Things that can't be so, but—"

"We can all do some of that at any age, Harp."

That remark was a stupid brush-off, a stone for bread, because I was cold, impatient, wanted in. Harp had always a tense one-way sensitivity. His face chilled. "Well, come in, warm up. Leda ain't feeling too good. Getting a cold or something."

When she came downstairs and made me welcome, her eyes were reddened. I don't think the wind made that noise. Droopy waddled from her basket behind the stove to snuff my feet and give me my usual low passing mark.

Leda never had it easy there, young and passionate with scant mental resources. She was twenty-eight that year, looking tall because she carried her firm body handsomely. Some of the sullenness in her big mouth and lucid gray eyes was sexual challenge, some pure discontent. I liked Leda; her nature was not one for animosity or meanness. Before her marriage the Darkfield News Bureau used to declare with its customary scrupulous fairness that Leda had been covered by every goddamn thing in pants within thirty miles. For once the Bureau may have spoken a grain of truth in the malice, for Leda did have the smoldering power that draws men without word or gesture. After her abrupt marriage to Harp—Sam told me all this: I wasn't living in Darkfield then and hadn't met her—the garbage-gossip went hastily underground: enraging Harp Ryder was never healthy.

The phone wires weren't down, yet. While I waited for the garage to answer, Harp said, "Ben, I can't let you walk back in that. Stay over, huh?"

I didn't want to. It meant extra work and inconvenience for Leda, and I was ancient enough to crave my known safe burrow. But I felt Harp wanted me to stay for his own sake. I asked Jim Short at the garage to go ahead with Bolt-Bucket if I wasn't there to meet him. Jim roared: "Know what it's doing right now?"

"Little spit of snow, looks like."

"Jesus!" He covered the mouthpiece imperfectly. I heard his enthusiastic voice ring through cold-iron echoes: "Hey, old Ben's got that thing into the ditch again! Ain't that something...? Listen, Ben, I can't make no promises. Got both tow trucks out already. You better stop over and praise the Lord you got that far."

"Okay," I said. "It wasn't much of a ditch."

Leda fed us coffee. She kept glancing toward the landing at the foot of the stairs where a night-darkness already prevailed. A closed-in stairway slanted down at a never-used front door; beyond that landing was the other ground floor room—parlor, spare, guest room—where I would sleep. I don't know what Leda expected to encounter in that shadow. Once when a chunk of firewood made an odd noise in the range, her lips clamped shut on a scream.

The coffee warmed me. By that time the weather left no loophole for argument. Not yet 3:30, but west and north were lost in furious black. Through the hissing white flood I could just see the front of the barn forty feet away. "Nobody's going no place into that," Harp said. His little house shuddered, enforcing the words. "Led,' you don't look too brisk. Get you some rest."

"I better see to the spare room for Ben."

Neither spoke with much tenderness, but it glowed openly in him when she turned her back. Then some other need bent his granite face out of its normal seams. His whole gaunt body leaning forward tried to help him talk. "You wouldn't figure me for a man'd go off his rocker?" he asked.

"Of course not. What's biting, Harp?"

"There's something in the woods, got no right to be there." To me that came as a letdown of relief: I would not have to listen to another's marriage problems. "I wish, b' Jesus Christ, it would hit somebody else once, so I could say what I know and not be laughed at all to hell. I ain't one for dumb fancies."

You walked on eggs with Harp. He might decide any minute that *I* was laughing. "Tell me," I said. "If anything's out there now it must feel a mite chilly."

"Ayah." He went to the north window, looking out where we knew the road lay under the white confusion. Harp's land sloped down on the other side of the road to the edge of a mighty evergreen forest. Mount Katahdin stands more than fifty miles north and a little east of us. We live in a withering, shrinking world, but you could still set out from Harp's farm and, except for the occasional country road and the rivers—not many large ones—you could stay in deep forest all the way to the tundra, or Alaska. Harp said, "This kind of weather is when it comes." He sank into his beat-up kitchen armchair and reached for *Kabloona*. He had barely glanced at the book while Leda was with us. "Funny name."

"Kabloona's an Eskimo word for white man."

"He done these pictures . . . ? Be they good, Ben?"

"I like 'em. Photographs in the back."

"Oh." He turned the pages hastily for those, but studied only the ones that showed the strong Eskimo faces, and his interest faded. Whatever he wanted was not here. "These people, be they—civilized?"

"In their own way, sure."

"Ayah, this guy looks like he could find his way in the woods."

"Likely the one thing he couldn't do, Harp. They never see a tree unless they come south, and they hate to do that. Anything below the Arctic is too warm."

"That a fact . . . ? Well, it's a nice book. How much was it?" I'd found it second-hand; he paid me to the exact penny. "I'll be glad to read it." He never would. It would end up on the shelf in the parlor with the Bible, an old almanac, a Longfellow, until some day this place went up for auction and nobody remembered Harp's way of living.

"What's this all about, Harp?"

"Oh . . . I was hearing things in the woods, back last summer. I'd think, fox, then I'd know it wasn't. Make your hair stand right on end. Lost a cow, last August, from the north pasture acrost the rud. Section of board fence tore out. I mean, Ben, the two top boards was *pulled out from the nail holes*. No hammer marks."

"Bear?"

"Only track I found looked like bear except too small. You know a bear wouldn't *pull* it out, Ben."

"Cow slamming into it, panicked by something?"

He remained patient with me. "Ben, would I build a cow pasture fence nailing the crosspieces from the outside? Cow hit it with all her weight she might bust it, sure. And kill herself doing it, be blood and hair all over the split boards, and she'd be there, not a mile and a half away into the woods. Happened during a big thunderstorm. I figured it had to be somebody with a spite ag'inst me, maybe some son of a bitch wanting the prop'ty, trying to scare me off that's lived here all my life and my family before me. But that don't make sense. I found the cow a week later, what was left. Way into the woods. The head and the bones. Hide tore up and flang around. Any *person* dressing off a beef, he'll cut whatever he wants and take off with it. He don't sit down and chaw the meat off the *bones*, b' Jesus Christ. He don't tear the thighbone out of the joint . . . All right, maybe bear. But no bear did that job on that fence and then driv old Nell a mile and a half into the woods to kill her. Nice little jersey, clever's a kitten. Leda used to make over her, like she don't usually do with the stock . . . I've looked plenty in the woods since then, never turned up anything. Once and again I did smell something. Fishy, like bear-smell but—*different.*"

"But Harp, with snow on the ground—"

"Now you'll really call me crazy. When the weather is clear, I ain't once found his prints. I hear him then, at night, but I go out by daylight where I think the sound was, there's no trail. Just the usual snow tracks. I know. He lives in the trees and don't come down except when it's storming, I got to believe that. Because then he does come, Ben, when the weather's like now, like right now. And old Ned and Jerry out in the stable go wild, and sometimes we hear his noise under the window. I shine my flashlight through the glass—never catch sight of him. I go out with the ten-gauge if there's any light to see by, and there's prints around the house—holes filling up with snow. By morning there'll be maybe some marks left, and they'll lead off to the north woods, but under the trees you won't find it. So he gets up in the branches and travels thataway? . . . Just once I have seen him, Ben. Last October. I better tell you one other thing fast. A day or so after I found what was left of old Nell, I lost six roaster chickens. I made over a couple box stalls, maybe you remember, so the birds could be out on range and roost in the barn at night. Good doors, and I always locked 'em. Two in the morning, Ned and Jerry go crazy, I got out through the barn into the stable, and they was spooked, Ned trying to kick his way out. I got 'em quiet, looked all over the stable—loft, harness room, everywhere. Not a thing. Dead quiet night, no moon. It had to be something the horses smelled. I come back into the barn, and found one of the chicken-pen doors open—*tore* out from the lock. Chicken thief would bring along something to pry with—wouldn't he be a Christly idjut if he didn't . . . ? Took six birds, six nice eight-pound roasters, and left the heads on the floor—bitten off."

"Harp—some lunatic. People *can* go insane that way. There are old stories—"

"Been trying to believe that. Would a man live the winter out there? Twenty below zero?"

"Maybe a cave—animal skins."

"I've boarded up the whole back of the barn. Done the same with the hen-loft windows—two-by-fours with four-inch spikes driv slant-wise. They be twelve feet off the ground, and he ain't come for 'em, not yet . . . . So after that happened I sent for Sheriff Robart. Son of a bitch happens to live in Darkfield, you'd think he might've took an interest."

"Do any good?"

Harp laughed. He did that by holding my stare, making no sound, moving no muscle except for a disturbance at the eye corners. A New England art; maybe it came over on the *Mayflower*. "Robart, he come by, after a while. I showed him that door. I showed him them chicken heads. Told him how I'd been spending my nights out there on my ass, with the ten-gauge." Harp rose to unload tobacco juice into the range fire; he has a theory it purifies the air. "Ben, I might've showed him them chicken heads a shade close to his nose. By the time he got here, see, they wasn't all that fresh. He made out he'd look around and let me know. Mid-September. Ain't seen him since."

"Might've figured he wouldn't be welcome?"

"Why, he'd be welcome as shit on a tablecloth."

"You spoke of—seeing it, Harp?"

"Could call it seeing . . . All right. It was during them Indian summer days—remember? Like June except them pretty colors, smell of wind-falls—God, I like that, I like October. I'd gone down to the slope acrost the rud where I mended my fence after losing old Nell. Just leaning there, guess I was tired. Late afternoon, sky pinking up. You know how the fence cuts acrost the slope to my east wood lot. I've let the bushes grow free—lot of elder, other stuff the birds come for. I was looking down to-ward that little break between the north woods and my wood lot, where a bit of old growed-up pasture shows through. Pretty spot. Painter fella come by a few years ago and done a picture of it, said the place looked like a coro, dunno what the hell that is, he didn't say."

I pushed at his brown study. "You saw it there?"

"No. Off to my right in them elder bushes. Fifty feet from me, I guess. By God I didn't turn my head. I got it with the tail of my eye and turned the other way as if I meant to walk back to the rud. Made like busy with something in the grass, come wandering back to the fence some nearer. He stayed for me, a brownish patch in them bushes by the big yellow birch. Near the height of a man. No gun with me, not even a stick . . . Big shoulders, couldn't see his goddamn feet. He don't stand more'n five feet tall. His hands, if he's got real ones, hung out of my sight in a tangle of elder branches. He's got brown fur, Ben, reddy-brown fur all over him. His face too, his head, his big thick neck. There's a shine to fur in sunlight, you can't be mistook. So—I did look at him direct. Tried to act like I still didn't see him, but he knowed. He melted back and got the birch between him and me. Not a sound." And then Harp was listening for Leda upstairs. He went on softly: "Ayah, I ran back for a gun, and searched the woods, for all the good it did me. You'll want to know about his face. I ain't told Led' all this part. See, she's scared, I don't want to make it no worse, I just said it was some animal that snuck off before I could see it good. A big face, Ben. Head real human except it sticks out too much around the jaw. Not much nose—open spots in the fur. Ben, the—the *teeth!* I seen his mouth drop open and he pulled up one side of his lip to show me them stabbing things. I've seen as big as that on a full-growed bear. That's what I'll hear, I ever try to tell this. They'll say I seen a bear. Now I shot my first bear when I was sixteen and Pa took me over toward Jackman. I've got me one maybe every other year since then. I know 'em, all their ways. But that's what I'll hear if I tell the story."

I am a frustrated naturalist, loaded with assorted facts. I know there aren't any monkeys or apes that could stand our winters except maybe the harmless Himalayan langur. No such beast as Harp described lived anywhere on the planet. It didn't help. Harp was honest; he was rational; he wanted reasonable explanation as much as I did. Harp wasn't the village atheist for nothing. I said, "I guess you will, Harp. People mostly won't take the—unusual."

"Maybe you'll hear him tonight, Ben."

Leda came downstairs, and heard part of that. "He's been telling you, Ben. What do you think?"

"I don't know what to think."

"Led', I thought, if I imitate that noise for him—"

"No!" She had brought some mending and she was about to sit down with it, but froze as if threatened by attack. "I couldn't stand it, Harp. And—it might bring them."

"Them?" Harp chuckled uneasily. "I don't guess I could do it that good he'd come for it."

"Don't *do* it, Harp!"

"All right, hon." Her eyes were closed, her head drooping back. "Don't get nerved up so."

I started wondering whether a man still seeming sane could dream up such a horror for the unconscious purpose of tormenting a woman too young for him, a woman he could never imagine he owned. If he told her a fox bark wasn't right for a fox, she'd believe him. I said, "We shouldn't talk about it if it upsets her."

He glanced at me like a man floating up from under water. Leda said in a small, aching voice: "I wish to *God* we could move to Boston."

The granite face closed in defensiveness. "Led', we been over all that. Nothing is going to drive me off of my land. I got no time for the city at my age. What the Jesus would I do? Night watchman? Sweep out somebody's back room, b' Jesus Christ? Savings'd be gone in no time. We been all over it. We ain't moving nowhere."

"I could find work." For Harp of course that was the worst thing she could have said. She probably knew it from his stricken silence. She said clumsily, "I forgot something upstairs." She snatched up her mending and she was gone.

We talked no more of it the rest of the day. I followed through the milking and other chores, lending a hand where I could, and we made everything as secure as we could against storm and other enemies. The long-toothed furry thing was the spectral guest at dinner, but we cut him, on Leda's account, or so we pretended. Supper would have been awkward anyway. They weren't in the habit of putting up guests, and Leda was a rather deadly cook because she cared nothing about it. A Darkfield girl, I suppose she had the usual twentieth-century mishmash of television dreams until some impulse or maybe false signs of pregnancy tricked her into marrying a man out of the nineteenth. We had venison treated like beef and overdone vegetables. I don't like venison even when it's treated right.

At six Harp turned on his battery radio and sat stone-faced through the day's bad news and the weather forecast—"a blizzard which may prove the worst in forty-two years. Since 3:00 P.M., eighteen inches have fallen at Bangor, twenty-one at Boston. Precipitation is not expected to end until tomorrow. Winds will increase during the night with gusts up to seventy miles per hour." Harp shut it off, with finality. On other evenings I had spent there he let Leda play it after supper only kind of soft, so there had been a continuous muted bleat and blatter all evening. Tonight Harp meant to listen for other sounds. Leda washed the dishes, said an early good night, and fled upstairs.

Harp didn't talk, except as politeness obliged him to answer some blah of mine. We sat and listened to the snow and the lunatic wind. A hour of it was enough for me; I said I was beat and wanted to turn in early. Harp saw me to my bed in the parlor and placed a new chunk of rock maple in the pot-bellied stove. He produced a difficult granite smile, maybe using up his allowance for the week, and pulled out a bottle from a cabinet that had stood for many years below a parlor print—George Washington, I think, concluding a treaty with some offbeat sufferer from hepatitis who may have been General Cornwallis if the latter had two left feet. The bottle contained a brand of rye that Harp sincerely believed to be drinkable, having charred his gullet forty-odd years trying to prove it. While my throat, healed Harp said, "Shouldn't've bothered you with all this crap, Ben. Hope it ain't going to spoil your sleep." He got me his spare flashlight, then let me be, and closed the door.

I heard him drop back into his kitchen armchair. Under too many covers, lamp out, I heard the cruel whisper of the snow. The stove muttered, a friend, making me a cocoon of living heat in a waste of outer cold. Later I heard Leda at the head of the stairs, her voice timid, tired, and sweet with invitation: "You comin' up to bed, Harp?" The stairs creaked under him. Their door closed; presently she cried out in that desired pain that is brief release from trouble.

I remembered something Adelaide Simmons had told me about this house, where I had not gone upstairs since Harp and I were boys. Adelaide, one of the very few women in Darkfield who never spoke unkindly of Leda, said that the tiny west room across from Harp's and Leda's bedroom was fixed up for a nursery, and Harp wouldn't allow anything in there but baby furniture. Had been so since they were married seven years before.

Another hour dragged on, in my exasperations of sleeplessness. Then I heard Longtooth.

The noise came from the west side, beyond the snow-hidden vegetable garden. When it snatched me from the edge of sleep, I tried to think it was a fox barking, the ringing, metallic shriek the little red beast can belch dragon-like from his throat. But wide awake, I knew it had been much deeper, chestier. Horned owl? —no. A sound that belonged to ancient times when men relied on chipped stone weapons and had full reason to fear the dark.

The cracks in the stove gave me firelight for groping back into my clothes. The wind had not calmed at all. I stumbled to the west window, buttoning up, and found it a white blank. Snow had drifted above the lower sash. On tiptoe I could just see over it. A light appeared, dimly illuminating the snowfield beyond. That would be coming from a lamp in the Ryders' bedroom, shining through the nursery room and so out, weak and diffused, into the blizzard chaos.

Yaaarrhh!

Now it had drawn horribly near. From the north windows of the parlor I saw black nothing. Harp squeaked down to my door. "Wake, Ben?"

"Yes. Come look at the west window."

He had left no light burning in the kitchen, and only a scant glow came down to the landing from the bedroom. He murmured behind me. "Ayah, snow's up some. Must be over three feet on the level by now."

Yaaarrhh!

The voice had shouted on the south side, the blinder side of the house, overlooked only by one kitchen window and a small one in the pantry where the hand pump stood. The view from the pantry window was mostly blocked by a great maple that overtopped the house. I heard the wind shrilling across the tree's winter bones.

"Ben, you want to git your boots on? Up to you—can't ask it. I might have to go out." Harp spoke in an undertone as if the beast might understand him through the tight walls.

"Of course." I got into my knee boots and caught up my parka as I followed him into the kitchen. A .30-caliber rifle and his heavy shotgun hung on deerhorn over the door to the woodshed. He found them in the dark.

What courage I possessed that night came from being shamed into action, from fearing to show a poor face to an old friend in trouble. I went through the Normandy invasion. I have camped out alone, when I was younger and healthier, in our moose and bear country, and slept nicely. But that noise of Longtooth stole courage. It ached along the channel of the spine.

I had the spare flashlight, but knew Harp didn't want me to use it here. I could make out the furniture, and Harp reaching for the gun rack. He already had on his boots, fur cap, and mackinaw. "You take this'n," he said, and put the ten-gauge in my hands. "Both barrels loaded. Ain't my way to do that, ain't right, but since this thing started—"

Yaaarrhh!

"Where's he got to now?" Harp was by the south window. "Round this side?"

"I thought so . . . Where's Droopy?"

Harp chuckled thinly. "Poor little shit! She come upstairs at the first sound of him and went under the bed. I told Led' to stay upstairs. She'd want a light down here. Wouldn't make sense."

Then, apparently from the east side of the hen-loft and high, booming off some resonating surface: *Yaaarrhh!*

"He can't! Jesus, that's twelve foot off the ground!" But Harp plunged out into the shed, and I followed. "Keep your light on the floor, Ben." He ran up the narrow stairway. "Don't shine it on the birds, they'll act up."

So far the chickens, stupid and virtually blind in the dark, were making only a peevish tut-tutting of alarm. But something was clinging to the outside of the barricaded east window, snarling, chattering teeth, pounding on the two-by-fours. With a fist?—it sounded like nothing else. Harp snapped, "Get your light on the window!" And he fired through the glass.

We heard no outcry. Any noise outside was covered by the storm and the squawks of the hens scandalized by the shot. The glass was dirty from their continual disturbance of the litter; I couldn't see through it. The bullet had drilled the pane without shattering it, and passed between the two-by-fours, but the beast could have dropped before he fired. "I got to go out there. You stay, Ben." Back in the kitchen he exchanged rifle for shotgun. "Might not have no chance to aim. You remember this piece, don't y'?—eight in the clip."

"I remember it."

"Good. Keep your ears open." Harp ran out through the door that gave on a small paved area by the woodshed. To get around under the east loft window he would have to push through the snow behind the barn, since he had blocked all the rear openings. He could have circled the house instead, but only by bucking the west wind and fighting deeper drifts. I saw his big shadow melt out of sight.

Leda's voice quavered down to me: "He—get it?"

"Don't know. He's gone to see. Sit tight..."

I heard that infernal bark once again before Harp returned, and again it sounded high off the ground; it must have come from the big maple. And then moments later—I was still trying to pierce the dark, watching for Harp—a vast smash of broken glass and wood, and the violent bang of the door upstairs. One small wheezing shriek cut short, and one scream such as no human being should ever hear. I can still hear it.

I think I lost some seconds in shock. Then I was groping up the narrow stairway, clumsy with the rifle and flashlight. Wind roared at the opening of the kitchen door, and Harp was crowding past me, thrusting me aside. But I was close behind him when he flung the bedroom door open. The blast from the broken window that had slammed the door had also blown out the lamp. But our flashlights said at once that Leda was not there. Nothing was, nothing living.

Droopy lay in a mess of glass splinters and broken window sash, dead from a crushed neck—something had stamped on her. The bedspread had been pulled almost to the window—maybe Leda's hand had clenched on it. I saw blood on some of the glass fragments, and on the splintered sash, a patch of reddish fur.

Harp ran back downstairs. I lingered a few seconds. The arrow of fear was deep in me, but at the moment it made me numb. My light touched up an ugly photograph on the wall, Harp's mother at fifty or so, petrified and acid-faced before the camera, a puritan deity with shallow, haunted eyes. I remembered her.

Harp had kicked over the traces when his father died, and quit going to church. Mrs. Ryder "disowned" him. The farm was his; she left him with it and went to live with a widowed sister in Lohman, and died soon, unreconciled. Harp lived on as a bachelor, crank, recluse, until his strange marriage in his fifties. Now here was Ma still watchful, pucker-faced, unforgiving. In my dullness of shock I thought: Oh, they probably always made love with the lights out.

But now Leda wasn't there.

I hurried after Harp, who had left the kitchen door to bang in the wind. I got out there with rifle and flashlight, and over across the road I saw his torch. No other light, just his small gleam and mine. I knew as soon as I had forced myself beyond the corner of the house and into the fantastic embrace of the storm that I could never make it. The west wind ground needles into my face. The snow was up beyond the middle of my thighs. With weak lungs and maybe an imperfect heart, I could do nothing out here except die quickly to no purpose. In a moment Harp would be starting down the slope to the woods. His trail was already disappearing under my beam. I drove myself a little farther, and an instant's lull in the storm allowed me to shout: "Harp! I can't follow!"

He heard. He cupped his mouth and yelled back: "Don't try! Git back to the house! Telephone!" I waved to acknowledge the message and struggled back.

I only just made it. Inside the kitchen doorway I fell flat, gun and flashlight clattering off somewhere, and there I stayed until I won back enough breath to keep myself living. My face and hands were ice-blocks, then fires. While I worked at the task of getting air into my body, one thought continued, an inner necessity: *There must be a rational cause. I do not abandon the rational cause.* At length I hauled myself up and stumbled to the telephone. The line was dead.

I found the flashlight and reeled upstairs with it. I stepped past poor Droopy's body and over the broken glass to look through the window space. I could see that snow had been pushed off the shed roof near the bedroom window; the house sheltered that area from the full drive of the west wind, so some evidence remained. I guessed that whatever came must have jumped to the house roof from the maple, then down to the shed roof, and then hurled itself through the closed window without regard for it as an obstacle. Losing a little blood and a little fur.

I glanced around and could not find that fur now. Wind must have pushed it out of sight. I forced the door shut. Downstairs, I lit the table lamps in kitchen and parlor. Harp might need those beacons—if he came back. I refreshed the fires, and gave myself a dose of Harp's horrible whisky. It was nearly one in the morning. If he never came back?

It might be days before they could plow out the road. When the storm let up I could use Harp's snowshoes, maybe . . . .

Harp came back, at 1:20, bent and staggering. He let me support him to the armchair. When he could speak he said, "No trail. No trail." He took the bottle from my hands and pulled on it. "Christ Jesus! What can I do? Ben . . . ? I got to go to the village, get help. If they got any help to give."

"Do you have an extra pair of showshoes?"

He stared toward me, battling confusion. "Hah? No, I ain't. Better you stay anyhow. I'll bring yours from your house if you want, if I can get there." He drank again and slammed in the cork with the heel of his hand. "I'll leave you the ten-gauge."

He got his snowshoes from a closet. I persuaded him to wait for coffee. Haste could accomplish nothing now; we could not say to each other that we knew Leda was dead. When he was ready to go, I stepped outside with him into the mad wind. "Anything you want me to do before you get back?" He tried to think about it.

"I guess not, Ben . . . God, ain't I *lived* right? No, that don't make sense. God? That's a laugh." He swung away. Two or three great strides and the storm took him.

That was about two o'clock. For four hours I was alone in the house. Warmth returned, with the bedroom door closed and fires working hard. I carried the kitchen lamp into the parlor, and then huddled in the nearly total dark of the kitchen with my back to the wall, watching all the windows, the ten-gauge near my hand, but I did not expect a return of the beast, and there was none.

The night grew quieter, perhaps because the house was so drifted in that snow muted the sounds. I was cut off from the battle, buried alive.

Harp would get back. The seasons would follow their natural way, and somehow we would learn what had happened to Leda. I supposed the beast would have to be something in the human pattern—mad, deformed, gone wild, but still human.

After a time I wondered why we had heard no excitement in the stable. I forced myself to take up gun and flashlight and go look. I groped through the woodshed, big with the jumping shadows of Harp's cord-wood, and into the barn. The cows were peacefully drowsing. In the center alley I dared to send my weak beam swooping and glimmering through the ghastly distances of the hayloft. Quiet, just quiet; natural rustling of mice. Then to the stable, where Ned whickered and let me rub his brown cheeks, and Jerry rolled a humorous eye. I suppose no smell had reached them to touch off panic, and perhaps they had heard the barking often enough so that it no longer disturbed them. I went back to my post, and the hours crawled along a ridge between the pits of terror and exhaustion. Maybe I slept.

No color of sunrise that day, but I felt paleness and change; even a blizzard will not hide the fact of day-shine. I breakfasted on bacon and eggs, fed the hens, forked down hay and carried water for the cows and horses. The one cow in milk, a jumpy Ayrshire, refused to concede that I meant to be useful. I'd done no milking since I was a boy, the knack was gone from my hands, and relief seemed less important to her than kicking over the pail; she was getting more amusement than discomfort out of it, so for the moment I let it go. I made myself busywork shoveling a clear space by the kitchen door. The wind was down, the snowfall persistent but almost peaceful. I pushed out beyond the house and learned that the stuff was up over my hips.

Out of that, as I turned back, came Harp in his long, snowshoe stride, and down the road three others. I recognized Sheriff Robart, overfed but powerful; and Bill Hastings, wry and ageless, a cousin of Harp's and one of his few friends; and last, Curt Davidson, perhaps a friend to Sheriff Robart but certainly not to Harp.

I'd known Curt as a thick-witted loudmouth when he was a kid; growing to man's years hadn't done much for him. And when I saw him I thought, irrationally perhaps: Not good for our side. A kind of absurdity, and yet Harp and I were joined against the world simply because we had experienced together what others were going to call impossible, were going to interpret in harsh, even damnable ways; and no help for it.

I saw the white thin blur of the sun, the strength of it growing. Nowhere in all the white expanse had the wind and the new snow allowed us any mark of the visitation in the night.

*   *   *

The men reached my cleared space and shook off snow. I opened the woodshed. Harp gave me one hopeless glance of inquiry and I shook my head.

"Having a little trouble?" That was Robart, taking off his snowshoes. Harp ignored him. "I got to look after the chores." I told him I'd done it except for that damn cow. "Oh, Bess, ayah, she's nervy, I'll see to her." He gave me my snowshoes that he had strapped to his back. "Adelaide, she wanted to know about your groceries. Said I figured they was in the ca'."

"Good as an icebox," says Robart, real friendly.

Curt had to have his pleasures, too: "Ben, you sure you got hold of old Bess by the right end, where the tits was?" Curt giggles at his own jokes, so nobody else is obliged to. Bill Hastings spat in the snow.

"Okay if I go in?" Robart asked. It wasn't a simple inquiry: he was present officially and meant to have it known. Harp looked him up and down.

"Nobody stopping you. Didn't bring you here to stand around, I suppose."

"Harp," said Robart pleasantly enough, "don't give me a hard time. You come tell me certain things has happened, I got to look into it is all." But Harp was already striding down the woodshed to the barn entrance. The others came into the house with me, and I put on water for fresh coffee. "Must be your ca' down the rud a piece, Ben? Heard you kind of went into a ditch. All's you can see now is a hump in the snow. Deep freeze might be good for her, likely you've tried everything else." But I wasn't feeling comic, and never had been on those terms with Robart. I grunted, and his face shed mirth as one slips off a sweater. "Okay, what's the score? Harp's gone and told me a story I couldn't feed to the dogs, so what about it? Where's Mrs. Ryder?"

Davidson giggled again. It's a nasty little sound to come out of all that beef. I don't think Robart had much enthusiasm for him either, but it seems he had sworn in the fellow as a deputy before they set out. "Yes, sir," said Curt, "that was *really* a story, that was."

"Where's Mrs. Ryder?"

"Not here," I told him. "We think she's dead."

He glowered, rubbing cold out of his hands. "Seen that window. Looks like the frame is smashed."

"Yes, from the outside. When Harp gets back you'd better look. I closed the door on that room and haven't opened it. There'll be more snow, but you'll see about what we saw when we got up there."

"Let's look right now," said Curt.

Bill Hastings said, "Curt, ain't you a mite busy for a dep'ty? Mr. Dane said when Harp gets back." Bill and I are friends; normally he wouldn't mister me. I think he was trying to give me some flavor of authority.

I acknowledged the alliance by asking: "You a deputy, too, Bill?" Giving him an opportunity to spit in the stove, replace the lid gently, and reply: "Shit no."

Harp returned and carried the milk pail to the pantry. Then he was looking us over. "Bill, I got to try the woods again. You want to come along?"

"Sure, Harp. I didn't bring no gun."

"Take my ten-gauge."

"Curt here'll go along," said Robart. "Real good man on snowshoes. Interested in wild life."

Harp said, "That's funny, Robart. I guess that's the funniest thing I heard since Cutler's little girl fell under the tractor. You joining us, too?"

"Fact is, Harp, I kind of pulled a muscle in my back coming up here. Not getting no younger neither. I believe I'll just look around here a little. Trust you got no objection? To me looking around a little?"

"Coffee's dripped," I said.

"Thing of it is, if I'd've thought you had any objection, I'd've been obliged to get me a warrant."

"Thanks, Ben." Harp gulped the coffee scalding. "Why, if looking around the house is the best you can do, Sher'f, I got no objection. Ben, I shouldn't be keeping you away from your affairs, but would you stay? Kind of keep him company? Not that I got much in the house, but still— you know—"

"I'll stay." I wished I could tell him to drop that manner; it only got him deeper in the mud.

Robart handed Davidson his gun belt and holster. "Better have it, Curt, so to be in style."

Harp and Bill were outside getting on their snowshoes; I half heard some remark of Harp's about the sheriff's aching back. They took off. The snow had almost ceased. They passed out of sight down the slope to the north, and Curt went plowing after them. Behind me Robart said, "You'd think Harp believed it himself."

"That's how it's to be? You make us both liars before you've even done any looking?"

"I got to try to make sense of it is all." I followed him up to the bedroom. It was cruelly cold. He touched Droopy's stiff corpse with his foot. "Hard to figure a man killing his own dog."

"We get nowhere with that kind of idea."

"Ben, you got to see this thing like it looks to other people. And keep out of my hair."

"That's what scares me, Jack. Something unreasonable did happen, and Harp and I were the only ones to experience it—except Mrs. Ryder."

"You claim you saw this—animal?"

"I didn't say that. I heard her scream. When we got upstairs this room was the way you see it." I looked around, and again couldn't find that scrap of fur, but I spoke of it, and I give Robart credit for searching. He shook out the bedspread and blankets, examined the floor and the closet. He studied the window space, leaned out for a look at the house wall and the shed roof. His big feet avoided the broken glass, and he squatted for a long gaze at the pieces of window sash. Then he bore down on me, all policemen personified, a massive, rather intelligent, conventionally honest man with no patience for imagination, no time for any fact not already in the books. "Piece of fur, huh?" He made it sound as if I'd described a jabberwock with eyes of flame. "Okay, we're done up here." He motioned me downstairs—all policemen who'd ever faced a crowd's dangerous stupidity with their own.

As I retreated I said, "Hope you won't be too busy to have a chemist test the blood on that sash."

"We'll do that." He made move-along motions with his slab hands. "Going to be a pleasure to do that little thing for you and your friend."

Then he searched the entire house, shed, barn, and stable. I had never before watched anyone on police business; I had to admire his zeal. I got involved in the farce of holding the flashlight for him while he rooted in the cellar. In the shed I suggested that if he wanted to restack twenty-odd cords of wood he'd better wait till Harp could help him; he wasn't amused. He wasn't happy in the barn loft, either. Shifting tons of hay to find a hypothetical corpse was not a one-man job. I knew he was capable of returning with a crew and machinery to do exactly that. And by his lights it was what he ought to do. Then we were back in the kitchen, Robart giving himself a manicure with his jackknife, and I down to my last cigarette, almost the last of my endurance.

Robart was not unsubtle. I answered his questions as temperately as I could—even, for instance: "Wasn't you a mite sweet on Leda yourself?" I didn't answer any of them with flat silence; to do that right you need an accompanying act like spitting in the stove, and I'm not a chewer. From the north window he said: "Comin' back. It figures." They had been out a little over an hour.

Harp stood by the stove with me to warm his hands. He spoke as if alone with me: "No trail, Ben." What followed came in an undertone: "Ben, you told me about a friend of yours, scientist or something, professor—"

"Professor Malcolm?" I remembered mentioning him to Harp a long while before; I was astonished at his recalling it. Johnny Malcolm is a professor of biology who has avoided too much specialization. Not a really close friend. Harp was watching me out of a granite despair as if he had asked me to appeal to some higher court. I thought of another acquaintance in Boston, too, whom I might consult—Dr. Kahn, a psychiatrist who had once seen my wife Helen through a difficult time . . . .

"Harp," said Robart, "I got to ask you a couple, three things. I sent word to Dick Hammond to get that goddamn plow of his into this road as quick as he can. Believe he'll try. Whiles we wait on him, we might's well talk. You know I don't like to get tough."

"Talk away," said Harp, "only Ben here, he's got to get home without waiting on no Dick Hammond."

"That a fact, Ben?"

"Yes. I'll keep in touch."

"Do that," said Robart, dismissing me. As I left he was beginning a fresh manicure, and Harp waited rigidly for the ordeal to continue. I felt morbidly that I was abandoning him.

Still—corpus delicti—nothing much more would happen until Leda Ryder was found. Then if her body were found dead by violence, with no acceptable evidence of Longtooth's existence—well, what then?

I don't think Robart would have let me go if he'd known my first act would be to call Short's brother Mike and ask him to drive me in to Lohman where I could get a bus for Boston.

Johnny Malcolm said, "I can see this is distressing you, and you wouldn't lie to me. But, Ben, as biology it won't do. Ain't no such animal. You know that."

He wasn't being stuffy. We were having dinner at a quiet restaurant, and I had of course enjoyed the roast duckling too much. Johnny is a rock-ribbed beanpole who can eat like a walking famine with no regrets. "Suppose," I said, "just for argument and because it's not biologically inconceivable, that there's a basis for the Yeti legend."

"Not inconceivable. I'll give you that. So long as any poorly known corners of the world are left—the Himalayan uplands, jungles, tropic swamps, the tundra—legends will persist and some of them will have little gleams of truth. You know what I think about moon flights and all that?" He smiled; privately I was hearing Leda scream. "One of our strongest reasons for them, and for the bigger flights we'll make if we don't kill civilization first, is a hunt for new legends. We've used up our best ones, and that's dangerous."

"Why don't we look at the countries inside us?" But Johnny wasn't listening much.

"Men can't stand it not to have closed doors and a chance to push at them. Oh, about your Yeti—he might exist. Shaggy anthropoid able to endure severe cold, so rare and clever the explorers haven't tripped over him yet. Wouldn't have to be a carnivore to have big ugly canines—look at the baboons. But if he was active in a Himalayan winter, he'd have to be able to use meat, I think. Mind you, I don't believe any of this, but you can have it as a biological not-impossible. How'd he get to Maine?"

"Strayed? Tibet—Mongolia—Arctic ice."

"Maybe." Johnny had begun to enjoy the hypothesis as something to play with during dinner. Soon he was helping along the brute's passage across the continents, and having fun till I grumbled something about alternatives, extraterrestrials. He wouldn't buy that, and got cross. Still hearing Leda scream, I assured him I wasn't watching for little green men.

"Ben, how much do you know about this—Harp?"

"We grew up along different lines, but he's a friend. Dinosaur, if you like, but a friend."

"Hardshell Maine bachelor picks up dizzy young wife—"

"She's not dizzy. Wasn't. Sexy, but not dizzy."

"All right. Bachelor stewing in his own juices for years. Sure he didn't get up on that roof himself?"

"Nuts. Unless all my senses were more paralyzed than I think, there wasn't time."

"Unless they were more paralyzed than you think."

"Come off it! I'm not senile yet . . . What's he supposed to have done with her? Tossed her into the snow?"

"Mph," said Johnny, and finished his coffee. "All right. Some human freak with abnormal strength and the endurance to fossick around in a Maine blizzard stealing women. I liked the Yeti better. You say you suggested a madman to Ryder yourself. Pity if you had to come all the way here just so I could repeat your own guesswork. To make amends, want to take in a bawdy movie?"

"Love it."

The following day Dr. Kahn made time to see me at the end of the afternoon, so polite and patient that I felt certain I was keeping him from his dinner. He seemed undecided whether to be concerned with the traumas of Harp Ryder's history or those of mine. Mine were already somewhat known to him. "I wish you had time to talk all this out to me. You've given me a nice summary of what the physical events appear to have been, but—"

"Doctor," I said, "it *happened*. I heard the animal. The window *was* smashed—ask the sheriff. Leda Ryder did scream, and when Harp and I got up there together, the dog had been killed and Leda was gone."

"And yet, if it was all as clear as that, I wonder why you thought of consulting me at all, Ben. I wasn't there. I'm just a headshrinker."

"I wanted . . . Is there any way a delusion could take hold of Harp *and* me, disturb our senses in the same way? Oh, just saying it makes it ridiculous."

Dr. Kahn smiled. "Let's say, difficult."

"Is it possible Harp could have killed her, thrown her out through the window of the *west* bedroom—the snow must have drifted six feet or higher on that side—and then my mind distorted my time sense? So I might've stood there in the dark kitchen all the time it went on, a matter of minutes instead of seconds? Then he jumped down by the shed roof, came back into the house the normal way while I was stumbling upstairs? Oh, hell."

Dr. Kahn had drawn a diagram of the house from my description, and peered at it with placid interest. "Benign" was a word Helen had used for him. He said, "Such a distortion of the time sense would be unusual . . . Are you feeling guilty about anything?"

"About standing there and doing nothing? I can't seriously believe it was more than a few seconds. Anyway that would make Harp a monster out of a detective story. He's not that. How could he count on me to freeze in panic? Absurd. I'd've heard the struggle, steps, the window of the west room going up. Could he have killed her and I known all about it at the time, even witnessed it, and then suffered amnesia for that one event?"

He still looked so patient I wished I hadn't come. "I won't say any trick of the mind is impossible, but I might call that one highly improbable. Academically, however, considering your emotional involvement—"

"I'm not emotionally involved!" I yelled that. He smiled, looking much more interested. I laughed at myself. That was better than poking him in the eye. "I'm upset, Doctor, because the whole thing goes against reason. If you start out knowing nobody's going to believe you, it's all messed up before you open your mouth."

He nodded kindly. He's a good joe. I think he'd stopped listening for what I didn't say long enough to hear a little of what I did say. "You're not unstable, Ben. Don't worry about amnesia. The explanation, perhaps some human intruder, will turn out to be within the human norm. The norm of possibility does include such things as lycanthropic delusions, maniacal behavior, and so on Your police up there will carry on a good search for the poor woman. They won't overlook that snowdrift. Don't underestimate them, and don't worry about your own mind, Ben."

"Ever seen our Maine woods?"

"No, I go away to the Cape."

"Try it some time. Take a patch of it, say about fifty miles by fifty, that's twenty-five hundred square miles. Drop some eager policemen into it, tell 'em to hunt for something they never saw before and don't want to see, that doesn't want to be found."

"But if your beast is human, human beings leave traces. Bodies aren't easy to hide, Ben."

"In those woods? A body taken by a carnivorous animal? Why not?" Well, our minds didn't touch. I thanked him for his patience and got up. "The maniac responsible," I said. "But whatever we call him, Doctor, he was *there*."

Mike Short picked me up at the Lohman bus station, and told me something of a ferment in Darkfield. I shouldn't have been surprised. "They're all scared, Mr. Dane. They want to hurt somebody." Mike is Jim Short's younger brother. He scrapes up a living with his taxi service and occasional odd jobs at the garage. There's a droop in his shaggy ringlets, and I believe thirty is staring him in the face. "Like old Harp he wants to tell it like it happened and nobody buys. That's sad, man. You been away what, three days? The fuzz was pissed off. You better connect with Mister Sheriff Robart like soon. He climbed all over my ass just for driving you to the bus that day, like I should've known you shouldn't."

"I'll pacify him. They haven't found Mrs. Ryder?"

Mike spat out the car window, which was rolled down for the mild air. "Old Harp he never got such a job of snow-shoveling done in all his days. By the c'munity, for free. No, they won't find her." In that there was plenty of I-want-to-be-asked, and something more, a hint of the mythology of Mike's generation.

"So what's your opinion, Mike?"

He maneuvered a fresh cigarette against the stub of the last and drove on through tiresome silence. The road was winding between ridged mountains of plowed, rotting snow. I had the window down on my side, too, for the genial afternoon sun, and imagined a tang of spring. At last Mike said, "You prob'ly don't go along . . . Jim got your ca' out, by the way. It's at your place . . . Well, you'll hear 'em talking it all to pieces. Some claim Harp's telling the truth. Some say he killed her himself. They don't say how he made her disappear. Ain't heard any talk against you, Mr. Dane, nothing that counts. The sheriff's peeved, but that's just on account you took off without asking." His vague, large eyes watched the melting landscape, the ambiguous messages of spring. "Well, I think, like, a demon took her, Mr. Dane. She was one of his own, see? You got to remember, I knew that chick. Okay, you can say it ain't scientific, only there is a science to these things, I read a book about it. You can laugh if you want."

I wasn't laughing. It wasn't my first glimpse of the contemporary medievalism and won't be my last if I survive another year or two. I wasn't laughing, and I said nothing. Mike sat smoking, expertly driving his twentieth-century artifact while I suppose his thoughts were in the seventeenth, sniffing after the wonders of the invisible world, and I recalled what Johnny Malcolm had said about the need for legends. Mike and I had no more talk.

Adelaide Simmons was dourly glad to see me. From her I learned that the sheriff and state police had swarmed all over Harp's place and the surrounding countryside, and were still at it. Result, zero. Harp had repeatedly told our story and was refusing to tell it any more. "Does the chores and sets there drinking," she said, "or staring off. Was up to see him yesterday, Mr. Dane—felt I should. Couple days they didn't let him alone a minute, maybe now they've eased off some. He asked me real sharp, was you back yet. Well, I redd up his place, made some bread, least I could do."

When I told her I was going there, she prepared a basket, while I sat in the kitchen and listened. "Some say she busted that window herself, jumped down and run off in the snow, out of her mind. Any sense in that?"

"Nope."

"And some claim she deserted him. Earlier. Which'd make you a liar. And they say whichever way it was, Harp's made up this crazy story because he can't stand the truth." Her clever hands slapped sandwiches into shape. "They claim Harp got you to go along with it, they don't say how."

"Hypnotized me, likely. Adelaide, it all happened the way Harp told it. I heard the thing, too. If Harp is ready for the squirrels, so am I."

She stared hard, and sighed. She likes to talk, but her mill often shuts off suddenly, because of a quality of hers that I find good as well as rare: I mean that when she has no more to say, she doesn't go on talking.

I got up to Ryder's Ridge about suppertime. Bill Hastings was there. The road was plowed slick between the snow ridges, and I wondered how much of the litter of tracks and crumpled paper and spent cigarette packages had been left by sight-seers. Ground frost had not yet yielded to the mud season, which would soon make normal driving impossible for a few weeks. Bill let me in, with the look people wear for serious illness. But Harp heaved himself out of that armchair, not sick in body at least. "Ben, I heard him last night. Late."

"What direction?"

"North."

"You hear it, Bill?" I set down the basket.

My pint-size friend shook his head. "Wasn't here." I couldn't guess how much Bill accepted of the tale.

Harp said, "What's the basket?—oh. Obliged. Adelaide's a nice woman." But his mind was remote. "It was north, Ben, a long way, but I think I know about where it would be. I wouldn't've heard it except the night was so still, like everything had quieted for me. You know, they been a-deviling me night and day. Robart, state cops, mess of smart little buggers from the papers. I couldn't sleep, I stepped outside like I was called. Why, he might've been the other side of the stars, the sky so full of 'em and nothing stirring. Cold . . . You went to Boston, Ben?"

"Yes. Waste of time. They want it to be something human, anyhow something that fits the books."

Whittling, Bill said neutrally, "Always a man for the books yourself, wasn't you, Ben?"

I had to agree. Harp asked, "Hadn't no ideas?"

"Just gave me back my own thoughts in their language. We have to find it, Harp. Of course some wouldn't take it for true even if you had photographs."

Harp said, "Photographs be goddamned."

"I guess you got to go," said Bill Hastings. "We been talking about it, Ben. Maybe I'd feel the same if it was me...I better be on my way or supper'll be cold and the old woman raising hell-fire." He tossed his stick back in the woodbox.

"Bill," said Harp, "you won't mind feeding the stock couple, three days?"

"I don't mind. Be up tomorrow."

"Do the same for you some time. I wouldn't want it mentioned anyplace."

"Harp, you know me better'n that. See you, Ben."

"Snow's going fast," said Harp when Bill had driven off. "Be in the woods a long time yet, though."

"You wouldn't start this late."

He was at the window, his lean bulk shutting off much light from the time-seasoned kitchen where most of his indoor life had been passed. "Morning, early. Tonight I got to listen."

"Be needing sleep, I'd think."

"I don't always get what I need," said Harp.

"I'll bring my snowshoes. About six? And my carbine—I'm best with a gun I know."

He stared at me a while. "All right, Ben. You understand, though, you might have to come back alone. I ain't coming back till I get him, Ben. Not this time."

*   *   *

At sunup I found him with Ned and Jerry in the stable. He had lived eight or ten years with that team. He gave Ned's neck a final pat as he turned to me and took up our conversation as if night had not intervened. "Not till I get him. Ben, I don't want you drug into this ag'inst your inclination."

"Did you hear it again last night?"

"I heard it. North."

The sun was at the point of rising when we left on our snowshoes, like morning ghosts ourselves. Harp strode ahead, down the slope to the woods without haste, perhaps with some reluctance. Near the trees he halted, gazing to his right where a red blaze was burning the edge of the sky curtain; I scolded myself for thinking that he was saying good-bye to the sun.

The snow was crusted, sometimes slippery even for our web feet. We entered the woods along a tangle of tracks, including the fat tire marks of a snow scooter. "Guy from Lohman," said Harp. "Hired the goddamn thing out to the state cops and hisself with it. Goes pootin' around all over hell, fit to scare everything inside eight, ten miles." He cut himself a fresh plug to last the morning. "I b'lieve the thing is a mite farther off than that. They'll be messing around again today." His fingers dug into my arm. "See how it is, don't y'? They ain't looking for what we are. Looking for a dead body to hang onto my neck. And if they was to find her the way I found—the way I found—"

"Harp, you needn't borrow trouble."

"I know how they think," he said. "Was I to walk down the road beyond Darkfield, they'd pick me up. They ain't got me in shackles because they got no—no body, Ben. Nobody needs to tell me about the law. They got to have a body. Only reason they didn't leave a man here overnight, they figure I can't go nowhere. They think a man couldn't travel in three, four foot of snow . . . Ben, I mean to find that thing and shoot it down . . . We better slant off thisaway."

He set out at a wide angle from those tracks, and we soon had them out of sight. On the firm crust our snowshoes left no mark. After a while we heard a grumble of motors far back, on the road. Harp chuckled viciously. "Bright and early like yesterday." He stared back the way we had come. "They'll never pick up our trail without dogs. That son of a bitch Robart did talk about borrying a hound somewhere, to sniff Leda's clothes. More likely give 'em a sniff of mine, now."

We had already come so far that I didn't know the way back. Harp would know it. He could never be lost in any woods, but I have no mental compass such as his. So I followed him blindly, not trying to memorize the route. It was a region of uniform old growth, mostly hemlock, no recent lumbering, few landmarks. The monotony wore down native patience to a numbness, and our snowshoes left no more impression than our thoughts.

An hour passed, or more, after that sound of motors faded. Now and then I heard the wind move peacefully overhead. Few bird calls, for most of our singers had not yet returned. "Been in this part before, Harp?"

"Not with snow on the ground, not lately." His voice was hushed and careful. "Summers. About a mile now, and the trees thin out some. Stretch of slash where they was taking out pine four, five years back and left everything a Christly pile of shit like they always do."

No, Harp wouldn't get lost here, but I was well lost, tired, sorry I had come. Would he turn back if I collapsed? I didn't think he could, now, for any reason. My pack with blanket roll and provisions had become infernal. He had said we ought to have enough for three or four days. Only a few years earlier I had carried heavier camping loads than this without trouble, but now I was blown, a stitch beginning in my side. My wristwatch said only nine o'clock.

The trees thinned out as he had promised, and here the land rose in a long slope to the north. I looked up across a tract of eight or ten acres where the devastation of stupid lumbering might be healed if the hurt region could be let alone for sixty years. The deep snow, blinding out here where only scrub growth interfered with the sunlight, covered the worst of the wreckage. "Good place for wild ras'berries," Harp said quietly. "Been time for 'em to grow back. Guess it was nearer seven years ago when they cut here and left this mess. Last summer I couldn't hardly find their logging road. Off to the left—"

He stopped, pointing with a slow arm to a blurred gray line that wandered up from the left to disappear over the rise of ground. The nearest part of that gray curve must have been four hundred feet away, and to my eyes it might have been a shadow cast by an irregularity of the snow surface; Harp knew better. Something had passed there, heavy enough to break the crust. "You want to rest a mite, Ben? Once over that rise I might not want to stop again."

I let myself down on the butt of an old log that lay tilted toward us, cut because it had happened to be in the way, left to rot because they happened to be taking pine. "Can you really make anything out of that?"

"Not enough," said Harp. "But it could be him." He did not sit by me, but stood relaxed with his load, snowshoes spaced so he could spit between them. "About half a mile over that rise," he said, "there's a kind of gorge. Must've been a good brook, former times, still a stream along the bottom in summer. Tangle of elders and stuff. Couple, three caves in the bank at one spot. I guess it's three summers since I been there. Gloomy goddamn place. There was foxes into one of them caves. Natural caves, I b'lieve. I didn't go too near, not then."

I sat in the warming light, wondering whether there was any way I could talk to Harp about the beast—if it existed, if we weren't merely a pair of aging men with disordered minds. Any way to tell him the creature was important to the world outside our dim little village? That it ought somehow to be kept alive, not just shot down and shoveled aside? How could I say this to a man without science, who had lost his wife and also the trust of his fellow men?

Take away that trust and you take away the world. Could I ask him to shoot it in the legs, get it back alive? Why, to my own self, irrationally, that appeared wrong, horrible, as well as beyond our powers. Better if he shot to kill. Or if I did. So in the end I said nothing, but shrugged my pack into place and told him I was ready to go on.

With the crust uncertain under that stronger sunshine, we picked our way slowly up the rise, and when we came at length to that line of tracks, Harp said matter-of-factly, "Now you've seen his mark. It's him."

Sun and overnight freezing had worked on the trail. Harp estimated it had been made early the day before. But wherever the weight of Long-tooth had broken through, the shape of his foot showed clearly down there in its pocket of snow, a foot the size of a man's, but broader, shorter. The prints were spaced for the stride of a short-legged person. The arch of the foot was low, but the beast was not actually flatfooted. Beast or man. I said, "This is a man's print, Harp. Isn't it?"

He spoke without heat. "No. You're forgetting, Ben. I seen him."

"Anyhow there's only one."

He said slowly, "Only one set of tracks."

"What d' you mean?"

Harp shrugged. "It's heavy. He could've been carrying something. Keep your voice down. That crust yesterday, it would've held me without no web feet, but he went through, and he ain't as big as me." Harp checked his rifle and released the safety. "Half a mile to them caves. B'lieve that's where he is, Ben. Don't talk unless you got to, and take it slow."

I followed him. We topped the rise, encountering more of that lumberman's desolation on the other side. The trail crossed it, directly approaching a wall of undamaged trees that marked the limit of the cutting. Here forest took over once more, and where it began, Longtooth's trail ended. "Now you seen how it goes," Harp said. "Any place where he can travel above ground he does. He don't scramble up the trunks, seems like. Look here—he must've got aholt of that branch and swung hisself up. Knocked off some snow, but the wind knocks off so much, too, you can't tell nothing. See, Ben, he—he figures it out. He knows about trails. He'll have come down out of these trees far enough from where we are now so there ain't no chance of us seeing the place from here. Could be anywhere in a half-circle, and draw it as big as you please."

"Thinking like a man."

"But he ain't a man," said Harp. "There's things he don't know. How a man feels, acts. I'm going on to them caves." From necessity, I followed him . . . .

I ought to end this quickly. Prematurely I am an old man, incapacitated by the effects of a stroke and a damaged heart. I keep improving a little—sensible diet, no smoking, Adelaide's care. I expect several years of tolerable health on the way downhill. But I find, as Harp did, that it is even more crippling to lose the trust of others. I will write here once more, and not again, that my word is good.

It was noon when we reached the gorge. In that place some melancholy part of night must always remain. Down the center of the ravine between tangles of alder, water murmured under ice and rotting snow, which here and there had fallen in to reveal the dark brilliance. Harp did not enter the gorge itself, but moved slowly through tree-cover along the left edge, eyes flickering for danger. I tried to imitate his caution. We went a hundred yards or more in that inching advance, maybe two hundred. I heard only the occasional wind of spring.

He turned to look at me, with a sickly triumph, a grimace of disgust and of justification, too. He touched his nose and then I got it also, a rankness from down ahead of us, a musky foulness with an ammoniacal tang and some smell of decay. Then on the other side of the gorge, off in the woods, but not far, I heard Longtooth.

A bark, not loud. Throaty, like talk.

Harp suppressed an answering growl. He moved on until he could point down to a black cave-mouth on the opposite side. The breeze blew the stench across to us. Harp whispered, "See, he's got like a path. Jumps down to that flat rock, then to the cave. We'll see him in a minute." Yes, there were sounds in the brush. "You keep back." His left palm lightly stroked the underside of his rifle barrel.

So intent was he on the opening where Longtooth would appear, I may have been first to see the other who came then to the cave mouth and stared up at us with animal eyes. Longtooth had called again, a rather gentle sound. The woman wrapped in filthy hides may have been drawn by that call or by the noise of our approach.

Then Harp saw her.

He knew her. In spite of the tangled hair, scratched face, dirt, and the shapeless deer-pelt she clutched around herself against the cold, I am sure he knew her. I don't think she knew him, or me. An inner blindness, a look of a beast wholly centered on its own needs. I think human memories had drained away. She knew Longtooth was coming. I think she wanted his warmth and protection, but there were no words in the whimper she made before Harp's bullet took her between the eyes.

Longtooth shoved through the bushes. He dropped the rabbit he was carrying and jumped down to that flat rock, snarling, glancing sidelong at the dead woman who was still twitching. If he understood the fact of death, he had no time for it. I saw the massive overdevelopment of thigh and leg muscles, their springy motions of preparation. The distance from the flat rock to the place where Harp stood must have been fifteen feet. One spear of sunlight touched him in that blue-green shade, touched his thick red fur and his fearful face.

Harp could have shot him. Twenty seconds for it, maybe more. But he flung his rifle aside and drew out his hunting knife, his own long tooth, and had it waiting when the enemy jumped.

So could I have shot him. No one needs to tell me I ought to have done so.

Longtooth launched himself, clawed fingers out, fangs exposed. I felt the meeting as if the impact had struck my own flesh. They tumbled roaring into the gorge, and I was cold, detached, an instrument for watching.

It ended soon. The heavy brownish teeth clenched in at the base of Harp's neck. He made no more motion except the thrust that sent his blade into Longtooth's left side. Then they were quiet in that embrace, quiet all three. I heard the water flowing under the ice.

I remember a roaring in my ears, and I was moving with slow care, one difficult step after another, along the lip of the gorge and through mighty corridors of white and green. With my hard-won detachment I supposed this might be the region where I had recently followed poor Harp Ryder to some destination or other, but not (I thought) one of those we talked about when we were boys. A band of iron had closed around my forehead, and breathing was an enterprise needing great effort and caution, in order not to worsen the indecent pain that clung as another band around my diaphragm. I leaned against a tree for thirty seconds or thirty minutes, I don't know where. I knew I mustn't take off my pack in spite of the pain, because it carried provisions for three days. I said once: "Ben, you are lost."

I had my carbine, a golden bough, staff of life, and I recall the shrewd management and planning that enabled me to send three shots into the air. Twice.

It seems I did not want to die, and so hung on the cliff-edge of death with a mad stubbornness. They tell me it could not have been the second day that I fired the second burst, the one that was heard and answered—because, they say, a man can't suffer the kind of attack I was having and then survive a whole night of exposure. They say that when a search party reached me from Wyndham Village (eighteen miles from Darkfield), I made some garbled speech and fell flat on my face.

I woke immobilized, without power of speech or any motion except for a little life in my left hand, and for a long time memory was only a jarring of irrelevancies. When that cleared I still couldn't talk for another long deadly while. I recall someone saying with exasperated admiration that with cerebral hemorrhage on top of coronary infarction, I had no damn right to be alive; this was the first sound that gave me any pleasure. I remember recognizing Adelaide and being unable to thank her for her presence. None of this matters to the story, except the fact that for months I had no bridge of communication with the world; and yet I loved the world and did not want to leave it.

One can always ask: What will happen next?

Some time in what they said was June my memory was (I think) clear. I scrawled a little, with the nurse supporting the deadened part of my arm. But in response to what I wrote, the doctor, the nurses, Sheriff Robart, even Adelaide Simmons and Bill Hastings, looked—sympathetic. I was not believed. I am not believed now, in the most important part of what I wish I might say: that there are things in our world that we do not understand, and that this ignorance ought to generate humility. People find this obvious, bromidic—oh, they always have!—and therefore they do not listen, retaining the pride of their ignorance intact.

Remnants of the three bodies were found in late August, small thanks to my efforts, for I had no notion what compass direction we took after the cut-over area, and there are so many such areas of desolation I couldn't tell them where to look. Forest scavengers, including a pack of dogs, had found the bodies first.

Water had moved them, too, for the last of the big snow melted suddenly, and for a couple of days at least there must have been a small river raging through that gorge. The head of what they are calling the "lunatic" got rolled downstream, bashed against rocks, partly buried in silt. Dogs had chewed and scattered what they speak of as "the man's fur coat."

It will remain a lunatic in a fur coat, for they won't have it any other way. So far as I know, no scientist ever got a look at the wreckage, unless you glorify the coroner by that title. I believe he was a good vet before he got the job. When my speech was more or less regained, I was already through trying to talk about it. A statement of mine was read at the inquest—that was before I could talk or leave the hospital. At this ceremony society officially decided that Harper Harrison Ryder, of this township, shot to death his wife Leda and an individual, male, of unknown identity, while himself temporarily of unsound mind, and died of knife injuries received in a struggle with the said individual of unknown, and so forth.

I don't talk about it because that only makes people more sorry for me, to think a man's mind should fail so, and he not yet sixty.

I cannot even ask them: "What is truth?" They would only look more saddened, and I suppose shocked, and perhaps find reasons for not coming to see me again.

They are kind. They will do anything for me, except think about it.

THE HERMIT GENIUS
OF MARSHVILLE

Tom Tolnay

WARNING: This exclusive report is fully protected by copyright and appears in this magazine for the first time anywhere.

EDITOR'S NOTE: The documents, tape recordings, articles, and investigative accounts herein represent, to our knowledge, the first published effort to draw into an intelligible whole the emerging story of Griswold Masterson, popularly known as "The Hermit Genius of Marshville." While admittedly incomplete, these materials provide a framework through which our readers may gain an impression of the ideas and life of the secretive, eccentric, self-made philosopher/scientist.

EQMM (*Ellery Queen's Mystery Magazine*) became aware of the Hermit Genius the way many scientific discoveries are made—by chance. Last summer an editorial assistant, on vacation in Maine, went fishing in a ten-foot powerboat near the mouth of the Peace River. The young man got caught in a squall, and it looked as though he was going to be swamped, when a returning lobster boat spotted him and pulled his craft to safety. Afterwards, the assistant insisted the lobsterman join him for something to eat and drink. In a local tavern the two men had their tongues loosened by several mugs of ale, and that's when the strange doings at Marshville first came up.

When the story of the Hermit Genius got back to us, naturally we were highly skeptical. But having let more than one major story get away from us over the years, we reluctantly decided to send a reporter[†] up to Maine to check it out. The decision proved to be well worth the investment, for she uncovered a story of international—we might even say, universal—implications.

At a very early age—three or four—legend has it that Griswold Masterson got hold of several science fiction magazines and within a period of months had taught himself to read. By five or six, it is said, he had gone through much of Jules Verne and H. G. Wells at a local lending library outside Marshville. Masterson apparently was greatly moved by the realization that each of us is stuck in our own time—that our finiteness precludes our partaking of the scientific advantages of succeeding ages. And at some point he must have made a childhood pledge to himself that one day he would overcome such limitations in his own life.

Before attaining maturity, Masterson began conducting experiments in the basement of the house in which he was born. He worked fifteen to twenty hours a day in what turned out to be a lifelong attempt to find a means by which he could experience firsthand the technological promises of ages to come. Late in his career, he apparently made a discovery that enabled him to realize his childhood dream.

In the years to come, as the world gradually pieces together more of Masterson's remarkable adventure, all human beings may find their lives altered for the better. In the meantime, we must content ourselves with having at least begun to study and, hopefully, learn from this one solitary life.

Wanda Pierce
Editor

EQMM's reporter began her investigation by visiting the local elementary school, on the road between Machias and Marshville, in the township of Harrington, Maine. Requesting access to school records, she was turned down summarily by school officials. But the reporter followed the school secretary home, explained her mission, and, finally, managed to elicit her aid. Griswold Masterson's grades turned out to be rather poor, and the only noteworthy entry in school records was that he had been expelled on May 17, 1946, at the age of eleven. Mrs. Martha Tuttle, the principal, wrote the following comments in her report of this incident:

"The student is totally uncooperative. He never raises his hand, never erases the blackboard, never recites in class, never does his homework . . . . His teacher, Maryanne Wilson, reports that all he does is read formulas on desk top . . . . Elsie and Josiah Masterson were called up to school, and they indicated he was the same way at home . . . . 'Doesn't seem to hear a thing we say,' according to Mrs. Masterson.... 'That boy's head is in the clouds,' said Mr. Masterson."

Our reporter visited Washington County High School outside Marshville. There she found one instructor—physics teacher Groden Catlege—who was willing to discuss Griswold. Nearly eighty years old and weighing about the same, Catlege was feisty, fearless, but forgetful: "Wasn't he the kid who tried to burn down the post office 'cause he didn't receive a package of books? Or was he the one who quit school at sixteen to study astrophysics on his own? One of those rascals in my class trapped stray cats for experiments. Could that have been Masterson?" (*Editor's Note: Masterson may have been all three.*) "Well, sir, whichever of those things he did, he was no weirdo the way people tried to make out. Hell, it was the town that drove him to shut himself away.... Yes, sir, he had a grasp of the physical and theoretical sciences that defied normal capacities for knowledge. Uncanny it was, the way he could join opposing elements in his mind. And his curiosity was insatiable—climbed a tree in a storm to study lightning and sure enough got struck to the ground! . . . Yes, sir, I laughed it off at the time, but now, who knows, maybe the feller was right when he said to me, one day after school: 'Einstein is interesting, but he misses the point.' "

If young "Grist," as the town called him, was advanced mentally beyond most of us, physically he was a poor specimen. The only photograph of him known to exist, snapped by a local, now-deceased shutterbug, shows Masterson passing the general store, attempting to cover his face with his hands. He was probably in his early twenties and, obviously, had not yet entirely shut himself away. The photo, judging from its faded sepia, was taken with an old box camera—and under far from cooperative conditions. But it did provide a glimpse of his stubby teeth and drastically receding hair, along with the bony slabs that served for shoulders. Accounts of Masterson's height differ greatly—some say over six feet, others say under five feet. (Judging from the size of his shoes, the latter seems more likely.) Whatever the truth, that disagreement dramatizes the misunderstanding and mythmaking that surrounded him all his life. *EQMM's* attempt to obtain that photograph to publish with these materials was thwarted by Butch White, who oversees the community's grange hall. White "accidentally" dropped it into a lighted potbelly stove moments after our reporter—who had discovered it tacked under a wad of announcements on the hall's bulletin board—asked White who it was. The snapshot must've been put up as a joke so long ago that people had stopped seeing it. Our reporter protested, but White told her: "You better clear out of here if you know what's good for that pretty neck of yours."

Why would the people of Marshville want to suppress information about a man who had no contact with (or interest in) them? From the cold shoulders and slammed doors and outright threats aimed at her, our reporter suspected that people in this solemn, oak-locked town were afraid of drawing attention to themselves—of disrupting their simple way of life. But as she found out more about Masterson, she thought it more likely that the townspeople were behaving peculiarly out of an irrational terror they felt toward the secret experiments that had been conducted in the sagging house on Cobalt Hill (a name that may come from its steely hue at dusk). They seemed to think that if the reporter stirred up the strange dust of Masterson's work, it might contaminate them all.

One person who seemed anxious to speak out cast a more specific focus on the nature of the town's fear. The pastor of the First Presbyterian (and only) Church, Rev. Leopold Ossip, suggested that being mentally ahead and physically less appealing than the "local folks" made it impossible for Grist to make friends or even casual connections. Ossip decided this had led Masterson to seek out and establish an unholy alliance with "dark supernatural forces." Here is his statement, slightly edited, as taped by our reporter:

"Facts all point in that direction. Grist came into town less and less, barricading himself in the broken-down house left by his folks—Josiah and Elsie died more or less simultaneously some years back, you know. (By the way, no one's been able to figure out how it happened. And I would not entirely discount the talk that Grist's ma and pa perished in one of his mad experiments.) Living off his folks' savings, and on vegetables he grew in vats in the house, under heat lamps, using kerosene for heat and power (he'd welded himself a huge tank and has it filled once a year, you know), Grist was more or less self-sufficient. Near as anyone in the congregation can figure, he never did anything but read, perform experiments in that fiendish cellar, and tend his indoor garden. (They say he grew tomatoes the size of cantaloupes!) God knows he didn't come to church! Queer thing is, you know, people passing near his place some nights could hear him reciting the Bible loud and clear, like he was committing it to memory. That gave me hope that there was an ounce of religion left in him, so one afternoon I walked up Cobalt Hill, stepped onto the Masterson porch bold as you please, and knocked—hard. But he wouldn't open the door. When it comes to saving souls I can be pretty stubborn, though, so I stood there and called out in the name of the Lord: 'Now, Grist,' I said, 'you know darn well that business you're engaged in is contrary to a moral life, contrary to the laws of God.' And you know what he said to me? With his door still locked, mind you, he said in that scratchy hiss of his: 'The secret of all that was, all that is, and all that will be lies in my experiments.' I never tried to save him again, you know, for he'd convinced me I'd been right all along: He was in cahoots with the devil!"

When Rev. Ossip had said all he was going to say, our reporter asked him: "What exactly was the nature of Griswold Masterson's experiments?" The God-fearing man, a "well-dried pastorly type," stared at the reporter as if she'd spoken a dead language, then turned on his heel and moved down the aisle, kneeling at the altar to pray.

Griswold Masterson was not entirely successful in escaping human involvement. By sheer perversity of personality, and an overpowering loneliness, Beryl Ward of Columbia Falls managed to gain access to his house, if not his heart. Having been abandoned by her husband after one year of marriage, and having spent the subsequent decade growing grim and frustrated—having lost both her parents, too—Miss Ward, at well past forty, decided that a life alone was no life at all. At the very least she needed someone to look after. And since there were no other prospects within reach, she set her cap on Griswold Masterson—sight unseen, though with plenty of tales about him in her head: His isolation constituted a local legend. If nothing else, she could be sure he wouldn't pack up and run off on her.

A former neighbor of Miss Ward's, whom the editors tracked down in Boston, apparently felt far enough removed from the scene to speak to us over the phone (though not far enough to authorize us to use her name) on the unusual courtship of Griswold and Beryl:

"I mean that Beryl Ward was always sniffing 'round Mr. Masterson's house. And even though he fired off a shotgun on the roof one night to scare her off, that hussy just kept on going back. All the way down on Main Street, we could hear her calling to him—she was going to wait forever, she'd shout loud as a loon, so he might as well open up. But he didn't; so what does she do?—that hussy starts sleeping out on an old sofa on the porch. I mean the town really got upset with her, but what could we do? Then one morning the door of the house opened, just like that, and Beryl Ward moseyed inside. Nothing but a rusty-headed hussy! After that there sure was plenty of talk about what they were doing up there on Cobalt Hill, if you know what I mean. Personally I doubt it very much—he was all mind and no body. Besides, what would any man see in Beryl Ward?"

EQMM's theory is that Mr. Masterson gave in to Miss Ward for two reasons: (1) It gave him more time and energy for his work, rather than expending physical and mental resources worrying about what she was doing out on the porch; (2) There were probably many items he needed on a continual basis for his experiments, goods she could procure from the local general store while he worked: candles, jars, nails, copper tubing, alcohol, matches, wire, batteries, welding rods, and who knows what else? How Beryl Ward reacted upon setting eyes on him for the first time is not known, and what she found inside the huge, unpainted, crumbling place is open to speculation. But the large shopping list she turned over to the store clerk that first month—including ammonia, detergent, scouring pads, and a mop—confirmed what most believed to be the case: Griswold Masterson, already being referred to as one of the great unheralded minds of this century, apparently lived like a farm animal. Probably the biggest housekeeping problem Beryl Ward had were the science fiction magazines, the technical books, and the philosophical tracts he'd collected over the decades. According to our Boston source:

"He had so many books you could see them from the footpath—stacked up every which way; I mean, they just blocked out the living room windows; I mean, you could smell the moldiness all the way down to Jill's beauty shop! . . . Thousands of rats and mice must've been nesting in that house. Ugh!"

It did not occur to Miss Ward's former neighbor that the Hermit Genius may have been consciously attempting to attract those rodents, for they might have served an important function in his work. In any case, she indicated further that sometimes there were empty packing cartons scattered on the porch. The local postmaster/general store proprietor confirmed that a few times each year Griswold Masterson received shipments from laboratory supply companies around the country. But when our reporter asked the gray-faced postmaster what he could tell us about the weight and size of those boxes, and about what might have been inside them, his voice hardened:

"Didn't pay attention, and I wouldn't want to know. And *stop* coming around here botherin' me! I got work to do."

The fire that destroyed the two-story, stick-built house on Cobalt Hill may indeed have gotten started through spontaneous combustion, as Marshville residents contended—those dried-out magazines springing into flames. Or maybe a bolt of lightning set it off. Or a kerosene lamp left lit by mistake may have been knocked over by the wind. An act of nature may well have been the cause. But with the attitude the town maintained toward Masterson and his work, one had to wonder. Certainly our reporter did. However, she was unable to come up with any evidence of arson, conspiratorial or otherwise. Of course, Rev. Ossip saw it as neither an act of nature nor man:

"God was righting a grievous wrong."

Sifting through the ashy remains in the Masterson basement, *EQMM*'s reporter made an important find: a few fragments of yellow, lined manuscript pages, written in what is undoubtedly the hand of Griswold Masterson. Tragically, most of Masterson's papers must have been destroyed by flames, and even sections of the fragments salvaged—preserved by mere chance under a slab of fallen boilerplate—were damaged by heat and water. In attempting to piece together a skeleton of Masterson's thoughts, the editors have bracketed words that were obliterated or not entirely readable, corrected misspellings and obvious grammatical oversights, and are publishing the fragments in the order that seems to offer the greatest continuity. But the total sense of these elements will probably never be known:

> . . . in the Practical Future—a psychological response to immediate human needs, the second is the Theoretical Future—a cry for more time to experience Man's potential. In pursuing the Practical Future we are expressing a [desire to preview particu-

lar] events so that we might alter their outcome in some way that is meaningful to our existence. In pondering the Theoretical [Future], we are attempting to break out of the [limitations of our flesh]—to participate in a time beyond our physical life span . . . .

After countless attempts to discard faulty reasoning, it became clear that bridging the Practical and Theoretical would have to be accomplished not entirely physically, not entirely spiritually, but through a journey involving mind and body . . . .

. . . and still another discipline, that of philosophy. Specifically the question of an immortal presence in the universe. If the world as we know it was indeed shaped through a process of evolution, certainly that development had to be set into motion. It needed a Prime Mover. But how events are shaped in the future will depend on Man . . . .

There is no more. While we suspect hundreds of these handwritten sheets were destroyed (bear in mind the technical aspects of his experiments have barely been alluded to in these fragments), who can say for sure?

In searching the ruins of the house, our reporter came across the remains of jars and test tubes—apparently smashed by the volunteer firemen. She also recovered a charred corner of a schematic drawing that seems to correspond to the stainless-steel cylinder the sheriff and his deputy reputedly found in Masterson's basement the morning before the fire. That was the day Beryl Ward reported the Hermit Genius missing. The reporter didn't get to see the cylinder itself, and there was much too little of the schematic to infer anything meaningful. (This was confirmed by the International Institute of Scientific Phenomena in New York, to whom we later turned it over.) So the editors of this magazine contacted the Washington County sheriff's office by telephone, requesting permission to inspect the cylinder in person. Deputy Durham Stone told us:

"Save yourself the trip. Thing's missing. Me and the sheriff, we went back to the office to get the pickup truck, so's we could haul it to the compound, but when we got back up to the house it was gone. Plain disappeared! . . . Say, how come you city folks want to come all the way out to these parts to see that thing anyway? It's just an old liquid propane gas tank, if you ask me."

The deputy's comments made us all the more curious—not to mention suspicious—so our managing editor drove up anyway. And while he could not locate the cylinder at the compound, or at the ruins, or even in the nearby woods, the trip was amply rewarded. Through certain inducements, *EQMM* managed to borrow (and re-record) the tape of the official statement made to Sheriff Joe Bartheme by Beryl Ward the day she reported Masterson missing. In a quavering voice that frequently broke down (as indicated by ellipses), here's what she said:

"When Grist didn't come upstairs for the dinner I left by the door—did that every day for him—I called but he didn't answer. That got me worried . . . . He kept the basement door locked, so I went round to the side of the house to look in a window—but they were painted black. I'd never noticed that before. I knocked and knocked on the glass; still there was no answer. That really got me upset; I thought he'd had a heart attack or something so I got an axe out of the shed and started hitting the lock on the storm-shelter door. Finally the lock fell apart and I went in . . . . Didn't see Griswold anywhere. All I found were a bunch of tubes and wires and gadgets, plus some weird charts on the wall . . . What really amazed me was the big Bible on the stand: It was opened to Genesis." (*Editor's note: no trace of a Bible was ever found.*) "In the back room of the basement I found this . . . kind of a cylinder, I guess . . . set up on a log-cutting horse. And it was glowing. So help me! . . . Top and bottom were rounded off; looked like a huge vitamin pill, or a miniature rocket ship. . . . I did what I knew would've made Griswold very angry, but I couldn't help myself. Guess I wanted to know once and for all what he was up to—why he stayed up night after night—why his work was more important to him than . . . anything else in the world. I started unscrewing the cap . . . . All of a sudden there was a tremendous *whoosh* and I heard this weird, high-pitched squeal: Scared the daylights out of me, but I looked inside and saw . . . I couldn't believe it—I found a baby . . . . Just a few months old—a naked baby! It looked up at me as if I were its mother. I was confused, I was frightened . . . . First I wanted to run away, but instincts much deeper took hold of me, I guess. I reached in and pulled the baby out. A fine child, with purplish eyes and silky skin. It didn't even cry. Just looked at me—poor thing!—and stopped breathing . . . . I wondered where Griswold had gotten the baby, what he was doing with it—all sorts of weird things I wondered until I spotted, off in a black corner... I saw Griswold's gray trousers and lab smock, his underwear and socks all neatly folded on a bench . . . ."

At this point Miss Ward became silent, and when Sheriff Bartheme asked (more than once) what she did next, she broke down and cried hysterically. Nothing else on the tape was coherent. Later that afternoon Beryl Ward had to be removed from the house in a state police straightjacket, kicking and screaming. That night, the house went up in flames.

In the aftermath of these events—the disappearance of Griswold Masterson, the discovery of the cylinder, the loss of Miss Ward's grip on reality, the destruction of the house—and as news spread out into the world, scientists and sociologists and theologians hastily began postulating theories. A few of these ideas were incorporated into the summary presented at a recent meeting of the American Board of Science in Washington, D.C.:

"Due to the absence of conclusive data, and the seclusion and secrecy in which Griswold Masterson chose to work throughout his life, and because so much of his research was destroyed, our inquiry, though arduous, has been, in many ways, unsatisfactory. Nevertheless, it is our shared opinion that Mr. Masterson achieved the ability to project himself into the physical form and mental development of his own infancy, and that he used this means to renew his future. That is to say, he opened the door to what he called the 'Theoretical Future' not by achieving longevity, but by reducing his age as the framework of life around him progressed at its usual rate. This means that Masterson, who was sixty-three years old at the time of this experiment, by regressing, made available to himself another seventy-two years (based on current life expectancy for a male in this country) . . . . The idea seems to have been to enable himself to observe the future at least seventy years hence, with his records of his first sixty-three years meant to serve as the link between his lifetimes. Of course, this would leave open the possibility of his regressing to infancy again and again—a capability he may not have originally anticipated . . . . Tragically, however, we will probably never know precisely how he accomplished this, for the machine Beryl Ward found has disappeared, and the baby Griswold is dead."

While the theory of the American Board of Science has the weight of evidence behind it, the editors of this magazine must point out that there is an important consideration that has not yet been addressed: the human element. Beryl Ward had apparently fallen desperately in love with Griswold Masterson. And faced with the prospect of having to watch the man she loved slowly bloom into a youngster—and then into a young man—while she grew shriveled and weak (unaware of the universal implications of his experiments), she may have placed a pillow over the child's mouth until it wailed and clawed no longer. (Miss Ward is locked behind bars in an institution for the criminally insane.) Thus a basic human emotion may have been responsible for our being separated forever from the full implications of Masterson's experiments. This, as we see it, is the ultimate irony, the ultimate tragedy of the life and times of Griswold Masterson.

The sheriff's office is much too close to the real world to bend to the hypotheses of the intellectual community, so they have simply listed Griswold Masterson as a missing person. The child in the cylinder? From the pulpit Rev. Leopold Ossip has rendered the opinion, on more than one occasion, that the infant was the illegitimate offspring of Mr. Masterson and Miss Ward, and that in her madness she murdered her own son. The story she told to the sheriff, Ossip proclaimed, was the invention of an unholy "and therefore diseased" mind. While much of Marshville seems to have accepted the reverend's view, the rest of the world does not agree—judging from the many interpretations that have surfaced on the significance of the child. The most remarkable aspect of the entire affair, however, may be the steel cylinder. While its whereabouts has never been firmly established, a newspaper article (no date was indicated) clipped from the *Brattleboro Gazette*, published in Saskatchewan, Canada, and sent to our offices by an anonymous reader, could well have some bearing on the mystery:

CAVE PEOPLE IN STRANGE VIGIL

People have begun to gather on a hillside outside Brattleboro, Saskatchewan, and each morning there seems to be more of them, speaking in a growing variety of tongues.

All day these people do little more than sit and stare at an object partially imbedded in the earth, which blocks off the mouth of a natural cave—one of a series in the area. The stainless-steel capsule, apparently catching the gleam of the sun, seems to glow as if from its own internal light.

Toward evening, the cave people can be heard chanting. Once the sun is down, they build campfires, and the chanting stops. Lately they have been entering the catacombs of surrounding caves to shelter themselves for the night and, it is said, to pray.

Brattleboro police told the *Gazette* that the cave people are orderly and are breaking no laws. "That hill is part of a huge national forest preserve, open to all Canadians," said Chief Judd Nooson. "There's nothing much we can do about them, legally."

A professor of philosophy at the University of Saskatchewan, Stanley Nihlin, offered a possible explanation: "In these times of rapid change, when religious belief is at such a low level, people try on cults like new shoes. And discard them just as quickly."

A curious postscript to that newspaper item and, indeed, to this entire investigation, is that the editorial assistant who first heard about the Hermit Genius of Marshville, and the reporter who covered the story for *EQMM*, have resigned. Reportedly she left her husband and children and he left his fiancée and friends behind to join the cave people. But this has not been confirmed.

† At their request, the identities of the assistant and the reporter are being withheld.

BASS FISHING
WITH THE ENEMY

Daniel Hatch

Some people said we were heroes and some said we were traitors, but we were just a few old Mainers, with scruffy white beards and tussled white hair, in the right place at the right time—or maybe the wrong place at the wrong time, depending on your point of view.

Either way, the place we were at was a little seafood and ice cream shack called The Cabana at the southeast end of a little lake outside of Auburn. My brother, Ben, and I had been out fishing since the sun came up.

I love the lake first thing in the morning, when great clouds of steam rise up into the sky and a dazzling glare sparkles across the water. I was trying out a new bass lure—yellow and red with little flukes on the side. We didn't have much to show for the effort, but it was a wicked good way to keep a couple of old men out of their wives' way for a few hours.

It wasn't much of a lake—only a couple miles long and less than a mile across and pretty rectangular down at our end. Nothing like its bigger neighbors, Sebago and Thompson, but sufficient it was to the purpose of the day.

Our cottage was at one corner of the lake—now a duplex with my wife and I on one side and Ben and his wife on the other. The Cabana was over at the other corner, set just far enough back to be out of view from our porch.

It was one of those aging gems you find around Maine, with red-and-white-striped awnings outside and dark wood paneling inside. A juke box sat in the corner with little units at each booth where you could drop your quarter and pick your song. There was an old Coca-Cola sign on one wall and a Moxie sign on the other—the real thing from the factory in Lisbon Falls, not one of those phony Americana factory fakes. The place had the smell of moss and old grease and pine oil. It was a monument to the heyday of Maine's Golden Age, a century ago, before the rest of the country moved on and it stayed behind. ("Hea'd you had a Depression down theah," my father used to say to the tourists, with a heavy Down East cant. "Hea'd it was ovah.")

We tied our little boat at the dock and walked across a deep green dew-soaked lawn, through the sunroom and into the dining room proper.

And there we found Ted, the owner of the place, perched atop a stepladder, poking around in the space above the acoustic ceiling.

"What you up to, Ted?" Ben asked.

Ted must not have heard us come in, because he was so startled he gave a quick shudder that threw him off balance, making him lose his grip on whatever he was working on and nearly falling off the ladder. Ted was a good cook and he ate way too much of his own cooking, so climbing to the top of a stepladder was always a challenge to the laws of gravity—more so if anything broke his concentration.

I rushed forward and grabbed him by the arm before he completed the disaster and helped him regain his balance as he climbed down the steps to the floor.

"Jeezum, Ben, don't ever sneak up like that on me again," Ted said when he regained his composure. "I thought you was one of those Homeland Stupidity guys."

"Why would you think I was one of them?" Ben asked.

"Because he's got a guilty conscience."

We turned our heads to the table in the corner where Dan Adams was sitting, tapping away at a beat-up old laptop that looked nearly as old as Ben and me—and him. Ted turned white, then red, then sputtered briefly.

"Do you want to tell them or should I?" Dan asked.

"You're being so clever this morning, why don't you?" Ted said. "It was your idea."

"He's hooking up the satellite dish," Dan said.

"What for?" I asked. "Hockey season doesn't start until the end of next month." Since they cut off the cable from Canada a few years back, Ted had been running a pirate dish to pick up the CBC satellite feed so folks could watch the games from Montreal and Quebec—you know, real hockey for real hockey fans. He kept the dish in the attic, under a skylight, where it couldn't be seen from outside, and he had a cousin who was a state trooper who would give a day's warning whenever the Homeland Stupidity guys got the idea someone might be watching foreign videos and they needed to do a sweep of the countryside.

"We were watching CNN a little while ago when they broke in with a report from Juneau, Alaska. Something about a communications blackout—maybe a natural disaster, they weren't sure. Then one of those Homeland Security announcers came on and said we couldn't watch the Juneau story any more."

"Hey, Ted, doesn't your sister live in Juneau?" Ben asked as he poured himself a cup of coffee from the big chrome-plated urn behind the counter.

"Yeah," Ted said. "Dan couldn't find anything on the Internet about it."

"Just 'Error 999' screens," Dan said. "Security blackouts."

"So I figured I'd hook up the satellite dish and see if there was anything on the Canadian news. It was only going to be for a few minutes, then I was going to disconnect it. I just wanted to find out if anything might have happened to my sister."

"Then don't let us hold you up," I said. "Finish what you were doing. Ben and I will spot you on the ladder. We'd do it for you, but our wives told us when we turned 70 that we couldn't go climbing ladders any more."

"Thanks, Toby," Ted said. "Say, what have you two been up to this morning?"

"We were trying to find that big old bass over there near our cottage, the one that's been hiding all summer long over where the reeds are thick and the rocks stick out of the water."

"That fella's been hiding there for three or four summers now, hasn't he?" Dan asked.

"Ayuh," Ben said. "And one of these days we're going to catch him."

Ted started to climb the stepladder, but was interrupted before he got two steps up by a tremendous buzzsaw roar that rattled the windows and the silverware and the dishes and the coffee cups, starting in the front of the dining room and rushing over the sunroom.

"What was that?" Ted asked. But we were already rushing out into the sunroom and then out onto the lawn in time to see a bright yellow float plane zoom on overhead towards the lake—no more than fifty or sixty feet above the ground.

"Jeezum!" Ted cried when he caught up with us—just in time to see the plane touch down on the lake's surface.

The plane tipped left, then right, and it seemed like the pilot was having problems. We could see he was going to have bigger problems as he veered towards a little island that sits a hundred feet from the shore. The pilot must have seen the island, because we could see the rudder flip and the plane tip as he tried to come about before running out of room.

He should have cut the engine, but that was probably one thing too many to think of—and the next thing we knew, the plane was on its side.

"Come on, Toby!" Ben called to me. "Get in the boat!"

For a couple of old Mainers, we managed to move surprisingly fast.

All we had was a little twenty-horsepower gas motor, so it took us about five minutes to get our aluminum boat across the water to where the plane went down.

And the dangest thing about it was that my mind wasn't on the poor guy thrashing around in the water as the yellow tail fins slipped lower and lower, surrounded by green water and bubbles. It was across the lake, in the shallow water full of reeds and flat rocks with that big old largemouth bass that we'd been after all morning.

I pictured him down there in the shadows, behind the big rocks, in the reeds, laying in wait for some little minnow to make his breakfast— the great lake hunter waiting in ambush. And my lure kept running past him, trying to bring him out of hiding, ready to turn the hunter into the hunted. Somehow my deception wasn't enough, or he just wasn't hungry enough, and we went our separate ways once again.

Then we were on top of the sinking float plane, and Ben throttled back the motor to come alongside the pilot. He must have been a half-way decent swimmer, because he hadn't gone under yet. But he was struggling.

We pulled him in over the side, being careful not to swamp the boat in the process. He kind of rolled over the thwarts, water running off his green coveralls and nylon jacket. His heavy boots were soaked, and I wondered for a moment how he had managed to keep his head above water with a couple of anchors like those on his feet. I could see that he had a cut across his forehead, the blood mixing with the lakewater and running freely down the side of his face.

Then Ben cranked up the throttle and we headed back to the dock at The Cabana.

Dan and Ted met us there and helped us out, half-carrying, half-dragging the pilot across the lawn and into the restaurant.

Once inside, Dan and Ben sat the man down and started pouring coffee into him. Ben took his jacket off him and Dan went out into the kitchen where he found a pile of dish towels, which he used to wipe his face and hands.

The pilot, a young guy compared to us, no more than forty or so, was dazed and his few attempts at speech weren't effective. About all he managed at first was a weak "Thank you, thank you," which set him to coughing up some of the lakewater that he'd managed to get into his lungs.

Meanwhile, Ted clambered up the stepladder to finish what he'd started earlier. I stood by to keep him from falling down, and a few minutes later we had a picture on the television—one of those big flat things with the Perfect Crystal screen on the dining room wall—with a pretty blonde newscaster and pretty red and blue graphics.

The only problem was that she was speaking French.

"Any idea what she's saying, Dan?" Ted asked.

"Sorry, I never did know much French," he said.

"Don't look at me," Ben chipped in. "All I ever learned was enough to get in trouble with the girls down on Lisbon Street."

"Ayuh, and now you'd have to know Somalian to get into trouble down there," I said.

"Shouldn't we call the state police or someone about this guy?" Dan asked as he wrung the water from one of the dish towels.

"You mean so they can catch us watching Canadian news and lock us up?" Ted said.

"It's not like you'd be that far away," Ben said. "They turned that old Girl Scout camp at the north end of the lake into a detention center, you know."

"No," Ted said. "I didn't know that."

"You bet," Ben said. "They chased the Tripp girls away from there last month when they went up to pick blueberries. Followed them home in a big boat and brought them in for questioning. The girls told them that terrorists don't eat blueberries. They didn't seem too amused, from what I heard."

"They grabbed Emma Tripp a week later after she sounded off at Cormier's," I said. Cormier's was the little general store at the top of the hill from our cottage. It had a little post office in the back where we got our mail every day—after we got back from fishing. That was their excuse for grabbing Emma: Causing a disturbance at a federal facility, to wit, the post office at Cormier's.

"I heard about that, but none of the details," Ted said.

"Well, they can come for me any time they want," Ben said. "I'm their worst nightmare—a baby boomer from Maine with nothing to lose."

"Except your Social Security," Dan said.

"They take that away and I'll just go build myself a tarpaper mansion out in the woods and live by candlelight," Ben said. "I've done it before, you know, and I can do it again."

"You know what they say—you can tell someone from Maine, but you can't tell them much," I said.

"And it only gets worse when we get old," Dan said. "I've told you before about my father's uncle down in Wiscassett. He was 95 years old and the oldest plumber in America. Had to walk to work because they took away his car. He hung up on Barbara Walters because she kept asking so many dumb questions. His son worked for him. When he turned 65, he said, 'Dad, I want to retire.' His father said, 'Not 'til I do.'"

"If you ask me, they've been locking up way too many people for no reason at all," Ted said. "Just for things like watching hockey on Canadian TV. And I still don't know why they cut off the cable."

"The government's been pissed at them ever since they shot at that icebreaker trying to run the Northwest Passage after the Canadians told them not to," Dan said.

"Hey, look!" Ben said. "They're talking about Alaska."

He pointed at the television where a map of Alaska had popped up beside the newscaster's face. It zoomed in on the southeast panhandle, that narrow strip that sticks down towards the continental U.S., with a star marking Juneau.

The star turned into one of those red circles with a slash through it. A few words in French were inscribed below it, but not any that I recognized.

Then I noticed that the half-drowned pilot was watching the TV with us, reaching out with one hand to point at the screen.

"Alaska," he said. "I'm from Alaska. Sitka, Alaska."

"Well good for you," Ted said. "You sound like you're getting your wits back after that crash."

"But this isn't Alaska?" the pilot asked.

"Afraid not," said Dan.

"Then where am I?

Only in Maine could you give him an honest answer that would only confuse him, and Ben did just that, quickly and without thinking.

"West Poland," he said.

The pilot's jaw dropped and his eyes grew large and round.

"Maine," I added quickly. "West Poland, Maine. Near Auburn and Lewiston."

It didn't help.

"You mean I'm not in Alaska?" the pilot asked weakly. "But . . . but . . . that's impossible. I took off from Sitka this morning. I can't be in Maine."

His name was Norm Reynolds and he lived in Sitka, the first Russian settlement in Alaska, down in the panhandle, about 90 miles from Juneau.

"I took off from there before dawn," he said. "Headed over to Prince of Wales Island. The sun was coming up and I flew into a bright cloud. When I came out the other side, it didn't look like Alaska anymore. So I came down on the lake out there. Messed that up good, didn't I."

"You hit your head pretty hard," I said. "Are you sure you aren't just confused?"

"Today's Thursday, August 23rd isn't it?"

"All day," Ben said.

"I'm not confused about that," Norm said with a pained smile. He put his face in his hands, rubbed his eyes, then added: "This is impossible."

"Not exactly," Dan said.

"Not exactly?" I asked.

"Not if you look at the physics of it," he replied.

When Dan was a boy, he wanted to go to college somewhere where people didn't have an accent. So his folks packed him up in an old Volvo station wagon and sent him off to Boston. He didn't like Harvard much. He was too smart for BU and BC and all them little schools. But he liked MIT just fine. Stuck around and went through an ungodly amount of money until he dropped out a semester before graduating. That was the year they were shooting college students. He generally kept his education to himself. I kind of wished he'd done it that morning. But he didn't.

"Scientists have known for years about how the universe is constructed," he said. "There's eleven dimensions—maybe more, depending on how you do your math. Three of them are the ones we know. The ones that tell you where you are. And then there's time, that's another dimension. But all the rest of them are infinitesimally small. They're all folded up inside the others."

Ben grinned, and said: "I know that, Dan. You've explained it to us before."

Dan shrugged him off and continued. "Well it stands to reason that if most of the dimensions are infinitesimally small, then down there everything is already connected to everything else, all in the same place, all together. So if something slips—like across one of those extra dimensions—it could easily end up someplace else."

"Aren't there laws against that?" Ben asked. "Conservation of stuff or something?"

"Ayuh," Dan said. "But there's loopholes."

"Loopholes?" Ted asked credulously.

"If something's too small to measure or happens too quick, it can violate the laws."

"But Dan, that float plane out there at the bottom of the lake doesn't look too small to measure, does it?"

"I don't know, Dan," Ben said. "Sounds like an episode of 'Twilight Zone' to me." He hummed a few bars of the theme song to the old TV show, "Dee-dee-dee-dee, dee-dee-dee-dee."

"Old Rod did love those disappearing airplane stories," I said.

"I remember those," Ted said. "There was one where the pilot came from World War I and landed in Canada or somewhere."

"France," said Dan.

"What?" Ted asked.

"He landed in France."

"Ayuh," Ben said. "And another one where an airliner flew over Central Park and saw dinosaurs."

"What about the one where the bomber crashed in the desert and Bob Cummings spent an hour trying to find the rest of his crew?" I asked.

"That was a special one-hour show with a write-up in *TV Guide*," Ben said.

"What about all those stories about people who disappeared?" Ted asked. "That judge who walked around a horse and vanished into thin air? Or the man who came out of nowhere and ended up getting murdered in a snowy graveyard with no one else's footprints around?"

"We all grew up hearing those stories," I said. "It comes from living up here in the woods with nothing else to do at night."

"You fellows can laugh all you want," Dan said dryly. "But there's one thing you need to consider."

"What's that?" Ted asked.

"There's something going on out in Alaska that the government doesn't want us to hear about on the news."

"I think I need to see a doctor," Norm moaned, putting a hand to his head where Dan had placed one of those big Band-Aids on the cut.

"Or a physicist," Ben quipped.

"He's probably right, you know," I said. "Maybe it's time to call the EMTs."

"If we do, they'll bring the state troopers," Ted said. "And they'll bring the Homeland Stupidity. And I'll end up at the other end of the lake with Emma Tripp in the old Girl Scout camp."

"Ted, by now someone's probably already called everyone," Ben said. "There's forty cottages around the lake, and I'll bet everyone saw that plane go down."

Ted turned white, then scrambled over to the stepladder, which we'd folded up in the corner after he hooked up the satellite dish.

"You know, Ted," I said, "if you're so worried about Homeland Security, you can always turn the TV off before they get here. They won't know you've been watching the Canadian news."

Ted's shoulders sagged under the weight of the painfully obvious and he looked embarrassed at not thinking of it himself.

"I guess I could," he said.

"But not just yet," Dan said. "The English-language broadcast just came on. Turn it up, will you, Ted."

Everyone turned their attention to the screen as a new newscaster, a mousy brunette with her hair in a flip, repeated the top story for the non-Quebecois who were tuned in.

"And in Alaska, the government today announced a daring surprise raid by the Canadian Defense Force into the Juneau area just before dawn. Aided by the RCMP, more than five hundred special forces crossed the border near the Alaskan state capital and secured several detention camps in the area. More than a thousand political prisoners held in the camps were freed and transported back across the border before U.S. forces were able to respond. In Ottawa, government spokesmen said the action was taken at the urging of the European Union, the United Nations, and a number of Latin American governments. U.S. officials lodged a protest at the Canadian embassy and threatened unspecified retaliatory actions."

"Well I'll be damned," Ben said.

"Hooray for the Canadians," Dan said, raising a fist into the air.

"I can see why they don't want that getting out on CNN," I said.

And then all of a sudden I had that image again of the old largemouth bass hiding out in the reeds and the shadows at the bottom of the lake, with my bright, shiny lure flashing through the sunlight, trying to attract his attention.

I turned to Norm.

"Something tells me that you know more about this thing in Alaska than you're letting on," I said. "You know what they say. You can tell someone from Maine, but you can't tell them much."

Norm looked up and shook his head. "I took off from Sitka this morning before dawn and flew into a cloud. When I came out, I was over your lake."

"If you're going to stick with that story, then the rest of us have a decision to make," I said.

I could see the lights come on in Ben's eyes, but Ted looked confused. "What are you saying, Toby?" he asked.

"Despite Dan's explanation of eleven-dimensional space-time physics, I just don't think Norm is telling us the truth," I said. "I don't think he's from Alaska. And I don't think he flew out of any mysterious cloud over our lake."

"He's a Canadian," Ben said.

Norm wasn't budging. "I'm from Alaska," he said. "Sitka, Alaska."

"Ted, turn off that television," I said. "We don't want anyone to know we've been watching Canadian news."

"We don't?" asked Ben.

"Not if we're going to stick to Norm's story, we aren't. Besides, we don't want to get Ted into trouble when Homeland Security gets here, do we?"

"We sure don't," Ted said.

"The way I see it, if Norm is a Canadian and not an Alaskan, he's got a good reason for making up a wild story like this. We've got two choices. We can tell the Homeland Security people what we think—and let on that we've been watching the news from Canada. Or we can keep our mouths shut and let whatever is going to happen happen."

We looked at one another without saying a word for a long moment.

And a couple minutes later, Dan was on his cell phone to the state police, asking for help for a downed pilot. "And the damndest thing is," he said, "the guy says he took off from Alaska before dawn, flew into a cloud, and came out over the lake."

About twenty minutes after that, all the state troopers in southern Maine rolled into the parking lot in front of The Cabana with their blue lights flashing. An EMT rescue truck followed them up. And then a pair of black helicopters that didn't make any noise were landing on the lawn beside the lake, full of Homeland Security officers.

They rounded us up, put each of us in a different police car and Norm in the rescue truck, and headed off towards Auburn, with the helicopters keeping close escort all the way.

They were still asking us questions when the Canadian helicopters came in low out of the north and dropped in on the old Girl Scout camp, with their special forces and Mounties, to liberate Emma Tripp and all the others they had locked up there.

Norm was just a decoy. A lure to pull the Homeland Security guys out of the reeds and shadows and keep them busy while the real mission was on its way.

He was still telling them about that mysterious cloud—and we were still backing him up right up until the end. Until it was too late.

Eventually they let us go.

They told us not to tell anyone what had happened. They told us it wouldn't matter, because the newspapers and TV wouldn't be allowed to cover it. And they told us that if we did go talking about it, they'd take away our Social Security and put us in that Girl Scout camp.

But word got out anyway. It's hard to keep secrets up here.

And some thought we were heroes, while some thought we were traitors. But we were just a few old Mainers in the right place at the right time.

DREAMS OF
VIRGINIA DARE

John P. O'Grady

I was there the night it all began, but the greater part of this story I've had to piece together over the years from reports of others, mostly friends of mine, who are usually pretty honest. It's customary in these situations to start by saying something like, "Verily, this tale is true." At least that's how all the old books begin. They claim that the power of enchantment—whether a magical charm, or an eloquent poem, or a good story told around the table—is so great that it is able to overwhelm all of nature. I don't know about that, but just try saying "I love you" to someone for the first time and see how the world is changed, for good or ill.

Nostalgia, too, must be something like this. After a couple of decades, people look back on their college years and say, "That was a magical time." Those folks are speaking figuratively and from a distance. What I'm trying to do is figure *out* some things, and thereby draw a little closer to the offbeat phenomena of the world, which, if they aren't magic in a literal sense are without a doubt "wicked," as they say in Maine, "wicked weird."

It was a college bull session. First day back for the fall semester and everybody was excited because there was a big football game the next day to kick off the new school year. A bunch of people were sitting around in the dorm lounge introducing themselves to each other or catching up on the summer's news with old friends. Among them was a new guy named Leo LaHapp, a freshman, who was on the cross-country team. Talk got around to the courses people were taking and a couple said they were enrolled in Early American History. So Barb Taylor asked, "Does anybody remember Virginia Dare? I just love that name."

Virginia Dare, you may recall, was the first child born of English parents in the New World: August 18, 1587, on Roanoke Island in North Carolina. Not a good place to be from, all things considered, since not long after her birth everybody there disappeared without a trace. A few years later, when a long-delayed supply ship finally showed up from England, all they found were abandoned buildings overgrown with vines and a single word carved into a tree: *Croatoan*. Nobody knew what it meant, and there were no further signs of what happened to those unfortunate souls. All of them, including the baby Virgina Dare, were gone, never to be heard from again.

We were in Maine, so North Carolina seemed a pretty exotic topic—warm weather, sunny beaches, spring breaks—and it gave rise that evening to all kinds of fantastic speculations and associations. Somebody said that he knew of a bar called Croatoan—he thought that was the name—but it was down in South Boston. Somebody else said he was going to start a rock band and call it Croatoan. He imagined that none of the members in this band would ever take the stage and nobody would know what they look like; instead they'd play in some hidden location far removed from the audience and pipe in the music via speakers so it would all be very mysterious, and rumors could start that the band was really led by Jim Morrison, who hadn't died after all.

That's when Leo LaHapp spoke up. He wasn't called "The Bugman" yet. It was the first time anybody there had heard from him, so he was given the floor, and he surprised us by going on at length. Not a person in the room could have anticipated the succession of events after that. I realize that those of you who were there at the University of Maine will remember some of the incidents I'm about to recall—especially the infamous Witch Hunt—but so far as I know, the strange and disparate occurrences of those days have never been brought together in an adequate account. I don't make any great claims for my own story, but it must suffice until a more satisfactory version is put forth.

Anyway, Leo LaHapp launched into his story, telling the group—all of whom were strangers to him—that he had once been to Roanoke Island and had seen there a marble statue of Virginia Dare. It was sculpted in the nineteenth century by Maria Louise Lander, a friend of Nathaniel Hawthorne, and it was the most exquisite work of art he had ever seen. This statue was life sized, presenting Virginia Dare as a beautiful young woman, mostly naked, a detail Leo delivered with great relish. He described her as standing, scantily clad, in the midst of a fancy garden, with flowering trees and sweet-smelling shrubs all around. It was as if the baby Virginia Dare had somehow escaped from the ill-fated colony and had grown up and was now living in Eden or Arcadia or maybe, as Leo believed, Croatoan.

Then he spoke of a legend concerning this statue, how on certain nights of the year it comes to life and starts walking around. "If only it were so," Leo sighed. "Something like that is very hard to believe, I know, and I don't go for it myself, but she does come to me in my special dream."

That got a few snickers from the audience, but we all wanted to hear more about this special dream, so we encouraged him to continue.

"I'm at home and for some reason my family has this huge dead bear in the middle of the living room. It's stuffed like it came from the taxidermist, so I ask around but nobody can tell me why this bear is here. 'Who killed it?' I keep asking my father, but he just tells me to go ask my mother, but I can't find her anywhere. Next thing you know, a big tree starts growing out of the bear's head. It's huge and already very old, even though it just sprouted. As it rises up, I think it's going to break through the roof of the house, but when I look up, there is no roof—it's gone and everything's just night sky with stars blazing and the tree soaring up there so high it looks like its leaves are the stars. Then way up there I see a woman swinging on a swing. She's naked and her skin is shiny white like marble. It's Virginia Dare. But she's not a statue anymore, she's alive and she's swinging and smiling and waving down to me. She wants me to climb up the tree, but the trunk is so big I can't get my arms around it. There's no place to grab hold. I get all upset because I can't climb the tree and I won't be able to go up there and sit on the swing and swing back and forth among the starry leaves with Virginia Dare. It's really frustrating. But she keeps swinging and smiling and waving down, as if to urge me on, so I try once more. Then I wake up."

He finished his recitation by expressing the wistful hope that one day, if that statue of Virginia Dare really does come to life and go for walks, she might make the trip up to Maine and pay him a visit. "In the meantime," he concluded, "at least I have my special dream."

A couple of the women in the audience thought the story quite romantic, but mostly people just snickered some more and exchanged knowing looks or the cuckoo sign with each other. When some of the guys started teasing him about being in love with a chunk of rock, Leo just got up and left, insulted.

But the talking went on well into the night, moving away from Leo and his statue to related topics of magic potions and amulets. "Wouldn't it be fun," Westphal suggested, "to find some way to grant Leo his wish and have that statue stop by and give him a thrill?" More plotting and scheming followed. At last somebody—I think it was Crilly Fritz (a real name by the way)—said: "Let's go find the Magician!"

The Magician was the nickname of a guy whose real name was Forrest Woodroe, an otherwise lackluster accounting major save for one curious fact: he came from a part of Maine that, at the time we're talking about, still had a vibrant folk tradition of magic. It was somewhere up near Solon or Carrabassett maybe. The joke around campus was that while other kids were growing up playing with dolls or chemistry sets, the Magician was concocting potions and working out incantations. The bookshelves in his dorm room were lined with volumes by Albert the Great, Cornelius Agrippa, and Giordano Bruno. Forrest regularly wrote cryptic letters to the college newspaper interpreting current events in light of the prophecies of Nostradamus, signing his bizarre messages with the penname Nick Cusa. Guys like this show up every fall on college campuses all across America. What separated Forrest Woodroe, what kept him from being just another freshman goofball, was the fact that people actually witnessed him alter the course of the 1975 World Series. It happened the year before I got there, but here's what they say about it.

Going into the sixth game of the series, the Red Sox are down three games to two against the Reds, playing at home in Fenway. Everybody in New England is barnacled to their TV screen. The game goes into extra innings. Now it's past midnight. Bottom of the twelfth and leading off for the Sox is Carlton Fisk. On Pat Darcy's second pitch—a low inside sinker—Fisk takes a mighty swipe. The ball goes soaring up in a meteoric arc toward the wall in left field. It's a crisis, a moment when the past has least hold on the present and the present has greatest hold on the future. The ball becomes a lifeboat with all of New England's hopes crammed into it, and it's drifting dangerously toward the foul line.

Fisk takes a tentative step down the line toward first; stops; watches.

Time stops and watches, too. That's when the guys watching the game in the dorm lounge notice Forrest is standing performing this strange rhythmic motion with his arms, waving to the right as if to urge the lifeboat to keep from running afoul. Each wave is joined with a hop, so he's waving as he's bouncing his way across the room. Everybody's seized with wonder, looking at Forrest, when suddenly a loud "Hey, look!" rings out in the room. Eyes return to the TV screen, where Carlton Fisk is now doing the exact same thing as Forrest—waving his arms as he hops, in just the same fashion, even keeping exactly in sync. Three waves with three hops: whoosh, whoosh, whoosh. It is a very strange moment and it's going on even still: Forrest Woodroe leading Carlton Fisk in this weird dance across 250 miles and all of eternity.

But everything changes when the lifeboat hits the yellow foul pole above the wall—"Fair ball!"—and becomes a game-winning home run. The day is saved and Carlton Fisk is a hero! And to those sitting in the lounge of York Hall at the University of Maine on this faraway October night, so is Forrest Woodroe.

Even though the Red Sox would go on the next day to drop the ball and lose the series to the Reds, that sixth game—capped by Fisk's unforgettable performance—went down as the greatest in World Series history. And Forrest Woodroe, for his part, stepped into campus history and was known ever after as the Magician.

As for what went wrong with the Sox in that remaining game, the Magician had a role in that, too. Much to everybody's dismay, he was unable to make it back from some unspecified business in time for the game. The guys were counting on his working the magic one more time. They were plenty mad when he didn't show. Somebody even suggested that they burn the Magician at the stake for his failure, but death threats are ordinary in the mouths of disappointed Red Sox fans. Just ask Bob Stanley.

Cooler heads, though, prevailed that night in Maine, especially once it was reasoned that if this guy can sway the course of a World Series game, there's no telling what he might do to anybody who tried to mess with him. No one was willing to take that chance. Indeed, there are those who say that the Magician was so indignant about even the mild rudeness he suffered from those Red Sox fans when he finally did show up, that he put a hex on their team so they would never win another World Series.

One can only conclude that this, combined with the Babe Ruth curse, adds up to some pretty potent hoodoo.

And so the Magician now enters this story about Leo LaHapp and the statue of Virginia Dare. I myself have no part in the rest of it, save for the gathering of details after the fact. I have to admit that I did play a small role in hatching the scheme that called for the Magician's services, and it was me who came up with the idea to carve *Croatoan* into the Hollow Tree, thinking it might work as a kind of navigation beacon for Virginia Dare—but I didn't think anybody would take it seriously. Come on, this was a bull session.

When those guys from the dorm lounge—including, among others, Crilly Fritz, Peter Snell, and a muscle-bound guy that everybody called Animal—went off looking for the Magician, I stayed behind and so did Westphal. For a little while we sat around trying to impress the women by making fun of how gullible those nitwits were. But then I got tired and went off to bed, leaving Westphal still trying to impress the women.

What went down next at the Hollow Tree came to light just this past Christmas—Westphal filled me in. Turns out the Magician was perfectly willing to help those guys help Leo get his girl. Carving the word *Croatoan* into the Hollow Tree was a great idea, the Magician said, but to cast an effective love charm—especially if it involved animating a marble statue—*that* would require a more formal ritual, for which the presence of all these guys was required. They eagerly agreed to it.

So it must have been at that point the Magician went to his closet, grabbed the blue denim laundry bag and shook out a bunch of dirty clothes onto the floor. Then he gathered a few items from a drawer, stashed them into the bag in a big clatter, and the whole crew set off for the Hollow Tree.

The Hollow Tree was a beloved campus landmark, a huge old cottonwood on the long, sloping lawn above the Penobscot River. It was the biggest tree around, and some people even claimed it was the largest in the state of Maine. At the base of its immense trunk was a gaping hole, wide as a church door, that led into an immense, rotted-out interior. Inside was cozy as a chapel, with space vaulting upward into the dim rafters of the world, where statues of angels and Madonnas might lurk unseen in dark niches. There was room enough in there you could celebrate a mass if you wanted, or have a party, or—more intimately—bring a date and make out. Most everybody who attended the university in those days sooner or later did. It was a rite of passage and widely held that if you didn't make out in the Hollow Tree at least once before graduation, you couldn't really call yourself a University of Maine alum. Over the decades, the aura of all those comings together inside the tree must have inhered into the very xylem and phloem of that venerable monarch; if tree rings were a record of lovers' trysts rather than years, then this cottonwood easily qualified as the oldest living thing on earth.

I like to imagine that when the Magician and his band of dorm rats showed up there in the wee hours of the night, a pair of terrified lovebirds were flushed from cover, bolting out from the Hollow Tree as the truth sometimes does in the course of things. There they go, a couple of quail, bobbing as they weave, hopping and tripping as they tug up on jeans, open shirt and open blouse unfurling behind them in a ghostly flutter. They flee across the dark lawn toward still darker reaches in the distance, until their fantastic forms fade into the same stuff from which everything after midnight is made, two blurs in the blur of darkness.

The Magician and company now stood in front of the Hollow Tree. Preparations were made for the ritual. The Magician emptied out the clattering contents of the blue denim bag: a can of Sterno, a camping pot, a potholder, some matches, and another item, hard to see. The Magician instructed Crilly Fritz to go inside the tree and carve *Croatoan* somewhere in its heart. With gusto Crilly pulled out his pocketknife and vanished into the cottonwood.

By the time he emerged from his task, the Magician had things set up on the grass. The can of Sterno was going. The guys stood in a semi- circle around him. Using the potholder, the Magician suspended the camping pot over the blue flame. He had begun his conjuring. I guess you could call it that.

All of the guys now went drop-jawed, looking back and forth between what the Magician was doing and one another, or maybe they were just looking for the exit sign. The Magician's spell, performed in a tone of voice that seemed to rise directly out of a catacomb, went something like this:

Draw Virginia from the wild,

> *Home, my song, draw Virginia home,*
> *Home to Leo, home, my song, and pray:*
> *These words I weave as Venus bands*
> *Will draw, draw Virginia home!*

Most people are discomfitted by poetry in one way or another, and these guys were no exception. But they were thoroughly undone when the Magician started to lower into the camp pot a waxen figure—some say it was in the shape of an angel, others say it was a bear, and there is one report that insists it was just a handful of birthday candles—and proceeded with his incantation:

> *Draw Virginia from the wild,*
> *Home, my song, draw Virginia home.*
> *As Croatoan takes its hold*
> *Deep in the heart of this tree,*
> *Draw Virginia home, my song,*
> *Draw Virginia home.*
> *As this wax melts in one*
> *And the selfsame fire,*
> *Even so let Virginia melt,*
> *Melt with love for Leo—*
> *And to others' love let loose all hold*
> *And draw Virginia home!*

By no academic standard can this be called good verse. You won't find stuff like this in a *Norton Anthology.* But if a poem is measured by the effect it has in the world, then this one reversed the magnetic pole of reality.

First thing the guys hear after the Magician finishes is the growling. It erupts from somewhere deep inside the tree, then pounces out like a panther or a really mad Bigfoot. Everybody, including the Magician, goes lime white and starts trembling like an aspen grove. The Magician himself is the first one to break, taking off like a barn-sour rental horse. The rest of them are right on his tail.

Given what happened over the next few days, it's no wonder these guys fell into tacit agreement never to mention this episode again. The whole thing is embarrassing. Even today if you manage to track one of them down and ask about that night around the Hollow Tree and how it might have been connected to the Witch Hunt that followed, they will deny any knowledge of the topic. It's the main reason the story didn't get out before this.

Here's the next part.

The other famous campus landmark was in front of the gym: a bigger-than-life-size statue of a black bear. The black bear is the University of Maine mascot and this one had been around since the days of Rudy Vallee. I've seen a yellowed photo of old Rudy standing next to this bear. The singer is wearing a long raccoon coat and is crooning something through a megaphone, probably the "Maine Stein Song." So this picture would have to have been taken in the late Twenties. Otherwise pretty ferocious looking, the bear was made out of wood and plaster, so by the time we got to college in the Seventies he had been chewed up by termites and was looking pretty mangy.

On the very next morning after the high jinks around the Hollow Tree, Peter Snell was heading to the gym when he was shocked to discover the bear was gone! There was the empty pedestal, and all around it he could see footprints and deep ruts leading off in the direction of the woods. Peter Snell had flunked basic math a couple of times, but this two-and-two he could put together. He ran back to the dorm, terror stricken, with the whole pack of junkyard dogs that was his imagination nipping at his heels.

He found the rest of the Magician's assistants from the night before and warned them of the big trouble afoot. Whatever level-headedness had remained among them had now been dropped into a vat of acid. Greg Downing, another dorm resident, happened to be walking past the room where they were in heated deliberation. What he overheard didn't make much sense, so he thought it was just another bunch of Saturday morning drunks. He wasn't able to say who said what, but among the fragments of conversation preserved in his report are these:

"Shit! Do you really think that bear's name was Croatoan?"

"Shit! Is *that* what we heard growling in the tree?"

"Shit, we gotta get that bear back—the football team's gonna kill us!"

And lastly: "That Magician is a dead man!"

Then the guys charged out of the room—no need to repeat their names, you know them by now—and went off, presumably to grab the Magician and force him to set matters aright. One of the things we learned in political science class was that the solution to the problems of democracy is more democracy; the same might be said, at least in this case, when it comes to folly.

Now, believing that a ratty old statue of a bear, some dilapidated university mascot, could be conjured—even by mistake—into life, and that its name would just happen to be Croatoan, is by no means as far fetched as you may think. Wacky behavior stemming from wayward belief happens all the time in America. It may be the only story we've got.

Compare, for instance, the man from Plymouth, Massachusetts, who, a couple hundred years ago, had an idea about how to bring in a few more tourist dollars to his pretty how town. He went down to the harbor and walked out onto the strand of dreams. Or maybe it was a mudflat. The place was strewn with unremarkable boulders dropped there about ten thousand years ago—a heap of junk a glacier didn't want anymore. It had been lying there like this for millennia. But he walked around for a while, like people do in Fairly Reliable Bob's Used Car Lot, and at last selected a boulder, perhaps the least remarkable of them all, into which he chiseled four numerals: "1620." Next thing you know, the rock exploded into myth.

Historians assure us that the picture of Pilgrims stepping off the *Mayflower* onto this rock as if it were a welcome mat to the New World is little more than a charming bit of Thanksgiving lore, but it nevertheless translates into some overly firm belief. In 1835, Alexis de Tocqueville (that shrewd Frenchman) observed just how obsessed Americans had already become with this coffin-size piece of glacier trash: "I have seen fragments of this rock carefully preserved in several American cities, where they are venerated, and tiny pieces distributed far and wide." Today Plymouth Rock is housed in a kind of Greek temple, and it draws millions of people a year to an otherwise unexceptional place surrounded by sour cranberry bogs, lonesome pine woods, and smelly salt marshes. Talk about conjuring!

Well, the guys did find the Magician that day, sometime around sunset, and hauled him back to the Hollow Tree, where they planned to make him cancel the faulty spell cast the night before. But when they got there a lot of angry people were swarming about on campus—the football team had just lost—and the Hollow Tree was in plain sight, so our boys beat a hasty detour to the forest behind the university and went down the woods path that the cross-country team trained on.

At some point they left the trail and pushed into the dark spruce and fir forest where they found hundreds of small cheesecloth bags festooned from nearly every branch of the evergreens. The guys thought this a little strange, but they had bigger and stranger worries: they had to get that bear back before somebody got hurt—namely them—at the hands of a superstitious football team and its angry fans.

By the time they reached a spot secluded enough to perform whatever crazy ritual deemed proper by the Magician, dusk had settled in.

"Get going," Animal said as he gave the Magician a nasty shove. "Get that bear to go back where it belongs."

"Look," the Magician said, "I'm not sure I can. I don't know any spells that work on bears."

"What do you mean? Look what happened last night. Sure as hell looked like it worked to me. Just say the same thing, and make sure you mention the bear's name again."

"What are you talking about? What name?"

"Croatoan, you idiot!"

"I don't have my magic kit," the Magician said, "I left it at that tree last night. When I went back this morning to get it, all the stuff was gone."

"We don't have time for that crap. This is serious. Look, here's some candles. We'll light them and stand around holding them and you just sing that damn bear back to where the hell it belongs. Now do it!"

Alas the Magician, wanting his bag of tricks, did the only thing any performer can do in such a situation—he winged it. Who knows exactly what words he chanted, but they came through in that same catacomb tone, only now they tumbled along through the dusky forest like empty trash cans in a Halloween wind.

Little is understood anymore about the relation between word and world. In sounding it out, you might think there is some vast separation between them, starting with the letter *L* and reaching out to every level of meaning. But this would be an error. There is no separation, or so they say. To the artists who work in this medium—which goes by the name of magic—there is a conviction that nothing happens by chance or luck. These people align their actions with some bigger principle, in some cases bright and shining, and in others very dark indeed. All of them use the human voice to express the inner nature of the mind, to draw forth its secret manifestations and to declare the will of the speaker or a guardian angel or whatever demon might have stowed away for the course of any particular human life.

Maybe, as you say, all of this is just a load of hooey. You wouldn't be wrong. But if it had been *you* jogging down the woods path that evening on your way back to the fieldhouse after a strenuous and solitary training run because you showed up late for cross-country practice, and you heard that creepy chanting coming from the dark woods and had seen the candlelight flickering among the somber spruce and fir boughs, then maybe *you* would have been struck as poor Leo LaHapp was struck that evening: with the firm impression that there was a coven of witches out there in the University Forest and they were conducting some dark ritual, probably a black mass.

"Holy shit!" you would say, picking up the pace and running the fastest mile you'd ever run in your whole life (and nobody there to see), just so you can get back to campus in time and sound the alarm: "There's witches out there—I mean it—and they're doing animal sacrifices and who knows what all! We gotta stop it!"

Yes, had all this actually happened to you, then a few pages in the underground history of the University of Maine would have been devoted to your exploits. That is, if anybody bothered to write it.

But this is Leo's story and here's what happened to him.

He emerged from the forest and Paul-Revered it around campus, hustling from dorm to dorm and shouting about witches. At first people just dismissed Leo as a rowdy or a drunk, but then he managed to convince a couple of resident assistants at the dorm to go into the woods with him to investigate.

Flashlights in hand, they retraced Leo's path. Along the way, they saw the cheesecloth bags hanging in the trees. Nobody knew what they meant, but everybody agreed they looked pretty sinister, like little ghosts that had snagged themselves in the branches. Then they found some smoking candles lying in the forest duff. But what clinched it was when they heard, from deep in the recesses of the night woods, a horrible racket of breaking branches and snorting animals and demonic cursing, as if a bunch of people were running away. It sounded like a coven of witches!

There's no telling where in the human mind the switch is that, if thrown, turns on mob mentality, but Leo, groping around in there for anything to throw some light on his experience, managed on that memorable Friday night to trip it.

The whole campus lit up in a frenzy. It was like a kindergarten game of telephone gone haywire, or an adult game that politicians used to play called the domino effect. Whatever it was, it was nuts and it was fast. As Westphal describes it: "Next thing you know there's two hundred guys with baseball bats and hockey sticks pouring out of the dorms and heading for the woods. God help anybody they found out there. I think they killed a couple of black cats, I'm not sure, but a lot of those guys were already drunk and pissed off that the football team had lost, so when they couldn't find any witches, they started beating each other up. That witch-hunt was the scariest thing I've ever seen, and it went on all weekend."

It was as though the campus had sent up a weather balloon into Cloud Cuckoo-land. It stayed up there for a day and a half. In the meantime, the Witch Hunt was big news and almost everybody was taking it seriously.

Since Leo was the first one to spot the trouble, he became a hero of sorts, as well as the de facto spokesman for what was going on. He was now the Cotton Mather of UMaine, demanding the purge of baneful influences. He thought people would be interested in what he had to say, so he set up a makeshift press room in the dorm lounge.

At first it was just a single reporter from the campus newspaper, but as the scope of the events widened, press from off campus started showing up. In eastern Maine, any fuss is big news. Soon there were rumors that TV cameras were on their way and maybe Huntley and Brinkley, too. Lucky for Leo, those who knew the real story, including the fine points of his special dream, had their own problems and were lying low.

With Leo at the helm, all kinds of fools started making report. Stories came in about strange mounds of earth discovered out in the forest. "It must be where the witches buried their victims," exclaimed one sociology major on Sunday morning. For the rest of the day you saw guys heading off into the woods with shovels. Then came the psychology major who said he saw a bunch of naked people, obviously witches, darting among the trees. "And if you don't believe it, here's a shirt I found out there!" This sent even more people out into the woods; nobody wanted to miss out on a chance to lay hands on these witches. Finally, there were several UFO sightings that weekend, and one thoroughly besotted philosophy major claimed to have been abducted by the aliens, vicious beings who—he insisted—had robbed him of everything. "I can't even remember my name," he sobbed over and over to the reporters, as Leo stood there with a comforting arm around the poor scholar's shoulders. "We must recover this good man's name," Leo intoned for the record.

Monday morning was when that weather balloon came crashing down. It dropped in the form of a graduate student in forest entomology who came bursting into Leo's "press room" with a bug up his ass. He said he had been away for the weekend and just gotten back. He had this big experiment going for his dissertation research on spruce budworm. It involved setting up cheesecloth traps out in the forest to catch the insects. When he went out to the site this morning, he found all the traps had been ripped from the trees. Three years of research down the drain. Or up in smoke as the case may be, because he learned that students from one of the Christian organizations had pulled them down and burned them in a ritual bonfire out in the forestry school's stump dump.

"They thought my traps had something to do with witchcraft!" the bewildered grad student declared, as reporters busily scribbled down notes. He also said something about finding a badly charred bear's head nearby. "What the hell's going on around here?" he demanded.

"Oh shit," said Leo, as he bolted out of there before the grad student could grab him or any TV cameras showed up.

The next day the campus newspaper headline read: "Witch Hunt Proves a Witch Hunt. Campus Bugged by False Report." Many humiliating details found their way into that story, but somehow Leo was spared public exposure of his special dream. At least he still had that. Also, there was no mention of the Magician, Crilly Fritz, Peter Snell, Animal, or any of those other mischief-makers from the dorm.

Even today very few know about Virginia Dare's role in all this. For Leo's sake, I'm glad. I hope he forgives me for invoking her one more time, but I think these things can now be laid to rest. Everybody should know that the Witch Hunt wasn't really Leo's fault; he was just caught up in a swirl of circumstances. Once that story broke, his reputation on campus was ruined. Nobody called him a hero after that. They didn't even call him Leo anymore. Instead, he was simply "the Bugman." And the Bugman he remains.

There's a mawkish pleasure one takes in calling to mind events such as these. Sometimes I think my college years were misspent in pulling pranks and cutting classes so I could sit around and write stories like this to entertain my friends. Then I comfort myself by thinking that nothing that happened back there, no matter how silly, was far removed from anything else going on in the world. It was the Seventies and everybody was doing this kind of thing. Call it the "spirit of the times." Every age has one.

"What a waste!" people say when I tell them the kinds of things we did in those days. "How did you ever make anything of yourselves?" Well, maybe it's like the millions of seeds a cottonwood tree flings out into the world each spring, those tiny, feathery parcels of hope that float together in the air for a while, just drifting around in companionable oblivion. Only one or two of them might ever come down to earth and find a nurturing spot to take root, someplace where they might indeed "make something of themselves."

After all, while we were sitting around a University of Maine dorm on that Friday evening a quarter century ago, concocting schemes to animate a statue and put a love spell on it, at the same time, on the other side of the continent, there were others with names like Jobs and Wozniak sitting around conjuring up a computer that would be named for a fruit that comes from a tree in Eden; a computer small enough and friendly enough that everybody in the world might own one, a magical box to be connected to millions of other boxes all over the world, so that in the end, no matter whatever else might be said of any individual, each would be a node in some infinite web, each an electric sparkle in the eye of Indra.

And thus my wayward college days are redeemed—because they were never lost in the first place, never removed from the center of things in this center-less universe. In fact, so far as this story goes, they *are* the center. It's mind boggling to consider: whatever it is that causes one idea or name to gain purchase in the wider world while another fades away just may be what ultimately distinguishes a college prank from true magic. Or, as some are inclined to see it, history from myth.

In any case, you may be wondering how it came about that I should now have all these details. Perhaps you're curious as to what happened to the people who appeared in this sketch, or maybe you'd just like to check out these places for yourself, much as literary tourists do when they rummage around the Catskill Mountains looking for Rip Van Winkle's bed, or when they scour Wall Street trying to find the building Bartleby worked in. There's no going back to such places, except by the way we just came. But if you insist on historical accuracy, I'll do my best, though this particular bag of tricks is nearly empty.

First of all, the Magician. He did graduate from UMaine and went on to Harvard Law School. After that he got a job with some Big Eight accounting firm and got busted in the Eighties for insider trading. Last I heard he's selling furniture in Farmington, Maine. The rest of those guys from the dorm I haven't seen or heard about in years, but with names like Crilly and Animal, you can be sure they are well known in their respective neighborhoods, wherever they may be. As for the Bugman, he dropped out of college after one semester, to chase his special dream elsewhere, maybe in Croatoan.

Speaking of Croatoan, for several years after these events, lovers and other visitors to the heart of the Hollow Tree were baffled by this odd word they found carved there. It became part of the campus folklore. There was even a story about a young couple who, not long after graduation, had a baby they named Croatoan, no doubt because she was conceived in the Hollow Tree.

Ah, the Hollow Tree. Sad to say, but even mythical giants must fall. Sometime after I left Maine, the Hollow Tree came down. I can only hope that it wasn't rudely toppled as if it were just another piece of timber, sliced up into logs, and hauled off for target practice in the stump dump, where junior lumberjacks fling axes at old carved hearts and one mysterious word—or worse, carted away to the Old Town mill and pulped into the paper you're reading this on. I would hate to think that this book is all that remains of a million "I love yous" and one special dream. Whatever, the Hollow Tree is gone from UMaine. I wonder if anybody there even remembers it anymore.

As for that old black bear mascot that disappeared—his name wasn't Croatoan. As far as I can determine, he never had a name. Nor did he ever stand up from his pedestal and stalk the campus. Turns out that on the Friday evening before the disappointing football game, the Alumni Association had held a little ceremony. The old bear was being retired. The president of the university said some gold-watch words, then a crane hoisted the crumbling bear onto a flatbed truck that carried it away and unceremoniously dropped it off in the stump dump, for lack of a better paddock. Given the mayhem of the next few days, it's not surprising that nobody ever asked about its mysterious disappearance from the stump dump. But there's an aging entomology grad student—still trying to repair the damage to his career after the disastrous spruce budworm experiments—who could tell you a thing or two about that bear's fate.

So if you had your heart set on seeing a bear at the University of Maine, don't fret—they replaced it. The new mascot is a bit smaller—"leaner and meaner" as the Alumni Association likes to say—and it's made of cast bronze. Some say bronze was chosen so as to prevent the rotted-out destiny that overtook its predecessor. But there are a few—and you know their names—who believe that using heavy metal was the only way to ensure that if *this* mascot should ever come to life, its own weight would keep it from going anywhere. Thus this bear is now fixed in place more firmly than most treasured beliefs.

At long last, there is the mystery of the growl. As I said, I was only able to pick up the threads of this story thanks to Westphal. I paid him a visit over Christmas down on Mount Desert Island and we got to talking about our college days. The Witch Hunt came up, as it sometimes does when we get together. This time he provided all of the details of the events at the Hollow Tree and I wondered how he came upon this expanded version. I knew he hadn't gone along with the Magician and company that fateful night. I pressed him.

"So what gives?"

"Come on down in the cellar with me." He grinned impishly, an expression I know all too well.

Westphal lives in an old house. Cellars in these places are spooky. They're dimly lit and smell like the earth's dirty laundry. As he led me over to some dark shelves on a back wall, he said, "Hey, O'Grady—that growl? It was me. I beat those guys to the Hollow Tree and was hiding inside, up in one of those dark places you can't see from below. I scared the shit out of them—you should have seen it."

"No way!" I said.

"Well then, how do you explain this?" He reached up to the highest shelf and brought down an old blue denim bag, clattering with stuff inside. He handed it over to me. We were a couple of bank robbers and here was my share of the loot.

And that's all I got.

ECHO

Elizabeth Hand

This is not the first time this has happened. I've been here every time it has. Always I learn about it the same way, a message from someone five hundred miles away, a thousand, comes flickering across my screen. There's no TV here on the island, and the radio reception is spotty: the signal comes across Penobscot Bay from a tower atop Mars Hill, and any kind of weather—thunderstorms, high winds, blizzards—brings the tower down. Sometimes I'm listening to the radio when it happens, music playing, Nick Drake, a promo for the Common Ground Country Fair; then a sudden soft explosive hiss like damp hay falling onto a bonfire. Then silence.

Sometimes I hear about it from you. Or, well, I don't actually hear anything: I read your messages, imagine your voice, for a moment neither sardonic nor world-weary, just exhausted, too fraught to be expressive. Words like feathers falling from the sky, black specks on blue.

The Space Needle. The Sears Tower. LaGuardia Airport. The Golden Gate Bridge. The Millennium Eye. The Bahrain Hilton. Sydney, Singapore, Jerusalem.

Years apart at first; then months; now years again. How long has it been since the first tower fell? When did I last hear from you?

I can't remember.

This morning I took the dog for a walk across the island. We often go in search of birds, me for my work, the wolfhound to chase for joy. He ran across the ridge, rushing at a partridge that burst into the air in a roar of copper feathers and beech leaves. The dog dashed after her fruitlessly, long jaw open to show red gums, white teeth, a panting unfurled tongue.

"Finn!" I called and he circled round the fern brake, snapping at bracken and crickets, black splinters that leapt wildly from his jaws. "Finn, get back here."

He came. Mine is the only voice he knows now.

There was a while when I worried about things like food and water, whether I might need to get to a doctor. But the dug well is good. I'd put up enough dried beans and canned goods to last for years, and the garden does well these days. The warming means longer summers here on the island, more sun; I can grow tomatoes now, and basil, scotch bonnet peppers, plants that I never could grow when I first arrived. The root cellar under the cottage is dry enough and cool enough that I keep all my medications there, things I stockpiled back when I could get over to Ellsworth and the mainland—albuterol inhalers, alprazolam, amoxicillin, Tylenol and codeine, ibuprofen, aspirin; cases of food for the wolfhound. When I first put the solar cells up, visitors shook their heads: not enough sunny days this far north, not enough light. But that changed, too, as the days got warmer.

Now it's the wireless signal that's difficult to capture, not sunlight. There will be months on end of silence and then it will flare up again, for days or even weeks, I never know when. If I'm lucky, I patch into it, then sit there, waiting, holding my breath until the messages begin to scroll across the screen, looking for your name. I go downstairs to my office every day, like an angler going to shore, casting my line though I know the weather's wrong, the currents too strong, not enough wind or too much, the power grid like the Grand Banks scraped barren by decades of trawlers dragging the bottom. Sometimes my line would latch onto you: sometimes, in the middle of the night, it would be the middle of the night where you were, too, and we'd write back and forth. I used to joke about these letters going out like messages in bottles, not knowing if they would reach you, or where you'd be when they did.

London, Paris, Petra, Oahu, Moscow. You were always too far away. Now you're like everyone else, unimaginably distant. Who would ever have thought it could all be gone, just like that? The last time I saw you was in the hotel in Toronto, we looked out and saw the spire of the CN Tower like Cupid's arrow aimed at us. You stood by the window and the sun was behind you and you looked like a cornstalk I'd seen once, burning, your gray hair turned to gold and your face smoke.

I can't see you again, you said. *Deirdre is sick and I need to be with her.* I didn't believe you. We made plans to meet in Montreal, in Halifax, Seattle. Gray places; after Deirdre's treatment ended. After she got better. But that didn't happen. Nobody got better. Everything got worse.

In the first days I would climb to the highest point on the island, a granite dome ringed by tamaracks and hemlock, the gray stone covered with lichen, celadon, bone white, brilliant orange: as though armfuls of dried flowers had been tossed from an airplane high overhead. When evening came, the aurora borealis would streak the sky, crimson, emerald, amber; as though the sun were rising in the west, in the middle of the night, rising for hours on end. I lay on my back wrapped in an old Pendleton blanket and watched, the dog, Finn, stretched out alongside me. One night the spectral display continued into dawn, falling arrows of green and scarlet, silver threads like rain or sheet lightning racing through them. The air hummed, I pulled up the sleeve of my flannel shirt and watched as the hairs on my arm rose and remained erect; looked down at the dog, awake now, growling steadily as it stared at the trees edging the granite, its hair on end like a cat's. There was nothing in the woods, nothing in the sky above us. After perhaps thirty minutes I heard a muffled sound to the west, like a far-off sonic boom; nothing more.

After Toronto we spoke only once a year; you would make your annual pilgrimage to mutual friends in Paris and call me from there. It was a joke, that we could only speak like this.

I'm never closer to you than when I'm in the seventh arrondissement at the Bowlses', you said.

But even before then we'd seldom talked on the phone. You said it would destroy the purity of our correspondence, and refused to give me your number in Seattle. We had never seen that much of each other anyway, a handful of times over the decades. Glasgow once, San Francisco, a long weekend in Liverpool, another in New York. Everything was in the letters; only of course they weren't actual letters but bits of information, code, electrical sparks; like neurotransmitters leaping the chasm between synapses. When I dreamed of you, I dreamed of your name shining in the middle of a computer screen like a ripple in still water. Even in dreams I couldn't touch you: my fingers would hover above your face and you'd fragment into jots of gray and black and silver. When you were in Basra

I didn't hear from you for months. Afterward you said you were glad; that my silence had been like a gift.

* * *

For a while, the first four or five years, I would go down to where I kept the dinghy moored on the shingle at Amonsic Cove. It had a little two-horsepower engine that I kept filled with gasoline, in case I ever needed to get to the mainland.

But the tides are tricky here, they race high and treacherously fast in the Reach; the *Ellsworth American* used to run stories every year about lobstermen who went out after a snagged line and never came up, or people from away who misjudged the time to come back from their picnic on Egg Island and never made it back. Then one day I went down to check on the dinghy and found the engine gone. I walked the length of the beach two days running at low tide, searching for it, went out as far as I could on foot, hopping between rocks and tidal pools and startling the cormorants where they sat on high boulders, wings held out to dry like black angels in the thin sunlight. I never found the motor. A year after that the dinghy came loose in a storm and was lost as well, though for months I recognized bits of its weathered red planking when they washed up on shore.

The book I was working on last time was a translation of Ovid's *Metamorphoses*. The manuscript remains on my desk beside my computer, with my notes on the nymph "whose tongue did not still when others spoke," the girl cursed by Hera to fall in love with beautiful, brutal Narkissos. He hears her pleading voice in the woods and calls to her, mistaking her for his friends.

But it is the nymph who emerges from the forest. And when he sees her, Narkissos strikes her, repulsed; then flees. *Emoriar quam sit tibi copia nostri!* he cries; and with those words condemns himself.

Better to die than be possessed by you.

And see, here is Narkissos dead beside the woodland pool, his hand trailing in the water as he gazes at his own reflection. Of the nymph,

> *She is vanished, save for these:*
> *her bones and a voice that calls out*
> *amongst the trees.*
> *Her bones are scattered in the rocks.*

*She moves now in the laurels and beeches, she moves unseen
across the mountaintops.*
*You will hear her in the mountains and wild places,
but nothing of her remains save her voice,
her voice alone, alone upon the mountaintop.*

Several months ago, midsummer, I began to print out your letters. I was afraid something would happen to the computer and I would lose them forever. It took a week, working off and on. The printer uses a lot of power and the island had become locked in by fog; the rows of solar cells, for the first time, failed to give me enough light to read by during the endless gray days, let alone run the computer and printer for more than fifteen minutes at a stretch. Still, I managed, and at the end of a week held a sheaf of pages. Hundreds of them, maybe more; they made a larger stack than the piles of notes for Ovid.

I love the purity of our relationship, you wrote from Singapore. *Trust me, it's better this way. You'll have me forever!*

There were poems, quotes from Cavafy, Sappho, Robert Lowell, W. S. Merwin. *It's hard for me to admit this, but the sad truth is that the more intimate we become here, the less likely it is we'll ever meet again in real life.* Some of the letters had my responses copied at the beginning or end, imploring, fractious; lines from other poems, songs.

Swept with confused alarms of
I long and seek after
You can't put your arms around a memory.

The first time, air traffic stopped. That was the eeriest thing, eerier than the absence of lights when I stood upon the granite dome and looked westward to the mainland. I was used to the slow constant flow overhead, planes taking the Great Circle Route between New York, Boston, London, Stockholm, passing above the islands, Labrador, Greenland, gray space, white. Now, day after day after day the sky was empty. The tower on Mars Hill fell silent. The dog and I would crisscross the island, me throwing sticks for him to chase across the rocky shingle, the wolfhound racing after them and returning tirelessly, over and over.

After a week the planes returned. The sound of the first one was like an explosion after that silence, but others followed, and soon enough I grew accustomed to them again. Until once more they stopped.

I wonder sometimes, how do I know this is all truly happening? Your letters come to me, blue sparks channeled through sunlight; you and your words are more real to me than anything else. Yet how real is that? How real is all of this? When I lie upon the granite I can feel stone pressing down against my skull, the trajectory of satellites across the sky above me a slow steady pulse in time with the firing of chemical signals in my head. It's the only thing I hear, now: it has been a year at least since the tower at Mars Hill went dead, seemingly for good.

One afternoon, a long time ago now, the wolfhound began barking frantically and I looked out to see a skiff making its way across the water. I went down to meet it: Rick Osgood, the part-time constable and volunteer fire chief from Mars Hill.

"We hadn't seen you for a while," he called. He drew the skiff up to the dock, but didn't get out. "Wanted to make sure you were okay."

I told him I was, asked him up for coffee, but he said no. "Just checking, that's all. Making a round of the islands to make sure everyone's okay."

He asked after the children. I told him they'd gone to stay with their father. I stood waving, as he turned the skiff around and it churned back out across the dark water, a spume of black smoke trailing it. I have seen no one since.

Three weeks ago I turned on the computer and, for the first time in months, was able to patch into a signal and search for you. The news from outside was scattered and all bad. Pictures, mostly; they seem to have lost the urge for language, or perhaps it is just easier this way, with so many people so far apart. *Some things take us to a place where words have no meaning.* I was readying myself for bed when suddenly there was a spurt of sound from the monitor. I turned and saw the screen filled with strings of words. Your name: they were all messages from you. I sat down, elated and trembling, waiting as for a quarter-hour they cascaded from the sky and moved beneath my fingertips, silver and black and gray and blue. I thought that at last you had found me; that these were years of words and yearning, that you would be back. Then, as abruptly as it had begun, the stream ceased; and I began to read.

They were not new letters; they were all your old ones, decades old, some of them. 2009, 2007, 2004, 2001, 1999, 1998, 1997, 1996. I scrolled backward in time, a skein of years, words; your name popping up again and again like a bright bead upon a string. I read them all, I read them until my eyes ached and the floor was pooled with candle wax and broken light bulbs. When morning came I tried to tap into the signal again, but it was gone. I go outside each night and stare at the sky, straining my eyes as I look for some sign that something moves up there, that there is something between myself and the stars. But the satellites, too, are gone now, and it has been years upon years since I have heard an airplane.

In fall and winter I watch those birds that do not migrate. Chickadees, nuthatches, ravens, kinglets. This last autumn I took Finn down to the deep place where in another century they quarried granite to build the Cathedral of Saint John the Divine. The quarry is filled with water, still and black and bone-cold. We saw a flock of wild turkeys, young ones; but the dog is so old now he can no longer chase them, only watch as I set my snares. I walked to the water's edge and gazed into the dark pool, saw my reflected face, but there is no change upon it, nothing to show how many years have passed for me here, alone. I have burned all the old crates and cartons from the root cellar, though it is not empty yet. I burn for kindling the leavings from my wood bench, the hoops that did not curve properly after soaking in willow-water, the broken dowels and circlets. Only the wolfhound's grizzled muzzle tells me how long it's been since I've seen a human face. When I dream of you now I see a smooth stretch of water with only a few red leaves upon its surface.

We returned from the cottage, and the old dog fell asleep in the late afternoon sun. I sat outside and watched as a downy woodpecker, *Picus pubesens*, crept up one of the red oaks, poking beneath its soft bark for insects. They are friendly birds, easy to entice, sociable; unlike the solitary wrynecks they somewhat resemble. The wrynecks do not climb trees, but scratch upon the ground for the ants they love to eat. "Its body is almost bent backward," Thomas Bewick wrote more than two hundred years ago in his *History of British Birds:*

> whilst it writhes its head and neck by a slow and almost
> involuntary motion, not unlike the waving wreaths of a

serpent. It is a very solitary bird, never being seen with any other society but that of its female, and this is only transitory, for as soon as the domestic union is dissolved, which is in the month of September, they retire and migrate separately.

It was this strange involuntary motion, perhaps, that so fascinated the ancient Greeks. In Pindar's fourth Pythian Ode, Aphrodite gives the wryneck to Jason as the magical means to seduce Medea, and with it he binds the princess to him through her obsessive love. Aphrodite of many arrows: she bears the brown-and-white bird to him, "the bird of madness," its wings and legs nailed to a four-spoked wheel.

> *And she shared with Jason*
> *the means by which a spell might blaze*
> *and burn Medea, burning away all love she had for her family*
> *a fire that would ignite her mind, already aflame*
> *so that all her passion turned to him alone.*

The same bird was used by the nymph Simaitha, abandoned by her lover in Theokritos's *Idyll:* pinned to the wooden wheel, the feathered spokes spin above a fire as the nymph invokes Hecate. The isle is full of voices: they are all mine.

Yesterday the wolfhound died, collapsing as he followed me to the top of the granite dome. He did not get up again, and I sat beside him, stroking his long gray muzzle as his dark eyes stared into mine and, at last, closed. I wept then as I didn't weep all those times when terrible news came, and held his great body until it grew cold and stiff between my arms. It was a struggle to lift and carry him, but I did, stumbling across the lichen-rough floor to the shadow of the thin birches and tamaracks overlooking the Reach. I buried him there with the others, and afterward lit a fire.

This is not the first time this has happened. There is an endless history of forgotten empires, men gifted by a goddess who bears arrows, things in flight that fall in flames. Always, somewhere, a woman waits alone for news. At night I climb to the highest point of the island. There I make a little fire and burn things that I find on the beach and in the woods. Leaves, bark, small bones, clumps of feathers, a book. Sometimes I think of you and stand upon the rock and shout as the wind comes at me, cold and smelling of snow. A name, over and over and over again.

Farewell, Narkissos said, and again Echo sighed and whispered Farewell.

Good-bye, good-bye.

Can you still hear me?

MRS. TODD'S SHORTCUT

Stephen King

"There goes the Todd woman," I said.

Homer Buckland watched the little Jaguar go by and nodded. The woman raised her hand to Homer. Homer nodded his big, shaggy head to her, but didn't raise his own hand in return. The Todd family had a big summer home on Castle Lake, and Homer had been their caretaker since time out of mind. I had an idea that he disliked Worth Todd's second wife every bit as much as he'd liked 'Phelia Todd, the first one.

This was just about two years ago and we were sitting on a bench in front of Bell's Market, me with an orange soda-pop, Homer with a glass of mineral water. It was October, which is a peaceful time in Castle Rock. Lots of the lake places still get used on the weekends, but the aggressive, boozy summer socializing is over by then and the hunters with their big guns and their expensive nonresident permits pinned to their orange caps haven't started to come into town yet. Crops have been mostly laid by. Nights are cool, good for sleeping, and old joints like mine haven't yet started to complain. In October the sky over the lake is passing fair, with those big white clouds that move so slow; I like how they seem so flat on the bottoms, and how they are a little gray there, like with a shadow of sundown foretold, and I can watch the sun sparkle on the water and not be bored for some space of minutes. It's in October, sitting on the bench in front of Bell's and watching the lake from afar off, that I still wish I was a smoking man.

"She don't drive as fast as 'Phelia," Homer said. "I swan I used to think what an old-fashion name she had for a woman that could put a car through its paces like she could."

Summer people like the Todds are nowhere near as interesting to the year-round residents of small Maine towns as they themselves believe. Year-round folk prefer their own love stories and hate stories and scandals and rumors of scandal. When that textile fellow from Amesbury shot himself, Estonia Corbridge found that after a week or so she couldn't even get invited to lunch on her story of how she found him with the pistol still in one stiffening hand. But folks are still not done talking about Joe Camber, who got killed by his own dog.

Well, it don't matter. It's just that they are different race-courses we run on. Summer people are trotters; us others that don't put on ties to do our week's work are just pacers. Even so there was quite a lot of local interest when Ophelia Todd disappeared back in 1973. Ophelia was a genuinely nice woman, and she had done a lot of things in town. She worked to raise money for the Sloan Library, helped to refurbish the war memorial, and that sort of thing. But *all* the summer people like the idea of raising money. You mention raising money and their eyes light up and commence to gleam. You mention raising money and they can get a committee together and appoint a secretary and keep an agenda. They like that. But you mention *time* (beyond, that is, one big long walloper of a combined cocktail party and committee meeting) and you're out of luck. Time seems to be what summer people mostly set a store by. They lay it by, and if they could put it up in Ball jars like preserves, why, they would. But 'Phelia Todd seemed willing to *spend* time—to do desk duty in the library as well as to raise money for it. When it got down to using scouring pads and elbow grease on the war memorial, 'Phelia was right out there with town women who had lost sons in three different wars, wearing an overall with her hair done up in a kerchief. And when kids needed ferrying to a summer swim program, you'd be as apt to see her as anyone headed down Landing Road with the back of Worth Todd's big shiny pickup full of kids. A good woman. Not a town woman, but a good woman. And when she disappeared, there was concern. Not grieving, exactly, because a disappearance is not exactly like a death. It's not like chopping something off with a cleaver; more like something running down the sink so slow you don't know it's all gone until long after it is.

"'Twas a Mercedes she drove," Homer said, answering the question I hadn't asked. "Two-seater sportster. Todd got it for her in sixty-four or sixty-five, I guess. You remember her taking the kids to the lake all those years they had Frogs and Tadpoles?"

"Ayuh."

"She'd drive 'em no more than forty, mindful they was in the back. But it chafed her. That woman had lead in her foot and a ball bearing sommers in the back of her ankle."

It used to be that Homer never talked about his summer people. But then his wife died. Five years ago it was. She was plowing a grade and the tractor tipped over on her and Homer was taken bad off about it. He grieved for two years or so and then seemed to feel better. But he was not the same. He seemed waiting for something to happen, waiting for the next thing. You'd pass his neat little house sometimes at dusk and he would be on the porch smoking a pipe, with a glass of mineral water on the porch rail. The sunset would be in his eyes and pipe smoke around his head and you'd think—I did, anyway—*Homer is waiting for the next thing.* This bothered me over a wider range of my mind than I liked to admit, and at last I decided it was because if it had been me, I wouldn't have been waiting for the next thing, like a groom who has put on his morning coat and finally has his tie right and is only sitting there on a bed in the up-stairs of his house and looking first at himself in the mirror and then at the clock on the mantel and waiting for it to be eleven o'clock so he can get married. If it had been me, I would not have been waiting for the next thing; I would have been waiting for the last thing.

But in that waiting period—which ended when Homer went to Vermont a year later—he sometimes talked about those people. To me, to a few others.

"She never even drove fast with her husband, s'far as I know. But when I drove with her, she made that Mercedes strut."

A fellow pulled in at the pumps and began to fill up his car. The car had a Massachusetts plate.

"It wasn't one of these new sports cars that run on unleaded gasoline and hitch every time you step on it; it was one of the old ones, and the speedometer was calibrated all the way up to a hundred and sixty. It was a funny color of brown and I ast her one time what you called that color and she said it was champagne. Ain't that *good*, I says, and she laughs fit to split. I like a woman who will laugh when you don't have to point her right at the joke, you know."

The man at the pumps had finished getting his gas.

"Afternoon, gentlemen," he says as he comes up the steps.

"A good day to you," I says, and he went inside.

"'Phelia was always lookin for a shortcut," Homer went on as if we had never been interrupted. "That woman was mad for a shortcut. I never saw the beat of it. She said if you can save enough distance, you'll save time as well. She said her father swore by that scripture. He was a salesman, always on the road, and she went with him when she could, and he was always lookin for the shortest way. So she got in the habit.

"I ast her one time if it wasn't kinda funny—here she was on the one hand, spendin' her time rubbin' up that old statue in the square and takin' the little ones to their swimmin' lessons instead of playing tennis and swimming and getting boozed up like normal summer people, and on the other hand bein' so damn set on savin' fifteen minutes between here and Fryeburg that thinkin' about it probably kep' her up nights. It just seemed to me the two things went against each other's grain, if you see what I mean. She just looks at me and says, 'I like being helpful, Homer. I like driving, too—at least sometimes, when it's a challenge—but I don't like the *time* it takes. It's like mending clothes—sometimes you take tucks and sometimes you let things out. Do you see what I mean?'

"'I guess so, missus,' I says, kinda dubious.

"'If sitting behind the wheel of a car was my idea of a really good time *all* the time, I would look for long-cuts,' she says, and that tickled me s'much I had to laugh."

The Massachusetts fellow came out of the store with a six-pack in one hand and some lottery tickets in the other.

"You enjoy your weekend," Homer says.

"I always do," the Massachusetts fellow says. "I only wish I could afford to live here all year 'round."

"Well, we'll keep it all in good order for when you *can* come," Homer says, and the fellow laughs.

We watched him drive off toward someplace, that Massachusetts plate showing. It was a green one. My Marcy says those are the ones the Massachusetts Motor Registry gives to drivers who ain't had a accident in that strange, angry, fuming state for two years. If you have, she says, you got to have a red one so people know to watch out for you when they see you on the roll.

"They was in-state people, you know, the both of them," Homer said, as if the Massachusetts fellow had reminded him of the fact.

"I guess I did know that," I said.

"The Todds are just about the only birds we got that fly north in the winter. The new one, I don't think she likes flying north too much."

He sipped his mineral water and fell silent a moment, thinking.

"*She* didn't mind it, though," Homer said. "At least, I *judge* she didn't, although she used to complain about it something fierce. The complaining was just a way to explain why she was always lookin' for a shortcut."

"And you mean her husband didn't mind her traipsing down every wood-road in tarnation between here and Bangor just so she could see if it was nine-tenths of a mile shorter?"

"He didn't care piss-all," Homer said shortly, and got up and went in the store. There now, Owens, I told myself, you know it ain't safe to ast him questions when he's yarning, and you went right ahead and ast one, and you have buggered a story that was starting to shape up promising.

I sat there and turned my face up into the sun and after about ten minutes he come out with a boiled egg and sat down. He ate her and I took care not to say nothing and the water on Castle Lake sparkled as blue as something as might be told of in a story about treasure. When Homer had finished his egg and had a sip of mineral water, he went on. I was surprised, but still said nothing. It wouldn't have been wise.

"They had two or three different chunks of rolling iron," he said. "There was the Cadillac, and his truck, and her little Mercedes go-devil. A couple of winters he left the truck, 'case they wanted to come down and do some skiin'. Mostly when the summer was over he'd drive the Caddy back up and she'd take her go-devil."

I nodded but didn't speak. In truth, I was afraid to risk another comment. Later I thought it would have taken a lot of comments to shut Homer Buckland up that day. He had been wanting to tell the story of Mrs. Todd's shortcut for a long time.

"Her little go-devil had a special odometer in it that told you how many miles was in a trip, and every time she set off from Castle Lake to Bangor she'd set it to 000-point-0 and let her clock up to whatever. She had made a game of it, and she used to chafe me with it."

He paused, thinking that back over.

"No, that ain't right."

He paused more and faint lines showed up on his forehead like steps on a library ladder.

"She *made* like she made a game of it, but it was a serious business to her. Serious as anything else, anyway." He flapped a hand and I think he meant the husband. "The glovebox of the little go-devil was filled with maps, and there was a few more in the back where there would be a seat in a regular car. Some was gas station maps, and some was pages that had been pulled from the Rand-McNally Road Atlas; she had some maps from Appalachian Trail guidebooks and a whole mess of topographical survey-squares; too. It wasn't her having those maps that made me think it wa'n't a game; it was how she'd drawed lines on all of them, showing routes she'd taken or at least tried to take.

"She'd been stuck a few times, too, and had to get a pull from some farmer with a tractor and chain.

"I was there one day laying tile in the bathroom, sitting there with grout squittering out of every damn crack you could see—I dreamed of nothing but squares and cracks that was bleeding grout that night—and she come stood in the doorway and talked to me about it for quite a while. I used to chafe her about it, but I was also sort of interested, and not just because my brother Franklin used to live down-Bangor and I'd traveled most of the roads she was telling me of. I was interested just because a man like me is always uncommon interested in knowing the shortest way, even if he don't always want to take it. You that way, too?"

"Ayuh," I said. There's something powerful about knowing the shortest way, even if you take the longer way because you know your mother-in-law is sitting home. Getting there quick is often for the birds, although no one holding a Massachusetts driver's license seems to know it. But *knowing* how to get there quick—or even knowing how to get there a way that the person sitting beside you don't know . . . that has power.

"Well, she had them roads like a Boy Scout has his knots," Homer said, and smiled his large, sunny grin. "She says, 'Wait a minute, wait a minute,' like a little girl, and I hear her through the wall, rummaging through her desk, and then she comes back with a little notebook that looked like she'd had it a good long time. Cover was all rumpled, don't you know, and some of the pages had pulled loose from those little wire rings on one side.

" 'The way Worth goes—the way *most* people go—is Route 97 to Mechanic Falls, then Route 11 to Lewiston, and then the Interstate to Bangor. 156.4 miles.' "

I nodded.

" 'If you want to skip the turnpike—and save some distance—you'd go to Mechanic Falls, Route 11 to Lewiston, Route 202 to Augusta, then up Route 9 through China Lake and Unity and Haven to Bangor. That's 144.9 miles.'

" 'You won't save no time that way, missus,' I says, 'not going through Lewiston *and* Augusta. Although I will admit that drive up the Old Derry Road to Bangor is real pretty.'

" 'Save enough miles and soon enough you'll save time,' she says. 'And I didn't say that's the way I'd go, although I have a good many times; I'm just running down the routes most people use. Do you want me to go on?'

" 'No,' I says, 'just leave me in this cussed bathroom all by myself, starin' at all these cussed cracks until I start to rave.'

" 'There are four major routes in all,' she says. 'The one by Route 2 is 163.4 miles. I only tried it once. Too long.'

" 'That's the one I'd hosey if my wife called and told me it was left-overs,' I says, kinda low.

" 'What was that?' she says.

" 'Nothin', I says. 'Talkin' to the grout.'

" 'Oh. Well, the fourth—and there aren't too many who know about it, although they are all good roads—paved, anyway—is across Speckled Bird Mountain on 219 to 202 *beyond* Lewiston. Then, if you take Route 19, you can get around Augusta. Then you take the Old Derry Road. That way is just 129.2.'

"I didn't say nothing for a little while and p'raps she thought I was doubting her because she says, a little pert, 'I know it's hard to believe, but it's so.'

"I said I guessed that was about right, and I thought—looking back—it probably was. Because that's the way I'd usually go when I went down to Bangor to see Franklin when he was still alive. I hadn't been that way in years, though. Do you think a man could just—well—forget a road, Dave?"

I allowed it was. The turnpike is easy to think of. After a while it almost fills a man's mind, and you think not how could I get from here to there, but how can I get from here to the turnpike ramp that's *closest* to there. And that made me think that maybe there are lots of roads all over that are just going begging; roads with rock walls beside them, real roads with blackberry bushes growing alongside them but nobody to eat the berries but the birds, and gravel pits with old rusted chains hanging down in low curves in front of their entryways, the pits themselves as forgotten as a child's old toys with scrumgrass growing up their deserted, unremembered sides. Roads that have just been forgot except by the people who live on them and think of the quickest way to get off them and onto the turnpike, where you can pass on a hill and not fret over it. We like to joke in Maine that you can't get there from here, but maybe the joke is on us. The truth is there's about a damn thousand ways to do it and man doesn't bother.

Homer continued: "I grouted tile all afternoon in that hot little bathroom and she stood there in the doorway all that time, one foot crossed behind the other, bare-legged, wearin' loafers and a khaki-colored skirt and a sweater that was some darker. Hair was drawed back in a hosstail. She must have been thirty-four or -five then, but her face was lit up with what she was tellin' me and I swan she looked like a sorority girl home from school on vacation.

"After a while she musta got an idea of how long she'd been there cuttin' the air around her mouth because she says, 'I must be boring the hell out of you. Homer.'

"'Yes'm,' I says, 'you are. I druther you went away and left me to talk to this damn grout.'

"'Don't be sma'at, Homer,' she says.

"'No, missus, you ain't borin' me,' I says.

"So she smiles and then goes back to it, pagin' through her little notebook like a salesman checkin' his orders. She had those four main ways—well, really three because she gave up on Route 2 right away—but she must have had forty different other ways that were play-offs on those. Roads with state numbers, roads without, roads with names, roads without. My head fair spun with 'em. And finally she says to me, 'You ready for the blue-ribbon winner, Homer?'

"'I guess so,' I says.

"'At least it's the blue-ribbon winner *so far*,' she says. 'Do you know,

Homer, that a man wrote an article in *Science Today* in 1923 proving that no man could run a mile in under four minutes? He *proved* it, with all sorts of calculations based on the maximum length of the male thigh muscles, maximum length of stride, maximum lung capacity, maximum heart rate, and a whole lot more. I was *taken* with that article! I was so taken that I gave it to Worth and asked him to give it to Professor Murray in the math department at the University of Maine. I wanted those figures checked because I was sure they must have been based on the wrong postulates, or something. Worth probably thought I was being silly—"Ophelia's got a bee in her bonnet" is what he says—but he took them. Well, Professor Murray checked through the man's figures quite carefully . . . and do you know what, Homer?'

" 'No, missus.'

" 'Those figures were *right*. The man's criteria were *solid*. He proved, back in 1923, that a man couldn't run a mile in under four minutes. He *proved* that. But people do it all the time, and do you know what that means?'

" 'No, missus,' I said, although I had a glimmer.

" 'It means that no blue ribbon is forever,' she says. 'Someday—if the world doesn't explode itself in the meantime—someone will run a *two*-minute mile in the Olympics. It may take a hundred years or a thousand, but it will happen. Because there is no ultimate blue ribbon. There is zero, and there is eternity, and there is mortality, but there is no *ultimate*.'

"And there she stood, her face clean and scrubbed and shinin', that darkish hair of hers pulled back from her brow, as if to say 'Just you go ahead and disagree if you can.' But I couldn't. Because I believe something like that. It is much like what the minister means, I think, when he talks about grace.

" 'You ready for the blue-ribbon winner *for now?*' she says.

" 'Ayuh,' I says, and I even stopped groutin' for the time bein'. I'd reached the tub anyway, and there wasn't nothing left but a lot of those frikkin' squirrelly little corners. She drawed a deep breath and then spieled it out at me as fast as that auctioneer goes over in Gates Falls when he has been putting the whiskey to himself, and I can't remember it all, but it went something like this."

Homer Buckland shut his eyes for a moment, his big hands lying perfectly still on his long thighs, his face turned up toward the sun. Then he opened his eyes again and for a moment I swan he *looked* like her, yes he did, a seventy-year-old man looking like a woman of thirty-four who was at that moment in her time looking like a college girl of twenty, and I can't remember exactly what he said any more than he could remember exactly what she said, not just because it was complex but because I was so fetched by how he looked sayin' it, but it went close enough like this:

"'You set out Route 97 and then cut up Denton Street to the Old Townhouse Road and that way you get around Castle Rock downtown but back to 97. Nine miles up you can go an old logger's road a mile and a half to Town Road #6, which takes you to Big Anderson Road by Sites' Cider Mill. There's a cut-road the old-timers call Bear Road, and that gets you to 219. Once you're on the far side of Speckled Bird Mountain you grab the Stanhouse Road, turn left onto the Bull Pine Road—there's a swampy patch there but you can spang right through it if you get up enough speed on the gravel—and so you come out on Route 106. 106 cuts through Alton's Plantation to the Old Derry Road—and there's two or three woods roads there that you follow and so come out on Route 3 just beyond Derry Hospital. From there it's only four miles to Route 2 in Etna, and so into Bangor.'

"She paused to get her breath back, then looked at me. 'Do you know how long that is, all told?'

"'No'm,' I says, thinking it sounds like about a hundred and ninety miles and four busted springs.

"'It's 116.4 miles,' she says."

I laughed. The laugh was out of me before I thought I wasn't doing myself any favor if I wanted to hear this story to the end. But Homer grinned himself and nodded.

"I know. And *you* know I don't like to argue with anyone, Dave. But there's a difference between having your leg pulled and getting it shook like a damn apple tree.

"'You don't believe me,' she says.

"'Well, it's *hard* to believe, missus,' I said.

"'Leave that grout to dry and I'll show you,' she says. 'You can finish behind the tub tomorrow. Come on, Homer. I'll leave a note for Worth—he may not be back tonight anyway—and you can call your wife! We'll be sitting down to dinner in the Pilot's Grill in'—she looks at her watch—'two hours and forty-five minutes from right now. And if it's a minute longer, I'll buy you a bottle of Irish Mist to take home with you. You see, my dad was right. Save enough miles and you'll save time, even if you have to go through every damn bog and sump in Kennebec County to do it. Now what do you say?'

"She was lookin at me with her brown eyes just like lamps, there was a devilish look in them that said turn your cap around back'rds, Homer, and climb aboard this hoss, I be first and you be second and let the devil take the hindmost, and there was a grin on her face that said the exact same thing, and I tell you, Dave, I wanted to *go.* I didn't even want to top that damn can of grout. And I *certain* sure didn't want to drive that go-devil of hers. I wanted just to sit in it on the shotgun side and watch her get in, see her skirt come up a little, see her pull it down over her knees or not, watch her hair shine."

He trailed off and suddenly let off a sarcastic, choked laugh. That laugh of his sounded like a shotgun loaded with rock salt.

"Just call up Megan and say, 'You know 'Phelia Todd, that woman you're halfway to being so jealous of now you can't see straight and can't ever find a good word to say about her? Well, her and me is going to make this speed-run down to Bangor in that little champagne-colored go-devil Mercedes of hers, so don't wait dinner.'

"Just call her up and say that. Oh *yes.* Oh *ayuh.*"

And he laughed again with his hands lying there on his legs just as natural as ever was and I seen something in his face that was almost hateful and after a minute he took his glass of mineral water from the railing there and got outside some of it.

"You didn't go," I said.

"Not *then.*"

He laughed, and this laugh was gentler.

"She must have seen something in my face, because it was like she found herself again. She stopped looking like a sorority girl and just looked like 'Phelia Todd again. She looked down at the notebook like she didn't know what it was she had been holding and put it down by her side, almost behind her skirt.

"I says, 'I'd like to do just that thing, missus, but I got to finish up here, and my wife has got a roast on for dinner.'

"She says, 'I understand. Homer—I just got a little carried away. I do that a lot. All the time, Worth says.' Then she kinda straightened up and says, 'But the offer holds, any time you want to go. You can even throw your shoulder to the back end if we get stuck somewhere. Might save me five dollars.' And she laughed.

"'I'll take you up on it, missus,' I says, and she seen that I meant what I said and wasn't just being polite.

"'And before you just go believing that a hundred and sixteen miles to Bangor is out of the question, get out your own map and see how many miles it would be as the crow flies.'

"I finished the tiles and went home and ate leftovers—there wa'n't no roast, and I think 'Phelia Todd knew it—and after Megan was in bed, I got out my yardstick and a pen and my Mobil map of the state, and I did what she had told me . . . because it had laid hold of my mind a bit, you see. I drew a straight line and did out the calculations accordin' to the scale of miles. I was some surprised. Because if you went from Castle Rock up there to Bangor like one of those little Piper Cubs could fly on a clear day—if you didn't have to mind lakes, or stretches of lumber company woods that was chained off, or bogs, or crossing rivers where there wasn't no bridges, why, it would just be seventy-nine miles, give or take."

I jumped a little.

"Measure it yourself, if you don't believe me," Homer said. "I never knew Maine was so small until I seen that."

He had himself a drink and then looked around at me.

"There come a time the next spring when Megan was away in New Hampshire visiting with her brother. I had to go down to the Todds' house to take off the storm doors and put on the screens, and her little Mercedes go-devil was there. She was down by herself.

"She come to the door and says: 'Homer! Have you come to put on the screen doors?'

"And right off I says: 'No, missus, I come to see if you want to give me a ride down to Bangor the short way.'

"Well, she looked at me with no expression on her face at all, and I thought she had forgotten all about it. I felt my face gettin' red, the way it will when you feel you just pulled one hell of a boner. Then, just when I was getting ready to 'pologize, her face busts into that grin again and she says, 'You just stand right there while I get my keys. And don't change your mind. Homer!'

"She come back a minute later with 'em in her hand. 'If we get stuck, you'll see mosquitoes just about the size of dragonflies.'

'I've seen 'em as big as English sparrows up in Rangely, missus,' I said, 'and I guess we're both a spot too heavy to be carried off.'

"She laughs. 'Well, I warned you, anyway. Come on, Homer.'

"'And if we ain't there in two hours and forty-five minutes,' I says, kinda sly, 'you was gonna buy me a bottle of Irish Mist.'

"She looks at me kinda surprised, the driver's door of the go-devil open and one foot inside. 'Hell, Homer,' she says, 'I told you that was the Blue Ribbon for *then*. I've found a way up there that's *shorter*. We'll be there in two and a half hours. Get in here. Homer. We are going to roll.'"

He paused again, hands lying calm on his thighs, his eyes dulling, perhaps seeing that champagne-colored two-seater heading up the Todds' steep driveway.

"She stood the car still at the end of it and says, 'You sure?'

"'Let her rip,' I says. The ball bearing in her ankle rolled and that heavy foot come down. I can't tell you nothing much about whatall happened after that. Except after a while I couldn't hardly take my eyes off her. There was somethin wild that crep' into her face, Dave—something *wild* and something *free*, and it frightened my heart. She was beautiful, and I was took with love *for* her, anyone would have been, any man, anyway, and maybe any woman, too, but I was scairt *of* her, too, because she looked like she could kill you if her eye left the road and fell on you and she decided to love you back. She was wearin' blue jeans and a old white shirt with the sleeves rolled up—I had a idea she was maybe fixin' to paint somethin on the back deck when I came by—but after we had been goin' for a while, seemed like she was dressed in nothin' but all this white billowy stuff like a pitcher in one of those old gods-and-goddesses books."

He thought, looking out across the lake, his face very somber.

"Like the huntress that was supposed to drive the moon across the sky."

"Diana?"

"Ayuh. Moon was her go-devil. 'Phelia looked like that to me and I just tell you fair out that I was stricken in love for her and never would have made a move, even though I was some younger then than I am now. I would not have made a move even had I been twenty, although I suppose I might of at sixteen, and been killed for it—killed if she looked at me was the way it felt.

"She was like that woman drivin' the moon across the sky, halfway up over the splashboard with her gossamer stoles all flyin' out behind her in silver cobwebs and her hair streamin' back to show the dark little hollows of her temples, lashin' those horses and tellin' me to get along faster and never mind how they blowed, just faster, faster, *faster*.

"We went down a lot of woods roads—the first two or three I knew, and after that I didn't know none of them. We must have been a sight to those trees that had never seen nothing with a motor in it before but big old pulp trucks and snowmobiles; that little go-devil that would most likely have looked more at home on the Sunset Boulevard than shooting through those woods, spitting and bulling its way up one hill and then slamming down the next through those dusty green bars of afternoon sunlight—she had the top down and I could smell everything in those woods, and you know what an old fine smell that is, like something which has been mostly left alone and is not much troubled. We went on across corduroy that had been laid over some of the boggiest parts, and black mud squelched up between some of those cut logs and she laughed like a kid. Some of the logs was old and rotted, because there hadn't been nobody down a couple of those roads—except for her, that is—in I'm going to say five or ten years. We was *alone*, except for the birds and whatever animals seen us. The sound of that go-devil's engine, first buzzin' along and then windin' up high and fierce when she punched in the clutch and shifted down . . . that was the only motor sound I could hear. And although I knew we had to be close to *someplace* all the time—I mean, these days you always are—I started to feel like we had gone back in time, and there wasn't *nothing*. That if we stopped and I climbed a high tree, I wouldn't see nothing in any direction but woods and woods and more woods. And all the time she's just *hammering* that thing along, her hair all out behind her, smilin', her eyes flashin'. So we come out on the Speckled Bird Mountain Road and for a while I known where we were again, and then she turned off and for just a little bit I *thought* I knew, and then I didn't even bother to kid myself no more. We went cut-slam down another woods road, and then we come out—I swear it—on a nice paved road with a sign that said MOTORWAY B. You ever heard of a road in the state of Maine that was called MOTORWAY B?"

"No," I says. "Sounds English."

"Ayuh. *Looked* English. These trees like willows overhung the road. 'Now watch out here, Homer,' she says, 'one of those nearly grabbed me a month ago and gave me an Indian burn.'

"I didn't know what she was talkin' about and started to say so, and then I seen that even though there was no wind, the branches of those trees was dippin' down—they was *waverin'* down. They looked black and wet inside the fuzz of green on them. I couldn't believe what I was seein'. Then one of 'em snatched off my cap and I knew I wasn't asleep. 'Hi!' I shouts. 'Give that back!'

"'Too late now. Homer,' she says, and laughs. 'There's daylight, just up ahead . . . we're okay.'

"Then another one of 'em comes down, on her side this time, and snatches at her—I swear it did. She ducked, and it caught in her hair and pulled a lock of it out. 'Ouch, dammit, that *hurts!*' she yells, but she was laughin', too. The car swerved a little when she ducked and I got a look into the woods and holy God, Dave! *Everythin'* in there was movin'. There was grasses wavin' and plants that was all knotted together so it seemed like they made faces, and I seen somethin sittin' in a squat on top of a stump, and it looked like a tree-toad, only it was as big as a full-growed cat.

"Then we come out of the shade to the top of a hill and she says, 'There! That was exciting, wasn't it?' as if she was talkin about no more than a walk through the Haunted House at the Fryeburg Fair.

"About five minutes later we swung onto another of her woods roads. I didn't want no more woods right then—I can tell you that for sure—but these were just plain old woods. Half an hour after that, we was pulling into the parking lot of the Pilot's Grill in Bangor. She points to that little odometer for trips and says, 'Take a gander, Homer.' I did, and it said 111.6. 'What do you think now? Do you believe in my shortcut?'

"That wild look had mostly faded out of her, and she was just 'Phelia Todd again. But that other look wasn't entirely gone. It was like she was two women, 'Phelia and Diana, and the part of her that was Diana was so much in control when she was driving the back roads that the part that was 'Phelia didn't have no idea that her shortcut was taking her through places . . . places that ain't on any map of Maine, not even on those survey squares.

"She says again, 'What do you think of my shortcut, Homer?'

"And I says the first thing to come into my mind, which ain't something you'd usually say to a lady like 'Phelia Todd. 'It's a real piss-cutter, missus,' I says.

"She laughs, just as pleased as punch, and I seen it then, just as clear as glass: She didn't remember none of the funny stuff. Not the willow-branches—except they weren't willows, not at all, not really anything like 'em, or anything else—that grabbed off m'hat, not that MOTORWAY B sign, or that awful-lookin toad-thing. *She didn't remember none of that funny stuff!* Either I had dreamed it was there or she had dreamed it wasn't. All I knew for sure, Dave, was that we had rolled only a hundred and eleven miles and gotten to Bangor, and that wasn't no daydream; it was right there on the little go-devil's odometer, in black and white.

"'Well, it is,' she says. 'It *is* a piss-cutter. I only wish I could get Worth to give it a go sometime . . . but he'll never get out of his rut unless someone blasts him out of it, and it would probably take a Titan II missile to do that, because I believe he has built himself a fallout shelter at the bottom of that rut. Come on in, Homer, and let's dump some dinner into you.'

"And she bought me one hell of a dinner, Dave, but I couldn't eat very much of it. I kep' thinkin' about what the ride back might be like, now that it was drawing down dark. Then, about halfway through the meal, she excused herself and made a telephone call. When she came back she ast me if I would mind drivin' the go-devil back to Castle Rock for her. She said she had talked to some woman who was on the same school committee as her, and the woman said they had some kind of problem about somethin' or other. She said she'd grab herself a Hertz car if Worth couldn't see her back down. 'Do you mind awfully driving back in the dark?' she ast me.

"She looked at me, kinda smilin', and I knew she remembered *some* of it all right—Christ knows how much, but she remembered enough to know I wouldn't want to try her way after dark, if ever at all . . . although I seen by the light in her eyes that it wouldn't have bothered her a bit.

"So I said it wouldn't bother me, and I finished my meal better than when I started it. It was drawin' down dark by the time we was done, and she run us over to the house of the woman she'd called. And when she gets out she looks at me with that same light in her eyes and says, 'Now, you're sure you don't want to wait, Homer? I saw a couple of side roads just today, and although I can't find them on my maps, I think they might chop a few miles.'

"I says, 'Well, missus, I would, but at my age the best bed to sleep in is my own, I've found. I'll take your car back and never put a ding in her . . . although I guess I'll probably put on some more miles than you did.'

"Then she laughed, kind of soft, and she give me a kiss. That was the best kiss I ever had in my whole life, Dave. It was just on the cheek, and it was the chaste kiss of a married woman, but it was as ripe as a peach, or like those flowers that open in the dark, and when her lips touched my skin I felt like . . . I don't know exactly what I felt like, because a man can't easily hold on to those things that happened to him with a girl who was ripe when the world was young or how those things felt—I'm talking around what I mean, but I think you understand. Those things all get a red cast to them in your memory and you cannot see through it at all.

" 'You're a sweet man, Homer, and I love you for listening to me and riding with me,' she says. 'Drive safe.'

"Then in she went, to that woman's house. Me, I drove home."

"How did you go?" I asked.

He laughed softly. "By the turnpike, you damned fool," he said, and I never seen so many wrinkles in his face before as I did then.

He sat there, looking into the sky.

"Came the summer she disappeared. I didn't see much of her . . . that was the summer we had the fire, you'll remember, and then the big storm that knocked down all the trees. A busy time for caretakers. Oh, I *thought* about her from time to time, and about that day, and about that kiss, and it started to seem like a dream to me. Like one time, when I was about sixteen and couldn't think about nothing but girls. I was out plowing George Bascomb's west field, the one that looks acrost the lake at the mountains, dreamin' about what teenage boys dream of. And I pulled up this rock with the harrow blades, and it split open, and it *bled*. At least, it looked to me like it bled. Red stuff come runnin' out of the cleft in the rock and soaked into the soil. And I never told no one but my mother, and I never told her what it meant to me, or what happened to me, although she washed my drawers and maybe she knew. Anyway, she suggested I ought to pray on it. Which I did, but I never got no enlightenment, and after a while something started to suggest to my mind that it had been a dream. It's that way, sometimes. There is holes in the *middle*, Dave. Do you know that?"

"Yes," I says, thinking of one night when I'd seen something. That was in '59, a bad year for us, but my kids didn't know it was a bad year; all they knew was that they wanted to eat just like always. I'd seen a bunch of whitetail in Henry Brugger's back field, and I was out there after dark with a jacklight in August. You can shoot two when they're summer-fat; the second'll come back and sniff at the first as if to say *What the hell? Is it fall already?* and you can pop him like a bowlin' pin. You can hack off enough meat to feed yowwens for six weeks and bury what's left. Those are two whitetails the hunters who come in November don't get a shot at, but kids have to eat. Like the man from Massachusetts said, *he'd* like to be able to afford to live here the year around, and all I can say is sometimes you pay for the privilege after dark. So there I was, and I seen this big orange light in the sky; it come down and down, and I stood and watched it with my mouth hung on down to my breastbone and when it hit the lake the whole of it was lit up for a minute a purple-orange that seemed to go right up to the sky in rays. Wasn't nobody ever said nothing to me about that light, and I never said nothing to nobody myself, partly because I was afraid they'd laugh, but also because they'd wonder what the hell I'd been doing out there after dark to start with. And after a while it was like Homer said—it seemed like a dream I had once had, and it didn't signify to me because I couldn't make nothing of it which would turn under my hand. It was like a moonbeam. It didn't have no handle and it didn't have no blade. I couldn't make it work so I left it alone, like a man does when he knows the day is going to come up nevertheless.

"There are *holes* in the middle of things," Homer said, and he sat up straighter, like he was mad. "Right in the damn *middle* of things, not even to the left or right where your p'riph'ral vision is and you could say 'Well, but hell—' They are there and you go around them like you'd go around a pothole in the road that would break an axle. You know? And you forget it. Or like if you are plowin', you can plow a dip. But if there's somethin' like a *break* in the earth, where you see darkness, like a cave might be there, you say 'Go around, old hoss. Leave that alone! I got a good shot over here to the left'ards.' Because it wasn't a cave you was lookin' for, or some kind of college excitement, but good plowin'.

"*Holes* in the *middle* of things."

He fell still a long time then and I let him be still. Didn't have no urge to move him. And at last he says:

"She disappeared in August. I seen her for the first time in early July, and she looked . . ." Homer turned to me and spoke each word with careful, spaced emphasis. "Dave Owens, she looked *gorgeous!* Gorgeous and wild and almost untamed. The little wrinkles I'd started to notice around her eyes all seemed to be gone. Worth Todd, he was at some conference or something in Boston. And she stands there at the edge of the deck—I was out in the middle with my shirt off—and she says, 'Homer, you'll never believe it.'

" 'No, missus, but I'll try,' I says.

" 'I found two new roads,' she says, 'and I got up to Bangor this last time in just sixty-seven miles.'

"I remembered what she said before and I says, 'That's not possible, missus. Beggin' your pardon, but I did the mileage on the map myself, and seventy-nine is tops . . . as the crow flies.'

"She laughed, and she looked prettier than ever. Like a goddess in the sun, on one of those hills in a story where there's nothing but green grass and fountains and no puckies to tear at a man's forearms at all. 'That's right,' she says, 'and you can't run a mile in under four minutes. It's been mathematically *proved*.'

" 'It ain't the same,' I says.

" 'It's the same,' she says. 'Fold the map and see how many miles it is then, Homer. It can be a little less than a straight line if you fold it a little, or it can be a lot less if you fold it a lot.'

"I remembered our ride then, the way you remember a dream, and I says, 'Missus, you can fold a map on paper but you can't fold *land*. Or at least you shouldn't ought to try. You want to leave it alone.'

" 'No sir,' she says. 'It's the one thing right now in my I life that I won't leave alone, because it's *there*, and it's *mine*.'

"Three weeks later—this would be about two weeks before she disappeared—she give me a call from Bangor. She says, 'Worth has gone to New York, and I am coming down. I've misplaced my damn key, Homer. I'd like you to open the house so I can get in.'

"Well, that call come at eight o'clock, just when it was starting to come down dark. I had a sanwidge and a beer before leaving—about twenty minutes. Then I took a ride down there. All in all, I'd say I was forty-five minutes. When I got down there to the Todds', I seen there was a light on in the pantry I didn't leave on while I was comin' down the driveway. I was lookin at that, and I almost run right into her little go-devil. It was parked kind of on a slant, the way a drunk would park it, and it was splashed with muck all the way up to the windows, and there was this stuff stuck in that mud along the body that looked like seaweed . . . only when my lights hit it, it seemed to be *movin'*. I parked behind it and got out of my truck. That stuff wasn't seaweed, but it *was* weeds, and it *was* movin' . . . kinda slow and sluggish, like it was dyin'. I touched a piece of it, and it tried to wrap itself around my hand. It felt nasty and awful. I drug my hand away and wiped it on my pants. I went around to the front of the car. It looked like it had come through about ninety miles of splash and low country. Looked *tired*, it did. Bugs was splashed all over the wind-shield—only they didn't look like no kind of bugs *I* ever seen before. There was a moth that was about the size of a sparrow, its wings still flap-pin' a little, feeble and dyin'. There was things like mosquitoes, only they had real eyes that you could see—and they seemed to be seein' *me*. I could hear those weeds scrapin' against the body of the go-devil, dyin', tryin' to get a hold on somethin'. And all I could think was, Where in the hell has she been? And how did she get here in only three-quarters of an hour? Then I seen somethin' else. There was some kind of a animal half-smashed onto the radiator grille, just under where that Mercedes orna-ment is—the one that looks kinda like a star looped up into a circle? Now most small animals you kill on the road is bore right under the car, be-cause they are crouching when it hits them, hoping it'll just go over and leave them with their hide still attached to their meat. But every now and then one will jump, not away, but right at the damn car, as if to get in one good bite of whatever the buggardly thing is that's going to kill it—I have known that to happen. This thing had maybe done that. And it looked mean enough to jump a Sherman tank. It looked like something which come of a mating between a woodchuck and a weasel, but there was other stuff thrown in that a body didn't even want to look at. It hurt your eyes, Dave; worse'n that, it hurt your *mind*. Its pelt was matted with blood, and there was claws sprung out of the pads on its feet like a cat's claws, only longer. It had big yellowy eyes, only they was glazed. When I was a kid I had a porcelain marble—a croaker—that looked like that. And teeth. Long thin needle teeth that looked almost like darning needles, stickin' out of its mouth. Some of them was sunk right into that steel grillwork. That's why it was still hanging on; it had hung its *own* self on by the teeth. I looked at it and knowed it had a headful of poison just like a rattlesnake, and it jumped at that go-devil when it saw it was about to be run down, tryin' to bite it to death. And I wouldn't be the one to try and yonk it offa there because I had cuts on my hands—hay-cuts—and I thought it would kill me as dead as a stone parker if some of that poison seeped into the cuts.

"I went around to the driver's door and opened it. The inside light come on, and I looked at that special odometer that she set for trips . . . and what I seen there was 31.6.

"I looked at that for a bit, and then I went to the back door. She'd forced the screen and broke the glass by the lock so she could get her hand through and let herself in. There was a note that said: 'Dear Homer—got here a little sooner than I thought I would. Found a shortcut, and it is a dilly! You hadn't come yet so I let myself in like a burglar. Worth is coming day after tomorrow. Can you get the screen fixed and the door reglazed by then? Hope so. Things like that always bother him. If I don't come out to say hello, you'll know I'm asleep. The drive was very tiring, but I was here in no time! Ophelia.'

"'*Tirin'!* I took another look at that bogey-thing hangin' offa the grille of her car, and I thought, Yessir, it *must* have been tiring. By God, *yes.*"

He paused again, and cracked a restless knuckle.

"I seen her only once more. About a week later. Worth was there, but he was swimmin' out in the lake, back and forth, back and forth, like he was sawin' wood or signin' papers. More like he was signin' papers, I guess.

"'Missus,' I says, 'this ain't my business, but you ought to leave well enough alone. That night you come back and broke the glass of the door to come in, I seen somethin hangin' off the front of your car—'

"'Oh, the chuck! I took care of that,' she says.

"'Christ!' I says. 'I hope you took some care!'

"'I wore Worth's gardening gloves,' she said. 'It wasn't anything anyway, Homer, but a jumped-up woodchuck with a little poison in it.'

"'But missus,' I says, 'where there's woodchucks there's bears. And if that's what the woodchucks look like along your shortcut, what's going to happen to you if a bear shows up?'

"She looked at me, and I seen that other woman in her—that Diana-woman. She says, 'If things are different along those roads, Homer, maybe I am different, too. Look at this.'

"Her hair was done up in a clip at the back, looked sort of like a butterfly and had a stick through it. She let it down. It was the kind of hair that would make a man wonder what it would look like spread out over a pillow. She says, 'It was coming in gray, Homer. Do you see any gray?' And she spread it with her fingers so the sun could shine on it.

"'No'm,' I says.

"She looks at me, her eyes all a-sparkle, and she says, 'Your wife is a good woman, Homer Buckland, but she has seen me in the store and in the post office, and we've passed the odd word or two, and I have seen her looking at my hair in a kind of satisfied way that only women know. I know what she says, and what she tells her friends . . . that Ophelia Todd has started dyeing her hair. But I have not. I have lost my way looking for a shortcut more than once . . . lost my way . . . and lost my gray.' And she laughed, not like a college girl but like a girl in high school. I admired her and longed for her beauty, but I seen that other beauty in her face as well just then . . . and I felt afraid again. Afraid *for* her, and afraid *of* her.

"'Missus,' I says, 'you stand to lose more than a little sta'ch in your hair.'

"'No,' she says. 'I tell you I am different over there . . . I am *all myself* over there. When I am going along that road in my little car I am not Ophelia Todd, Worth Todd's wife who could never carry a child to term, or that woman who tried to write poetry and failed at it, or the woman who sits and takes notes in committee meetings, or anything or anyone else. When I am on that road I am in the heart of myself, and I feel like—'

"'*Diana*,' I said.

"She looked at me kind of funny and kind of surprised, and then she laughed. 'Oh, like some goddess, I suppose,' she said. 'She will do better than most because I am a night person—I love to stay up until my book is done or until the national anthem comes on the TV, and because I am very pale, like the moon—Worth is always saying I need a tonic, or blood tests or some sort of similar bosh. But in her heart what every woman wants to be is some kind of goddess, I think—men pick up a ruined echo of that thought and try to put them on pedestals (a woman, who will pee down her own leg if she does not squat! it's funny when you stop to think of it)—but what a man senses is not what a woman wants. A woman wants to be in the clear, is all. To stand if she will, or walk . . .' Her eyes turned toward that little go-devil in the driveway, and narrowed. Then she smiled. 'Or to *drive*, Homer. A man will not see that. He thinks a goddess wants to loll on a slope somewhere on the foothills of Olympus and eat fruit, but there is no god or goddess in that. All a woman wants is what a man wants—a woman wants to *drive*.'

"'Be careful where you drive, missus, is all,' I says, and she laughs and give me a kiss spang in the middle of the forehead.

"She says, 'I will, Homer,' but it didn't mean nothing, and I known it, because she said it like a man who says he'll be careful to his wife or his girl when he knows he won't . . . can't.

"I went back to my truck and waved to her once, and it was a week later that Worth reported her missing. Her and that go-devil both. Todd waited seven years and had her declared legally dead, and then he waited another year for good measure—I'll give the sucker that much—and then he married the second Missus Todd, the one that just went by. And I don't expect you'll believe a single damn word of the whole yarn."

In the sky one of those big flat-bottomed clouds moved enough to disclose the ghost of the moon—half-full and pale as milk. And something in my heart leaped up at the sight, half in fright, half in love.

"I do though," I said. "Every frigging damned word. And even if it ain't true, Homer, it ought to be."

He give me a hug around the neck with his forearm, which is all men can do since the world don't let them kiss but only women, and laughed, and got up.

"Even if it *shouldn't* ought to be, it is," he said. He got his watch out of his pants and looked at it. "I got to go down the road and check on the Scott place. You want to come?"

"I believe I'll sit here for a while," I said, "and think."

He went to the steps, then turned back and looked at me, half-smiling.

"I believe she was right," he said. "She was different along those roads she found . . . wasn't nothing that would dare touch her. You or me, maybe, but not her.

"And I believe she's young."

Then he got in his truck and set off to check the Scott place.

That was two years ago, and Homer has since gone to Vermont, as I think I told you. One night he come over to see me. His hair was combed, he had a shave, and he smelled of some nice lotion. His face was clear and his eyes were alive. That night he looked sixty instead of seventy, and I was glad for him and I envied him and I hated him a little, too. Arthritis is one buggardly great old fisherman, and that night Homer didn't look like arthritis had any fishhooks sunk into his hands the way they were sunk into mine.

"I'm going," he said.

"Ayuh?"

"Ayuh."

"All right; did you see to forwarding your mail?"

"Don't want none forwarded," he said. "My bills are paid. I am going to make a clean break."

"Well, give me your address. I'll drop you a line from one time to another, old hoss." Already I could feel loneliness settling over me like a cloak . . . and looking at him, I knew that things were not quite what they seemed.

"Don't have none yet," he said.

"All right," I said. "*Is* it Vermont, Homer?"

"Well," he said, "it'll do for people who want to know."

I almost didn't say it and then I did. "What does she look like now?"

"Like Diana," he said. "But she is kinder."

"I envy you, Homer," I said, and I did.

I stood at the door. It was twilight in that deep part of summer when the fields fill with perfume and Queen Anne's lace. A full moon was beating a silver track across the lake. He went across my porch and down the steps. A car was standing on the soft shoulder of the road, its engine idling heavy, the way the old ones do that still run full bore straight ahead and damn the torpedoes. Now that I think of it, that car *looked* like a torpedo. It looked beat-up some, but as if it could go the ton without breathin' hard. He stopped at the foot of my steps and picked something up—it was his gas can, the big one that holds ten gallons. He went down my walk to the passenger side of the car. She leaned over and opened the door. The inside light came on and just for a moment I saw her, long red hair around her face, her forehead shining like a lamp. Shining like the *moon*. He got in and she drove away. I stood out on my porch and watched the taillights of her little go-devil twinkling red in the dark . . . getting smaller and smaller. They were like embers, then they were like flickerflies, and then they were gone.

Vermont, I tell the folks from town, and Vermont they believe, because it's as far as most of them can see inside their heads. Sometimes I almost believe it myself, mostly when I'm tired and done up. Other times I think about them, though—all this October I have done so, it seems, because October is the time when men think mostly about far places and the roads that might get them there. I sit on the bench in front of Bell's Market and think about Homer Buckland and about the beautiful girl who leaned over to open his door when he come down that path with the full red gasoline can in his right hand—she looked like a girl of no more than sixteen, a girl on her learner's permit, and her beauty *was* terrible, but I believe it would no longer kill the man it turned itself on; for a moment her eyes lit on me, I was not killed, although part of me died at her feet.

Olympus must be a glory to the eyes and the heart, and there are those who crave it and those who find a clear way to it, mayhap, but I know Castle Rock like the back of my hand and I could never leave it for no shortcuts where the roads may go; in October the sky over the lake is no glory but it is passing fair, with those big white clouds that move so slow; I sit here on the bench, and think about 'Phelia Todd and Homer Buckland, and I don't necessarily wish I was where they are . . . but I still wish I was a smoking man.

A VISION OF BANGOR, IN THE TWENTIETH CENTURY

Edward Kent

I am not a nervous man, or one addicted to seeing visions and dreaming dreams, but once, as I journeyed through the wilderness of this world, I had a dream, "which was not all a dream," but partly a vision of the future, like those vouchsafed to the clairvoyant in his magnetic state. I do not know that I had been magnetized, and yet, I half suspect that some distant passes had been made at me, or some charmed toothpick or pencil case had been charged with subtle essence, and put under my pillow to work the wondrous devilment. I would charge no one rashly, yet truth compels me to state facts, and then, as the newspapers say, a candid public will judge, whether or not I have been fairly dealt with. I am one of the unfortunate victims, selected, I know not on what principle, who were months since penciled down on gilt-edged note paper in a fair Italian hand, as the masculine contributors to the "Bangor Book" to "do" the rough and solid work in this superstructure of the wit and wisdom of Down East. The list was soon exhibited thereon, like the marks on the death roll of the Roman triumvirate. At first, I laughed outright, and snapped my fingers in defiance and indignant resistance. I write in a book!! A Bangor book! I, of all men!

"The dog star rages."

For a wonder, like the wonder in heaven, the woman said nothing, but looked calm, confident, and secure, and I began to feel like the entwined fly in the web of the spider. I was left alone, after a significant nod, and the single words,—"prepare, the time is short." I mused awhile, and then rushed into business. In its vortex I actually drove, at times, from my mind the injunction and the warning. But time passed, and I felt a gentle pull, and "is it ready?" in a low, soft, musical voice, fell upon my ear.

"What?" said I.

"The contribution in prose or verse," said she.

"Ready, my dear woman—no, and never will be."

"Yes, it will be. The paper is made on which it will be written; the pen and ink are waiting. Beware of the third time of asking."

And she turned away to speak to another of the unfortunate *listed* men. I only heard her say the printers will reach your page next week— and there can be no delay—the boy will call for copy— "I defy the *devil* and all his works," said the incipient author.

I could not resist whispering in his ear, "So you may, but who can stand against the determined purpose of a woman?" (His article appears in the volume, and stands the voluntary offering of an unpracticed author, to the great curse of humanity.) I turned again to my fair dictator, deter- mined to break away from the strange enchantment, for I began actually to feel a sort of itching in my fingers, and to look with unwonted interest towards the ink stand and the writing desk. I found myself parting my hair and smoothing it down and opening my vest and turning down my collar *à la Byron*. I saw myself in the mirror, and there was a new and most ludicrously grotesque, sentimental, half-poetic and half-transcendental, and altogether lackadaisical stare of the eyes, and dropping of the eye- brows. The case began to look alarming. Everything about me looked "blue." The "*cacoethes scribendi*" was developing its symptoms, and whether taken in the natural way or by inoculation, it threatened a fatal result.

I roused myself for an impressive appeal. I knew that woman was ever ready to succor and relieve distressed humanity. "My good friend," said I, "listen to reason."

"Listen to a fiddlestick!" (She did not say a "fool," but she did look a little contemptuous, and more impatient.) "Why do you resist? Are you not 'listed,' and booked, and have we not devoted ten pages to you?"

"But how can I write? I never wrote a line for a book in my life; and the idea of having my words, written by my hands, actually printed, and hot-pressed, and screwed and bound in real hard covers, is entirely over- whelming."

"Now does not this pass all endurance?" said she; "that you, and others like you, self-styled 'lords of the creation,' with fierce whiskers, and broad shoulders, and the assumed air of independence, and with the roughness of bears, should not have the heart of a hen partridge—whilst we women, timid, delicate, and retiring, as is our nature and destiny, are ready to go boldly forth to the public, and to write our prettiest and our best, and have it printed, too, *solely* from our love for the cause of the fatherless and the destitute?"

"But think of the Bangor public, and the cynical and severe critics in our midst, who, not being willing to write, are yet over-willing to carp, ridicule, and disparage."

"Think of the orphans," said she!

"Think of the reviewers," said I!

"What *reviewers*," said she, "would ever think our Down East book worthy of notice?"

"That's true again," said I. "Then write your article, not having the fear of the reviewers before your eyes."

I went home, feeling like one spellbound. "Seven women shall take hold of one man," was the text of scripture for this night's meditation. Must I write! And if so, what shall I write? I was in a fix, and as a last resort I went to bed.

I did not search for witch hazel or magnetized implements, as I before said, but I soon fell asleep, and my last thoughts were of steel pens, paper manufactories and printers' ink. I have an indistinct remembrance of a half-sleeping and half-waking vision of a ragged and suffering orphan, which held up to me a ream of foolscap, and he asked me, in plaintive tones, to write, and then he strangely vanished, repeating the lines of the children's play, "He can do little that can't do this." I turned, but my destiny was before me. Methought I arose, determined to escape in the open air, from the sight of objects calculated to remind me of the unperformed task, and with the lurking thought that perchance I might gather materials or suggestions to be brain-woven into the fatal "article."

In a moment I was in "the square," but it was strangely altered. I could not recognize a single tenement. I gazed upward and saw on one granite front the letters "Erected 1938." There was an appearance of age about the building. It looked discolored and gray. As far as the eye could reach were ranges of high and splendid stores. What does this all mean?

I involuntarily asked; and as I spoke, I saw a man the exact image of T———-, and felt relieved. He was a tall, lank, long-sided Yankee, six feet and two inches in height. I addressed him familiarly.

He gave me a keen and independent look, as such a Yankee only can give, and replied, "You have the advantage of me."

"How so?"

"You seem to know me, but I do not know you."

In the sauciness of a dream I thought, I am not sure that it is for the advantage of anyone to know you. But I was polite and said nothing of the kind. "Why, certainly, your name is T———-."

"O yes."

"You know *me*, A———-?"

"Never heard the name in these parts."

"Why, did we not board together at the old Hatch house, in the times of Thomas?"

"Never heard of such a house."

"Pray," said I, utterly confounded, "who was your great grandfather?"

"I don't know," but like an American, always looking ahead, he added, "I know who my son is, and there he stands."

"Who are your relations?"

"I don't know as I ever had any relations nearer than uncles."

"Do you live in Bangor?"

"Yes, I was born and grew up here, man and boy, sixty odd years."

"Where is Taylor's corner?"

"There," he said, pointing to a splendid block, covered with signs of banks, insurance offices and brokers. "It has been so named for more than a hundred years—and is still owned by descendents of the original possessor."

"I am glad of it," said I, "if the successors are as honest men as he was. Can you show me the mark of high water in the great freshet of 1846?"

"No," said he, "I have heard of that great rise, and there have been a great many attempts to find some stone or mark to show the height, but strange to say, the antiquarians of that day were so busy in hunting up antediluvian relics, and taking the measure of the Buskahegian giant, that they forgot that they, and their days, would ever become antiquity."

"But where," said I, "is the Kenduskeag Stream?"

"Under those buildings and bridges," said he; "if you will go up above the 'Lovers Leap,' you can see it—and you can get a glimpse of it near the market." As we passed along, I saw Jerome's X press office in large letters, and then I at once felt at home. "And there," said he, "is the man himself—a little stiff in the joints, for he is our oldest inhabitant, and nobody knows how old he is. But he is as good as new, and ready always *expressly* for the occasion. He says he hopes to live until he discovers something a little quicker than lightning, and then he shall be ready to be gathered in."

A familiar nod and ready smile from my old friend assured me that in him there was "no mistake."

The market, a long and commodious building, extending up the middle of the stream, reminded me of the plan I saw in 1836. It was well filled up with fat carcasses, and fatter men. "Oleaginous" was written on every side—man and beast.

"How many people have you in this city?"

"About one hundred thousand," said he, "according to the last census in 1970."

I began to be wearied, and stept into an office to rest. I took up the paper of the day, Sept. 10, 1978, and called "the Bangor Daily News." It was one of twelve dailies and numerous able weeklies, as I was told. I read, as I could, the news column, but I found many new words, and many old ones strangely altered. I gathered from the paragraphs, that the southern portion of the South American continent, including Cape Horn, had yielded to the inevitable destiny of the Saxon race, and had been conquered and annexed, because they would not give up without fighting. "Later news from the State of Peru," a paragraph headed, "Presidential election," attracted my attention. It contained a column of states, fifty-six in number, and at the bottom, "We have partial returns by telegraph, of the voting yesterday at Oregon City. One of the candidates residing in that region, gives great interest to the votes of the Pacific states." The editor, who was evidently a little of an antiquarian, had hunted up an old file of newspapers, and had copied as curiosities some of the notices of the year 1848, of the "Whig, Democratic and Liberty" parties, and their stirring appeals—and the editor adds, "Can it be believed, that in 1848, men were actually held as chattels, and sold at auction like oxen? We yesterday saw a shipmaster, who told us that he had seen and talked with black men in the south, who were once slaves, and they and their children had been sold by an auctioneer. Thank heaven, we have seen the last of that horrid system." I took up another paper, in phonographic words. The editor complained, that, although the reformers had worked diligently more than a century, yet the mass of men would persist in rejecting their improvements. As far as I could judge, the parties in politics were divided mainly on the question of the union of the States.

In an adjoining building was the telegraph office. I looked and saw that instead of wires, they had, near the ground, rails of a small size. I asked why this change, and was told that they sent passengers on them, driven by electricity, to Boston in four minutes.

"But how can the human system stand such velocity?"

"O, we 'stun' them," the fellow said, "with the Letheon, and then tie them in boxes on little wheels, and they go safely, and come out bright. There are rival lines," he continued, "and great efforts are being made to bring the passage within three minutes. We have to put on rather a large dose of Letheon when we attempt this, but the passengers all say they will run the risk of never waking again, rather than be beat. We have had to bury a few, but what is that to saving a minute, and beating the rascally opposition line? The people all say 'go ahead.'"

By a sudden transition, I remember not how, I found myself at Mount Hope, the final resting place of the dead. The avenue was shaded delightfully. At the base of the conical hill were two beautiful ponds, surrounded by the weeping willow—that long cherished emblem of sadness and mourning. The garden in front was full of beautiful and fragrant plants. And the grounds sacred to sepulture were filled with all the varied monuments which affectionate love could devise, from the uprising shaft and costly sculpture, to the single rose tree, or the modest violet. I gazed around on the forest, natural and transplanted, which covered all the public and private grounds, and the solid masonry of the stone wall which enclosed the whole area. I sought for familiar names, but long in vain. I found old tombstones at last, some lying on the ground, and others all but illegible. I traced names once familiar and dear, and many, that, had it not been the confusion of a dream, I should have known were now young and full of life and promise. On the tombstone of one who was daily in my sight, the beautiful, the admired in the midst of the years of young existence, I read—"Sacred to the memory of ———- ———-, who died aged 85 years: bowed down with the weight of years, she was ready to depart."

I saw a funeral procession enter the grounds, and the tears of heartfelt anguish which fell fast and freely from those parents' eyes as they saw the child of their affections consigned to the silent tomb, testified to me, that as of yore "man was made to mourn," and that the same hearts yet beat in human bosoms. I saw my *own* name on a marble headstone, but the tall rank grass hid the date from my vision; but I read such a long list of unremembered virtues, that a smile which covered my face was very near being turned into a hearty laugh at this to me, tangible evidence of the *value* of monumental epitaphs.

Anon the scene changed, and I was on the shore of the Kenduskeag, looking upward to that firm pile of the everlasting rocks, rising perpendicularly from the shore. Man had not changed this, and *here* I was on my own ground. I saw two lovers in their quiet, slow, and absorbed walk—as they talked in low and touching tones—and watched the eyes, which spoke more effective language than the tongue, and heard them utter vows and build airy castles of future happiness, and I felt that, although art had wrought such mighty revolutions all around me, there was the same interchange of the soft affections of the heart as in my own youthful days, the same undoubting trust and unclouded hopes for the future, which no experience of others could ever calm or conquer.

Again I was in the busy haunts of men. I heard them conversing at the corners—"*Dollars,*—thousands!—great bargain!—worth his hundred thousand," were the emphatic words. This sounded as familiar talk to my ears. The dollar still remained the representative of value, and the idol of men.

And now I seemed to feel and know that I was in the midst of the twentieth century, and that I was but a spectator, looking at posterity. I was not awed, but curious. The man I had seen before was at my side.

"My friend!" said I, "do boards sell readily at 21—14—8."

He opened wide his eyes, but said nothing.

"What is the price of stumpage? Does the lumber hold out of a good quality, or is it shaky and concosy? Is Veazie's boom large enough to hold all that comes down? How does the wood scale hold out?" I poured these questions upon him, but he shook his head in despair.

"I don't know what you mean—your terms are all Greek or Indian to me."

"You can at least tell me how many million feet of boards are sawed and shipped yearly on the rivers?

"Million feet!" said he, "I have never heard of such a quantity!"

"Is not lumber your great staple for export?"

"Lumber! . . . why, we have not shipped a cargo for fifty years. We have to search closely to get hemlock enough to use here, and as to good pine, we have to depend on Oregon."

"And how do you get it?"

"O," said he, "by the Oregon railroad, and the lakes, and the St. Lawrence railroad. You see the depot over there."

"And what *is* your business here?"

"All kinds of trading, and great manufacturing establishments of cotton, woolen and mixed goods, to supply the markets of the world. Do you think we could have built up such a city as this, by chipping up logs with a saw? That might have helped our great-grandfathers, when they lived along side of the Indians. But the vast factories at Treat's Falls, on the costly dam, and these long rows of warehouses—these extended streets—were never built by the lumber trade. See, yonder, the cathedral, and near to it the spire of the stone church, and all around you the evidences of thrift, and industry, and improvement. See that splendid granite front; within those walls is the Bangor Public Library, open to all, and free to the poor and rich alike, containing seventy thousand volumes, founded in 1848—and ever honored by the name of Vattemare, who first started the plan—and thanks to those, our predecessors, who followed his suggestions."

"Permit me," said I, "to inquire as to the social arrangements; do men and women yet live in families, or did the reformers of my day succeed in introducing the community system."

"O," said he, "that nonsense died a natural death, and with it the kindred absurdities of women's rights to participate in government and to direct affairs outdoors as well as in—all this was given up long ago, except, that now and then some old, cross-grained or disappointed maid, sets up a sort of snarl, but nobody minds her, our women bake and darn stockings and tend the babies, and mend their husbands' clothes, teach their children the way they should go, and walk with them in it, and read their Bibles and as many books as they can find time to. They tried those schemes to which you allude, a great while ago—but nature was too strong for abstract theories, and after a considerable struggle between the sexes, they both became satisfied that it was best to compromise, and let the *women* rule indoors and the *men* out."

"Not much of a compromise," said I, "for women always did that."

"Well," said he, "they were satisfied to give up the new schemes (the man somehow seemed now to be aware of my actual condition), for they tried their hands at a little government."

"Pray, tell me about it."

"Why, they fretted and teased until in several of the states the people, for the sake of quiet, admitted them to a participation on equal footing with men. The first difficulty was in voting at the polls. It was impossible to keep the women within party lines. They would vote for the youngest and handsomest and most agreeable man; and they would see and hear all the candidates, and insisted upon good looks and genteel clothes; and when their own sex were candidates, it was almost impossible to make one woman vote for another. They all liked the men best. But when the legislature met it was impossible to get along at all. One lady had her hair to dress, and could not be in that day. Another was shopping—there were such *dear* beauties of silks just imported. Another must have leave of absence, for her baby must be looked after. Another would not attend because there was no looking glasses in committee rooms. And yet another because her milliner had made a horrid fit. And those that were there would not observe any rules, but each insisted on talking without stint or limit. And then on committees, the reports were not forthcoming, for the bachelors had been making love to the maids.

"The members of both sexes were all good looking, but the public business needed some rougher outsides and some better heads than those that belonged to the Adonises of the halls.

"They once held a private session on matters which required the most profound secrecy. The doors were closed, windows barred; but the next day, before the morning papers were out, the whole matter was the town talk. Upon investigation, it was found that each of the female members had told it, but in strict confidence, as they all declared, to a female friend."

I found myself strolling on Broadway, and stood beneath the shade of aged and venerable and wide-spreading elms, "still wearing proudly their panoply of green," extending as far as the eye could reach on each side of the spacious central walk. I saw the children at their sports beneath the arching canopy, and heard the same animated cries and joyous shouts, and earnest vociferations, which had always been the characteristics of childhood. I saw the marbles and the hoops, and the bat and ball—all familiar and unaltered. A bevy of girls and boys were engaged in reading books. I looked over their shoulders and saw "Mother Goose's Melodies," with the old pictures, "Robinson Crusoe," in his hairy skin suit, and one sober miss intent on the "Pilgrim's Progress." It seemed there were some books that would *never* been consigned to oblivion.

I passed into a bookstore, but I remember only that I saw the old Saxon Bible in King James's translation, Shakespeare, and Milton, and Robert Burns, and Don Quixote. I asked if they had a copy of the Bangor Book?

"O yes," said the shopman, and handed me a thick octavo. It was the Bangor Directory for 1978.

"I mean," said I, "the work published in 1847; surely that must have survived, for it was preserved by attic salt in *blue* covers, and contained the best efforts of the Penobscot mind in prose and verse; we all looked to posterity for our reward."

"Never heard of it," said the man.

A little dried-up specimen of a man who was poring over a book in a corner, addressing me, said, "I have seen that book, I am quite sure, at least the outside of it, in one of the alcoves of the rooms of the Antiquarian Society, labeled 'the day of small things,' where are kept the relics and curiosities of the first settlements on the river, and also Indian gouges, axes and hatchets, miniature birch canoes, and the portrait of the Buskahegian Giant, so called."

"Is there not also one of the striped pig?"

"I never saw any," quoth he.

"Speaking of the striped pig," said I, "have you any licensed grogshops?"

"O no, we have conquered King Alcohol, and are all temperance men now; and the ladies of the present time look with wonder and dismay in their countenances, when they are informed that their sex did once even *here* by their example countenance the use of wine as a beverage in their evening levees!"

Once more in the street I moved toward my home as I remembered it. As I passed onward, I was attracted by a beautiful arch at the entrance of a substantial, elegant, and commodious building, bearing this inscription: "The Bangor Female Orphan Asylum, founded in 1839, and sustained by the benevolence of its citizens." I looked with interest on the groups of healthy, happy, and well conditioned children, but alas! I was reminded of the dreaded "article," and the faces before so pleasant seemed to change into looks of reproach and regret. I involuntarily exclaimed—"Where shall I find a subject, and finish the task appointed me?" I looked up and recognized the same orphan face that appeared at my bedside, tranquil and satisfied; and the little urchin with a triumphant smile replied,—"It is completed."

BY THE LAKE

Jeff Hecht

"How do you keep your little lake so peaceful and quiet, Rachel?" Jennifer asked, as the younger woman opened a bottle of California red wine. The vintage was drinkable, but nothing Jennifer would serve to guests.

"It's taken a lot of work over the last few years," Rachel replied, setting the bottle on a tray with two wine glasses, brie, and crackers. "Nothing like setting up the company, of course, but it does have a connection. We stock it with our own fish."

"I hadn't realized that." Jennifer's investment firm had taken Aquatic Genosynthesis public, and she thought she knew all the company's major projects.

"It's under research and development on the balance sheet," Rachel said, sliding open a wide glass door and leading the way onto the deck.

"It sounds like a nice little tax dodge," Jennifer said. She had to keep alert for CEOs siphoning too much cash out of their companies; it might depress the stock value.

"No, it's one of Ron's projects. He thinks recreational fishing could become quite a large market. He's working quite hard on it; he takes his father out on the lake almost every weekend to evaluate the results, like he took your husband."

That had amused Jennifer. Her husband was an accountant, and after her twenty-five years in investment banking, he normally didn't set foot on anything smaller than a yacht. "Do you think Ron can help him catch something? The poor dear hasn't been fishing since his eighth birthday." She could see their boat near the shore, moving slowly, although she couldn't hear a sound from its little engine.

Rachel set the tray down on a glass-topped table between two chairs. "I'm sure Ron can help him, but Ron's father was really the one who had the idea. Ron's dad was a biologist at the state fish hatchery for forty years before he retired last year. He knows an amazing amount about the feeding instincts of various fish, and what sort of lures can attract what sort of fish."

Jennifer settled into a lounge chair. "What does that have to do with genetically modified fish?"

"Ron's dad thought the feeding cues were genetically controlled, so when Ron was at the university he had his grad students look for genes that control what the fish respond to. They found several genes for specific responses, like striking at something that moved in a certain way, or generated specific noises."

Jennifer got the idea. "Is that how the fish recognizes its dinner?"

"Exactly. For fish farming we engineer in fast growth and limit breeding outside of the environment we control, to protect our investment. For recreational fishing, we modify other genes to modify feeding response."

"How does that make them more attractive for fishing?"

"Ron designed an artificial lure—a kind of high-tech fly—that creates a pattern the fish are programmed to strike at. We've tested it and the fish go for it every time. At the company we were able to step up their growth rate, and our latest trick is to adjust this behavior so the fish don't start striking at the lures until they are large enough to impress the fishermen. We stocked them in this lake last year, and they're already big enough to start striking. A few of the old-time purists don't like it, but it attracts the casual fisherman."

"And how big a market is this?" Jennifer asked. A big market could justify a secondary offering, which could earn her a fat commission.

"Billions," replied Rachel, then paused and looked onto the water, evidently distracted.

Jennifer's eyes followed and saw a wake far down the lake. Her ears picked up the whine of a jet ski motor.

"Damned moron!" Rachel said. "We had the public boat ramp blocked, but they still manage to get in."

"The noise is annoying," Jennifer said, glad to see that Rachel's lake wasn't perfect. "Our lake association keeps lobbying our state legislators to ban jet skis, but they want more campaign contributions before they introduce a bill."

"This isn't just an aesthetic issue, Jennifer. The wakes damage the delicate shore ecology, and the noise chases off birds and frogs, and upsets the fish."

"Can you use your genetic technology to make the fish less sensitive, so it wouldn't bother them?"

"I suppose that's possible, but we're going in a different direction." Rachel picked up a pair of Zeiss binoculars from the table to look more closely at the water. "We have a new experiment with pike, and if it works, you might see something in a minute."

"Why pike?" Jennifer knew only the fish that came on plates.

"They are voracious predators. We've speeded up their growth rate, and now are fine-tuning their instinctive striking response to just the right noise level. Watch over there," she said, pointing.

The jet ski sped uncomfortably close to a small child on a raft as it changed course, turning back up the lake. Jennifer followed Rachel's gesture and saw a dark shape moving from the middle of the lake. Suddenly it broke the surface and a huge mouth gaped open in front of the jet ski. There was a huge splash, with water spraying in all directions and blocking their view. Then the giant mouth, the jet ski, and the kid riding it were gone. Waves spread silently outward from the spot.

"The response threshold is perfect. That should show the bastards," Rachel said, putting down her binoculars.

Jennifer picked her glass of wine from the table and sipped. It was a much better vintage than she had realized. She had underestimated Rachel. "I can see a very big market. I'm sure our lake association will be interested."

AWSKONOMUK

Gregory Feeley

From the footpath above Overlook he could imagine them entering the harbor, envision the island and its mountain in their wondering eyes. Even the bow would rise just above the water line, and their low perspective (he had studied pictures of longships for years before he finally got to the museum at Oslo) would disclose Cadillac first, and then, only after they had made for it, the curve of the bay beyond and the astonishing greenery. They would know fjords, so not be surprised at a peak abutting the sea, whose nakedness—he remembered Champlain's observation that the island summits were bare of vegetation when seen from the sea—would likelier shock with familiarity. But the mountain (they would have their own name for it, now lost) would prove unique, and the densely forested interior, with its meadows, berries, and game, would draw them in.

The undisputed Viking site is northeast in Newfoundland; the "Maine Penny" was found farther down, on Penobscot Bay. They could have come here. Exploring south, the longships would have hugged the coast, bringing them into the gulf and sight of the island—perhaps more plainly an island then, for the Medieval Warm Period was in force, and the narrow strait that prevents Mount Desert Island from being a peninsula may have been wider. The Wabanaki Indians would have scattered the remains of any encampment, and the elements had centuries to destroy the rest, wash them into the sea, bury them in the silt that slowly turned lakes to meadows.

Even if L'Anse aux Meadows was the true Vinland, they would have quickly discovered the nearby mainland and ventured farther, beguiled by the inviting coastline that led them westward as well as south. How far, in the absence of seafaring resistance, would they have continued? Enough to assure themselves that no threat existed, no marauding powers beyond the Skræling settlements they raided at will. The coast of Maine is long; they may well have turned back before reaching Portsmouth. But until they had satisfied themselves that Nova Scotia was not another island—until they had touched the continent that Leif, who had traveled to Norway, knew lay beyond every large øy but his own—the Norsemen would have sailed on. They really could have come here.

He had bought a timetable in Bar Harbor and was on the beach by seven, walking the sodden strip just uncovered by low tide and soon to be submerged once more. Best was the lip of clear water as it receded before curling into the next wave: in that final quarter second, Jay could see declivities of sand and rock no beachcomber would glimpse. He had long since relinquished the hope that the tides would cast up anything heavy enough to have survived a millennium in the bay, but their clawing at the sands might conceivably uncover something washed away in storms and shallowly buried.

He tied his shoelaces together and hung them round his neck, then waded up to his shins in the ever-cold water. Parts of the *Denbigh* had been visible for decades at extreme low tide in Galveston Bay, and the *Amsterdam*, buried in English mud for more than a century longer, was discovered during an exceptional tide only in 1969, the year of his birth. Though he knew better, Jay found himself looking not for the gleam of metal at his feet, but—shielding his eyes—farther out, to the edge of refractivity, for the foreshortened outlines of a just-uncovered ship.

Breakfast a few miles outside the park, and when the visitors' center opened he was inside looking at the maps. A thousand years is nothing, and save perhaps for the shoreline, the contours of the topographical models displayed at ping-pong table height showed the island as the Norsemen would have found it. Jay wanted to know where the Indians had settled, so he knew where the Norsemen hadn't. He was browsing the book section for new information on pre-Wabanaki settlements when he noticed a woman holding a copy of *Vikings in America*.

"That isn't very good," he said, nodding at the familiar cover.

She flipped it over and looked at it, as though he was speaking of someone in the illustration. "What, this?"

"It's not a great book. I mean, I like the theory, but he can't tell good evidence from bad; he just accepts everything."

The woman frowned, and Jay realized with a stab of dismay that she wasn't sure what he was talking about. "But they came before Columbus, didn't they?"

"Centuries before Columbus, but the only site that has ever been found is up in Canada. If they ventured down this far, nobody knows where."

"He says they've found things, coins and stone carvings."

Jay made a face. "It's hard to date runes scratched in a rock, and you can't tell who dropped a coin, or when." The woman looked surprised, and he added, "No, I think he's right: the Vikings must have come down here. But we won't prove it until a settlement is found."

She opened the book again, to the middle pages where the photo section was. A ring on each finger, but neither a diamond: he noted these things automatically, realizing it only when a voice reminded him that he was two hundred miles from home. She looked perhaps thirty-five, and he liked her intelligent, inquiring expression as she scanned a photograph, then looked down to read the caption. The captions, he knew, oversold every point.

"Hm," she said. "Too bad." And she put back the book in a manner that did not particularly invite further discussion. Jay saw two more copies on the shelf, but nothing better. He returned to his perusal of the Indian section, which contained (like last fall) no new information on the island's prehistoric inhabitants.

The afternoon was spent south of town, where he would pull off the road every few miles to compare a site that had looked good on the topo map with the real thing. He knew enough not to bother tramping over the grounds, let alone trying to dig, but the experience of standing off the turnout and looking down on a coastal flatland or an especially hospitable cove and imagining how it might have looked a millennium earlier held its own complex pleasures, which he had long since given up trying to analyze.

He was on Route 3 heading north when his cell phone trilled, evidence that he was back within range of the watchtowers that stood at the borders of empire. He glanced down to see two messages waiting, blinks between pauses on a unit he knew better than to open here. One of the messages would be work, maybe both. Jay wasn't about to answer questions on the road, and let the phone content itself with having announced their arrival.

The Vikings showed no desire to "colonize" the new land, evidently seeing it simply as a source of lumber and other resources for its Greenland settlements. Jay pondered the logistics of sailing a thousand miles in order to collect as many planks as a longship would carry. Total costs are hard to calculate, a reflection that brought him back to work, where questions of drainage, soil mechanics, thin drift, and winter transport danced like arcade Whac-a-Moles.

He was pondering coffee in Ellsworth, a bad town for foundations but notable for the Agassiz Outcrop, which he remembered from college geology. Jay wondered what the Indians had made of its striations, like the claw marks (he remembered then thinking) of a giant bear. The Norsemen had no mythology of giant animals, though Fenrir would eventually grow large enough to touch the sky and berserks, of course, became bears. If they noticed the signs of ice carving and wondered at their cause, it didn't show up in the *Eddas*.

The cell phone rang again, a third summons that, as in folk tales, must this time be answered. Without taking his eyes from the road, Jay found the unit and one-handedly flipped it open. Holding it up, he said, "I'm driving; can't really talk."

"I'll send you e-mail," the device replied in a fair approximation of Lynn's voice.

"Fine." Jay dropped it beside him and looked out at the businesses on High Street, brooding over base flood elevation and the growing popularity of manufactured homes. He ate at a diner that advertised homemade pie, persuaded the waitress to put on a fresh pot, and read a trade paperback about the Vinland map while he waited. A thatch of business cards covered a bulletin board next to the cash register, though he didn't see any for foundation contractors.

Continuing north, he passed the street of a house he had tested for radon two winters back, when the seasonal slowdown was straining his cash flow. He remembered the basement, whose owner had to be told how the collector worked, and who then stood on the stairs, squeezing her hands in distress at what the world was coming to. Jay had explained how radon accumulation had nothing to do with pollution or any human activity: that the Passamaquoddy would have suffered increased rates of lung cancer had they built underground chambers like the Pueblos or Plains Indians. The memory usually triggered an annoyed reflection on people who don't understand their business, but this time he found himself thinking about Nidavellr, the subterranean realm of mines and dwarves. Was the stone they dug somehow deadly, or was that a detail from *Age of Mythology* or some other game? Once matters left the tangible world of artifacts that could be excavated and handled, it was difficult for him to keep their categories apart.

It would be too late to call Janice when he got home, but he imagined telling her about his day, looking down from Overlook onto wheeling gulls and wading in shallows uncovered only certain days of the year. Didn't some Indiana Jones film use that device? Real archeologists, even amateurs, had nothing but disdain for the treasure-hunting celebrated in such movies, as he remembered telling her once and reminded himself not to say again.

The only artifact he owned was an iron trivet with a leg missing, which he had bought in Norway. He had been able to afford it (and take it out of the country) because it could not be confidently dated to the Viking era, meaning that it did have the look. Its homeliness had bemused his wife, but Jay merely shifted it from the coffee table to his study, hefting it lightly in his palm during phone conversations, its mottled surface ugly and reassuringly real.

An empty toolbox sat on a bench near the service shed door, where employees tossed odd bits that had come up during ground excavations. Every few weeks Lynn asked Jay to go through them, and he would line up the potsherds, rusted hinges, and glass beads and gauge their provenance for whoever was interested.

"This is ceramic," he said as he rolled an item between his fingers. "What does it look like?"

"A spool for thread?" asked a secretary.

"It's part of an old fuse, probably from the 1920s." It was dispiriting how much of the crap buried several feet underground dated from the early twentieth century, even in areas that had been sparsely settled. Jay had found a few century-old implements over the years, but only one of plausibly Indian origin and nothing truly old. "Does your sister still have that old green bottle?"

"She keeps flowers in it." Handmade nails were uncommon, but when you found one there would be more: the site where a building once stood.

Contractors work long days through early autumn, so the late Saturday afternoons after the end of mosquito season are prized, a last chance for swim parties and cookouts. Jay was holding a beer and watching patties sizzle when he heard his host's wife mention his interest in Vinland.

"Really?" exclaimed her next-door neighbor, a young bank executive with a Black Bears logo on his polo shirt. "I thought they had proved that Leif Ericson reached America."

"North America," said Jay, "but nobody knows where. The only settlement anyone has found is in Canada."

"Wasn't there a map?" someone asked.

"A map that included the New World, but with no settlements marked." By now Jay knew all the usual questions.

"Have *you* found anything?"

"Jay was in Bar Harbor for the July low tides, looking for artifacts along the shore," Stacy said helpfully. That sounded faintly inane, and to stave off questions about metal detectors, he shrugged and made a deprecating remark about the lowest tides being in January, when he had too much sense to go out.

The subject came up again a few hours later, when most of the guests had retreated indoors and were sitting with their drinks in the TV room. Jay, who had a fifty-minute drive ahead, was restricting himself to coffee and feeling pleasantly tired, and was only half listening to the conversation when it swerved his way. Some women had been talking about antiques and collectibles, the Maine topic that interested him least, and one mentioned the recent case of a rare map dealer who had been arrested stealing from the Yale Library. A man asked, with woozy irrelevance, whether Yale was where they had the map showing that Norsemen had discovered America, and another replied he thought that map had been proven a forgery. Then someone said, "Jay knows about this."

Jay, who had just begun to register the "Norsemen" that had bobbed past, looked up. "What do I know about?"

"Vikings in America. They were here before Columbus or the Irish, weren't they?"

The question always put him on his guard. "If by 'here' you mean North America, there was a definite Viking settlement in Newfoundland. It seems likely that they would have explored further, but no one knows." He added with caffeinated exactitude, "I don't really *know* about it; I'm *interested* in it."

"What about those beehive stone huts?" someone asked.

Jay made quick work of stone huts. "Yeah, there are lots of those things in northern New England, and some people say they were built by Irish monks around the twelfth century. Archeologists date them from the colonial era."

"What was his name, Saint Brendan . . . ?"

"Oh, he was even earlier. There's an account of him traveling across the ocean and reaching an island covered with vegetation. Of course, it also says that he encountered a sea monster." Alicia looked at him warningly, and Jay, who had been about to expound upon this, caught himself. "Lots of things are possible—Muslim explorers were supposed to be superb navigators—but unless you find some evidence, it's all just theories."

He was half-expecting someone to bring up tales of strange-looking petroglyphs or modern-day voyages in leather rafts, but the only response was a round of thoughtful nods. An archeology professor had once chided him for fancifulness, so he knew he could be provoked from either side. Smiling at Alicia, he raised his cup. The conversation, snagging briefly on a favorite subject, was beginning to loosen and drift when someone said, "I heard something about this."

"Yes?"

It was Chris, a gangly student who had been doing construction work over the summer. They had been introduced, but all Jay remembered was that he wasn't studying archeology.

"A friend of mine at UMaine," he said, a bit uncertain with people's attention now upon him, "he told me about a study he worked on, testing students for their DNA. He mentioned this one woman, a Native American, whose genetic background showed that she had a tiny bit of Scandinavian ancestry. She was surprised, and I guess kind of indignant, because she was from a reservation—she insisted that all of her ancestors were full-blooded Indian, I mean Native American, going back for centuries."

"So she has a tiny bit of Viking ancestry," Stacy said wonderingly.

"Well, yeah. I mean, they didn't tell her, but that's what everyone thought."

Jay thought: Is this how it happens? You look in the places that logic suggests, you watch for new articles by experts and remind yourself that the logic holds up, and one day the evidence comes out of the blue, from a direction no one had thought to look.

"The thing is," Chris added, as though apologetically, "she isn't from Maine at all. She's from a reservation across the border in Quebec, and was only taking classes because her boyfriend was a university employee. So I guess she was descended from the settlement in Newfoundland, not one in Maine."

Jay shook his head. "Most of the Wabanaki fled to Canada after English settlers threatened to annihilate them. Was she Wabanaki?"

Chris pantomimed ignorance. "No idea."

"They were testing women?" someone asked. "So this would be mitochondrial DNA?"

"I think so. That was part of the point—the ancestor with Scandinavian genes had to be a woman, so it wasn't some Viking marauder."

There was an interested murmur at this, but Jay wasn't listening. His gathering sense of excitement seemed more calming than agitating, a settling into alignment. Before they left he asked Chris for his friend's name, which the young man gave without demur. Alicia, however, wondered about it on the ride home. "What is he going to *give* you?"

"I want to know more about the test—what exactly it showed, and what it means. How reliable their conclusions are."

"No, I mean what is this going to give you? Sites to explore? You said that these Indians had been driven from their homes by early settlers; they won't know more about where their ancestors lived a thousand years ago than you do."

Jay sighed and wondered what to say. "It's a hit, you know? I dig in the sand, and get no hits." He was finding it hard to explain. "This is something scientists found."

"If scientists are studying this, you can Google it. But I don't think you should call up this kid and ask him about someone's test results." Alicia worked in physical therapy. "Are you looking for validation?"

Jay scowled. "I don't even know what that means." He pushed

slightly harder on the accelerator, a signal that he was concentrating on the road.

They didn't speak of the matter again, although Jay spent an evening reading online articles about genetic testing for ancestral DNA. Two nights later Alicia worked late, and he called the number Chris had given him. The young man who answered was very guarded, and a bit unhappy to hear that a friend had repeated something about an ongoing research project. Jay explained the source of his interest, and the student confirmed that one of the test subjects, a Native American, had had a match for haplogroup U5a1a, which was associated with Scandinavian ancestry. He declined to speculate on the reasons for this, and refused to confirm Chris's recollection that she had been Canadian.

Jay thanked him and hung up, then looked at the *U5a1a* scribbled on his note pad. A half-hour's browsing confirmed that it was recognized as a marker for Nordic ancestry. He poured himself a drink and returned to his study, where he began looking through websites for the University of Maine. There was an alumni locator service, but it promised little help if you didn't know someone's name. *The Maine Alumni Magazine* would keep mailing lists searchable by state and province, but he could think of no reason why anyone would give him the names of recent students with Quebec addresses. The Office of Multicultural Programs had links to a number of Native American resources, including (he was startled to see) a Wabanaki Center; but nothing he followed gave any hint of information about individuals.

Student directories might be indexed for place of origin, but he knew that their contents would not be available online, nor (he was sure) in the university library or public information office. Jay could call a student— the only one who came to mind was Chris—and ask if he could flip through his copy, but that probably sounded a bit creepy.

Alicia came home tired and went to bed right after her shower. Jay sat on the edge of the mattress while she set the clock radio, but she didn't want to talk, and ten minutes later he was back at his computer. It was after midnight when he discovered that the University of Maine had a second magazine, *UMaine Today*, that offered the contents of its back issues online. He clicked through the categories patiently and without particular hope until he came to an article, published four years ago, on the Native American Studies program. It came up, complete with photos, and sprinkled with quotations from various undergraduates. Two thirds of the way down he found one by Lucie Paguanquois, identified as belonging to the Nation Waban-Aki in Odanak, Centre-du-Québec.

He searched on the name and came up with four hits, two of them photo captions. Group shots on a student's blog and someone's photo page showed a woman in her early twenties, evidently uncomfortable in front of cameras, or rather (judging by the photos' quality) cell phones. One showed her as pretty plainly Native American. Jay then checked the text files, which turned out to be in French.

He went to bed thoughtful, and the next evening he wrote to her, care of Conseil de bande d'Odanak de la Nation Waban-Aki. He explained his interest in pre-Columbian contacts between Europe and the First Nations, and told her how he had heard about her test results. Though he did not wish to obtrude upon her privacy (Jay could imagine Alicia's disapproval as he typed), he wanted to ask her about this, whether the details he had heard were accurate, and if so, if she knew of any Wabanaki traditions involving very early contact with seafaring strangers.

He sent the file to work and printed it out on company letterhead, so it would not seem to have come from some solitary crank. Thinking it over as he drove from one building site to the next, he wondered what she might possibly have. It had been a couple years since he had found that old book on Wabanaki legends—an oversized Cambridge tome from the 1880s, with plates and a fussy title page—that suggested they had derived from Norse influence, and he knew enough to distrust any evidence that relied upon oral transmission over a millennium. What was she likely to produce—an unrecognized Viking brooch that had been in her family for centuries?

Jay didn't have an answer to this, one reason not to discuss it with Alicia. Daylight Saving Time expired, he began leaving the house even earlier to snatch at the dwindling sunlight, and Janice's soccer schedule sent him ranging across Penobscot County every Saturday. Standing afternoons in shafts of wan sunlight that had been balked a fortnight earlier by leaves, Jay looked from the excavations at his feet to the spongy crust of soil that bespoke night frost and thought: *What would they have done that first autumn?* The ferocity of winter would have been anticipated, but to gird for it in a still-strange land, with large animals and hostile natives such as Greenland signally lacked . . . They would have wondered when the first snow would fall, and looked uncertainly to the skies even as Jay checked www.weather.com.

When Alicia told him that she wanted to take her mother to Old Town the following weekend for an afternoon at the casino, he grimaced and shrugged, but later recalled the Penobscot museum there. He called and asked Janice's mother to take her to her game, then left Alicia a message saying he would be able to drive. Leaving them at the front curb where the charter buses disgorged their contents, Jay found a parking space among the avenues of packed vehicles and began the long walk to the museum.

The building was small, and its collection unsurprisingly emphasized the nation's post-colonial history—nineteenth-century photographs, weapons, head dresses, and ceremonial carvings. Jay was used to the paucity of ancient holdings in tribal museums, and studied the exhibits thoughtfully, wondering how greatly customs and tools would have changed over a thousand years. After more than an hour of careful reading while other visitors came and went, a young man behind the counter asked him whether he was a teacher, and Jay confessed himself interested in the first contact with European settlers.

"You mean English and French, or are we talking earlier?"

They chatted pleasantly about the ancient trading center excavated on Penobscot Bay, which the young man, an assistant curator, did not care to call "the Goddard site." He agreed that the Norwegian penny found there constituted insufficient evidence of Viking settlement, and nodded at Jay's explanation of why the Norsemen in Newfoundland would nonetheless have likely come this far. Ten centuries is a lot of time for a perhaps small body of artifacts to be scattered, and even the silver penny was badly corroded.

Emboldened, Jay told him what he had heard about the Quebec Abenaki who showed DNA evidence of Norse ancestry. The curator raised his eyebrows at that, though he added after a minute that even a full-blood might have a mixed ancestor centuries ago, and one would be enough. "The Odanak, though, they've been up there a long time. If there weren't any white ancestors in the last two hundred years—and they would know—then she's probably full."

"I'd like to confirm the story, since I heard it second hand," Jay admitted. "But I don't have her address. I sent a letter to the Nation, but it may never have reached her."

The young man frowned. "This is not necessarily something that would interest her, you know. And some Down Easter wanting to talk about the Viking in her heritage . . ." He looked at Jay closely. "What was her name again?"

Jay gave it, and the man went back to the front desk and set up a laptop next to the cash register. He worked on it for a few minutes, then looked up and said, "Okay."

Jay approached, uncertain. The assistant curator wrote something on a scrap of paper and pushed it toward him. It was an e-mail address, from an Abenaki domain in .ca, which he knew meant Canada. "I'm assuming you're not going to hassle her, since doing that across international borders brings real trouble. But take care how you ask. People aren't digs, you know."

He never told Alicia what had happened, though his plan had begun to set, like poured concrete, as it became apparent that the letter would go unanswered. By the time they set out, however, she had a fairly good idea what was going on, and sat without speaking as snowflakes beat against the windshield. Dawn was more than an hour away, and Jay's driving skills would be called upon for most of the trip—perhaps all of it, since his unadmitted intentions seemed to figure heavily in her mood.

He had resolved almost immediately to seek out Lucie Paguanquois, guessing that no e-mail exchange would really satisfy him. Very likely there was nothing she could tell him, but he didn't want to hear as much, not with the remote finality of a letter. He had e-mailed her in mid-December, explaining his fascination and apologizing for writing again. He would, he said, be visiting the Musée des Abénakis with his family the first weekend in January, and hoped to be able to speak with her over a cup of coffee. He promised no further contact should she not reply.

It was several days later before the answer appeared. In a single sentence, she said that if he was intent on coming, he could call her that Saturday. And she appended, by way of closing, a telephone number.

Alicia likely had no illusions concerning his interest in the Abenaki tribal museum, and her unspoken disapproval hung in the air, undispersed by the noisy heater. Only the first half hour would be highway, then they would be pushing northwest, through a succession of country roads and stop lights, for three hundred miles. The museum was in fact closed weekends this time of year—"Can you wonder why?" she asked—but he decided not to poke at what plans there were. He made good time on I-95, which gave a sense of impetus to their subsequent ascent into the Appalachians. Jay let Alicia choose the radio station, found a nice pancake house outside Eustis, and finally, as they were descending a pass, he said: "She wouldn't have agreed to meet if she didn't want to."

"Lord knows what she wanted, except not to be bothered."

Jay suspected that Alicia was angrier at being manipulated than she was on behalf of the student, but knew better than to say so. "Perhaps she's a bit curious herself. Or maybe she's just being nice."

It was after lunch when they crossed into Canada, and more than two hours—a light snow dusted the unfamiliar roads, slowing the hard-to-pass traffic on the provincial secondary routes—before Alicia announced that they were approaching Saint-François-du-Lac, and would soon cross a river.

"Not the Saint Lawrence," protested Jay, who knew they stopped short of that.

"Nothing so grand," she said.

From mid-span they could see the buildings of the Réserve, although Alicia had to point them out. These disappeared from sight as they neared the shore, and it was another half mile before they turned into the slushy parking lot of the Musée. A handsome building, larger than any tribal museum Jay had seen in Maine, it looked like the kind of place he would like to have taken Janice to. Other buildings, including the Fromagerie Odanak—a native cheese-making enterprise—still had lights on inside, but they had to drive into the village to find a coffee shop. Alicia looked meaningfully at him as he turned off the ignition, and with a sigh he took out his cell phone and called the number.

"*Allo?*" The voice was crackly, as though routed through a distant transmission tower.

"I would like to speak to Lucie Paguanquois, please," said Jay carefully.

"Speaking."

"Hi, this is Jay Furnivell." She said nothing, and he plunged ahead.

"We are in front of . . ." He paused uncertainly, and Alicia gave the name of the restaurant, which he repeated. "Would you like us to—"

"I will meet you there." She added something in French, and the connection ended.

They went inside and sat at a booth, where Alicia ordered them coffee. Snowflakes nestled in her hair, more than he would have guessed from the scant seconds they had spent crossing the parking lot. Alicia was looking at the collar of his parka, which he realized was thick with them. "Still plan on driving home tonight?" she asked.

"Perhaps not." He could register reproach implicit in everything she said, but all he felt was a fluttering excitement. The restaurant was about half full, and he could see that several of the patrons were Native American, if that (he suddenly thought) was what they were called here. He made a mental note not to use the term.

The coffee was hot, and the cream came out of a pitcher and might be local. They sat drinking thankfully, a moment of fellow-feeling that did not require (and would perhaps not bear) comment. Alicia told the waitress in careful French that they would not order yet, as they were waiting for a third person; Jay wondered how he could understand her.

"Do you know what it is you want? Because she's not going to tell you." Alicia was looking at him seriously. "This isn't her history, and she's not going to be interested in it."

"Well . . ." Jay thought of the respects in which he might argue the point, and decided not to. Did she think he was going to whip out his cell phone and take the woman's picture? He had a notebook in his pocket, but made no move to bring it out.

The door banged behind him, and he saw a change in Alicia's expression. Standing in the doorway, pulling off a knitted cap that was lopsided with snow, Lucie Paguanquois looked across the room and found their eyes.

Her boots clumped on the linoleum, and she was standing in front of them, looking at the third cup, empty, that Alicia had asked be set for them. "Thanks," she said. Snow slid off her parka as she shrugged out of it, and she walked away to hang it up. Jeans and a heavy knit sweater, jet black hair down her back. He wondered what she looked like under the layers.

The waitress had poured coffee by the time Lucie returned, and she sat without ceremony. "I suspect your English is better than my French," Alicia said after they had introduced themselves.

"I'm sure," Lucie replied. She turned to Jay. "So here I am. Why are you here?"

Jay had conducted enough negotiations in restaurant booths not to blink. "I wanted to speak with you. Thanks for meeting me."

She shrugged. "When I get married this spring, my phone will change. You won't be able to keep calling." A few snowflakes began to run down the front of her glasses, which she removed and cleaned with a napkin. When she replaced them, her black eyes fixed him keenly. "You like the idea of Indians having Viking blood?"

He smiled, unoffended. "If it's true, then that's interesting. I never thought about it before, because I like looking for artifacts. I heard about your test results by accident, and I won't tell anyone.

"Don't be offended by this—Alicia thinks I'll end up insulting you—but in a sense, your DNA is an artifact, or at least a record. So is mine, and everyone's, just as every site you excavate can be documented. But not all sites are interesting."

Lucie glanced sidelong toward Alicia. "If you told some anthropologist, he would simply say that I have a white ancestor five or six generations back whom I don't know about."

Jay was startled by the *whom*, then realized that she must have learned English in school. "But he would be wrong, wouldn't he? Your people have been here for three hundred years, and the first census was in 1822. You know who is and is not full-blood."

It seemed a reasonable reply, but she glared. "So you have been studying us, have you?"

"I studied what's on the Internet; come on. Should I come up here and waste time asking you things I could find out elsewhere?" He immediately changed tack. "Besides, a European ancestor that recent would have shown up all over those results. I've done a little reading there, too, and the researchers made a good inference."

The waitress returned, and Lucie spoke to her in rapid French, indicating the three of them. Watching her, Jay found himself not thinking of anticipated objections, but simply looking at the woman, an unremarkable Native American in her twenties whose mitochondrial DNA held, like a recently deciphered codex, the unlooked-for confirmation he had never expected to find. He had no doubt that this woman's great-to-the-forty-or-fiftieth grandmother had been a Viking settler—not of Newfoundland, where the Beothuk natives probably drove off the Norsemen after a few years, but from an unknown settlement, Vinland or another, that encountered the coastal Wabanaki of what is now called Maine. The fact that genealogists would doubtless find her mtDNA line suggestive rather than conclusive meant nothing: the immediacy of her being—before him, as he knew the drowned foundations never would be—sufficed to banish doubt.

"I ordered for you," she said, directing her look at Jay. Before he could thank her, she added, "You're just a typical American, unable to speak any language but your own?"

"I actually picked up a fair amount of Norwegian one summer," he replied mildly. Then, "Have you studied Abenaki?"

She gave a fractional nod, wary. "There aren't any Norse words in it, if you're wondering."

"Of course not." He decided not to tell her about the Victorian scholar who claimed that the Wabanaki trickster Lox derived from Loki, the wind eagle from something in the *Edda* and so on: who would certainly have pounced upon any linguistic echoes in the languages. The reasoning seemed sound, but he was beginning to understand how readily she felt his intrusion. "Is there an Abenaki word for 'exile'?"

She frowned, either at the question or his reasons for it. "*Nakasahozik* is the act of pushing out, but it doesn't really have a political sense. Perhaps *awskonomuk*—it means to displace. The Wabanaki were *awskonoak* by the English from their homeland—'wabanaki' means the eastern land."

"Did you visit Mount Desert Island when you were living in Maine? It was Wabanaki country a thousand years ago, their easternmost extent. The bay to the west was Penobscot—Penawapskewi—territory. That's the region where the Vikings would have landed."

"I don't care." She slashed across his point like a scythe. "The Wabanaki were driven into Québec centuries ago; do you think I am interested in details of *your* history, or its traces in that blood test? I did it for the sixty dollars."

The meal came then, three laden plates, different—he could see this as she set them down—from a Down East all-day breakfast. Thick cuts of what Jay would call ham, fries with gravy and what looked like half-melted cheese, beans atop scrambled eggs. The plates clacked down with reassuring solidity, and the three bent over them just as a chill gust blew from the door, a reminder of what was outside.

They ate in silence, finishing meat then starch and savoring the richness of the juices, which Jay did not hesitate to sop up. (Lucie, he saw, spread butter and then jam on her toast, a fearless Canadian practice he had unthinkingly associated with Anglophones.)

Eventually she pushed her plate away, and sat back to look at him with an amused expression. "And do you think you have Viking blood, too?"

"I have no idea." It had never occurred to him to get a DNA ancestry kit and try it on himself. "I grew up in Iowa."

She snorted. "And a thousand years ago your ancestors were where?"

"Well, not there. All over Europe, I guess." Someday genetic testing would tell more; he had read up on that, too. An uncovered potsherd was physical, and unique: these ghostly bits encoded in the tiniest structures of one's blood were neither—everyone had different proportions of the same innumerable scraps. Someday the tests would be so powerful and common that all would be known, the endless migrations of peoples, churning and recombining like seawater.

Nobody's story would please them, Jay thought; one more thing not to say right now. Flight, rapine, exile, all would be laid bare, plus bolts of more unremarkable lineage than anyone liked. We are all kings' bastards, for it is to them that our mothers were brought.

Lucie gestured as the plates were cleared away. "If you're planning to pay with American dollars, you'll need more than you think. It isn't worth more than ours any more."

"We have Canadian money," said Alicia, with perhaps a touch of reproof. "Maine isn't Mississippi."

"And Odanak isn't Maine." It would be interesting to know what had brought her to study in the States, and why she had returned to the reserve. But Jay felt he had maybe two questions left him, and that would not be one.

"Did it interest you," he asked, "to find that you have a Viking ancestor? I know it's not *important* to you, and I understand that it's nobody's business; but how did you feel to learn that something that happened so long ago, for which all other records are utterly gone, remains documented in your blood?"

She seemed to consider the question. "It's like an echo that bounced off a distant canyon. What produced the sound happened long ago. Some Indian graves are even older, but that doesn't mean you can handle the bones and put them on display. It's . . ." She looked at him in frank curiosity. "I don't know if you can understand it, Mister From-Everywhere."

"Meaning nowhere in particular. Okay, that's an answer." Dispelling her misapprehensions wasn't a priority for him, and Jay waved to the waitress to buy himself a few seconds. "Has anyone else on the reserve—"

A cell phone rang, not Jay's or Alicia's. Lucie stood up, lifted the hem of her sweater, and glanced at its display. "Goodbye," she said.

"You walked here," Alicia said. "Let us give you a ride back."

Jay was glad she offered—he knew it would be better if he didn't—but Lucie shook her head. "Finish your coffee; you have a long trip." She looked at Jay. "If you learn anything more, don't call me."

The door banged shut as the waitress poured their last cups and set down the bill. Jay and Alicia regarded each other, then he reached over and poured cream for her. "She doesn't want us to come out until she's gone from sight," he said.

"She probably has enough on her mind," Alicia replied. "Did you notice that she's pregnant?"

Jay stared and then shook his head. "How does that matter?" He stirred his own coffee, then sipped. The last swallow of warmth before they stepped out into the cold: he wondered if the Vikings had a word for it. Longships lacked cabins, but the Newfoundland excavations disclosed thick walls, so the act must have been significant.

"Her bloodline runs downstream, not up." The remark seemed to surprise her as much as him, and she smiled in embarrassment. Finishing her cup, Alicia picked up her purse and added: "She doesn't want to represent something."

The temperature had dropped outside, and the afternoon sky looked bruised. The surrounding flatland felt more like the Midwest than anywhere in Maine, and Jay wondered how far the Vikings had penetrated, up the Penobscot or St. Croix, into the continent's interior. The remains of such ventures might never be found.

The burial ship found at Ladby had entirely dissolved, its hull's outlines only discernible by a darkening of the soil. So the artifacts of Vinland, tokens one could lift and feel, were—he felt its truth bump hard—now vanished forever from human reach, their last traces, now copies of copies, diffusing in chemical memory like smoke.

THE COUNTY

Melanie Tem

That's a gorbey, him. Canada jay. Also known as gray jay, Whiskey Jack, moose-bird. See his furry feathers? For the cold. Put him back outside, *la*. You come up here to hunt moose, not gorbeys, you. Fog don't bother him. Funny-looking little thing, isn't he? Personally, *non*, I wouldn't call him cute.

Keep him? What for?

Sorry to hear that. But Jack won't make a pet for a sick child. Spirits of the dead, some say gorbeys are. Or just very smart birds that'll do to you what you do to them.

Oh, we got all sorts of such creatures up here, just like anywhere else. Papineau, big man like Paul Bunyan only meaner, goes from house to house begging for food, never can get full, him, puts a curse on you if you don't give him all the food you got. *Feux-follets*, spirits of the damned that wander around in the woods. You'll see 'em sometimes, little tiny flames in this thick old dark forest. Forest more like one solid tree, *n'est pas?* You boys ever seen anything like it?

Fairytales? Oh, I don't think so. So you best put that bird back outside, *la*. I'm telling you.

Pea soup? Hah! "Pea soup" don't come close to Maine fog. Thick enough you could cut it into bricks and build a house out of 'em like this one, easy. The wood all weathered gray, kind of dim and dark in here with those filmy curtains Lina likes, could just as well be made out of fog. Fog gets inside here, too. Can you see it, all shimmery between me and you? Feel it, like your skin and your hair might just dissolve any minute now? Taste it?

Lina. My daughter. This is her place.

Fog lifts, there'll be good hunting. More moose than people up here.

sonic moose deflectors like on my car. You saw how
'e and how the forest comes right up close. And moose
)n between human and non-human, you know who

's, "There's a tombstone every mile" along the road.
, - am not a singer. He's talking about right here in The
County.

So you gotta be careful. Don't mess with moose, okay? Don't mess
with gorbeys. We'll be waiting out the fog for a while here, my daughter
Lina's place, she won't mind, she went down to Bangor, *la*.

Leave him be, you. Let him go. Gorbey's nothing to fool around
with.

Born and raised here, me. Went down South to see what I could see,
nothing worth seeing, no reason to leave The County again. The Cyr
family goes back a long ways. Benoit's an old family name, too. Benoit.
B-e-n-o-i-t. Like I said at the beginning, just call me Ben.

Aroostook County. Bigger than a lot of states. Everybody in all of
New England knows it as just The County, like there's no other county
in the world. Potatoes. You saw the potato houses on those farms we went
by. Some of 'em are huge, potato mansions. You never thought of potatoes as beautiful? Hah. Beautiful white and purple blossoms. And you
have never tasted anything in your life like my Lina's potato cake.

Your basic wilderness. Everything manmade is very far from everything else manmade. That's the way we like it up here.

Well, I am a certified Maine Woods Guide, me. Not many of us.
Been leading hunting and fishing trips for longer than you've been alive.
Believe I'd have checked that out before I signed up for this trip. Best to
know who you're in the wilderness with, *non*?

This'll be my last trip, though. Retiring, me. Lucky for you boys you
come when you did, no telling who you'd've got.

So, Tim, how do you say your surname, with just the one vowel?
That Polish? In French, we have an abundance of vowels. Perhaps we
should give you some. Hah.

And Rob Thibideaux. You are Acadian, Rob? Ah, from Louisiana,
oui. Cajun. Perhaps we are related. From the Diaspora. You don't know
the Diaspora? Your own history? 1755, when our people were expelled
from the land and scattered like so many seeds, which is what "Diaspora"

means? We call it the Great Derangement.

You never heard of none of this. *Mon Dieu.* A man without a history is a man without a soul. You gotta do something about that, you. Maybe we can do something about that. Goes into making us who we are. You much as me. Like the Holocaust goes into making Tim who he is. Right, Tim?

My daughter Lina's quite the historian, her. Last winter she spent down in New Orleans, *la,* brought back Diaspora tales and Cajun recipes. Good cook. Pretty girl. You'd like my Lina, you. Don't know if she'd like you. She's picky. Says she's got no need for a man. Always been a little bit crazy, her.

Could be socked in for a while, can't say. Fog's part of the Maine experience you come here for. Third of this month was heavy fog, and some say that predicts the month. *Le trois fait le mois.* Don't know as I hold with that, but that's what some say. But then, some'll say practically anything. Gets thick enough, you can make fog angels. Hey, after a while you'll do anything to amuse yourself. Get to feeling sort of confined.

Like a gorbey in a box. Take that bird outside, you, let him go. Your kid won't like him, trust me. He won't like your kid, him.

What's your wife and kids think of you leaving 'em back there in Shreveport while you come up here to the fog and the moose? Ah, *oui, c'est vrai,* you got to get away sometimes. Heart grows fonder, like they say.

Divorced, me. One daughter. My Lina. Her husband's one of those tombstones along the road that Dick Curless fella sung about. Lonely for a woman up here, never mind what she says, just her old dad to talk to and me out in the woods half the year. Don't know why she didn't remarry. My sweet Lina. See how nice she keeps a house, her? Get your boots off the furniture.

Gotta take a leak. Leave the door open if you want, get some air in here. Sure, the fog'll come in, but it's already in, can't escape the fog, best you can do is hunker down and not get lost in it. Here, prop this up on the table, *la,* so the beam points up. Helps a little. Reflecting off the fog wisps like that, kind of looks like a wedding veil, don't it? Kind of pretty. Be right back.

Give me the damn box.

Rob Thibideaux, you are one stubborn Cajun, you. What is it with you and this gorbey? Stole your sandwich, did he? *Mais oui.* Camp robber's another name for him. Lina tells how a gorbey come right in her kitchen window and hooked his left foot through one of her doughnuts and his right foot through another one and his beak through another one and he flew off into a tree with all three doughnuts, him. Comes back now and sits outside her window every time she makes 'em. That's what she says. Complains, calls him names, but I'm not sure she altogether minds, being a young widow like she is and alone except for that woman comes up here sometimes from Bangor.

You think you're gonna teach him a lesson, trapping him like that? Let me tell you something. Nobody ever taught a gorbey nothing. Other way around. You think you're gonna take him home, put him in a cage, cheer up your little boy? Hah. Whatever you do to a gorbey'll be done to you. Now that's the honest truth.

Be right back.

Idiot.

So, Jack, you just remember, you, it's me letting you go. That Cajun boy, that *Robert* Thibodeaux, he's the one captured you, him. Made you stay in a box. You gonna do the same back to him, you? For my Lina? Once I know we got a deal, then I'll open this lid and you can fly off to wherever you fly to, *la.* We got a deal?

Merde. Got away, you! Without a deal. Too quick. Too tricky. Hey, Jack! You owe me, you! You hear me? *Merde.*

Ah, *monsieur!* You startled me, coming up out of the fog like that. Didn't see you, big as you are. Foggy enough for you?

Don't believe we've met. Name's Benoit Cyr.

Papineau. I heard of you. You're hungry, *c'est vrai?* That's what I figured. Well, you like potato doughnuts? Plenty of good food in that house, *la.* Couple of hunters in there with me, waiting out the fog. They won't mind. Come on in, you. Watch your head.

Boys, we got company. Allow me to introduce M. Papineau. Like I said before, he's pretty well known around here as a man with an appetite. This here's Tim Strand and Rob Thibodeaux. Rob's Cajun, though he don't know it, never been up this way before, him.

Help yourself, M. Papineau. Refrigerator, cupboards, pantry. Lina won't mind.

You boys come on outside, *la*, I'll show you about the Maine fog. Can't tell from in here. No, you come with me. *Pardonnez-nous, monsieur.* Now listen to me. Quiet, just listen. I know Papineau. I never met him, but I know him. Everybody around here knows him. You got Papineau in Louisiana? Wouldn't know that, would you? He goes from place to place, especially when the fog's in like this, and he begs for food, and he can't ever be filled up, him. He's big, you see how big he is, bigger'n a normal man by a long shot, had to duck and turn sideways coming through the door, *la*, you see that? Paul Bunyan's maybe bigger, but Papineau's meaner. You don't satisfy him, he can do bad things. Put a curse on. Go ahead, laugh. But give him whatever food you got. We can stop by the store in Limestone, *la.*

You got to what? Now? Best be careful where you piss, Rob Thibodeaux. This kind of fog, it'll come right back on you. And don't get yourself lost.

So, Tim. He's a handsome one, *non*? Your friend Rob? Betcha he turns the heads of the ladies. Betcha he'd turn my Lina's head, she could meet him, never mind she's so picky, her. Woman without a man is unnatural.

Oui. Bon. You give Papineau what you got and I give him what I got, maybe he goes on his way. Even if your handsome friend Rob wants to be stupid.

Hate to think of his wife and kids down there in Shreveport, *la.* But things happen, sometimes you can't help it, you gotta take what comes your way. Too bad you're not Cajun, you. You better go get him before he gets himself lost. I need to think some more about Papineau.

First the gorbey, then Papineau. Sometimes you gotta get beaned over the head before you see what's right there.

How's your supper, M. Papineau? See you found the moose steaks in the freezer. I was gonna point those out, me. See you found the Oreos. Can opener's in that drawer by the sink, *la.*

So, tell me something. You just happen on us in the fog, or did somebody send you? Whiskey Jack. That's what I figured. You're my payback, you. My return favor.

Wait, just thought of something else, be right back, don't go away. Hah.

Found 'em, right where I knew they'd be. My Lina's got a weakness, her. She thinks it's a secret, I don't know about her stash, I don't know she sits all alone by herself out here or with that woman friend of hers from Bangor and eats chocolate-covered cherries. That's not good, you know what I mean? Woman needs a man, no matter what she says.

Here you go, *mon ami.* Never opened. All yours.

Listen, I gotta talk to you about something, man to man. I'm afraid we got ourselves a little problem here. That boy Tim, that Polish boy, he's okay, he'll give you what food he's got, corn chips, juice in a box. But that Cajun kid Rob Thibodeaux, he's holding out on you, him. Power Bars and dried fruit in his pack. Trust me, I seen 'em. Just wanted you to know it's him.

There's something else. I'm sick, me. Real sick. Been failing for a while now, can't hide it much longer. My daughter Lina's down in Bangor, *la.* Visiting a friend, a woman friend, but she's gone too long. Gotta have Lina now, can't lose her to the outside. My wife, she just up and decided after thirty years up here it was too cold, too isolated for her, too empty. Like she didn't know that from the get-go. Man's gotta have somebody to come home to, *non?* Somebody to take care of him. Especially when he can't take care of himself.

And when I'm gone, me, Lina'll need a man.

We understand each other? We got ourselves a deal? Six, seven more boxes of chocolate-covered cherries where that one come from.

Tres bien. Here they come.

Well, boys, fog's burning off now. We can continue to the camp. M. Papineau, we must leave you now, with I hope enough sustenance to keep you going for a while. *Je regrette* we couldn't give you more, couldn't fill you up. *De rien.*

Robert? That's the French way, same spelling. You ready? Tim's already in the car. We want to get there before dusk, and we got to stop at Limestone, *la.*

Ah.

What's the matter with you, son? You can't move? You can't move out of this house, my Lina's house, which, when you think about it, is a lot like a box? Papineau got your tongue? Whiskey Jack got you stuck?

Well, you just stay right where you are, you. Not so cold you'll freeze. Little fog, that's all, mornings for the rest of the month. I'll send word to my Lina, she'll come back from Bangor and take care of you.

You'll like Lina, and maybe she'll like you. You'll like it up here, with your own people, you.

M. Papineau, look in the closet in that back bedroom. Whole stack of chocolates. *Merci.*

AND DREAM SUCH DREAMS

Lee Allred

Dedication of the 20th Maine Monuments at Gettysburg
October 3, 1889
> *Joshua Chamberlain read from the last page of his speech.*
> *"We know not of the future," he concluded, "and cannot plan for it much.*
But we can hold our spirits and our bodies so pure and high, we may cherish such
thoughts and such ideals, and dream such dreams of lofty purpose, that we can
determine and know what manner of men we will be whenever and wherever
the hour strikes, that calls to noble action."
> *The audience politely clapped and came up to shake his hand. The crowd*
milled about for a while until, as if on cue, it slowly melted away, leaving Cham-
berlain to stand silently alone.
> *The audience had not understood what it was he had been trying to say. Yes,*
today they might have listened to what had been done here and applauded at the
appropriate times, but tomorrow those deeds would quickly fade from memory.
> *He had tried to frame the words that would make them understand what*
had happened here, but for all his supposed classically trained skill at rhetoric and
oration, he had failed. Here, on the site of his greatest success, he had failed.
> *"Mr. Chamberlain, sir?" the young man from the Dedication Commit-*
tee prompted, hesitant to disturb him. "Shouldn't we be getting down off the
hill ourselves? I believe there's a luncheon prepared, and there's still tonight's
festivities—"
> *"He would have a found a way." Chamberlain said, as if the young man*
should know of whom he spoke without being told. "But he is gone. He is the one
who died, and I am the one who lived."
> *The young man, clearly not understanding, tried again, "The luncheon—"*
> *"It was many, many years after the war until Hay told me what that had*
happened."

"*Sir*—"

"'*We do not know the future.*' *But he knew. He knew before he ever left, knew standing on the back of that train. He told them in words plainer than any I've ever been able to fashion that he was not coming back.*"

His voice dropped to a whisper. "Parainesis *of the living,* epainesis *of the* dead."

I stood on the back of the train and looked out over the faces of my Springfield friends and neighbors one last time before I left. They wanted to hear the farewell from a President-elect. I could only give them a good-bye of plain ol' Abe.

My friends, I said to them, here I have lived a quarter of a century, have passed from a young man to an old man. Here my children have been born, and one is buried. I now leave, not knowing when, or whether ever, I may return.

I walked back into the train car they'd given us. Mrs. Lincoln and the children were waiting for me. I noticed crepe curtains on the window. Mother, I said to Mrs. Lincoln as I fingered them, black is a strange color for curtains on a train.

But Father, she said, looking at me sharply. The curtains are red.

John Hay's Diary
June 28, 1863

Lincoln quite morose tonight from the news that Robert E. Lee has pushed past Hooker, heading north into Maryland, perhaps even Pennsylvania. All we can do now is pray our Army will somehow stop him this time.

At least Lincoln has replaced that blowhard Hooker. George Meade's in command now, but will he be enough? I cannot help but fear Meade will only turn out to be another Burnside, another Hooker, another McClellan.

Lincoln shares my fear, I think, but even before the news he was troubled. I saw him this morning at his desk, even earlier than usual. His hair was mussed, his feet still in slippers, his hands absent-mindedly whittling a stick. When I walked in, he looked up and I knew at once that look in his eyes.

What dark dream was it this time?

I told Johnny about my new dream. He humored me, but I reckon he didn't believe me none, any more than he's believed me about any of the other dreams. He suggested in that college-boy way of his to recollect I'm President, not Pope. Reckon so, reckon so. The Almighty might be sending these dreams to the wrong feller. The dreams, though—they're real enough.

This new one was a mite different than the others. No death, no destruction, no railroad car at Springfield. Just the inside of a schoolroom. Some sort of boy's college. Tidy little buildings of red brick. Respectable, not rough-hewn like me.

A framed portrait of President James Buchanan hung on the wall. That's how I knowed it was a dream of the past. Nobody these days would hang a picture of Old Buck up on a wall, not even Mrs. Buchanan.

From what I could tell from the way the fellers in the dream talked, this school was up in New England somewhere. Pine trees out the window. Maine, maybe.

Anyway, this professor feller was teaching rhetoric and oratory, going on at length about the ancient Greeks. The books he was reading from were all written in little squiggles. Greek it was. Never studied it myself—not much call for it on the prairie—but I've brushed up agin it often enough that I can recognize it when I see it.

A harmless dream on the surface, yet it worries at me like a dog with a bone.

John Hay's Diary
July 1, 1863

News of a big scrap up in Pennsylvania. Lee collided with the Army of the Potomac in a sleepy little hamlet called Gettysburg. Entire city here in a panic.

Curious the way Lincoln reacted to the news this time, though. I remember how he fell to pieces after Chancellorsville. "What will the country say?" he cried out then. Today, though, Lincoln read the telegram without saying a word. He just went into his office alone and latched the door behind him.

A few minutes later he emerged. His hangdog look was gone. Instead, his face was as cool as block ice in a Vermont blizzard. Calm. Serene. The same face he sometimes wears after wresting a hard bargain from an opponent. There are times I think his harshest opponent is himself.

Lincoln's confident mood lasted the rest of the day. I just wish it were contagious. Heaven knows, I have a valise packed, just in case—and one for Lincoln as well (although I imagine he would put up a fuss if he knew).

John Hay's Diary
July 3, 1863—p.m.

Meade did it. I scarcely dared hope, but he did it. For the first time in this war our Army of the Potomac beat Robert E. Lee. Perhaps this war might actually end.

And yet, when the War Department handed Lincoln the telegram, I thought Lincoln would "whoop and holler" as he puts it, but instead he hardly even glanced at it, as if he already knew its contents.

I just do not understand him at times.

The one thing Lincoln did seem to react to was the news that General Sickles, one of our many politicians playing army, had been gravely wounded. Lincoln said, "I reckon I ought to go see him." No shrewd political calculation in his voice at all, just honest kindness for a man who has not always done Mr. Lincoln right.

I don't know why I told Sickles what I did when I visited him a couple days after the Gettysburg battle. Even started walking away from him, but then paused and turned back around. Don't know why, really. Maybe it was his pain. Maybe it was my own pain. Reckon I'll never know. But it came over me all of a sudden to tell him. Seemed important somehow.

So I told him. Told him I went to my room that day the battle had started and I got down on my knees before my Maker. I had tried my best to do my duty, but found myself unequal to the task. The burden was more than I could bear. I prayed, I begged. Give us victory now.

And suddenly I was sure. I rose up off my knees without a single doubt as to the outcome of the battle.

I didn't tell Sickles all of it, though. Not my bargain! That part I kept wrapped up in my heart as where it ought to stay. But I told Sickles the rest.

Then, caught up in the emotion of the event, I reckon, I reached down and patted the flat spot in the blanket where Sickles' leg should have been. I told him to get well, as if words alone could heal.

But then, I have always believed they could.

I have always believed they could.

> John Hay's Diary
> November 17, 1863
> Saunders, the man who planned the cemetery grounds and designed its layout, paid a call on the President today. I cannot believe it. A national graveyard designed by an *Agriculture Department*. How Europe must be laughing at us.

It's been four months since Gettysburg and yet my thoughts are never far from it. I dreamed of it again last night. The battle and my professor.

In this new dream, he wasn't wearing his specs. No fancy college robes. He wore Union blue instead, the uniform of an officer, a colonel. And he was there on a slope of a small rocky hill. His men were out of bullets and Lee's men were coming up the slope fast and hard.

I flew high above the entire battle sprawled across the countryside like a giant fishhook. My professor stood at shaft's end—the very end of the Union line. If he gave way, the entire Union Army and the entire Union cause—would give way and be lost. And my professor *must* give way. No hope for it.

And then he yells to his boys and orders the bayonet . . .

> John Hay's Diary
> November 17, 1863 con't

Lincoln spent quite a bit of time with Saunders talking over his plans for the cemetery. Odd. Lincoln not only asked questions about the maps and plans of the cemetery, but about the Gettysburg battlefield itself. At times Lincoln seemed to know more about some sections of the battlefield than Saunders—as if Lincoln could somehow see it clearly in his mind's eye.

Well, I guess we will have the chance to see if Lincoln's mind's eye is myopic or not. We leave for Gettysburg tomorrow.

My speech ain't even out of the barn yet. I try to write, but all I hear is my professor lecturing in Greek, lecturing until my ears ring with it. All I got to show for my troubles is a pile of crumpled foolscap at my feet.

Not as if the crowd will be coming to hear me, anyway.

This famous feller, Everett. He's already speechified at Bunker Hill and at Lexington and Concord cemeteries as well. Makes a regular business out of it.

Me, all I reckon to do is say enough to catch and hold Pennsylvania through the election. Hopefully, I won't need many words to do that.

John Hay's Diary
November 18, 1863
On the train

He asked me a curious question this morning. Said he: "Johnny, you're a college boy. What would you think if some professor knocked on your window every evening?"

"Is there a young lady involved?" I asked to which Lincoln only knocked his head back and laughed heartily.

I then said, "Well, his being a professor and all, I would think he came to lecture you."

Lincoln's face fell in one of his mercurial moods, somber and pensive. "So he has, Johnny," he said after some length, "so he has."

A different dream about my professor last night.

In my new dream, it was just before battle. My professor had a whole bunch of men in front of him, like an outdoor class, maybe, 'cept these boys (and most of them *were* boys) were wearing Army uniforms. And these boys had hard drawn faces of old men who'd seen too much of war, seen too much of death. It came to me that they'd thrown down their weapons and now they wanted to quit, wanted to just go home.

My professor, he hasn't time to heal what's hurting them. Hasn't any time at all. He has to go fight now. He needs these boys to go fight with him.

And all he has is words.

He has to talk to them boys, has just one chance to talk to them, has just time enough for a few, few words. He's got to talk to them so's to get them to fight again.

And I realize. I realize I got to do the same. I got to get these boys and all the other boys of the North, get them to fight again. And keep on fighting until they win.

And so my professor, he talks to these boys. But, really, he talks straight to me.

> John Hay's Diary
> November 18, 1863—p.m.
> We arrived at Gettysburg. Trains were all fouled up.
> Bridges out. A grand mess. If Lincoln had not been so
> anxious, had not been so insistent in leaving a day early,
> we would never have made it.
> Not that it matters. A week from now nobody will
> ever remember we were here.

The classroom dream again this time, but the meaning of my professor's words finally were clear. He was lecturing his boys about the grand funerary orations of the ancient Greeks. It seems Greek oration had an exact form and each specific part of that form had its own name.

A Greek funerary oration has two main sections, he said—*epainesis* or praise for the dead, and *parainesis* or admonishment for the living. He had the boys read Pericles out loud to he while he went through and named off all of them parts like a surgeon naming off the innards of his cadaver.

Funny thing was, them boys were reading in Greek and I was understanding them just fine. And the more they read, the more I begun to see how the battles those ancient Greeks fought and our Gettysburg weren't all that much apart from one another.

He's shown me what to do. Maybe not the exact words, but the tack I need to take.

One thing frets at me, though.

This business of praise for the dead and remembrance of the living: epainesis and parainesis. A couplet as indivisible as night and day. I can't shake the notion that one of us is to die, and one of us is to live, my professor and I. One must offer himself up in death so that the other can raise his memory up in life.

And I have already offered myself up as His instrumentality that dark, dark day in July . . .

> John Hay's Diary
> November 19, 1863—a.m.
> Lincoln was up well past two this morning, scribbling away again at the speech. I think he is finally finished now, but he still won't let me see it. Claims he's being "cow-ish" about it. "Need to ruminate," he said as he moved his jaw side to side like some heifer chewing its cud. Another of his homespun jokes, I guess. But he looks so haggard. I worry.

I deliver my speech, then sit down. I'm no Pericles, that's certain. Hardly even a scattering of applause—and that's mostly for politeness sake. They don't know what to make of my speech, I guess. I shake my head. That speech won't scour.

Johnny was right. I do feel bone tired. Maybe I can sleep on the train back.

> John Hay's Diary
> November 19, 1863—p.m.
> Writing this on the train back from Gettysburg. His great speech has been given—for all the good it did the Pennsylvania vote.

The cost was high enough: Lincoln is quite ill. The doctors said it's variola, a form of smallpox.

Lincoln is feverish, sometimes delirious and sometimes even babbling at times. I've ordered everybody out of his train compartment and turned it into a sickroom. I'm not thinking too clearly. Worried sick about Lincoln.

Lincoln has started mumbling again. Claims he's going to die. That was the bargain. Then he starts asking who's to be the dead, who's to be the living. Other questions, too, just as nonsensical as that.

Maybe I've come down with varioloid, too. I keep imaging Lincoln asks his questions in Greek.

I keep asking Johnny if he'd found the professor's grave yet. Didn't I come to dedicate it? Isn't it marked on the plans?

Johnny clucks at me and tells me I have a fever and to rest.

I cannot.

I cannot rest until I know which one of us is the dead, my professor or me.

Johnny tells me again I have a fever. Maybe I do. It's so hard to think. The train jounces and jars the life out of me. My joints ache. Why is it so dark in here?

I turn my head toward the windows. Why are the curtains black, Mary?

But she is not here. I am alone.

Alone with my professor.

John Hay's Diary
November 21, 1863

Lincoln still sick. Doctor says two or three more weeks. I do not know if I can last that long. Been getting little sleep. Lincoln was delirious throughout the night again. He told me about what he calls his professor dreams. Finally told me the whole sad story.

Would that I could believe it was all just part of the fever, pass it off as fever dreams. I can't. It's the Greek.

But for the Greek, I would laugh it away.

"One must die," he says repeatedly. "One must live.

Parainesis must have its *epainesis.*"

John Hay's Diary
November 23, 1863

Lincoln on the mend at last, but still too sick to read so he asks me to read the clippings to him.

Chicago Times tore the speech to shreds. There is no Constitutional promise of equality for the Negro, they thundered. How dare Lincoln stand on the graves of those dead and misstate the cause for which they had died? Lincoln has swindled the nation. They claim he has changed history to suit his needs.

Maybe he has.

John Hay's Diary
June 19, 1864

I was just on my way to his office, carrying some new dispatches, when I heard this terrific crash and the clatter of objects falling from Lincoln's desk. I entered to find his inkwell upset, books and things all scattered on the floor.

Lincoln was just sitting there, arms hanging at his side, staring off in the distance. Today's copy of *Harper's Illustrated Weekly* lay at his feet, blotched by a puddle of ink.

Lincoln, after some length, said simply, "Well, Johnny, I know my professor's name now."

I picked the newspaper up and scanned the opened pages. I saw the engraved portrait of a Brigadier General Chamberlain. The accompanying article said he'd been a professor of rhetoric and oration before the war. Said he'd been fatally wounded in one of those intermittent battles around Petersburg. The papers listed some of Chamberlain's previous services: Antietam. Fredericksburg. Gettysburg.

Chamberlain was not expected to survive his wounds.

Lincoln gave a little shrug. "It appears I shall be the one who lives after all."

John Hay's Diary
April 11, 1865
    I tried to hide the newspapers, but that fool Seward blundered in with some right in front of Lincoln's eyes. May God help him. May God help us all.

Johnny, I say. What's with this sad face? You look lower than a snake's belt buckle. Lee surrendered two days ago—hadn't you heard? Johnny won't answer.

Seward comes in carrying a stack of newspapers. Johnny tries to grab them away, but my reach is just a mite longer than he thought.

I didn't even have to open it up to see the headline Johnny was trying to hide. There it is. Page one.

GEN. JOSHUA CHAMBERLAIN RECEIVES
SURRENDER OF REBEL ARMS
15,000 STAND OF ARMS & 72 FLAGS SURRENDERED
THE DAY OF JUBILEE!

My professor lives after all.

I set the paper on the table. Johnny sees Seward out, leaving me alone with my professor.

John Hay's Diary
April 14, 1865
    All day today Lincoln was as giddy as a boy out of school. "Johnny," he says to me. "A great weight has been lifted off my shoulders. You know what I call that millstone that's dropped from around my neck?"
    I shake my head.
    "Uncertainty," he winks back at me.
    He held a cabinet meeting that morning. He was

positively . . . *buoyant* is the only word I can think of. He spoke openly about his barge dream, as he refers to it. He told them how he dreamed again last night of this singular, indescribable vessel, about his boarding it and moving with great rapidity towards an indefinite shore. He told them when he had that dream it always signified some portentous event. "Means good news," he said and smiled.

It is a solemn smile, a wistful one. Then he laughs and shakes their hands and claps them on the shoulders.

I imagine a meaning to his smile it cannot possibly hold. Men do not smile so at their own death. Or do they?

He goes to the theater tonight. I fear for him.

I have proved myself wrong and am glad for it.

I know my dream barge for what it is now: a ship crossing the River Styx, sailing on some stranger tides to a far distant shore.

I am ready.

I had thought for a short time that perhaps it had sailed past and had taken another passenger aboard, but the plans of Divine Providence are immutable. He has taken me, gripped me tightly in His hand as His instrument.

I was the one to offer up my life that day so long ago. My life for the Union's.

I am content with the bargain.

Dedication of the Maine Monuments at Gettysburg
Evening of October 3, 1889

Joshua Chamberlain stepped before the crowd to give his last speech of the day. The chill evening air condensed his breath. His old wound from Petersburg burned with fire from yet again climbing up this rock-strewn hill.

He blinked against the flickering torchlight. Squinting his eyes, he could almost imagine he saw Lincoln in the back of the crowd.

Someone coughed and Chamberlain realized the audience was shifting about nervously, waiting for him to start. The young man from the committee held up a lantern so Chamberlain could read.

He pulled a folded sheet of paper from his jacket. He started to unfold it, then slipped it back into his pocket unused. He knew what he needed to say.

"In great deeds . . ." Chamberlain began. His voice faltered.

Deeds, he thought to himself. Words and deeds, deeds and words. As indivisible a couplet as parainesis and epainesis. Wars are fought not just over the territory of maps, but the territory of hearts. Sometimes words are needed more than great deeds. And sometimes they exact just as high a price.

And Lincoln had paid that price.

Chamberlain's hand brushed his side. The wound from Petersburg should have killed him, but he had been spared for a reason, as if part of a bargain. It was up to the living to remember the dead and honor all that they had fought for. Lincoln had offered up his life; the least Chamberlain could do would be to offer up his heart.

His voice sure now, he spoke to the hearts of the crowd and felt them finally understand:

"In great deeds something abides. On great fields something stays. Forms change and pass; bodies disappear, but spirits linger, to consecrate ground for the vision-place of souls. And reverent men and women from afar, and generations that know us not and that we know not of, heart-drawn to see where and by whom great things were suffered and done for them, shall come to this deathless field to ponder and dream; And lo! the shadow of a mighty presence shall wrap them in its bosom, and the power of the vision pass into their souls."

"Parainesis of the living," he whispered to himself. "Epainesis of the dead."

FLASH POINT

Gardner Dozois

Ben Jacobs was on his way back to Skowhegan when he found the abandoned car. It was parked on a lonely stretch of secondary road between North Anson and Madison, skewed diagonally over the shoulder.

Kids again, was Jacobs' first thought—more of the road gypsies who plagued the state every summer until they were driven south by the icy whip of the first nor'easter. Probably from the big encampment down near Norridgewock, he decided, and he put his foot back on the accelerator. He'd already had more than his fill of outer-staters this season, and it wasn't even the end of August. Then he looked more closely at the car, and eased up on the gas again. It was too big, too new to belong to kids. He shifted down into second, feeling the crotchety old pickup shudder. It was an expensive car, right enough; he doubted that it came from within twenty miles of here. You didn't use a big-city car on most of the roads in this neck of the woods, and you couldn't stay on the highways forever. He squinted to see more detail. What kind of plates did it have? You're doing it again, he thought, suddenly and sourly. He was a man as aflame with curiosity as a magpie, and—having been brought up strictly to mind his own business—he considered it a vice. Maybe the car was stolen. It's possible, a'n't it? he insisted, arguing with himself. It could have been used in a robbery and then ditched, like that car from the bank job over to Farmington. It happened all the time.

You don't even fool yourself anymore, he thought, and then he grinned and gave in. He wrestled the old truck into the breakdown lane, jolted over a pothole, and coasted to a bumpy stop a few yards behind the car. He switched the engine off.

Silence swallowed him instantly.

Thick and dusty, the silence poured into the morning, filling the world as hot wax fills a mold. It drowned him completely, it possessed every inch and ounce of him. Almost, it spooked him.

Jacobs hesitated, shrugged, and then jumped down from the cab. Outside it was better—still quiet, but not preternaturally so. There was wind soughing through the spruce woods, a forlorn but welcome sound, one he had heard all his life. There was a wood thrush hammering at the morning, faint with distance, but distinct. And a faraway buzzing drone overhead, like a giant sleepy bee or bluebottle, indicated that there was a Piper Cub up there somewhere, probably heading for the airport at Norridgewock. All this was familiar and reassuring. Getting nervy, is all, he told himself, long in the tooth and spooky.

Nevertheless, he walked very carefully toward the car, flat footed and slow, the way he used to walk on patrol in 'Nam, more years ago than he cared to recall. His fingers itched for something, and after a few feet he realized that he was wishing he'd brought his old deer rifle along. He grimaced irritably at that, but the wish pattered through his mind again and again, until he was close enough to see inside the parked vehicle.

The car was empty.

"Old fool," he said sourly.

Snorting in derision at himself, he circled the car, peering in the windows. There were skid marks in the gravel of the breakdown lane, but they weren't deep—the car hadn't been going fast when it hit the shoulder; probably it had been already meandering out of control, with no foot on the accelerator. The hood and bumpers weren't damaged; the car had rolled to a stop against the low embankment, rather than crashing into it. None of the tires were flat. In the woods taking a leak, Jacobs thought. Damn fool didn't even leave his turn signals on. Or it could have been his battery, or a vapor lock or something, and he'd hiked on up the road looking for a gas station. "He still should have ma'ked it off someway," Jacobs muttered. Tourists never knew enough to find their ass in a snowstorm. This one probably wasn't even carrying any signal flags or flares.

The driver's door was wide open, and next to it was a child's plastic doll, lying facedown in the gravel. Jacobs could not explain the chill that hit him then, the horror that seized him and shook him until he was almost physically ill. Bristling, he stooped and thrust his head into the car.

There was a burnt, bitter smell inside, like onions, like hot metal. A layer of gray ash covered the front seat and the floor, a couple of inches deep; a thin stream of it was trickling over the doorjamb to the ground and pooling around the plastic feet of the doll. Hesitantly he touched the ash—it was sticky and soapy to the touch. In spite of the sunlight that was slanting into the car and warming up the upholstery, the ash was cold, almost icy. The cloth ceiling directly over the front seat was lightly blackened with soot—he scraped some of it off with his thumbnail—but there was no other sign of fire. Scattered among the ashes on the front seat were piles of clothing. Jacobs could pick out a pair of men's trousers, a sports coat, a bra, slacks, a bright child's dress, all undamaged. More than one person. They're all in the woods taking a leak, he thought inanely. Sta'k naked.

Sitting on the dashboard were a 35-mm Nikon SI with a telephoto lens and a new Leicaflex. In the hip pocket of the trousers was a wallet, containing more than fifty dollars in cash and a bunch of credit cards. He put the wallet back. Not even a tourist was going to be fool enough to walk off and leave this stuff sitting here, in an open car.

He straightened up and felt the chill again, the deathly noonday cold. This time he *was* spooked. Without knowing why, he nudged the doll out of the puddle of ash with his foot, and then he shuddered. "Hello!" he shouted, at the top of his voice, and got back only a dull, flat echo from the woods. Where in hell *had* they gone?

All at once, he was exhausted. He'd been out before dawn, on a trip up to Kingfield and Carrabassett, and it was catching up with him. Maybe that was why he was so jumpy over nothing. Getting old, c'n't take this kind of shit anymore. How long since you've had a vacation? He opened his mouth to shout again, but uneasily decided not to. He stood for a moment, thinking it out, and then walked back to his truck, hunch-shouldered and limping. The old load of shrapnel in his leg and hip was beginning to bother him again.

Jacobs drove a mile down the highway to a rest stop. He had been hoping he would find the people from the car here, waiting for a tow truck, but the rest area was deserted. He stuck his head into the wood-and-fieldstone latrine, and found that it was inhabited only by buzzing clouds of bluebottles and blackflies. He shrugged. So much for that. There was a pay phone on a pole next to the picnic tables, and he used it to call the sheriff's office in Skowhegan. Unfortunately, Abner Jackman answered the phone, and it took Jacobs ten exasperating minutes to argue him into showing any interest. "Well, if they did," Jacobs said grudgingly, "they did it without any clothes." *Gobblegobblebuzz*, said the phone. "With a *kid?*" Jacobs demanded. *Buzzgobblefttzbuzz*, the phone said, giving in. "Ayah," Jacobs said grudgingly, "I'll stay theah until you show up." And he hung up.

"Damned foolishness," he muttered. This was going to cost him the morning.

County Sheriff Joe Riddick arrived an hour later. He was a stocky, slab-sided man, apparently cut all of a piece out of a block of granite—his shoulders seemed to be the same width as his hips, his square-skulled, square-jawed head thrust belligerently up from his monolithic body without any hint of a neck. He looked like an old snapping turtle: ugly, mud colored, powerful. His hair was snow-white, and his eyes were bloodshot and ill-tempered. He glared at Jacobs dangerously out of red-rimmed eyes with tiny pupils. He looked ready to snap.

"Good morning," Jacobs said coldly.

"Morning," Riddick grunted. "You want to fill me in on this?"

Jacobs did. Riddick listened impassively. When Jacobs finished, Riddick snorted and brushed a hand back over his close-cropped snowy hair. "Some damn fool skylark more'n likely," he said, sourly, shaking his head a little. "*O*-kay, then," he said, suddenly becoming officious and brisk. "If this turns out to be anything serious, we may need you as a witness. Understand? All right." He looked at his watch. "All right. We're waiting for the state boys. I don't think you're needed anymore." Riddick's face was hard and cold and dull—as if it had been molded in lead. He stared pointedly at Jacobs. His eyes were opaque as marbles. "Good day."

Twenty minutes later Jacobs was passing a proud little sign, erected by the Skowhegan Chamber of Commerce, that said: HOME OF THE LARGEST SCULPTED WOODEN INDIAN IN THE WORLD! He grinned. Skowhegan had grown a great deal in the last decade, but somehow it was still a small town. It had resisted the modern tropism to skyscrape and had sprawled instead, spreading out along the banks of the Kennebec River in both directions. Jacobs parked in front of a dingy storefront on Water Street, in the heart of town. A sign in the window commanded: EAT; at night it glowed an imperative neon red. The sign belonged to an establishment that had started life as the Colonial Cafe, with a buffet and quaint rustic decor, and was finishing it, twenty years and three recessions later, as a greasy lunchroom with faded movie posters on the wall—owned and operated by Wilbur and Myna Phipps, a cheerful and indestructible couple in their late sixties. It was crowded and hot inside—the place had a large number of regulars, and most of them were in attendance for lunch. Jacobs spotted Will Sussmann at the counter, jammed in between an inverted glass bowl full of doughnuts and the protruding rear-end of the coffee percolator.

Sussmann—chief staff writer for the Skowhegan *Inquirer,* stringer and columnist for a big Bangor weekly—had saved him a seat by piling the adjacent stool with his hat, coat, and briefcase. Not that it was likely he'd had to struggle too hard for room. Even Jacobs, whose father had moved to Skowhegan from Bangor when Jacobs was three, was regarded with faint suspicion by the real oldtimers of the town. Sussmann, being originally an outer-stater and a "foreigner" to boot, was completely out of luck; he'd only lived here ten years, and that wasn't enough even to begin to tip the balance in his favor.

Sussmann retrieved his paraphernalia; Jacobs sat down and began telling him about the car. Sussmann said it was weird. "We'll never get anything out of Riddick," he said. He began to attack a stack of hotcakes. "He's hated my guts ever since I accused him of working over those gypsy kids last summer, putting one in the hospital. That would have cost him his job, except the higher echelons were being 'foursquare behind their dedicated law enforcement officers' that season. Still, it didn't help his reputation with the town any."

"We don't tolerate that kind of thing in these pa'ts," Jacobs said grimly. "Hell, Will, those kids are a royal pain in the ass, but—" But not in these pa'ts, he told himself, not that. There are decent limits. He was surprised at the depth and ferocity of his reaction. "This a'n't Alabama," he said.

"Might as well be, with Riddick. His idea of law enforcement's to take everybody he doesn't like down in the basement and beat the crap out of them." Sussmann sighed. "Anyway, Riddick wouldn't stop to piss on me if my hat was on fire, that's for sure. Good thing I got other ways of finding stuff out."

Jed Everett came in while Jacobs was ordering coffee. He was a thin, cadaverous man with a long nose; his hair was going rapidly to gray; put him next to short, round Sussmann and they would look like Mutt and Jeff. At forty-eight—Everett was a couple of years older than Jacobs, just as Sussmann was a couple of years younger—he was considered to be scandalously young for a small-town doctor, especially a GP. But old Dr. Barlow had died of a stroke three years back, leaving his younger partner in residency, and they were stuck with him.

One of the regulars had moved away from the trough, leaving an empty seat next to Jacobs, and Everett was talking before his buttocks had hit the upholstery. He was a jittery man, with lots of nervous energy, and he loved to fret and rant and gripe, but softly and goodnaturedly, with no real force behind it, as if he had a volume knob that had been turned down.

"What a morning!" Everett said. "Jesus H. Christ on a bicycle—'s-cuse me, Myna, I'll take some coffee, please, black—I swear it's psycho-somatic. Honest to God, gentleman, she's a case for the medical journals, dreams the whole damn shitbundle up out of her head just for the fun of it, I swear before all my hopes of heaven, swop me blue if she doesn't. *Definitely* psychosomatic."

"He's learned a new word," Sussmann said.

"If you'd wasted all the time I have on this nonsense," Everett said fiercely, "you'd be whistling a different tune out of the other side of your face, *I* call tell *you*, oh yes indeed. What kind of meat d'you have today, Myna? How about the chops—they good?—all right, and put some greens on the plate, please. Okay? Oh, and some homefrieds, now I think about it, please. If you have them."

"What's got your back up?" Jacobs asked mildly.

"You know old Mrs. Crawford?" Everett demanded. "Hm? Lives over to the island, widow, has plenty of money? Three times now I've di-agnosed her as having cancer, serious but still operable, and three times now I've sent her down to Augusta for exploratory surgery, and each time they got her down on the table and opened her up and couldn't find a thing, not a goddamned thing, old bitch's hale and hearty as a prize hog. Spontaneous remission. All psychosomatic, clear as mud. Three *times*, though. It's shooting my reputation all to hell down there. Now she thinks she's got an ulcer. I hope her kidney falls out, right in the street. Thank you, Myna. Can I have another cup of coffee?" He sipped his coffee, when it arrived, and looked a little more meditative. "Course, I think I've seen a good number of cases like that, I *think*, I said, ha'd to prove it when they're terminal. Wouldn't surprise me if a good many of the people who die of cancer—or a lot of other diseases, for that matter— were like that. No real physical cause, they just get tired of living, something dries up inside them, their systems stop trying to defend them, and one thing or another knocks them off. They become easy to touch off, like tinder. Most of them don't change their minds in the middle, though, like that fat old sow."

Wilbur Phipps, who had been leaning on the counter listening, ventured the opinion that modern medical science had never produced anything even half as good as the old-fashioned mustard plaster. Everett flared up instantly.

"You ever bejesus try one?" Phipps demanded.

"No, and I don't bejesus intend to!" Everett said.

Jacobs turned toward Sussmann. "Wheah you been, this early in the day?" he asked. "A'n't like you to haul yourself out before noon."

"Up at the factory. Over to West Mills."

"What was up? Another hearing?"

"Yup. Didn't stick—they aren't going to be injuncted."

"They never will be," Jacobs said. "They got too much money, too many friends in Augusta. The board'll never touch them."

"I don't believe that," Sussmann said. Jacobs grunted and sipped his coffee.

"As Christ's my judge," Everett was saying, in a towering rage, "I'll never understand you people, not if I live to be two hundred, not if I get to be so old my ass falls off and I have to lug it around in a handcart. I swear to God. Some of you ain' got a pot to piss in, so goddamned poor you can't afford to buy a bottle of aspirins, let alone, *let alone* pay your doctor bills from the past half-million years, and yet you go out to some godforsaken hick town too small to turn a horse around in proper and see an unlicensed practitioner, a goddamn back-woods quack, an un*mi*tigated phony, and *pay* through the nose so this witchdoctor can assault you with yarb potions and poultices, and stick leeches on your ass, for all *I* know—" Jacobs lost track of the conversation. He studied a bee that was bumbling along the putty- and-plaster edge of the storefront window, swimming through the thick and dusty sunlight, looking for a way out. He felt numb, distanced from reality. The people around him looked increasingly strange. He found that it took an effort of will to recognize them at all, even Sussmann, even Everett. It scared him. These were people Jacobs saw every day of his life. Some of them he didn't actually *like*—not in the way that big-city folk thought of liking someone—but they were all his neighbors. They belonged here, they were a part of his existence, and that carried its own special intimacy. But today he was beginning to see them as an intolerant sophisticate from the city might see them: dull, provincial, sunk in an iron torpor that masqueraded as custom and routine. That was valid, in its way, but it was a grossly one-sided picture, ignoring a thousand virtues, compensations and kindnesses. But that was the way he was seeing them. As aliens. As strangers.

Distractedly, Jacobs noticed that Everett and Sussmann were making ready to leave. "No rest for the weary," Everett was saying, and Jacobs found himself nodding unconsciously in agreement. Swamped by a sudden rush of loneliness, he invited both men home for dinner that night. They accepted, Everett with the qualification that he'd have to see what his wife had planned. Then they were gone, and Jacobs found himself alone at the counter.

He knew that he should have gone back to work also; he had some more jobs to pick up, and a delivery to make. But he felt very tired, too flaccid and heavy to move, as if some tiny burrowing animal had gnawed away his bones, as if he'd been hamstrung and hadn't realized it. He told himself that it was because he was hungry; he was running himself down, as Carol had always said he someday would. So he dutifully ordered a bowl of chili.

The chili was murky, amorphous stuff, bland and lukewarm. Listlessly, he spooned it up.

No rest for the weary.

"You know what I was nuts about when I was a kid?" Jacobs suddenly observed to Wilbur Phipps. "Rafts. I was a'ways making rafts out of old planks and sheet tin and whatevah other junk I could scrounge up, begging old rope and nails to lash them together with. Then I'd break my ass dragging them down to the Kennebec. And you know what? They a'ways sunk. Every goddamned time."

"Ayah?" Wilbur Phipps said.

Jacobs pushed the bowl of viscid chili away, and got up. Restlessly, he wandered over to where Dave Lucas, the game warden, was drinking beer and talking to a circle of men " . . . dogs will be the end of deer in these pa'ts, I swear to God. And I a'n't talking about wild dogs neither, I'm talking about your ordinary domestic pets. A'n't it so, every winter? Half-starved deer a'n't got a chance in hell 'gainst somebody's big pet hound, all fed-up and rested. The deer those dogs don't kill outright, why they chase 'em to death, and then they don't even eat 'em. Run 'em out of the forest covah into the open and they get pneumonia. Run 'em into the river and through thin ice and they get drowned. Remember last yeah, the deer that big hound drove out onto the ice? Broke both its front legs and I had to go out and shoot the poor bastid. Between those goddamn dogs and all the nighthunters we got around here lately, we a'n't going to have any deer left in this county . . . " Jacobs moved away, past a table where Abner Jackman was pouring ketchup over a plateful of scrambled eggs, and arguing about Communism with Steve Girard, a volunteer fireman and Elk, and Allen Ewing, a postman, who had a son serving with the Marines in Bolivia. " . . . let 'em win theah," Jackman was saying in a nasal voice, "and they'll be swa'ming all over us eventu'ly, sure as shit. Ain' no way to stop 'em then. And you're better off blowing your brains out than living under the Reds, don't ever think otherwise." He screwed the ketchup top back onto the bottle, and glanced up in time to see Jacobs start to go by.

"Ben!" Jackman said, grabbing Jacobs by the elbow. "You can tell 'em." He grinned vacuously at Jacobs—a lanky, loose-jointed, slack-faced man. "He can tell you, boys, what it's like being in a country overrun with Communists, what they do to everybody. You were in 'Nam when you were a youngster, weren't you?"

"Yeah."

After a pause, Jackman said, "You ain' got no call to take offense, Ben." His voice became a whine. "I didn't mean no ha'm. I didn't mean nothing."

"Forget it," Jacobs said, and walked out.

Dave Lucas caught up with Jacobs just outside the door. He was a short, grizzled man with iron-gray hair, about seven years older than Jacobs. "You know, Ben," Lucas said, "the thing of it is, Abner really doesn't mean any ha'm." Lucas smiled bleakly; his grandson had been killed last year, in the Retreat from La Paz. "It's just that he a'n't too bright, is all."

"They don't want him kicked ev'ry so often," Jacobs said, "then they shouldn't let him out of his kennel at all." He grinned. "Dinner tonight? About eight?"

"Sounds fine," Lucas said. "We're going to catch a nighthunter, out near Oaks Pond, so I'll probably be late."

"We'll keep it wa'm for you."

"Just the comp'ny'll be enough."

Jacobs started his truck and pulled out into the afternoon traffic. He kept his hands locked tightly around the steering wheel. He was amazed and dismayed by the surge of murderous anger he had felt toward Jackman; the reaction to it made him queasy, and left the muscles knotted all across his back and shoulders. Dave was right, Abner couldn't rightly be held responsible for the dumbass things he said—But if Jackman had said one more thing, if he'd done anything than to back down as quickly as he had, then Jacobs would have split his head open. He had been instantly ready to do it, his hands had curled into fists, his legs had bent slightly at the knees. He *would* have done it. And he would have enjoyed it. That was a frightening realization.

Y' touchy today, he thought, inanely. His fingers were turning white on the wheel.

He drove home. Jacobs lived in a very old wood-frame house above the north bank of the Kennebec, on the outskirts of town, with nothing but a clump of new apartment buildings for senior citizens to remind him of civilization. The house was empty—Carol was teaching fourth grade, and Chris had been farmed out to Mrs. Turner, the baby-sitter. Jacobs spent the next half hour wrestling a broken washing machine and a television set out of the pickup and into his basement workshop, and another fifteen minutes maneuvering a newly repaired stereo-radio console up out of the basement and into the truck. Jacobs was one of the last of the old-style Yankee tinkerers, although he called himself an appliance repairman, and also did some carpentry and general handywork when things got slow. He had little formal training, but he "kept up." He wasn't sure he could fix one of the new hologram sets, but then they wouldn't be getting out here for another twenty years anyway. There were people within fifty miles who didn't have indoor plumbing. People within a hundred miles who didn't have electricity.

On the way to Norridgewock, two open jeeps packed dangerously full of gypsies came roaring up behind him. They started to pass, one on each side of his truck, their horns blaring insanely. The two jeeps ran abreast of Jacobs' old pickup for a while, making no attempt to go by— the three vehicles together filled the road. The jeeps drifted in until they were almost touching the truck, and the gypsies began pounding the truck roof with their fists, shouting and laughing. Jacobs kept both hands on the wheel and grimly continued to drive at his original speed. Jeeps tipped easily when sideswiped by a heavier vehicle, if it came to that. And he had a tire-iron under the seat. But the gypsies tired of the game—they accelerated and passed Jacobs, most of them giving him the finger as they went by, and one throwing a poorly aimed bottle that bounced onto the shoulder. They were big, tough-looking kids with skin haircuts, dressed—incongruously—in flowered pastel luau shirts and expensive white bellbottoms.

The jeeps roared on up the road, still taking up both lanes. Jacobs watched them unblinkingly until they disappeared from sight. He was awash with rage, the same bitter, vicious hatred he had felt for Jackman. Riddick was right after all—the goddamned kids were a menace to everything that lived, they ought to be locked up. He wished suddenly that he *had* sideswiped them. He could imagine it all vividly: the sickening crunch of impact, the jeep overturning, bodies cartwheeling through the air, the jeep skidding upside down across the road and crashing into the embankment, maybe the gas tank exploding, a gout of flame, smoke, stink, screams—He ran through it over and over again, relishing it, until he realized abruptly what he was doing, what he was wishing, and he was almost physically ill.

All the excitement and fury drained out of him, leaving him shaken and sick. He'd always been a patient, peaceful man, perhaps too much so. He'd never been afraid to fight, but he'd always said that a man who couldn't talk his way out of most trouble was a fool. This sudden daydream lust for blood bothered him to the bottom of his soul. He'd seen plenty of death in 'Nam, and it hadn't affected him this way. It was the kids, he told himself. They drag everybody down to their own level. He kept seeing them inside his head all the way into Norridgewock—the thick, brutal faces, the hard reptile eyes, the contemptuously grinning mouths that seemed too full of teeth. The gypsy kids had changed over the years. The torrent of hippies and Jesus freaks had gradually run dry, the pluggers and the weeps had been all over the state for a few seasons, and then, slowly, they'd stopped coming, too. The new crop of itinerant kids were—hard. Every year they became more brutal and dangerous. They didn't seem to care if they lived or died, and they hated everything indiscriminately—including themselves.

In Norridgewock, he delivered the stereo console to its owner, then went across town to pick up a malfunctioning 75-hp Johnson outboard motor. From the motor's owner, he heard that a town boy had beaten an elderly storekeeper to death that morning, when the storekeeper caught him shoplifting. The boy was in custody, and it was the scandal of the year for Norridgewock. Jacobs had noticed it before, but discounted it: the local kids were getting mean, too, meaner every year. Maybe it was self-defense.

Driving back, Jacobs noticed one of the gypsy jeeps slewed up onto the road embankment. It was empty. He slowed, and stared at the jeep thoughtfully, but he did not stop.

A fire-rescue truck nearly ran him down as he entered Skowhegan. It came screaming out of nowhere and swerved onto Water Street, its blue blinker flashing, siren screeching in metallic rage, suddenly right on top of him. Jacobs wrenched his truck over to the curb, and it swept by like a demon, nearly scraping him. It left a frightened silence behind it, after it had vanished urgently from sight. Jacobs pulled back into traffic and continued driving. Just before the turnoff to his house, a dog ran out into the road. Jacobs had slowed down for the turn anyway, and he saw the dog in plenty of time to stop. He did not stop. At the last possible second, he yanked himself out of a waking dream, and swerved just enough to miss the dog. He had wanted to hit it; he'd liked the idea of running it down. There were too many dogs in the country anyway, he told himself, in a feeble attempt at justification. "Big, ugly hound," he muttered, and was appalled by how alien his voice sounded—hard, bitterly hard, as if it were a rock speaking. Jacobs noticed that his hands were shaking.

Dinner that night was a fair success. Carol had turned out not to be particularly overjoyed that her husband had invited a horde of people over without bothering to consult her, but Jacobs placated her a little by volunteering to cook dinner. It turned out "sufficient," as Everett put it. Everybody ate, and nobody died. Toward the end, Carol had to remind them to leave some for Dave Lucas, who had not arrived yet. The company did a lot to restore Jacobs' nerves, and, feeling better, he wrestled with curiosity throughout the meal. Curiosity won, as it usually did with him: in the end, and against his better judgment.

As the guests began to trickle into the parlor, Jacobs took Sussmann aside and asked him if he'd learned anything new about the abandoned car.

Sussmann seemed uneasy and preoccupied. "Whatever it was happened to them seems to've happened again this afternoon. Maybe a couple of times. There was another abandoned car found about four o'clock, up near Athens. And there was one late yesterday night, out at Livermore Falls. And a tractor-trailer on Route Ninety-five this morning, between Waterville and Benton Station."

"How'd you pry that out of Riddick?"

"Didn't." Sussmann smiled wanly. "Heard about that Athens one from the driver of the tow truck that hauled it back—that one bumped into a signpost, hard enough to break its radiator. Ben, Riddick can't keep me in the dark. I've got more stringers than he has."

"What d'you think it is?"

Sussmann's expression fused over and became opaque. He shook his head.

In the parlor, Carol, Everett's wife Amy—an ample, gray woman, rather like somebody's archetypical aunt but possessed of a very canny mind—and Sussmann, the inveterate bachelor, occupied themselves by playing with Chris. Chris was two, very quick and bright, and very excited by all the company. He'd just learned how to blow kisses, and was now practicing enthusiastically with the adults. Everett, meanwhile, was prowling around examining the stereo equipment that filled one wall. "You install this yourself?" he asked, when Jacobs came up to hand him a beer.

"Not only installed it," Jacobs said, "I built it all myself, from scratch. Tinkered up most of the junk in this house. Take the beah 'fore it gets hot."

"Damn fine work," Everett muttered, absently accepting the beer. "Better'n my own setup, I purely b'lieve, and that set me back a right sma't piece of change. Jesus Christ, Ben—I didn't know you could do quality work like that. What the hell you doing stagnating out here in the sticks, fixing people's radios and washing machines, f'chrissake? Y'that good, you ought to be down in Boston, New York mebbe, making some real money."

Jacobs shook his head. "Hate the cities, big cities like that. C'n't stand to live in them at all." He ran a hand through his hair. "I lived in New York for a while, seven-eight yeahs back, 'fore settling in Skowhegan again. It was terrible theah, even back then, and it's worse now. People down theah dying on their feet, walking around dead without anybody to tell 'em to lie down and get buried decent."

"We're dying here, too, Ben," Everett said. "We're just doing it slower, is all."

Jacobs shrugged. "Mebbe so," he said. "'Scuse me." He walked back to the kitchen, began to scrape the dishes and stack them in the sink. His hands had started to tremble again.

When he returned to the parlor, after putting Chris to bed, he found that conversation had almost died. Everett and Sussmann were arguing halfheartedly about the factory, each knowing that he'd never convince the other. It was a pointless discussion, and Jacobs did not join it. He poured himself a glass of beer and sat down. Amy hardly noticed him; her usually pleasant face was stern and angry. Carol found an opportunity to throw him a sympathetic wink while tossing her long hair back over her shoulder, but her face was flushed, too, and her lips were thin.

The evening had started off well, but it had soured somehow; everyone felt it. Jacobs began to clean his pipe, using a tiny knife to scrape the bowl. A siren went by outside, wailing eerily away into distance. An ambulance, it sounded like, or the fire-rescue truck again—more melancholy and mournful, less predatory than the siren of a police cruiser. " . . . brew viruses . . ." Everett was saying, and then Jacobs lost him, as if Everett were being pulled farther and farther away by some odd, local perversion of gravity, his voice thinning into inaudibility. Jacobs couldn't hear him at all now. Which was strange, as the parlor was only a few yards wide. Another siren. There were a lot of them tonight; they sounded like the souls of the dead, looking for home in the darkness, unable to find light and life.

Jacobs found himself thinking about the time he'd toured Vienna, during "recuperative leave" in Europe, after hospitalization in 'Nam. There was a tour of the catacombs under the Cathedral, and he'd taken it, limping painfully along on his crutch, the wet, porous stone of the tunnel roof closing down until it almost touched the top of his head. They came to a place where an opening had been cut through the hard, gray rock, enabling the tourists to come up one by one and look into the burial pit on the other side, while the guide lectured calmly in alternating English and German. When you stuck your head through the opening, you looked out at a solid wall of human bones. Skulls, arm and leg bones, rib cages, pelvises, all mixed in helter-skelter and packed solid, layer after uncountable layer of them. The wall of bones rose up sheer out of the darkness, passed through the fan of light cast by a naked bulb at eye-level, and continued to rise—it was impossible to see the top, no matter how you craned your neck and squinted.

This wall had been built by the Black Death, a haphazard but grandiose architect. The Black Death had eaten these people up and spat out their remains, as casual and careless as a picnicker gnawing chicken bones. When the meal was over, the people who were still alive had dug a huge pit under the Cathedral and shoveled the victims in by the hundreds of thousands. Strangers in life, they mingled in death, cheek by jowl, belly to backbone, except that after a while there were no cheeks or jowls. The backbones remained: yellow, ancient and brittle. So did the skulls—upright, upside down, on their sides, all grinning blankly at the tourists.

The doorbell rang.

It was Dave Lucas. He looked like one of the skulls Jacobs had been thinking about—his face was gray and gaunt, the skin drawn tightly across his bones; it looked as if he'd been dusted with powdered lime. Shocked, Jacobs stepped aside. Lucas nodded to him shortly and walked into the parlor without speaking. " . . . stuff about the factory is news," Sussmann was saying, doggedly, "and more interesting than anything else that happens up here. It sells papers—" He stopped talking abruptly when Lucas entered the room. All conversation stopped. Everyone gaped at the old game warden, horrified. Unsteadily, Lucas let himself down into a stuffed chair, and gave them a thin attempt at a smile. "Can I have a beah?" he said. "Or a drink?"

"Scotch?"

"That'll be fine," Lucas said mechanically.

Jacobs went to get it for him. When he returned with the drink,

Lucas was determinedly making small talk and flashing his new dead smile. It was obvious that he wasn't going to say anything about what had happened to him. Lucas was an old-fashioned Yankee gentleman to the core, and Jacobs—who had a strong touch of that in his own upbringing—suspected why he was keeping silent. So did Amy. After the requisite few minutes of polite conversation, Amy asked if she could see the new paintings that Carol was working on. Carol exchanged a quick, comprehending glance with her, and nodded. Grim-faced, both women left the room—they knew that this was going to be bad. When the women were out of sight, Lucas said, "Can I have another drink, Ben?" and held out his empty glass. Jacobs refilled it wordlessly. Lucas had never been a drinking man.

"Give," Jacobs said, handing Lucas his glass. "What happened?"

Lucas sipped his drink. He still looked ghastly, but a little color was seeping back into his face. "A'n't felt this shaky since I was in the a'my, back in Korea," he said. He shook his head heavily. "I swear to Christ, I don't understand what's got into people in these pa'ts. Used t'be decent folk out heah, Christian folk." He set his drink aside, and braced himself up visibly. His face hardened. "Never mind that. Things change, I guess, c'n't stop 'em no way." He turned toward Jacobs. "Remember that nighthunter I was after. Well we got 'im, went out with Steve Girard, Rick Barlow, few other boys, and nabbed him real neat—city boy, no woods sense at all. Well, we were coming back around the end of the pond, down the lumber road, when we heard this big commotion coming from the Gibson place, shouts, a woman screaming her head off, like that. So we cut across the back of their field and went over to see what was going on. House was wide open, and what we walked into—" He stopped; little sickly beads of sweat had appeared all over his face. "You remember the McInerney case down in Boston four-five yeahs back? The one there was such a stink about? Well, it was like that. They had a whatchamacallit there, a coven—the Gibsons, the Sewells, the Bradshaws, about seven others, all local people, all hopped out of their minds, all dressed up in black robes, and—blood, painted all over their faces. God, I—No, never mind. They had a baby there, and a kind of an altar they'd dummied up, and a pentagram. Somebody'd killed the baby, slit its throat, and they'd hung it up to bleed like a hog. Into cups. When we got there, they'd just

cut its heart out, and they were starting in on dismembering it. Hell—
they were tearing it apart, never mind that 'dismembering' shit. They
were so frenzied-blind they hardly noticed us come in. Mrs. Bradshaw
hadn't been able to take it, she'd cracked completely and was sitting in a
corner screaming her lungs out, with Mr. Sewell trying to shut her up.
They were the only two that even tried to run. The boys hung Gibson
and Bradshaw and Sewell, and stomped Ed Patterson to death—I just
couldn't stop 'em. It was all I could do to keep 'em from killing the other
ones. I shot Steve Girard in the arm, trying to stop 'em, but they took the
gun away, and almost strung me up, too. My God, Ben, I've known Steve
Girard a'most ten yeahs. I've known Gibson and Sewell all my life." He
stared at them appealingly, blind with despair. "What's happened to people up heah?"

No one said a word.

Not in these pa'ts, Jacobs mimicked himself bitterly. *There are decent
limits.*

Jacobs found that he was holding the pipe-cleaning knife like a
weapon. He'd cut his finger on it, and a drop of blood was oozing slowly
along the blade. This kind of thing—the Satanism, the ritual murders, the
sadism—was what had driven him away from the city. He'd thought it was
different in the country, that people were better. But it wasn't, and they
weren't. It was bottled up better out here, was all. But it had been coming for years, and they had blinded themselves to it and done nothing,
and now it was too late. He could feel it in himself, something long re-
pressed and denied, the reaction to years of frustration and ugliness and
fear, to watching the world dying without hope. That part of him had listened to Lucas' story with appreciation, almost with glee. It stirred
strongly in him, a monster turning over in ancient mud, down inside,
thousands of feet down, thousands of years down. He could see it spreading through the faces of the others in the room, a stain, a spider shadow
of contamination. Its presence was suffocating: the chalky, musty smell of
old brittle death, somehow leaking through from the burial pit in Vienna.
Bone dust—he almost choked on it, it was so thick here in his pleasant
parlor in the country.

And then the room was filled with sound and flashing, bloody light.

Jacobs floundered for a moment, unable to understand what was happening. He swam up from his chair, baffled, moving with dreamlike slowness. He stared in helpless confusion at the leaping red shadows. His head hurt.

"An ambulance!" Carol shouted, appearing in the parlor archway with Amy. "We saw it from the upstairs window—"

"It's right out front," Sussmann said.

They ran for the door. Jacobs followed them more slowly. Then the cold outside air slapped him, and he woke up a little. The ambulance was parked across the street, in front of the senior citizens' complex. The corpsmen were hurrying up the stairs of one of the institutional, cinderblock buildings, carrying a stretcher. They disappeared inside. Amy slapped her bare arms to keep off the cold. "Heart attack, mebbe," she said. Everett shrugged. Another siren slashed through the night, getting closer. While they watched, a police cruiser pulled up next to the ambulance, and Riddick got out. Riddick saw the group in front of Jacobs' house, and stared at them with undisguised hatred, as if he would like to arrest them and hold them responsible for whatever had happened in the retirement village. Then he went inside, too. He looked haggard as he turned to go, exhausted, hagridden by the suspicion that he'd finally been handed something he couldn't settle with a session in the soundproofed back room at the sheriff's office.

They waited. Jacobs slowly became aware that Sussmann was talking to him, but he couldn't hear what he was saying. Sussmann's mouth opened and closed. It wasn't important anyway. He'd never noticed before how unpleasant Sussmann's voice was, how rasping and shrill. Sussmann was ugly, too, shockingly ugly. He boiled with contamination and decay—he was a sack of putrescence. He was an abomination.

Dave Lucas was standing off to one side, his hands in his pockets, shoulders slumped, his face blank. He watched the excitement next door without expression, without interest. Everett turned and said something that Jacobs could not hear. Like Sussmann's, Everett's lips moved without sound. He had moved closer to Amy. They glanced uneasily around. They were abominations, too.

Jacobs stood with his arm around Carol; he didn't remember putting it there—it was seeking company on its own. He felt her shiver, and clutched her more tightly in response, directed by some small, distanced, horrified part of himself that was still rational—he knew it would do no good. There was a thing in the air tonight that was impossible to warm yourself against. It hated warmth, it swallowed it and buried it in ice. It was a wedge, driving them apart, isolating them all. He curled his hand around the back of Carol's neck. Something was pulsing through him in waves, building higher and stronger. He could feel Carol's pulse beating under her skin, under his fingers, so very close to the surface.

Across the street, a group of old people had gathered around the ambulance. They shuffled in the cold, hawking and spitting, clutching overcoats and nightgowns more tightly around them. The corpsmen reappeared, edging carefully down the stairs with the stretcher. The sheet was pulled up all the way, but it looked curiously flat and caved-in—if there was a body under there, it must have collapsed, crumbled like dust or ash. The crowd of old people parted to let the stretcher crew pass, then re-formed again, flowing like a heavy, sluggish liquid. Their faces were like leather or horn: hard, dead, dry, worn smooth. And *tired.* Intolerably, burdensomely tired. Their eyes glittered in their shriveled faces as they watched the stretcher go by. They looked uneasy and afraid, and yet there was an anticipation in their faces, an impatience, almost an envy, as they looked on death. Silence blossomed from a tiny seed in each of them, a total, primordial silence, from the time before there were words. It grew, consumed them, and merged to form a greater silence that spread out through the night in widening ripples.

The ambulance left.

In the hush that followed, they could hear sirens begin to wail all over town.

THE LOVES OF ALONZO
FITZ CLARENCE AND
ROSANNAH ETHELTON

Mark Twain

I

It was well along in the forenoon of a bitter winter's day. The town of Eastport, in the state of Maine, lay buried under a deep snow that was newly fallen. The customary bustle in the streets was wanting. One could look long distances down them and see nothing but a dead-white emptiness, with silence to match. Of course I do not mean that you could *see* the silence—no, you could only hear it. The sidewalks were merely long, deep ditches, with steep snow walls on either side. Here and there you might hear the faint, far scrape of a wooden shovel, and if you were quick enough you might catch a glimpse of a distant black figure stooping and disappearing in one of those ditches, and reappearing the next moment with a motion which you would know meant the heaving out of a shovelful of snow. But you needed to be quick, for that black figure would not linger, but would soon drop that shovel and scud for the house, thrashing itself with its arms to warm them. Yes, it was too venomously cold for snow-shovelers or anybody else to stay out long.

Presently the sky darkened; then the wind rose and began to blow in fitful, vigorous gusts, which sent clouds of powdery snow aloft, and straight ahead, and everywhere. Under the impulse of one of these gusts, great white drifts banked themselves like graves across the streets; a moment later another gust shifted them around the other way, driving a fine spray of snow from their sharp crests, as the gale drives the spume flakes from wave-crests at sea; a third gust swept that place as clean as your hand, if it saw fit. This was fooling, this was play; but each and all of the gusts dumped some snow into the sidewalk ditches, for that was business.

Alonzo Fitz Clarence was sitting in his snug and elegant little parlor, in a lovely blue silk dressing-gown, with cuffs and facings of crimson satin, elaborately quilted. The remains of his breakfast were before him, and the dainty and costly little table service added a harmonious charm to the grace, beauty, and richness of the fixed appointments of the room. A cheery fire was blazing on the hearth.

A furious gust of wind shook the windows, and a great wave of snow washed against them with a drenching sound, so to speak. The handsome young bachelor murmured:

"That means, no going out to-day. Well, I am content. But what to do for company? Mother is well enough, Aunt Susan is well enough; but these, like the poor, I have with me always. On so grim a day as this, one needs a new interest, a fresh element, to whet the dull edge of captivity. That was very neatly said, but it doesn't mean anything. One doesn't *want* the edge of captivity sharpened up, you know, but just the reverse."

He glanced at his pretty French mantel-clock.

"That clock's wrong again. That clock hardly ever knows what time it is; and when it does know, it lies about it—which amounts to the same thing. Alfred!"

There was no answer.

"Alfred! . . . Good servant, but as uncertain as the clock."

Alonzo touched an electric bell button in the wall. He waited a moment, then touched it again; waited a few moments more, and said:

"Battery out of order, no doubt. But now that I have started, I will find out what time it is." He stepped to a speaking-tube in the wall, blew its whistle, and called, "Mother!" and repeated it twice.

"Well, *that's* no use. Mother's battery is out of order, too. Can't raise anybody down-stairs—that is plain."

He sat down at a rosewood desk, leaned his chin on the left-hand edge of it and spoke, as if to the floor: "Aunt Susan!"

A low, pleasant voice answered, "Is that you, Alonzo?'

"Yes. I'm too lazy and comfortable to go downstairs; I am in extremity, and I can't seem to scare up any help."

"Dear me, what is the matter?"

"Matter enough, I can tell you!"

"Oh, don't keep me in suspense, dear! What is it?"

"I want to know what time it is."

"You abominable boy, what a turn you did give me! Is that all?"

"All—on my honor. Calm yourself. Tell me the time, and receive my blessing."

"Just five minutes after nine. No charge—keep your blessing."

"Thanks. It wouldn't have impoverished me, aunty, nor so enriched you that you could live without other means."

He got up, murmuring, "Just five minutes after nine," and faced his clock. "Ah," said he, "you are doing better than usual. You are only thirty-four minutes wrong. Let me see . . . let me see. . . . Thirty-three and twenty-one are fifty-four; four times fifty-four are two hundred and thirty-six. One off, leaves two hundred and thirty-five. That's right."

He turned the hands of his clock forward till they marked twenty-five minutes to one, and said, "Now see if you can't keep right for a while—else I'll raffle you!"

He sat down at the desk again, and said, "Aunt Susan!"

"Yes, dear."

"Had breakfast?"

"Yes, indeed, an hour ago."

"Busy?"

"No—except sewing. Why?"

"Got any company?"

"No, but I expect some at half past nine."

"I wish *I* did. I'm lonesome. I want to talk to somebody."

"Very well, talk to me."

"But this is very private."

"Don't be afraid—talk right along, there's nobody here but me."

"I hardly know whether to venture or not, but—"

"But what? Oh, don't stop there! You *know* you can trust me, Alonzo—you know, you can."

"I feel it, aunt, but this is very serious. It affects me deeply—me, and all the family—-even the whole community."

"Oh, Alonzo, tell me! I will never breathe a word of it. What *is* it?"

"Aunt, if I might dare—"

"Oh, please go on! I love you, and feel for you. Tell me all. Confide in me. What is it?"

"The weather!"

"Plague take the weather! I don't see how you can have the heart to serve me so, Lon."

"There, there, aunty dear, I'm sorry; I am, on my honor. I won't do it again. Do you forgive me?"

"Yes, since you seem so sincere about it, though I know I oughtn't to. You will fool me again as soon as I have forgotten this time."

"No, I won't, honor bright. But such weather, oh, such weather! You've *got* to keep your spirits up artificially. It is snowy, and blowy, and gusty, and bitter cold! How is the weather with you?"

"Warm and rainy and melancholy. The mourners go about the streets with their umbrellas running streams from the end of every whalebone. There's an elevated double pavement of umbrellas, stretching down the sides of the streets as far as I can see. I've got a fire for cheerfulness, and the windows open to keep cool. But it is vain, it is useless: nothing comes in but the balmy breath of December, with its burden of mocking odors from the flowers that possess the realm outside, and rejoice in their lawless profusion whilst the spirit of man is low, and flaunt their gaudy splendors in his face while his soul is clothed in sackcloth and ashes and his heart breaketh."

Alonzo opened his lips to say, "You ought to print that, and get it framed," but checked himself, for he heard his aunt speaking to someone else. He went and stood at the window and looked out upon the wintry prospect. The storm was driving the snow before it more furiously than ever; window-shutters were slamming and banging; a forlorn dog, with bowed head and tail withdrawn from service, was pressing his quaking body against a windward wall for shelter and protection; a young girl was plowing knee-deep through the drifts, with her face turned from the blast, and the cape of her waterproof blowing straight rearward over her head. Alonzo shuddered, and said with a sigh, "Better the slop, and the sultry rain, and even the insolent flowers, than this!"

He turned from the window, moved a step, and stopped in a listening attitude. The faint, sweet notes of a familiar song caught his ear. He remained there, with his head unconsciously bent forward, drinking in the melody, stirring neither hand nor foot, hardly breathing. There was a blemish in the execution of the song, but to Alonzo it seemed an added charm instead of a defect. This blemish consisted of a marked flatting of the third, fourth, fifth, sixth, and seventh notes of the refrain or chorus of the piece. When the music ended, Alonzo drew a deep breath, and said, "Ah, I never have heard 'In the Sweet By-and-by' sung like that before!"

He stepped quickly to the desk, listened a moment, and said in a guarded, confidential voice, "Aunty, who is this divine singer?"

"She is the company I was expecting. Stays with me a month or two. I will introduce you. Miss—"

"For goodness' sake, wait a moment, Aunt Susan! You never stop to think what you are about!"

He flew to his bedchamber, and returned in a moment perceptibly changed in his outward appearance, and remarking, snappishly:

"Hang it, she would have introduced me to this angel in that sky-blue dressing-gown with red-hot lapels! Women never think, when they get a-going."

He hastened and stood by the desk, and said eagerly, "Now, Aunty, I am ready," and fell to smiling and bowing with all the persuasiveness and elegance that were in him.

"Very well. Miss Rosannah Ethelton, let me introduce to you my favorite nephew, Mr. Alonzo Fitz Clarence. There! You are both good people, and I like you; so I am going to trust you together while I attend to a few household affairs. Sit down, Rosannah; sit down, Alonzo. Good-by; I sha'n't be gone long."

Alonzo had been bowing and smiling all the while, and motioning imaginary young ladies to sit down in imaginary chairs, but now he took a seat himself, mentally saying, "Oh, this is luck! Let the winds blow now, and the snow drive, and the heavens frown! Little I care!"

While these young people chat themselves into an acquaintanceship, let us take the liberty of inspecting the sweeter and fairer of the two. She sat alone, at her graceful ease, in a richly furnished apartment which was manifestly the private parlor of a refined and sensible lady, if signs and symbols may go for anything. For instance, by a low, comfortable chair stood a dainty, top-heavy workstand, whose summit was a fancifully embroidered shallow basket, with varicolored crewels, and other strings and odds and ends protruding from under the gaping lid and hanging down in negligent profusion. On the floor lay bright shreds of Turkey red, Prussian blue, and kindred fabrics, bits of ribbon, a spool or two, a pair of scissors, and a roll or so of tinted silken stuffs. On a luxurious sofa, upholstered with some sort of soft Indian goods wrought in black and gold threads interwebbed with other threads not so pronounced in color, lay a great square of coarse white stuff, upon whose surface a rich bouquet of flowers was growing, under the deft cultivation of the crochet-needle. The household cat was asleep on this work of art. In a bay-window stood an easel with an unfinished picture on it, and a palette and brushes on a chair beside it. There were books everywhere: Robertson's Sermons, Tennyson, Moody and Sankey, Hawthorne, *Rab and His Friends*, cookbooks, prayer-books, pattern-books—and books about all kinds of odious and exasperating pottery, of course. There was a piano, with a deck-load of music, and more in a tender. There was a great plenty of pictures on the walls, on the shelves of the mantelpiece, and around generally; where coigns of vantage offered were statuettes, and quaint and pretty gimcracks, and rare and costly specimens of peculiarly devilish china. The bay-window gave upon a garden that was ablaze with foreign and domestic flowers and flowering shrubs.

But the sweet young girl was the daintiest thing these premises, within or without, could offer for contemplation: delicately chiseled features, of Grecian cast; her complexion the pure snow of a japonica that is receiving a faint reflected enrichment from some scarlet neighbor of the garden; great, soft blue eyes fringed with long, curving lashes; an expression made up of the trustfulness of a child and the gentleness of a fawn; a beautiful head crowned with its own prodigal gold; a lithe and rounded figure, whose every attitude and movement was instinct with native grace.

Her dress and adornment were marked by that exquisite harmony that can come only of a fine natural taste perfected by culture. Her gown was of a simple magenta tulle, cut bias, traversed by three rows of light-blue flounces, with the selvage edges turned up with ashes-of-roses chenille; overdress of dark bay tarlatan with scarlet satin lambrequins; corn-colored polonaise, en *panier*, looped with mother-of-pearl buttons and silver cord, and hauled aft and made fast by buff velvet lashings; basque of lavender reps, picked out with valenciennes; low neck, short sleeves; maroon velvet necktie edged with delicate pink silk; inside handkerchief of some simple three-ply ingrain fabric of a soft saffron tint; coral bracelets and locket-chain; coiffure of forget-me-nots and lilies-of-the-valley massed around a noble calla.

This was all; yet even in this subdued attire she was divinely beautiful. Then what must she have been when adorned for the festival or the ball? All this time she had been busily chatting with Alonzo, unconscious of our inspection. The minutes still sped, and still she talked. But by and by she happened to look up, and saw the clock. A crimson blush sent its rich flood through her cheeks, and she exclaimed:

"There, good-by, Mr. Fitz Clarence; I must go now!"

She sprang from her chair with such haste that she hardly heard the young man's answering good-by. She stood radiant, graceful, beautiful, and gazed, wondering, upon the accusing clock. Presently her pouting lips parted, and she said:

"Five minutes after eleven! Nearly two hours, and it did not seem twenty minutes! Oh, dear, what will he think of me!"

At the self-same moment Alonzo was staring at his clock. And presently he said:

"Twenty-five minutes to three! Nearly two hours, and I didn't believe it was two minutes! Is it possible that this clock is humbugging again? Miss Ethelton! Just one moment, please. Are you there yet?"

"Yes, but be quick; I'm going right away."

"Would you be so kind as to tell me what time it is?"

The girl blushed again, murmured to herself, "It's right down cruel of him to ask me!" and then spoke up and answered with admirably counterfeited unconcern, "Five minutes after eleven."

"Oh, thank you! You have to go, now, have you?"

"I'm sorry."

No reply.

"Miss Ethelton!"

"Well?"

"You—you're there yet, *ain't* you?"

"Yes; but please hurry. What did you want to say?"

"Well, I—well, nothing in particular. It's very lonesome here. It's asking a great deal, I know, but would you mind talking with me again by and by—that is, if it will not trouble you too much?"

"I don't know but I'll think about it. I'll try."

"Oh, thanks! Miss Ethelton! . . . Ah, me, she's gone, and here are the black clouds and the whirling snow and the raging winds come again! But she said *good-bye*. She didn't say good morning, she said good-by! . . . The clock was right, after all. What a lightning-winged two hours it was!"

He sat down, and gazed dreamily into his fire for a while, then heaved a sigh and said:

"How wonderful it is! Two little hours ago I was a free man, and now my heart's in San Francisco!"

About that time Rosannah Ethelton, propped in the window-seat of her bedchamber, book in hand, was gazing vacantly out over the rainy seas that washed the Golden Gate, and whispering to herself, "How different he is from poor Burley, with his empty head and his single little antic talent of mimicry!"

II

Four weeks later Mr. Sidney Algernon Burley was entertaining a gay luncheon company, in a sumptuous drawing-room on Telegraph Hill, with some capital imitations of the voices and gestures of certain popular actors and San Franciscan literary people and Bonanza grandees. He was elegantly upholstered, and was a handsome fellow, barring a trifling cast in his eye. He seemed very jovial, but nevertheless he kept his eye on the door with an expectant and uneasy watchfulness. By and by a knobby lackey appeared, and delivered a message to the mistress, who nodded her head understandingly. That seemed to settle the thing for Mr. Burley; his vivacity decreased little by little, and a dejected look began to creep into one of his eyes and a sinister one into the other.

The rest of the company departed in due time, leaving him with the mistress, to whom he said:

"There is no longer any question about it. She avoids me. She continually excuses herself. If I could see her, if I could speak to her only a moment, but this suspense—"

"Perhaps her seeming avoidance is mere accident, Mr. Burley. Go to the small drawing-room up-stairs and amuse yourself a moment. I will despatch a household order that is on my mind, and then I will go to her room. Without doubt she will be persuaded to see you."

Mr. Burley went up-stairs, intending to go to the small drawing-room, but as he was passing "Aunt Susan's" private parlor, the door of which stood slightly ajar, he heard a joyous laugh which he recognized; so without knock or announcement he stepped confidently in. But before he could make his presence known he heard words that harrowed up his soul and chilled his young blood, he heard a voice say:

"Darling, it has come!"

Then he heard Rosannah Ethelton, whose back was toward him, say: "So has yours, dearest!"

He saw her bowed form bend lower; he heard her kiss something—not merely once, but again and again! His soul raged within him. The heartbreaking conversation went on:

"Rosannah, I knew you must be beautiful, but this is dazzling, this is blinding, this is intoxicating!"

"Alonzo, it is such happiness to hear you say it. I know it is not true, but I am so grateful to have you think it is, nevertheless! I knew you must have a noble face, but the grace and majesty of the reality beggar the poor creation of my fancy."

Burley heard that rattling shower of kisses again.

"Thank you, my Rosannah! The photograph flatters me, but you must not allow yourself to think of that. Sweetheart?"

"Yes, Alonzo."

"I am so happy, Rosannah."

"Oh, Alonzo, none that have gone before me knew what love was, none that come after me will ever know what happiness is. I float in a gorgeous cloud land, a boundless firmament of enchanted and bewildering ecstasy!"

"Oh, my Rosannah! for you are mine, are you not?"

"Wholly, oh, wholly yours, Alonzo, now and forever! All the day long, and all through my nightly dreams, one song sings itself, and its sweet burden is, 'Alonzo Fitz Clarence, Alonzo Fitz Clarence, Eastport, State of Maine!'"

"Curse him, I've got his address, anyway!" roared Burley, inwardly, and rushed from the place.

Just behind the unconscious Alonzo stood his mother, a picture of astonishment. She was so muffled from head to heel in furs that nothing of herself was visible but her eyes and nose. She was a good allegory of winter, for she was powdered all over with snow.

Behind the unconscious Rosannah stood "Aunt Susan," another picture of astonishment. She was a good allegory of summer, for she was lightly clad, and was vigorously cooling the perspiration on her face with a fan.

Both of these women had tears of joy in their eyes.

"So ho!" exclaimed Mrs. Fitz Clarence, "this explains why nobody has been able to drag you out of your room for six weeks, Alonzo!"

"So ho!" exclaimed Aunt Susan, "this explains why you have been a hermit for the past six weeks, Rosannah!"

The young couple were on their feet in an instant, abashed, and standing like detected dealers in stolen goods awaiting judge Lynch's doom.

"Bless you, my son! I am happy in your happiness. Come to your mother's arms, Alonzo!"

"Bless you, Rosannah, for my dear nephew's sake! Come to my arms!"

Then was there a mingling of hearts and of tears of rejoicing on Telegraph Hill and in Eastport Square.

Servants were called by the elders, in both places. Unto one was given the order, "Pile this fire high, with hickory wood, and bring me a roasting-hot lemonade."

Unto the other was given the order, "Put out this fire, and bring me two palm-leaf fans and a pitcher of ice-water."

Then the young people were dismissed, and the elders sat down to talk the sweet surprise over and make the wedding plans.

Some minutes before this Mr. Burley rushed from the mansion on Telegraph Hill without meeting or taking formal leave of anybody. He hissed through his teeth, in unconscious imitation of a popular favorite in melodrama, "Him shall she never wed! I have sworn it! Ere great Nature shall have doffed her winter's ermine to don the emerald gauds of spring, she shall be mine!

III

Two weeks later. Every few hours, during same three or four days, a very prim and devout-looking Episcopal clergyman, with a cast in his eye, had visited Alonzo. According to his card, he was the Rev. Melton Hargrave, of Cincinnati. He said he had retired from the ministry on account of his health. If he had said on account of ill-health, he would probably have erred, to judge by his wholesome looks and firm build. He was the inventor of an improvement in telephones, and hoped to make his bread by selling the privilege of using it. "At present," he continued, "a man may go and tap a telegraph wire which is conveying a song or a concert from one state to another, and he can attach his private telephone and steal a hearing of that music as it passes along. My invention will stop all that."

"Well," answered Alonzo, "if the owner of the music could not miss what was stolen, why should he care?"

"He shouldn't care," said the Reverend.

"Well?" said Alonzo, inquiringly.

"Suppose," replied the Reverend, "suppose that, instead of music that was passing along and being stolen, the burden of the wire was loving endearments of the most private and sacred nature?"

Alonzo shuddered from head to heel. "Sir, it is a priceless invention," said he; "I must have it at any cost."

But the invention was delayed somewhere on the road from Cincinnati, most unaccountably. The impatient Alonzo could hardly wait. The thought of Rosannah's sweet words being shared with him by some ribald thief was galling to him. The Reverend came frequently and lamented the delay, and told of measures he had taken to hurry things up. This was some little comfort to Alonzo.

One forenoon the Reverend ascended the stairs and knocked at Alonzo's door. There was no response. He entered, glanced eagerly around, closed the door softly, then ran to the telephone. The exquisitely soft and remote strains of the "Sweet By-and-by" came floating through the instrument. The singer was flatting, as usual, the five notes that follow the first two in the chorus, when the Reverend interrupted her with this word, in a voice which was an exact imitation of Alonzo's, with just the faintest flavor of impatience added:

"Sweetheart?"

"Yes, Alonzo?"

"Please don't sing that any more this week—try something modern."

The agile step that goes with a happy heart was heard on the stairs, and the Reverend, smiling diabolically, sought sudden refuge behind the heavy folds of the velvet window-curtains. Alonzo entered and flew to the telephone. Said he:

"Rosannah, dear, shall we sing something together?"

"Something *modern?*" asked she, with sarcastic bitterness.

"Yes, if you prefer."

"Sing it yourself, if you like!"

This snappishness amazed and wounded the young man. He said:

"Rosannah, that was not like you."

"I suppose it becomes me as much as your very polite speech became you, Mr. Fitz Clarence."

"*Mister* Fitz Clarence! Rosannah, there was nothing impolite about my speech."

"Oh, indeed! Of course, then, I misunderstood you, and I most humbly beg your pardon, ha-ha-ha! No doubt you said, 'Don't sing it any more *to-day.*'"

"Sing *what* any more to-day?"

"The song you mentioned, of course, How very obtuse we are, all of a sudden!"

"I never mentioned any song."

"Oh, you *didn't?*"

"No, I *didn't!*"

"I am compelled to remark that you *did.*"

"And I am obliged to reiterate that I *didn't.*"

"A second rudeness! That is sufficient, sir. I will never forgive you. All is over between us."

Then came a muffled sound of crying. Alonzo hastened to say:

"Oh, Rosannah, unsay those words! There is some dreadful mystery here, some hideous mistake. I am utterly earnest and sincere when I say I never said anything about any song. I would not hurt you for the whole world . . . . Rosannah, dear speak to me, won't you?"

There was a pause; then Alonzo heard the girl's sobbings retreating, and knew she had gone from the telephone. He rose with a heavy sigh, and hastened from the room, saying to himself, "I will ransack the charity missions and the haunts of the poor for my mother. She will persuade her that I never meant to wound her."

A minute later the Reverend was crouching over the telephone like a cat that knoweth the ways of the prey. He had not very many minutes to wait. A soft, repentant voice, tremulous with tears, said:

"Alonzo, dear, I have been wrong. You *could* not have said so cruel a thing. It must have been some one who imitated your voice in malice or in jest."

The Reverend coldly answered, in Alonzo's tones:

"You have said all was over between us. So let it be. I spurn your proffered repentance, and despise it!"

Then he departed, radiant with fiendish triumph, to return no more with his imaginary telephonic invention forever.

Four hours afterward Alonzo arrived with his mother from her favorite haunts of poverty and vice. They summoned the San Francisco household; but there was no reply. They waited, and continued to wait, upon the voiceless telephone.

At length, when it was sunset in San Francisco, and three hours and a half after dark in Eastport, an answer to the oft-repeated cry of "Rosannah!"

But, alas, it was Aunt Susan's voice that spake. She said:

"I have been out all day; just got in. I will go and find her."

The watchers waited two minutes—five minutes—ten minutes. Then came these fatal words, in a frightened tone:

"She is gone, and her baggage with her. To visit another friend, she told the servants. But I found this note on the table in her room. Listen: 'I am gone; seek not to trace me out; my heart is broken; you will never see me more. Tell him I shall always think of him when I sing my poor "Sweet By-and-by," but never of the unkind words he said about it.' That is her note. Alonzo, Alonzo, what does it mean? What has happened?"

But Alonzo sat white and cold as the dead. His mother threw back the velvet curtains and opened a window. The cold air refreshed the sufferer, and he told his aunt his dismal story. Meantime his mother was inspecting a card which had disclosed itself upon the floor when she cast the curtains back. It read, "Mr. Sidney Algernon Burley, San Francisco."

"The miscreant!" shouted Alonzo, and rushed forth to seek the false Reverend and destroy him; for the card explained everything, since in the course of the lovers' mutual confessions they had told each other all about all the sweethearts they had ever had, and thrown no end of mud at their failings and foibles for lovers always do that. It has a fascination that ranks next after billing and cooing.

IV

During the next two months many things happened. It had early transpired that Rosannah, poor suffering orphan, had neither returned to her grandmother in Portland, Oregon, nor sent any word to her save a duplicate of the woeful note she had left in the mansion on Telegraph Hill. Whosoever was sheltering her—if she was still alive—had been persuaded not to betray her whereabouts, without doubt; for all efforts to find trace of her had failed.

Did Alonzo give her up? Not he. He said to himself, "She will sing that sweet song when she is sad; I shall find her." So he took his carpet-sack and a portable telephone, and shook the snow of his native city from his arctics, and went forth into the world. He wandered far and wide and in many states. Time and again, strangers were astounded to see a wasted, pale, and woe-worn man laboriously climb a telegraph-pole in wintry and lonely places, perch sadly there an hour, with his ear at a little box, then come sighing down, and wander wearily away. Sometimes they shot at him, as peasants do at aeronauts, thinking him mad and dangerous. Thus his clothes were much shredded by bullets and his person grievously lacerated. But he bore it all patiently.

In the beginning of his pilgrimage he used often to say, "Ah, if I could but hear the 'Sweet By-and-by'!" But toward the end of it he used to shed tears of anguish and say, "Ah, if I could but hear something else!"

Thus a month and three weeks drifted by, and at last some humane people seized him and confined him in a private mad-house in New York. He made no moan, for his strength was all gone, and with it all heart and all hope. The superintendent, in pity, gave up his own comfortable parlor and bedchamber to him and nursed him with affectionate devotion.

At the end of a week the patient was able to leave his bed for the first time. He was lying, comfortably pillowed, on a sofa, listening to the plaintive Miserere of the bleak March winds and the muffled sound of tramping feet in the street below for it was about six in the evening, and New York was going home from work. He had a bright fire and the added cheer of a couple of student-lamps. So it was warm and snug within, though bleak and raw without; it was light and bright within, though outside it was as dark and dreary as if the world had been lit with Hartford gas. Alonzo smiled feebly to think how his loving vagaries had made him a maniac in the eyes of the world, and was proceeding to pursue his line of thought further, when a faint, sweet strain, the very ghost of sound, so remote and attenuated it seemed, struck upon his ear. His pulses stood still; he listened with parted lips and bated breath. The song flowed on— he waiting, listening, rising slowly and unconsciously from his recumbent position. At last he exclaimed:

"It is! it is she! Oh, the divine hated notes!"

He dragged himself eagerly to the corner whence the sounds proceeded, tore aside a curtain, and discovered a telephone. He bent over, and as the last note died away he burst forthwith the exclamation:

"Oh, thank Heaven, found at last! Speak to me, Rosannah, dearest! The cruel mystery has been unraveled; it was the villain Burley who mimicked my voice and wounded you with insolent speech!"

There was a breathless pause, a waiting age to Alonzo; then a faint sound came, framing itself into language:

"Oh, say those precious words again, Alonzo!"

"They are the truth, the veritable truth, my Rosannah, and you shall have the proof, ample and abundant proof!"

"Oh; Alonzo, stay by me! Leave me not for a moment! Let me feel that you are near me! Tell me we shall never be parted more! Oh, this happy hour, this blessed hour, this memorable hour!"

"We will make record of it, my Rosannah; every year, as this dear hour chimes from the clock, we will celebrate it with thanksgivings, all the years of our life."

"We will, we will, Alonzo!"

"Four minutes after six, in the evening, my Rosannah, shall henceforth—"

"Twenty-three minutes after twelve, afternoon shall—"

"Why; Rosannah, darling, where are you?"

"In Honolulu, Sandwich Islands. And where are you? Stay by me; do not leave me for a moment. I cannot bear it. Are you at home?"

"No, dear, I am in New York—a patient in the doctor's hands."

An agonizing shriek came buzzing to Alonzo's ear, like the sharp buzzing of a hurt gnat; it lost power in traveling five thousand miles. Alonzo hastened to say:

"Calm yourself, my child. It is nothing. Already I am getting well under the sweet healing of your presence. Rosannah?"

"Yes, Alonzo? Oh, how you terrified me! Say on."

"Name the happy day, Rosannah!"

There was a little pause. Then a diffident small voice replied, "I blush—but it is with pleasure, it is with happiness. Would—would you like to have it soon?"

"This very night, Rosannah! Oh, let us risk no more delays. Let it be now!—this very night, this very moment!"

"Oh, you impatient creature! I have nobody here but my good old uncle, a missionary for a generation, and now retired from service—nobody but him and his wife. I would so dearly like it if your mother and your Aunt Susan—"

"*Our* mother and *our* Aunt Susan, my Rosannah."

"Yes, *our* mother and *our* Aunt Susan—I am content to word it so if it pleases you; I would so like to have them present."

"So would I. Suppose you telegraph Aunt Susan. How long would it take her to come?"

"The steamer leaves San Francisco day after tomorrow. The passage is eight days. She would be here the 31st of March."

"Then name the 1st of April; do, Rosannah, dear."

"Mercy, it would make us April fools, Alonzo!"

"So we be the happiest ones that that day's suit looks down upon in the whole broad expanse of the globe, why need we care? Call it the 1st of April, dear."

"Then the 1st of April at shall be, with all my heart!"

"Oh, happiness! Name the hour, too, Rosannah."

"I like the morning, it is so blithe. Will eight in the morning do, Alonzo?"

"The loveliest hour in the day—since it will make you mine."

There was a feeble but frantic sound for some little time, as if wool-upped, disembodied spirits were exchanging kisses; then Rosannah said, "Excuse me just a moment, dear; I have an appointment, and am called to meet it."

The young girl sought a large parlor and took her place at a window which looked out upon a beautiful scene. To the left one could view the charming Nuuana Valley, fringed with its ruddy flush of tropical flowers and its plumed and graceful cocoa palms; its rising foothills clothed in the shining green of lemon, citron, and orange groves; its storied precipice beyond, where the first Kamehameha drove his defeated foes over to their destruction, a spot that had forgotten its grim history, no doubt, for now it was smiling, as almost always at noonday, under the glowing arches of a succession of rainbows. In front of the window one could see the quaint town, and here and there a picturesque group of dusky natives, enjoying the blistering weather; and far to the right lay the restless ocean, tossing its white mane in the sunshine.

Rosannah stood there, in her filmy white raiment, fanning her flushed and heated face, waiting. A Kanaka boy, clothed in a damaged blue necktie and part of a silk hat, thrust his head in at the door, and announced, "'Frisco haole!"

"Show him in," said the girl, straightening herself up and assuming a meaning dignity. Mr. Sidney Algernon Burley entered, clad from head to heel in dazzling snow—that is to say, in the lightest and whitest of Irish linen. He moved eagerly forward, but the girl made a gesture and gave him a look which checked him suddenly. She said, coldly, "I am here, as I promised. I believed your assertions, I yielded to your importune lies, and said I would name the day. I name the 1st of April—eight in the morning. Now go!"

"Oh, my dearest, if the gratitude of a lifetime—"

"Not a word. Spare me all sight of you, all communication with you, until that hour. No—no supplications; I will have it so."

When he was gone, she sank exhausted in a chair, for the long siege of troubles she had undergone had wasted her strength. Presently she said, "What a narrow escape! If the hour appointed had been an hour earlier—Oh, horror, what an escape I have made! And to think I had come to imagine I was loving this beguiling, this truthless, this treacherous monster! Oh, he shall repent his villainy!"

Let us now draw this history to a close, for little more needs to be told. On the 2d of the ensuing April, the Honolulu Advertiser contained this notice:

MARRIED.—In this city, by telephone, yesterday

morning—at eight o'clock, by Rev. Nathan Hays, assisted by Rev. Nathaniel Davis, of New York, Mr. Alonzo Fitz Clarence, of Eastport, Maine, U.S., and Miss Rosannah Ethelton, of Portland, Oregon, U.S. Mrs. Susan Howland, of San Francisco, a friend of the bride, was present, she being the guest of the Rev. Mr. Hays and wife, uncle and aunt of the bride. Mr. Sidney Algernon Burley, of San Francisco, was also present but did not remain till the conclusion of the marriage service. Captain Hawthorne's beautiful yacht, tastefully decorated, was in waiting, and the happy bride and her friends immediately departed on a bridal trip to Lahaina and Haleakala.

The New York papers of the same date contained this notice:

MARRIED.—In this city, yesterday, by telephone, at half-past two in the morning, by Rev. Nathaniel Davis, assisted by Rev. Nathan Hays, of Honolulu, Mr. Alonzo Fitz Clarence, of Eastport, Maine, and Miss Rosannah Ethelton, of Portland, Oregon. The parents and several friends of the bridegroom were present, and enjoyed a sumptuous breakfast and much festivity until nearly sunrise, and then departed on a bridal trip to the Aquarium, the bridegroom's state of health not admitting of a more extended journey.

Toward the close of that memorable day Mr. and Mrs. Alonzo Fitz Clarence were buried in sweet converse concerning the pleasures of their several bridal tours, when suddenly the young wife exclaimed: "Oh, Lonny, I forgot! I did what I said I would."

"Did you, dear?"

"Indeed, I did. I made *him* the April fool! And I told him so, too! Ah, it was a charming surprise! There he stood, sweltering in a black dress-suit, with the mercury leaking out of the top of the thermometer, waiting to be married. You should have seen the look he gave when I whispered it in his ear. Ah, his wickedness cost me many a heartache and many a tear, but the score was all squared up, then. So the vengeful feeling went right out of my heart, and I begged him to stay, and said I forgave him everything. But he wouldn't. He said he would live to be avenged; said he would make our lives a curse to us. But he can't, *can* he, dear?"

"Never in this world, my Rosannah!"

Aunt Susan, the Oregonian grandmother, and the young couple and their Eastport parents, are all happy at this writing, and likely to remain so. Aunt Susan brought the bride from the islands, accompanied her across our continent, and had the happiness of witnessing the rapturous meeting between an adoring husband and wife who had never seen each other until that moment.

A word about the wretched Burley, whose wicked machinations came so near wrecking the hearts and lives of our poor young friends, will be sufficient. In a murderous attempt to seize a crippled and helpless artisan who he fancied had done him some small offense, he fell into a caldron of boiling oil and expired before he could be extinguished.

TROPHY SEEKINS

Lucy Suitor Holt

O n September 25, just before midnight, a meteorite about the size of a sofa slipped overhead and landed, Dan told me, near Hollows Hill.

Dan lives near The Hollows, which is what we call a five-acre parcel of land near Pine Crest Reach, Maine. The reach juts out into the Atlantic Ocean and people like to picnic and dig clams there. No one ventures into The Hollows unless they like swamp gas and mosquitoes to go along with their sandwiches and soda pop.

Hollows Hill is really a mound of dirt with a couple of scraggy pines on it in the middle of The Hollows. A sluggish brook splits and goes around it, making Hollows Hill a sort of island in the middle of thick woods. Dan often went hunting in there, though that usually meant wet feet. But Dan always said to me, "Melvin, you can enjoy warming your feet by the fire more if you get them cold first."

Dan is Dan Seekins, my best friend. He watched the meteorite fall out of the sky and he figured it just about landed on Hollows Hill, or close by. He said no one else probably saw the thing, it being so late at night. He only saw it because he had gone out back of his house to quiet down his hunting dog, which was making all sorts of ruckus.

Dan looked around to see what was disturbing his dog, which was disturbing Dan's wife's sleeping, which disturbed Dan, and saw the meteorite sizzling right over his head. He called me up—I remember it was near on to two o'clock in the morning—as soon as he got back into the house, taking his dog with him just to be on the safe side.

Dan loves his long-legged Plott hound and named him Trophy Seekins. Dan always laughs at that. Anyway, when coon hunting time came near, we'd take Trophy out and practice a bit before getting to the real thing. Dan had me drag an old hat around on a long rope while the dog chased it. He did just fine, only getting a little distracted because the hat lining was rabbit fur and the earflaps were deerskin. We were sure the dog could tell the difference when the time came for the real thing, though.

Dan had a plan. He said he read somewhere that those meteorites were worth a good bit of money when sliced up into thin slivers. Some scientists needed them for experiments, thinking life started on Earth because of hitchhiking bugs. And other people paid good money to have a slice of cosmic jewelry. So Dan decided we shouldn't tell anyone about the one he saw. We should keep it our secret and just wait until hunting season started in two days, then go into the woods and find it for ourselves. He wanted me along because I could help carry it out. He figured that the rock had burned down some, from about the size of his couch, to about the size of his footstool. Since the thing was really dense though, it might take the two of us to carry out what was left. We eagerly waited the start of raccoon-hunting season.

We caught some luck when Mrs. Kolinsky called Dan and said she had gotten his name from someone who knew he had a coon dog. She explained that she had just put her birdfeeders out for the season and a raccoon was eating up the sunflower seeds and making a general wreck of things. Mrs. Kolinsky lived down at the farther edge of The Hollows, and could Dan come out and rid her of this pest? Oh, sure, yes indeed!

We had to wait until Saturday night because Dan's wife insisted he spend some time getting firewood cut for her kitchen stove, and put on a storm window or two in case it started snowing early. Dan was one to put off such things if a chance to hunt came up, but he got his honey-do chores done on Saturday afternoon and called me. Raccoons mostly sleep in the daytime and are more active at night, so all our hunting is done in the dark. Dan picked me up at dusk and we went to see the damage that the raccoon had done to Mrs. Kolinsky's bird feeders.

I don't know why Dan didn't have a cage for Trophy in the back of the truck. Instead, Trophy stood on the front seat, proud as punch, staring out the window over my elbow. The weather got cold and wet, and there's nothing like sitting in a closed up truck with a steaming wet Plott hound on your lap who's dripping drool into the windshield defroster. It also meant that I occasionally let out a stream of cussing meant to fit the electrifying jolts I got when that seventy-pound dog stepped where he shouldn't have. I'd shove Trophy around to sit between Dan and me, but as soon as that dog saw a strip of woods out the side window, he was treading all over me again, eager to stick his nose out. I really couldn't sit in the middle you see, because I tried it once and people sort of looked at us funny, what with me all close up to Dan, who weighs about 250 to my 160, and the dog drooling out the window, all besotted with the outdoor smells, his tail whipping me about the head and shoulders.

On this particular night in question, we got to The Hollows without much injury and saw Mrs. Kolinsky waiting for us on her stoop. She pointed out a whole ruination in her backyard where the feeders had been all upturned, birdbaths dumped over and cracked. This raccoon must be huge, judging by the claw marks up the side of a tree where the animal reached up to get at a greasy clump of beef fat hanging from a cord. Dan rubbed his hands together in what could only be described as delight. Tonight he might just get a two-fer: the biggest raccoon trophy he ever set eyes on, and a celestial rock to settle his income for the rest of his life.

We let Trophy sniff around the spot for a bit and then followed along as the dog loped off into the woods, nose to the ground. He wasn't baying yet, just trying to get an idea of where this bandit had gone. We hurried to get our equipment, which consisted of Dan's grandfather's old 30-30, all duct-taped on the stock. I decided not to take my old 12-gauge shotgun and let Dan have this prize, him being so eager for it. Instead, I grabbed up a couple of flashlights from the floor of the pickup and a large sack, being hopeful the meteorite had broken into bits so I could tote it out easier. By the time I got all that together, the dog gave a little yip to let us know he had found the trail. I got distracted and forgot my gloves, and I regret that mistake to this very day.

It was our usual plan to follow the dog well back and let him do his work. When Trophy wanted to let us know he was close to the raccoon, he would start to yodel, and when the dog finally treed the raccoon, he would bay up at the tree the coon had climbed.

This worked out fine as long as something else didn't cross the dog's path. Sometimes Trophy took a fling for himself and chased a deer for a bit before breaking off and returning to the raccoon scent. On those occasions, we just waited for him to get done with his silliness and get back to work, then followed him again.

The moon had started up, but the woods were as dark as the inside of a pocket, so we had to follow the cold yellow spots from the flashlights. I let Dan go ahead and tried to shine the lights either between his legs, or over his shoulder, though neither suited to show much. He showed his displeasure by whapping some branches back into my chest and I got myself caught up in the mess and dropped one of the lights. I couldn't find it again, and when I caught up to Dan, I shined the remaining flashlight beam at his feet, more proper like. That worked the best, as Dan's feet were the least shadow casting part of him.

We could hear the dog up ahead starting to bawl a little, meaning he got hold of a good sniff of raccoon. We tried to go faster, but the underbrush here was thicker and the moonlight and flashlight just couldn't get through. We had to slog through some trickle left in the brook that ran around the mound of dirt. Nothing prepared us for the sight when we broke out into the small clearing under the pine trees on Hollows Hill. The sky here had a blue flush from the moon, and all the trees cast shadows as black as aces. Weird thing was that all around our feet was this eerie greenish glow.

The flashlight dimmed and went out. I thunked it hard on my hand, but it wouldn't come back on except for a tiny orange button inside the bulb. We still had that strange glow all around our feet, though, that lit up the toes of our boots. I scraped my feet over the ground and stirred up more light. Dan stooped down and took a handful of it on his glove. "Worms," he said, and held his hand out to show me. "Just firefly larvae." He shook the dirt off his hand, but the fingers still glimmered from the crushed bugs.

We both saw something sitting right there in the center of that glowing mound. It was as large as a recliner, all bumpy on the outside, and crackling like a cat playing in a paper sack. Our meteorite! I looked at Dan, who looked at me, and we both looked at the burlap sack I'd brought, and we both sighed at the same time. The rock seemed to cave in on itself as we watched. Pretty soon there would be nothing left but a crumpled up husk too large even then to move.

We just started walking over to the strange shrinking rock, thinking a smaller piece might be nearby, when we heard Trophy circling around, baying like I never heard before. We had no light but what was on the ground, and couldn't make out anything in the trees a few feet away. We could only wait, turning to the sound of the dog's voice as he circled and spiraled in toward us. I noticed Dan raise up his 30-30 and follow the sounds all around in a circle, his elbow stuck out and his hat pushed way back on his head.

All of a sudden, something tore through the trees at us. I heard a shot as whatever it was pushed past Dan so fast that the rifle got shoved up and fired a neat hole into deepest space.

I backed up into a pine tree and ended up sandwiched between the tree and that thing that pounded through the woods, whatever it was. I felt the hard tree trunk behind me, something familiar and solid, and the thing in front of me like a rubbery mass that reminded me of the muck at the bottom of a stagnant pond I got my feet stuck in one time. But this thing wasn't cold like pond mud. It was in a fever, all sticky and smelling like burned tires. It peeled itself off me and I thought I was going to be sucked along with it, like my feet were sucked down into that pond bottom. It reached up and pushed at my face and then it was gone. That happened in a second, but seemed like forever.

Trophy tumbled through the trees, tripped over his own feet, and piled up on the ground in front of us. He got back up, shook himself off, spreading that glowworm crud all over his body, and then off he went again on the now luminous footprints of whatever it was he chased.

Dan gave me a jab in the ribs and we ran after the dog. We must have run a mile, maybe two; we got to zigzagging so much it's hard to tell. I know we ran back over Hollows Hill because I saw the tracks all scattered in the glowing dirt, and that hissing rock had disappeared into a small pile of blackened ash. We didn't stop.

Eventually we ran out the length of Pine Crest Reach and came out into the moonlight down by the ocean's edge. We followed the tracks in the sand along the shore. We could hear Trophy barking, which sounded more like a hysterical yowl by that time, and hurried to get to him. We found him all right. He glowed all green and sat on his haunches as he stared out over the moonlight sparkled ocean. He leaned his head back and howled at something up in the sky. We called and called, but Trophy wouldn't leave that shoreline, so we had to pick him up and take him home. All during the ride home, that dog whined and stared out the window at the sky.

We never went back to The Hollows, though we tried to take

Trophy out hunting one time after that. It didn't work out very well. We followed the dog into a farmer's cow pasture where Trophy was sitting, barking at a metal water tank. Trophy was ruined for a hunting dog, so Dan let his wife keep him as a pet, though she has to keep the dog in on moonlit nights or listen to the poor thing howl until daylight.

Mrs. Kolinsky called Dan and thanked him for ending her problem with the raccoon raids, but Dan and I never talked about it. We didn't want to talk about the smell of the thing as it went past us in the dark, a mixture of burned tires, musk, and old paper. I didn't want to tell Dan how the thing sucked on to me like hot pond mud as it rushed into me, or tell about the sticky, rubbery fingers covered in stiff bristles that brushed my face and hands as it pushed away from me.

We had both noticed the way the gleam from the crushed worms had stuck to the strange suckered feet and left tracks down the shoreline. Those glowing tracks, with the six-inch claw marks, went right off into the water. Thing is, we couldn't find a way to tell anyone, especially about the way those tracks just sort of floated on the surface. The only thing Dan actually ever said aloud about the situation, more to himself that to anyone else, was that it made him grateful old Trophy was a chasing dog and not a retriever.

THE AUTUMN OF SORROWS

Scott Thomas

Province of Maine, 1784

Frost had come in the night while Susanna Hayford and her children were sleeping. It whispered patterns against the windows of their house and silvered the uneven fields. It dulled the colors of turning leaves, left an icy dusting on bracken and spruce and coy September asters. Warm in their dreams, the family slept through it all, unaware as the year advanced impassively toward winter.

In the morning, Prudence, who was just ten, discovered the delicate impressions on the panes and ran to fetch her brother.

"Samuel! First frost . . . first frost!"

The boy, three years her senior, was rekindling the fire in the kitchen. He looked up and smiled. He knew what Prudence meant.

"Cranberries!" Samuel returned.

Both children turned and hurried up the tight staircase that nestled between the kitchen and pantry. There was chill enough for their breath to puff out before them as they made the top step and passed through a storage area to the door of the room where their mother slept. Susanna had moved to this chamber following the war. The handsome bed that she and her husband had shared, the most expensive thing in the house, remained down in the best room, little more than a monument to a cruelly interrupted marriage. Samuel stopped at the door and listened to make sure that he did not hear weeping on the other side before knocking.

"Yes?" a voice came.

Prudence bound in ahead of Samuel. The room was a simple whitewashed thing with a low ceiling that slanted on two sides. There was an unadorned fireplace (its contents burnt quiet) and two smallish windows on the gable side. A pretty dark-haired woman was sitting in bed with her back against the headboard. She was pale with chestnut eyes, and she was holding something in one of her hands, something that she did not want the children to notice. She tucked it beneath the rumpled tide of covers that obscured the lower half of her body, and smiled weakly.

"Hallo, my dears."

The woman's daughter sat down on the edge of the bed. "Mother, we've a frost! Might we *please* row out to Little Sorrow and pick the cranberries? They'll now be ripe."

Susanna Hayford looked from one eager child to the other. Much as she would have liked to keep them there at the house, safely in her sight at all times, she knew she could not.

"If you must, but heed to caution and should the sea be unruly, hasten back."

The hand under the blanket impulsively squeezed what it held.

"Thank you, Mother!" Prudence gushed, and her brother, hovering behind her, echoed the sentiment before they both rushed from the chamber. Susanna listened to them flying down the stairs, their steps and voices defying the silence that had overtaken the house in the last six months.

Not so long ago the humble structure had been filled with spirit and company. There had been a shifting family of occupants, from hired girls and hired men and boarders, to her widowed cousin Jennet (complete with three daughters). Susanna's maiden aunt Polly, as well an ailing grandsir, had also made a home of the place. And, of course, there had been her Abel. He had survived the fight against the French and Indians only to be lost in the rebellion.

But now the place was owned by shadows and painfully infused with memories. Life, about its inexplicable courses, had swept all but Susanna and her surviving children from the place. Her husband's grandfather had gone to his maker the previous winter. Jennet remarried and went to housekeeping in Machias; the spinster aunt had left to live with another relative, and there was not enough money to keep hired help. The last boarder, a Mr. Eaton, had moved out at the end of August, and the little west room behind the formal parlor had sat empty since.

Susanna pulled her fist out from under the blanket and opened her fingers. In her palm was a lock of hair curled up like a small sleeping thing. It was the hair of a six-year old child, blond, like Abel's had been. "Winter fever" had taken her Betsy in March.

Others in the village had remarked on Susanna's strength, praising her for tending the farm on her own, caring for two children after the loss of her husband and youngest daughter. They encouraged her to trust in God, to find comfort in her faith. But, she did not feel as strong as she appeared on the outside, and while the local Reverend Goodwin remained a dear friend, the force he served no longer garnered her devotion. Only days earlier, in her diary, she had written: *I lately see God in no thing. They speak of His mercy and compassion and His mysterious ways, but little mystery do I perceive. If there be a God then He puts thorns on flowers and allows that musket balls fly and the poor to starve and disease to whither. He has taken my child and my very heart with her.*

Susanna waited until she heard the back door shut, as the children headed out, before allowing herself to weep.

The sky was September blue, so clear and crisp that if one could hurl a stone high enough they would shatter it. Warm sunlight countered the chill air and made a strangely elongated shadow version of the house. The building itself looked smaller and plainer for the textured terrain rolling around it, a landscape shaped by a patient and astonishing violence. Stark rail fences conformed painfully to these rocky surroundings, defining crop fields and grazing land and orchard.

There was nothing pretentious about the house itself, little to make it stand apart from others in the vicinity. It was a one-story shingled structure with a substantial center chimney, the main door bordered by windows on the long side, facing the road.

The outbuildings were in need of repair. Samuel, who was not so handy when it came to carpentry, was outmatched by the effects of wind and temperature and gravity. Besides, much of his time was spent working at the shingle mill. There had been plenty of helpful men coming by following Abel's death, men from miles around (the majority of them married), men eager to assist with this or that task around the farm, but they soon vanished when they found that the pretty widow—unalterably clad in her black mourning gown—was not disposed to their desires to "console" her.

The Hayford children had dressed for a frosty morning, Samuel in a dead uncle's oversized coat and Prudence in her dull blue cloak and riding hood. They walked from the house and made their way along the cow path, cutting between cultivated fields and stony pasture. They passed leafy expanses that denoted sleeping turnips, and ripening pumpkins hunched amidst browning foliage. A dark wood waited at the end of the trail, its tall pines and solemn spruce crowded together, all but obscuring the oaks and reddened maples. The children looked small as they approached this wall of trees.

Once in the woods, Samuel led the way on a line of worn earth that was narrower and more crooked than the cow path. The air was moist, heavy with the scents of vegetation and dark soil, and it added to the sense of being enclosed. There was moss and shadow, and birds that were heard but not seen, and small red squirrels that chattered their agitation.

Prudence was prattling on about what she wanted to do with the cranberries once procured, inventing recipes as she maneuvered the ruts and roots and half-hidden stones that would have proved treacherous for the unfamiliar. She swung her empty basket like a pendulum. Samuel tired of her voice and began to whistle to himself.

"You would be well to save your vigor for the picking and less so for blathering," the boy cautioned over his shoulder.

This stirred the girl to defense. "I would blather and pick all at once, should it suit my fancy," she said, swatting away a little yellow leaf that had snared in the lacey trim of her day cap. "I would blather in my sleep as well, if it please me."

Samuel chuckled.

There were few indications that the young Hayfords were approaching the Atlantic, only quick glimpses of water through dense boughs.

"You sound a squirrel with that tireless tongue of yours," Samuel prodded.

"Were I a squirrel, I should bite you," Prudence returned.

The shaded spruce forest came to a sudden end, and there, startlingly expansive, was a glittering blue ocean. The border between water and trees was a steep jumble of overlapping pinkish boulders. They were smooth and jagged, broken and whole, randomly studded with periwinkles, and here and there cupping tidal pools lined with drowned green hair.

This rough crescent of granite shaped a small cove where the water, calmer than the open sea beyond, was an inscrutable gray. It was an inlet where ducks were known to bob and dive, and loons were apt to winter, away from their summer lakes. Betsy made her way down toward the waterline, beyond the hem of grass and scrub-plants, across a slanted swath of pebbles and shells, past the bleached remains of fallen pines like great broken antlers, over a crunching layer of dried brown seaweed. There was a gap in the natural stone rampart, allowing for a small area of gravely beach where a boat could gain access to the water.

Samuel's father's skiff was upside down, with oars beneath it, placed safely above the reach of high tide. Despite its worn appearance, the vessel was capable of floating, and so the boy flipped it onto its keel and pushed it down toward the surf, grunting the whole way.

"In with you," Samuel panted to his sister.

The girl climbed into the boat—so as not to soak her feet and skirts—and the boy gave it a shove. The skiff sloshed into the water with Samuel pushing behind it, until he himself scrambled in. The boat rocked as he took up position, setting his oars in their rowlocks and leaning back, dunking the blades, taking control. The tide was on its way out, which was to Samuel's favor, and just lightly caressed the stones along the shore.

A small island stood between the rowboat and the infinite Atlantic. Little Sorrow, they called it. The covering of trees gave it the look of a furred animal floating off the coast. It was the color of spruce, but for a rough line that dared above the blue water, a granite ridge the color of salmon. There were no homes or human residents on Little Sorrow.

It took only a short while to row across, and soon Samuel was dragging the skiff up a pebbled slope, slick with rockweed. Gulls had left pieces of ruined crabs about—a pale orange leg like a crooked skeleton finger, a hollow carapace, upside down and holding water; teacup for a mermaid.

The young Hayfords left the boat and marched up into the woods with their baskets, away from the cool air sighing in over the water. Autumn had preceded them, bringing its colors, and these showed brighter for the contrasting shadows under the spruce. Many of the small birches and maples appeared to be dead or dying, perhaps starved for light, their roots no rival for towering evergreens. Their branches were emaciated, and bore scratchy clots of ghostly-green moss instead of leaves.

The tree cover thinned and the children came to a marshy tract of land, thick with cranberry bushes. The plants were shrubby and low, with small green leaves and stark red fruit. Even from a distance the children could see that it was a good year for the berries.

Samuel and Prudence looked to one another, smiled, and went to their task. There was salt in the air and September in the air and the earthy scent of the shrubs as the children knelt in damp vines, eagerly plucking. Some of the elliptical fruits were still white, while others were blushing softly, but a good many had ripened to a deep red. Prudence sampled one of the tart berries, biting it in half to reveal its four hollow chambers.

When their baskets were full and bulging, the children started back for the skiff. They passed through the wooded expanse they had crossed to access the berries, but found a less steep route down toward where the boat awaited. Had they come this way initially, they would have seen what Prudence now spotted.

"Samuel, look there!"

The boy stopped and stared. "Do you suppose wasps fashioned it?"

It was gray and long and loosely shaped like a man, or more a shroud containing a man.

Samuel put his basket down on the grass above the rocks and, forsaking the path of smooth descent he had been on, made his way across undulating ledges to where the strange object lay wedged against an outcrop. He knelt by the gray object, which in size and shape was indeed suggestive of a man, all the more so for the rough shoulders and head. He reached down with his hand.

"Samuel!" Prudence called, "You mustn't touch it!"

Samuel touched it. He pressed his palm against the coarse slate-colored skin, which, though it looked as if it could have been some kind of stone, was not. It felt dry and somewhat yielding, like parchment hardened in layers, the outermost of which was flaking and frayed. He rapped his knuckles against the chest, then looked over at his sister.

"It seems hollow," he said.

"Leave it be, Samuel," Prudence pleaded.

The boy took the shape by the shoulders and gave it a shake. Whatever it was, it was relatively light, for it rocked with his effort, and he thought that he heard rattling.

"There is something within," Samuel reported.

He picked up a length of driftwood, which lay nearby, and stood above the form. The first blow crunched through the chest, making a hole as big as a fist, and dust puffed out. The encasing crust was hardly an inch thick. The second blow widened the opening, revealing some of what was inside. Birch branches, he thought at first.

"Have a look, Prudence," Samuel called, "there are bones!"

"I shouldn't like to look, Samuel. I am cold and I wish home." The girl had her hood pulled tight against her day cap, and held her cloak closed at the throat.

Samuel's fascination possessed him. He tore at the sides of the broken chest with his hands, and higher up to the featureless face of the cocoon, removing chunks, so as to get a better look at the dingy disheveled skeleton lying there in its womb of dust and shadow. The skull, the size of a man's, was tipped to one side, all teeth and pitted stare.

A flurry of thoughts went through the boy's mind. Whose bones were these? How did they get there? Had waves flung their container up onto the boulders? How old were the bones? Why were they sealed in that strange gray encasement? He wondered if maybe Indians were responsible, but then he had never heard of Indians tending to their dead in such a manner.

"There is something more," Samuel called.

A lumpy black cloth sack was tucked into the ribcage of the skeleton. The boy had to reposition himself, pressing his chest against the broken chest of the coffin, in order to angle his arm in to reach the bundle. Stale odors drifted up into his face and he snared a button on the sleeve of his coat while pulling the sack out through its tunnel of ribs. His prize secured, Samuel sat back on his heels and opened the cloth.

"I'm for home!" Prudence snapped, turning and walking off with her basket.

Samuel only half-noticed his sister's departure.

"A heart…" he said to himself.

It was a petrified heart, or a faithful carving of one, fashioned from pink granite and veined with cracks.

Samuel put the heart in the pocket of his coat and made a daring dash over the treacherous ledges, grabbing his basket of cranberries before rejoining his sister down below the tree line, where the boat awaited.

Prudence was standing there shivering, her knees imprinted on the skirt of her frock like damp shadows.

"May we now go?" The girl whined.

Samuel pulled out the heart and showed her. "See what I have found, Prudence . . . is it not a wonder?"

The girl frowned. "You mustn't take it, Samuel. To thieve from one's grave is improper."

"Mustn't take it? Silly! Those old bones have not a need for it."

With that Samuel stuffed his treasure back in his coat and loaded the baskets of berries into the skiff. Prudence was cold and in no mood to argue, knowing how stubborn her brother could be. She sat quietly in the back of the boat, hugging herself as Samuel rowed for the mainland.

Touches of autumn color stood out against dark spruce along the shore, and hazy mountains swelled in the distance. The young Hayfords were now more than halfway between Little Sorrow and the cove from which they'd launched. Samuel sat with his back to the prow, working the oars, while Prudence had a clear view of their progress. The water close to shore had lightened to a soft drowned green; its little waves stroked the breaching boulders like one soothing the head of a pet.

Prudence tucked her own head into her shoulders and gazed absently at the baskets of red fruit. Once again her mind was busy with imaginary recipes. Peripheral motion drew her eye back to the cove. She noticed the silvery agitation of displacement and a smallish pale figure lifting from under the surf. It rose up slowly, hunched, and only fully standing after a moment, as if adjusting to the pull of gravity. At first she thought it was some kind of animal, but it had long light hair pouring across its back, and limbs like a person, and once it had its footing it scurried up onto the jagged granite outcrops.

"Samuel, Samuel! Quick—see there—something from the water rises!"

The boy turned. He saw the naked back of a young blond girl as she reached the cliff above the stone embankment and plunged into gloomy forest.

"By God!" Samuel exclaimed.

Prudence stood up to try to get a better look and the boat rocked in protest. She felt something thump against the boards beneath her and glanced into the water, thinking they had struck a rock. Samuel felt it, too, and was distracted from looking for the child. An ashen blur passed alongside them, too low in the water to discern clearly, but whatever it was, it trailed long dark hair sinuous as seaweed.

"Samuel!" Prudence grabbed her brother by the arm.

The boy's eyes were wide and he craned his neck this way and that to try and see the thing in the water, but it had slipped out of sight. He shook free of his sister and slapped his oars in the surf to frighten off whatever might be below. When nothing unusual happened, he started rowing again, suddenly eager to be on dry land.

Prudence's gaze darted from side to side, behind the boat and in front, but the glare of sunlight on the surface of the waves made it difficult to distinguish anything. She looked back toward the mainland as they moved nearer to it. Some distance down the shore from where she had seen the child, a spindly naked figure walked out of the ocean onto an inadvertent staircase of stones. It was a stern-faced old man with long white hair plastered to his bony shoulders. Beyond him, a nude young woman pulled herself from the tide, grabbing onto rockweed and ledge, her skin glistening as she emerged.

Prudence cried out and her brother spun to look. More of them appeared at unequal intervals along the coastline. An infant wiggled out like a seal, then scrabbled up the gravely slope of the quiet cove. Here two young boys, there a lumbering unclothed man. They came up dripping, silent, strangely determined.

"How is it they are not drowned?" Prudence asked, incredulous.

Samuel was too distracted to respond. "See there," he said, "is it not Abner Tilden?"

The bulky, bearded man, like the rest, was oblivious of his observers and moved steadily up toward the wooded expanse.

Prudence replied, "Abner Tilden died Sunday last."

"And there!" Samuel pointed. "Polly Fisher! And old Mrs. Pratt... Look—Jedediah, the minister's son! It cannot be so, for they all are dead."

More children, a corpulent limping woman, and figures too far down the coast to distinguish, rose from the Atlantic and made their way up with the rest. They were all without clothes and all pale as chalk, and not a word came from any of them. They were like migrating birds returning to a place they knew, instinctively, single-mindedly. Off they went, into the swallowing green of the dark spruce forest.

Every one of them was gone before the Hayfords' skiff reached the gentle waters of the cove, but rather than go ashore, Samuel chose to float there. He and his sister looked at each other, then up into the trees, then at each other again. Knowing that those people, or ghosts, or whatever they were, might be in there, made them wonder if it would prove safer to stay in the boat.

"*We must tell Mother*," Prudence said after a long moment.

Samuel nodded and began to row. He felt the stone heart in his coat pocket pressing against his thigh. It suddenly felt very cold to him, as if it were a chunk of ice rather than granite.

Susanna Hayford worried. Winter was on the way and there was so much to do. So much preparation and relatively little time. So little money, and so few hands. The frost may have delighted her children, but to her it meant the cold season was upon them. Would there be food enough and wood to last? Was there a sufficient quantity of salt to preserve the meat that November's slaughter would provide? Would sickness come sneaking with fevers and coughs? Would she and her children survive to see the spring? While the sky boasted cloudless blue and the sun made the autumn colors pretty, there was indeed plenty to be concerned about.

It was hard enough carrying on after Abel's death, but the loss of her young Betsy had proved overwhelming. While once she had risen in the dark of day and whirled through the house, efficient and hardy, she now slept too long, and found the slightest task exhausting. It was as if the black of her mourning clothes had soaked deeply into her limbs and organs, a painful, unyielding weight. How, she wondered, could a creature in such a state provide for her children through a hard New England winter?

Following a quick breakfast of milk and bread, Susanna forced herself to get busy. Samuel and Prudence had already milked the cows, gathered eggs, fed the hens, and carried water into the kitchen, so she emptied her chamber pot, then went to the garden to see what the frost had done to the herbs that had yet to be harvested for drying. The situation did not seem so bad, the herbs being such sturdy plants, but time would tell. The frost was already melting off—she would wait for the sun to dry them and then gather the rest.

Next she worked in the formal parlor with its wainscot and paneled fireplace wall painted a warm mustard yellow. She took down the light curtains and put up the heavier winter ones in their place. She then did her sweeping and built up the kitchen fire to boil water for tea, having earned a few minutes rest.

If only her body had the vitality of her mind, she thought, for her head was a whirl of thoughts. She considered the possibility of selling off two of the cows, seeing as there probably would not be enough feed to last the lot of them all winter. That would give her some extra money, enough to hire a neighbor's girl to help with the fall whitewashing, and a man to repair the outbuildings and sow the winter hemp. Yes, Susanna thought, she might just be able to afford Bathsheba Hibbard's daughter for a few months, which would be a great help when it came time to cut up and salt meat, and make applesauce and cider to store.

After her tea, Susanna pushed herself to do more. She laundered the summer curtains and hung them to dry, thinking all the while about selling the long-handled bed warming pan, and—as much as she hated entertaining the idea—the tall clock in the parlor that had belonged to her father. That would give her money to stock up on molasses and nutmegs and cinnamon, and perhaps leave some to put by in case stores ran out and she needed to buy sugar and meat toward winter's end.

Susanna killed a chicken to prepare for the final meal of the day, and sat out in the dooryard on the milking stool, plucking it. She glanced over at the barn and thought that if she *did* sell the clock, the proceeds might better be spent fixing the building's leaky roof. The parson's son John would be agreeable for a reasonable sum, she imagined, and while slow-witted, he was known to put his back into whatever task came his way.

With the naked chicken sitting on the table, Susanna went back to the garden and quickly collected the rest of the herbs. She brought them into the kitchen and began stringing them up where there were already festoons of drying apples and red peppers and aromatic plumes of mint and savory. She was reaching above her head with a bundle of sage when she heard soft knocking at the front door. Only a stranger would use the front door, she thought, wiping her hands on her apron and adjusting her white day cap as she walked through the house. The rapping came again, more insistently. Susanna opened the door and looked down.

There stood her dead daughter Betsy, her soggy blond hair dripping down her small naked body.

*   *   *

Samuel and Prudence moved as quickly as they could without spilling their baskets of cranberries. By the time they came out of the woods it was afternoon, and the shortening September light was casting severe shadows. The Hayford house awaited, shingled and unadorned, surrounded on all sides by a horizon of jagged spruce trees. Wood smoke streamed from the big center chimney and pleasantly scented the air. The children panted up to the rear door and rushed in, calling to their mother, even before they saw her.

When they did see her, they were breathless and words of the strange and frightful emergence they had witnessed began to fly from their mouths. But then they fell silent. The pretty woman in her dark mourning clothes looked up and smiled, though her cheeks were wet with tears. She was sitting by the fire in the cozy family parlor with a child on her lap. It was a small pale girl with sodden blond hair, wrapped like a baby in Susanna's red riding cloak.

"Our Betsy has come back," Susanna said softly. "God has returned her to us."

The youngest of the Hayford children turned her head and gazed impassively at her siblings. She was healthy looking, but for her pallor. There was nothing to suggest that her breathing, blinking body had ever been decaying under earth, let alone for half a year. While the girl's hair was light like her father's had been, she had her mother's dark eyes, though there was something curious about them now. In each pupil there was a thread of moonlight loosely wound in a spiral. They glistened like periwinkles kissed by a sea.

There was little to distinguish the village of Newcomb from the expansive wilderness around it. No central cluster of shops and offices, no streets crowded with homes. The buildings were scattered, set apart from one another, divided by farmland and the undulating, heavily forested terrain that appeared as if it could swallow this humble attempt at civilization with a modicum of effort. The meetinghouse stood alone, as did the blacksmith's shop and the mills and the tavern. Some of the farms, which comprised the bulk of the buildings, were not even within view of neighbors.

One such farm belonged to Abner Tilden's widow, Mary. She didn't have the strength to finish sweeping her kitchen, so she sat down in the bow-back Windsor chair her spouse had been fond of and started to weep. Not a week had passed since she'd put Abner in the ground, and she still found herself expecting him to walk in at any time. When something tapped on the window, she turned to see her husband's pale, puffy face, with its beard like a clump of dark foam, gawking in at her through one of the small panes.

Another farm, belonging to Tolford Bird, dominated a rise that offered expansive views of bleeding maples and mountains. The property was encroached on its western side by wild-armed pines and an army of somber spruce trees. The farmer's orchard took up a good deal of the area at the bottom of the incline, close to a stream where he kept moose snares. This is where he and his five surviving children had spent the last hour, picking apples. Two sons, Henry and Owen, had died of "lung fever" the previous winter.

The youngest boy, Seth, who was seven, picked his way up and over a rise and now worked apart from the others. His small size allowed him to reach areas under gnarly branches where his father and older brothers would not have been able to fit. He was about to sample an apple when he lost his grip and it dropped at his feet. There was enough of a slant to allow the fruit to roll and Seth bent, grabbing as he chased after it, but the wayward fruit eluded him until it came to rest between two bony unshod feet. Seth lifted his head, his eyes passing over bare legs and an unclothed torso, on up to the gaunt, staring face of his dead brother Owen.

A group of men were bunching Indian-corn stalks into raggedy shocks when they noticed a nude old fellow with long white hair emerging from shady woods at the edge of the field. One of the men recognized the figure as his grandfather, Braddock Gliven.

Benjamin Fisher and his hired man Jeremiah were unloading a cartload of pumpkins and squash to put up for winter when they saw the landowner's young daughter Polly, her body uncovered and damp, walking slowly toward them through a yellow rain of twirling birch leaves. Polly, who died two years before, four days after falling off a ledge onto the rocks of Dunning's Point, moved numbly through complaining chickens in the dooryard, passing her stunned father and his worker as if they weren't there. She stopped at the entry of the simple one-story house and rapped with her small, faded fist.

By the time the sun lowered behind dark spruce hills, there was hardly a house in the village of Newcomb that went unvisited by the naked, sea-dripping dead.

Dusk fell and the low-ceilinged family parlor of the Hayford house was as homey as it could be, with a vigorous hardwood fire burning, and candle glow, and the woodwork of the mantel and doors and wainscoting a rich blue-gray that seemed to soak in the shadows. Susanna would not be torn away from her Betsy, and so Prudence prepared a meal using the chicken that the woman had plucked earlier.

The youngest child had been dressed in one of her own frocks, with which Susanna had not been able to part. The family, reunited, ate in that same room, safe from the September chill that floated an icy freckling of stars. Outside the innumerable trees had merged into a single darkness, a wall around the farm, the tops of evergreens like flaked-stone arrowheads against the indigo sky.

"Will you not speak?" Susanna said, with an ache in her voice.

She was in the dim second-best room, kneeling in front of Betsy, who regarded her mother with a blank stare, the silvery spirals in her eyes taking on a luminosity in the glow of the fireplace. The child had not spoken a word, nor had she reacted to the embraces and kisses her mother had delivered in quantity. The poor little thing was still mystified by her experience, Susanna reasoned, hoping that Betsy would come back to herself in time. For now it was enough that the girl was there in the flesh...breathing, tangible proof of a merciful God. Betsy's return, as far as Susanna was concerned, was a miracle.

"Did you see your father where you were, my dear?" Susanna asked.

The girl blinked, unresponsive, her face smooth and white as a doll's.

"Have you been in heaven for this time, Betsy?"

No answer was given. Leaning close to her daughter, Susanna thought that the silver spirals in the child's dark eyes had become more distinct than they had been earlier.

*   *   *

Samuel and Prudence were upstairs in their room, huddled over a candle. They had been banished from the back parlor when their mother tired of them emphatically recounting what they found on Little Sorrow, and the dead that rose from the water of the cove. It wasn't that she disbelieved what they had to say about the mass resurrection, for Betsy was corporeal proof; it was more that she was mesmerized by her little miracle, and everything else was a distraction, an annoyance.

"Betsy does not speak," Prudence whispered glumly to her brother, her shadow a long wobbling thing on the slanted ceiling.

"She is like to be afflicted yet, for being dead as she was," Samuel offered, "and she is cold something terrible to the touch. Her eyes are queer—did you not see?"

Prudence nodded. "Do you expect she will be well, Samuel?"

"I suppose she may, if God desire it."

"Let us pray so," the girl said.

"Yes."

Once their prayers were sent off into the night, the candle was put out and the children settled into bed. Sleep proved elusive, for their minds were full and busy with the events of the day, the confusion and terror of witnessing dead people coming up out of the sea, then the immeasurable joy of having their dear sister returned. The great excitement, though, eventually turned into exhaustion and sleep came on.

Susanna took Betsy by the hand and led her from the family parlor, up the back staircase, a modest chamberstick lighting the way. Their shadows formed a restless mural, lurching and twisting along the wall. A fire was waiting in the austere chamber on the west side of the house. Susanna had told Samuel to ready it before he retired. She added some pieces of quick-burning birch to rouse the flames, placing a heavier log of oak on top. The room retained its heat fairly well, but Betsy's skin felt clammy, like an autumn mushroom, and Susanna could not stand the thought of her becoming sick and dying *again*. She determined to stay awake and feed the fire all night if need be.

"Here, love, let's have you good and warm," Susanna said, tucking the child in bed.

Betsy looked up with a vacant expression, her small mouth closed tightly, her pretty little face framed by the waves of golden hair that spilled out the sides of her white cap. Susanna touched her cheek. It felt damp, and cooler than a child's face ought to feel. She leaned over the bed and hugged Betsy.

"*Please* be well, my dear," Susanna pleaded. "Do not leave me again."

So as not to tempt sleep by laying down, the woman pulled a chair up by the bed and sat holding her daughter's hand. She had to keep the fire high. Betsy closed her eyes at last, and was breathing softly. This is how the hours passed, with the worried mother sitting there in her white bed gown, praying, watching over her sleeping daughter, hearing the intermittent crackling of firewood, and the cricket under the bed, singing to the moon.

The sound of footsteps stirred Susanna from her sleep. Her body ached from her day's work, from containing storms of emotion, from having dozed in a stiff wooden chair with her head hanging over her bosom. The fire had burnt low and the room was cool and nearly dark. She looked immediately to the bed, which was empty.

"Betsy?"

A slight movement caught the woman's eye and she looked to see a small half-silhouetted figure on the opposite side of the room. Betsy was naked, standing at the window, peering up at the cold white moon. The girl's bed gown was a rumpled puddle at her feet and her cap was off, freeing her hair.

"Betsy?"

The girl turned slowly at the sound of her mother's voice, eyes like silver coins gleaming in her shadowy face. She took a step and her mother rushed to meet her, grabbing her up. The girl felt like ice.

"Tell, dearest, what troubles you?"

Susanna hastily put the child back under the covers and hurried to stir the fire. She revived the flames, then sat on the edge of the bed. Betsy was on her back, staring upward, her pale face beaded with moisture. Her lips twisted as if some horrible indecisive gravity were trying to sculpt her a new mouth, and when she wheezed, her breath was like a winter wind rasping through dark Maine woods.

Susanna rushed into the next room and shook her son awake.

"Samuel, you must get up and go quickly to fetch Reverend Goodwin. Betsy is sick!"

The boy was out of bed in an instant and within moments had stockings and breeches and shirt on and was heading downstairs to grab his coat. Prudence followed her mother across the upper floor of the house, into the dim chamber where a small figure lay still on the bed. She did not appear to be breathing.

"No!" Susanna gasped.

Her hands flew up to muffle a sob and she fell to her knees by the bed. Betsy's eyes were shut, her small mouth closed.

"Dearest! Betsy, my dearest!"

The little blond girl drew a quiet breath and opened her eyes. She sat up stiffly and swiveled her head to face her mother, who, with trembling lips, smiled in relief.

The horse echoed the pounding of Samuel's heart as it galloped along the moonlit road. Pines and spruce made an amorphous tunnel around boy and beast, and here and there leaves tumbled moth-like in the cool air. The weight of the pink granite heart in his coat pocket bounced against Samuel's thigh as he bounced in the saddle. The stone felt colder than the air.

Trees gave way to open farmland. A neighbor's house stood off in the distance, small and vulnerable looking with the expansive sky above and the night fields surrounding. The lighted windows were dimmer than stars and the screams that came from the place had largely faded before reaching Samuel's ears.

The boy reined the mare to a stop and turned to look out at Benjamin Fisher's house. Were those people running outside, a number of figures heading away from the main building with another chasing after? While the half-moon provided a fair amount of light, the distance was too great, and Samuel could not be sure just what he was seeing. Whatever the case, his sister's health was more pressing to him than any troubles the Fishers might be experiencing, and so he urged the horse forward along the track.

He passed craggy blueberry barrens, and chalky slashes of birch, and a pond that might have been a great hole for all its darkness. Musket shots sounded off in the dark somewhere, and more screams shrilled through the crisp air.

The sight of the parsonage brought Samuel a feeling of relief. There was no formal doctor in Newcomb, but Rev. Goodwin was knowledgeable about many medical problems, and had helped deliver babies on a number of occasions. Besides his skill and intellect, he was a reliable and trusted friend of Susanna Hayford, and one of the few men in the vicinity who had not tried to "solace" her after the loss of her husband. If anyone could help Betsy, it was him.

The shingled Goodwin house loomed pale in the moonlight—one of the few two-story houses in the settlement. The windows gleamed strangely and a ghostly stream of wood smoke was illuminated as it left the big center chimney and dissipated in the air. Samuel tied his mare to the front gate and approached the door.

Samuel heard shouts coming from upstairs. He stepped back and looked to a second-floor window where silhouetted figures reeled past. A man's voice boomed, the voice of Rev. Goodwin.

"No, Jed!"

Samuel remembered seeing the minister's son, Jedediah, coming out of the ocean earlier that day.

A man's horrible cry followed, and then came a shrieking chorus of young Goodwins, accompanied by the reverend's wife. Samuel shuddered and found himself backing away from the house. He was close enough to hear something stepping heavily down the front stairs, and then the sound of the door latch lifting. The boy did not remain to see what came through the door; he was back on his horse and off for home.

The road took Samuel alongside the sea, but a tract of forested land stood between him and the water. He could hear the hiss of the tide as it slid in upon the granite shore. He could smell the tide, too, the saltiness blending with the damp vegetative scent of an autumn night.

He felt exhausted, though the horse was doing the work, galloping through moonlight and falling leaves and dust from the road. The landscape was hilly and the closer Samuel got to home the closer the trees closed on either side. It was the darkness of the trees that made Abner

Tilden's naked flesh stand out so starkly, that and the moonlight. The great bearded man shambled out from the tree cover and walked numbly across the track, some yards ahead of Samuel's horse. The animal came to an abrupt stop and snorted.

Tilden, who had died the week before, was a bulky mass of white but for streaks and patches of dark, glistening liquid. He was carrying something in one hand, something that might have been mistaken for an apple.

Samuel gasped. He sat frozen in his saddle as others emerged from the murky wall of trees. An old bony man, nude and stained with wet ribbons, young Polly Fisher, her mouth a great red smear under silvery eyes, Tolford Bird's son Owen, unclothed and darkly splashed. They were all oblivious to their witness, or all sated, and not interested in troubling themselves with him. Up ahead, in the distance, more figures crossed the road, all carrying apples in hand, all passing to the other side, where the woods sloped down to the Atlantic. One of these was a small girl with blood in her mussed blond hair.

When the last had gone by, Samuel spurred the horse forward to a clearing in the trees through which he could see the dead descending slowly, purposefully back into the swallowing moon-glazed sea.

The boy rode on, his heart now faster than the hooves beating beneath him. He saw his own house in the distance, the windows dark but for the restless flickers of a fireplace in the upper gable-end windows of his mother's chamber. The horse had barely stopped before he dismounted and ran around to the door that led into the kitchen.

Samuel heard weeping coming from above and fumbled his way to the back stairs. He felt a sticky wetness on the banister as he pulled himself up. A shuddery light reached weakly to the top of the stairs, seeping out through the storage area from the doorway of his mother's room. Samuel followed the mournful sobbing, going to the humble room where the ceiling conformed to the slant of the roof. His sister Prudence met him at the door, looking up with watery eyes.

"She . . . "

Samuel could see a figure sprawled across the bed in the dim room behind his sister.

"She took Mother's heart."

*   *   *

Frost had come in the night. It left odd patterns on the windows of houses, whorls and shapes like fish skeletons and blurry ferns. It faded the crimson of maple leaves and mellowed the yellowing foliage of birches. It sat on the fields like moonlight that forgot that it was day.

The survivors came together, sharing their tears and terrible stories about the recent hours, the events that would change and haunt them forever. There were dead to bury and mourning clothes to be prepared. There was a quiet that seemed to radiate like a mist from the dense woods that surrounded Newcomb.

Some had the presence of mind to speculate on the horror that had been visited upon them. It was suggested that the murderous returnees had *not* in fact been their loved ones, but emanations of an evil that spied into the villagers' hearts so as to shape monsters in the guise of their familiar dead. This theory was furthered by accounts of those who had fought against the things, a man who shot one, and several who hacked into the attackers with bladed tools, claiming that the "dead" harbored eels and sticks and mud and damp leaves inside, instead of organs, muscle, bones and blood. Most feared the creatures would return, and quite a few villagers would eventually move away.

Samuel and Prudence Hayford were taken to live with Susanna's cousin Jennet in Machias. But before leaving Newcomb, Samuel, acting on an impulse that was more intuitive than conceptual, and his sister, rowed out to Little Sorrow where the cranberries were on their bushes like petrified drops of blood and the wind hissed a briny song in the tall sentinel spruce.

They found the curious gray figure, its chest wide where Samuel had broken it, resting on the rocks above the water, where it had been before. Samuel walked out across the perilous stones and stood over the thing. He took the icy broken heart of pinkish granite from his pocket and was about to return it to where he found it, when he stopped and turned to his sister with a look of dismay. He had expected to find the old yellow bones lying there in the hollow of that strange gray encasing, but instead found a heap of wilting human hearts.

ALTERNATE ANXIETIES

Karen Jordan Allen

mortal anxiety: anxiety based in the fear of death

mortal anxiety: anxiety rooted in/stemming from the uncertainty of life

rooted, stemming—significance of organic metaphors?

Possible book titles:
    Mortal Anxiety by Katherine Smith
    The Anxiety of Mortality by Katherine Smith

BIO (or introduction?)

Katherine Smith's life has been profoundly affected by mortal anxiety. She traces this back to the age of four, when the family beagle broke its leash while Katherine's mother was walking it. The dog ran in front of a dump truck and was flattened. The family got another dog, a docile and middle-aged shelter mutt, but thereafter Katherine gave herself the job of making sure the leash was in good repair and properly fastened before the dog got out the door. She didn't trust her mother, who had already proved herself incompetent in Katherine's eyes; she didn't trust her father, who claimed not to be a "dog person" and had grumbled about the new dog; and certainly her little brother, who was only one-and-a-half, couldn't be expected to keep the family dog safe. Thus Katherine appointed herself: She Who Makes Sure Bad Things Don't Happen.

But her anxiety was such that even when she grew old enough to walk the dog, she refused, because she did not think she could bear the pain if something happened to the dog while she was on the responsible end of the leash. Still, she inspected the leash and collar every time her mother (or father, or, later, her brother) took the dog for a walk. At least, she thought, if the dog gets away and gets hurt, it won't be my fault. I've done all I can.

This continued through a succession of family dogs.

mortal anxiety comes from:

1. the impossibility of knowing whether from moment to moment we (or our loved ones) shall continue to exist

—how can I relax and wash dishes, knowing that I could die any moment of a burst brain aneurysm, or that a stray undetected asteroid could kill me and most other life on Earth, or that one day the Earth will burn to cinders in the death throes of the Sun?

—note micro-concerns (personal death) vs. macro-concerns (fate of the Earth/Universe)

2. the impossibility of knowing when the simplest of daily choices (e.g. to leave the house at 4:04 instead of 4:03 or 4:05) is a life-or-death decision

—I could die in a car accident at the treacherous Outer Ave. blinking light at 4:08 that I might have missed at 4:07 or 4:09

—so how do I/we know when to leave the house? (consider relationship to agoraphobia)

Better title: *Living with Life's Great Impossibilities* by Katerina Smythe

could choice of title be a life-or-death decision?

—I could get up from this chair now and fall down the stairs and break my neck, whereas if I ponder titles for five seconds longer I might successfully negotiate the stairs to make a cup of coffee

—likely both trips will be safe; 99,999 times out of 100,000, I won't fall, but who knows when that 100,000th time will be?

(opening chapter: "Lessons from a Dead Squirrel")
A TRUE ANECDOTE

One Thursday morning the squirrel with the broken tail, surely the same that frolicked for weeks in my back yard, dove under my Honda's right front tire as I hurried to Deer Run Community College to give a lecture on apocalypticism to my World Religions class. The squirrel met its personal apocalypse with a sickening thump. I said "oh!" in a pained voice, and glanced into my rearview mirror, hoping that the gray lump on the pavement had suffered no mortal injury, and after a stunned moment would leap up and run into Mrs. Healy's lilac bushes. But no. I could see, even as they receded in the distance, four little paws, motionless, straight up in the air.

If only I had taken my usual route to work. Normally I pulled out from my driveway and turned right, but this morning a large semi-trailer had filled most of the street in that direction, and while I likely could have gotten by it, I decided instead to go left and around the block, and I was directly opposite my own house (though with three houses and their yards between) when the doomed squirrel threw itself under my radials.

The bright sunlight that had so lifted my spirits when I stepped out of the house suddenly fell flat and harsh, illuminating both happiness and tragedy with indifference. If I had taken my usual route, the squirrel would still be frolicking, I would still be smiling to the lively Haydn sonata playing on public radio, and all would be well in my world. At least as well as it ever was. But the event shadowed my day.

Just as the beagle's escape forever shadowed my life.

the eternal moment
the moment out of time
when the universe held its breath
when the universe stopped

definition of word to be coined: that pause identified only in retrospect, immediately before the life-altering/ending event, the point or fulcrum upon which all turns, before the phone call, the knock on the door, the breaking of the leash, the leap of a squirrel, when one feels certain that the disaster could have been averted had one just been alert enough to perceive that moment and turn it aside

BIO/INTRO cont'd.

Years later Katherine would awaken in the middle of the night, remembering the moment when the beagle strained at the leash, just before the leash snapped and the dog leapt away. That she could not go back and fix the leash, stop the disaster, change the story, seemed not only unfair, but wrong—as if she had been shoved in error into a fake world, a counterfeit world, a world that was a mistake. Somewhere, somehow, she thought, the dog must still be alive and happy.

the alternate universe theory: in some science fiction (and some science), it is posited that events may have more than one outcome, with each outcome spinning off its own universe, so that millions of universes are generated each day; perhaps the squirrel with the broken tail and/or the flattened beagle frolic still in some of those universes

—equally possible: I lie dead, having noticed the squirrel a half-second earlier, twisted my steering wheel to avoid it, and rammed myself into a tree

am I *in* an "alternate" universe? alternate to what?

A DISTRACTION/DISLOCATION

Mother called, told me to sit down. "They" found a lump (I didn't even know she was going for her mammogram); "they're" going to do a biopsy. But it's small, don't worry, it's a long way from Maine to California, it would be expensive. Your father and brother and his wife are all here, they'll look after me, I'll be fine. (But what about me? I'm not fine with this at all, I want to be there. No, that's not true, I don't want to be there, I don't want to be in this universe. But if I have to be, I want to be there, not here, not alone, waiting.)

the moment: there it was, before I answered the phone, distracted, absorbed in making my coffee, contemplating my book

I might have turned it aside, but I missed it —

what if I determine to be alert to those moments, those fulcrum moments (ah! a name!), those pauses in existence before the universe bifurcates, and bifurcates again?

eternal bifurcations
eternal, infinite bifurcations

take this universe back, please, I would like another—

(chapter title: "The Fulcrum Moment")
ANOTHER MOMENT MISSED

At the Goodwill store the skirts are jammed so tightly I can hardly wedge my hand between them. The metal skirt clips on the hangers catch on one another, locking all the skirts into a long, solid row. I wonder who hangs them, how they think customers can possibly browse with pleasure when they risk physical injury just getting the damn clothes off the rack.

Irritated, but determined not to be defeated, I claw at the hangers with both hands and force open a few inches of space. I jam my elbow against the skirts on the left and check the size of one on the right, a pretty thing of peach-colored chiffon. Yes, a 10. Just the thing to match a jacket I found here last week.

Then I see the blood well up under a flap of skin on my right index finger. It oozes out, trickles down my nail, and hangs perilously, a swelling crimson droplet.

With my other hand I dig in my pocket for a tissue. I catch the blood just as it falls. The peach-colored chiffon is saved.

In my mental rearview mirror, I glimpse again—belatedly—the moment, the fulcrum moment when in frustration and impatience I grabbed the hangers—not a mortal moment, but still. In another universe, I am already in the dressing room trying the skirt on.

I check to see if I left flesh or blood on the metal skirt clips. No, but the clips are discolored, rusty. Thoreau's brother died of tetanus after cutting himself with a rusty razor. I try to remember whether my tetanus booster is up-to-date. With a free-flowing wound like this, the danger is minimal. But what a bizarre and banal death that would be.

In another universe—

Perhaps a mortal moment, after all.

therapeutic value of the alternate universe theory:

—a sophisticated illusion (?) to help us manage the pain of uncertainty/finality

—helpful only if we believe we can choose the "better" universe (or does just the vision of, say, the squirrel still frolicking *somewhere* ease our pain?)

—not a defense against the eventuality of death, unless we posit universes of impossibly old people (and squirrels and beagles)

but mortal anxiety =/= anxiety about death
—the "good" death, quiet in bed at ninety or one hundred, that one is "ready" for (at least some have said they are ready); that death does not inspire mortal anxiety
—the young death, the accidental death, the "wrong" death that comes before we are finished, before we even know who we are; and the impossibility of foreseeing and avoiding that death, of controlling the terms of our existence—

New title: *Mortal Anxiety and the Alternate Universe* by E. K. Smythe (would appeal to multiple markets: psychology, philosophy, science, science fiction; the cover needn't tell that E. K. is a woman—if that matters)

BIO/INTRO cont'd.
Mortal, or existential, anxiety destroyed Katherine's marriage of five years to "Steve." He knew of her anxiety when he married her, but neither thought that it would come between them and having a family. "Steve" dreamed of becoming a father. At first Katherine wanted children, too, despite her terror of taking on responsibility for their safety (if she couldn't trust herself with a dog—then a child?). Then their friends "Bridget" and "Dennis" lost their infant son to the flu. Every year a few, very few, children succumb unpredictably to influenza; theirs was one. Katherine had never seen such intense grief. She kept waiting for time to bring healing, but it didn't. "Bridget" sank into depression. "Dennis" sought distraction in an affair. They divorced. "Bridget" moved in with her parents and spent her spare time drinking.

A bottomless well of anxiety opened up in Katherine's heart. How would she ever survive such a horrendous loss? She knew that people did, that not everyone destroyed themselves or their marriages. Some families circled, like wagons, embracing each other until they could move on. But could she?

"Steve" mourned the loss of his friends' child, even tried to help them patch up their marriage. He spoke with Katherine of the risk of that awful pain, the risk of loving as a parent loves. Still, his longing to be a parent survived his contemplation of the risk. Katherine admired his bravery, but could not find it in herself. "Steve" finally left. Now he has a new wife and a six-month-old son. He is happy. Katherine is glad he is happy. But when she contemplates having her own children she falls back into that terrible well of anxiety and only by promising herself childlessness forever can she pull herself out.

how can I with words open up that bottomless well?

perhaps I should keep it covered and let those who can maintain their illusions keep them

or is it the well itself that offers a way into other universes?

(chapter title: "Creating the Alternate Universe/s")
A TEST SITUATION

My mother awaits—hence I await—the biopsy results. I go online to check prices to fly to California. Then I realize this is the ideal test situation. How many universes can I create, spin off, as I make my reservations? I select "search by price" for a Boston–LA flight and am rewarded with a plethora of possibilities. Overwhelmed, I should say. Which airline? Which day? Which flight? My life will turn out differently depending on the choice—perhaps only a little differently, perhaps a lot. Perhaps end. But I cannot tell unless I peer into those other universes.

I select a date at random, choose another a week later, look for a flight leaving neither too early nor too late. I take it all the way up to "Click to buy ticket" and my hand freezes over the computer. This is it, a fulcrum moment, I can buy or not.

And even if I buy, I can go or not.

Which life, which universe do I choose? To buy this ticket, go on this flight? To buy this ticket, then choose later whether to go or not? To start over?

I hold my hand motionless, letting my thoughts pour into the moment and fill it, nudging me into this universe or that. Or at least opening a tiny window, a hatch, into other possible universes, so that I know what I am choosing.

The universes close up tight.

Tell me, God, tell me what to do.
God, as usual, is silent. Or not there.

segue to: "God and Mortal Anxiety"
    —are there universes in which God is, and universes in which He/She is not? or universes with many Gods? or one God for many universes?
    —religious people have been found to be happier, less depressed, less anxious; check research
    —is it the belief in God as such, or the existential certainty that accompanies such belief, that relieves anxiety?
    —atheists are likewise certain; are they less anxious?
    —agnostics, the uncertain, the know-nots: if uncertainty breeds anxiety, then anxiety must trail them like a hungry dog

(yet more) BIO/INTRO

Because Katherine teaches religion, her students—and others—assume her to be a religious person. She is a religious person in the sense that the deep questions of life concern her greatly, and she seeks the subjective responses of religion and philosophy, not just the objective answers of science. But so far her studies have shed no light on the question of God. Despite—or perhaps because of—years of religious study, Katherine finds herself a thoroughgoing agnostic. Faith in God and the prospect of heaven, being unreal to her, can neither comfort her nor calm her anxiety.

could it be belief in heaven, rather than spiritual certainty or belief in God, that relieves mortal anxiety?
    —heaven: a kind of alternate universe accessible primarily through death, perhaps also through trance or vision
    —carrying heavy moral weight (unlike most other alternate universes)
    —pre-existent to this universe? i.e. not a result of bifurcations of it or of universes preceding; or perhaps a very early bifurcation

but a universe accessible by death is not therapeutically useful when the interior aim is to *avoid* untimely death ways other than death to access alternate universes:

—inward: meditation, hypnosis, trance, aided by fasting, drugs, pain

—outward: specialized technology (not yet known), travel at a particular speed or direction, key geographical points/gateways, transitional objects

is *belief* in the alternate universe necessary to reach it (as perhaps to reach heaven)?

—then the agnostic is doomed; neither science nor theology can save her

(unless in writing this book I find a way—)

AN OUTSIDE TRIP

Despite Katherine's anxieties, she persists in the belief that only total immersion in the vagaries of life will eventually bring security. She knows she thinks too much. To get out of her head, out of her anxieties, she goes to the supermarket. Instead of imagining the universes that may be splitting off as she chooses to take this road instead of that, this parking space instead of that, this shopping cart instead of that, she focuses on the tastes she plans to bring home: mango, pineapple, strawberries. Plain first, then with vanilla yogurt, then whipped with a little sugar and spice into an East Indian lassi.

Her mouth waters.

The man in front of her in the checkout line has a basket full of hamburger, a dozen packages. None have been put into a protective plastic bag, although these are provided in the meat section. When Katherine buys hamburger, she pulls a plastic bag over her hand like a glove, picks up the package of meat, then pulls the bag back up, never touching the original plastic-wrap packaging. Who knows, a little juice might have dripped out, a little meat spilled, bacteria-filled, contaminated.

Katherine has never contracted food poisoning at home.

She watches the man load the hamburger onto the conveyor belt, notices the wet spot underneath when he shifts the packages to make room for more, a crumb of red that might have oozed out of the plastic-wrap. She looks at her mango and pineapple (there were no strawberries today). Alternate universes spin before her: Despite the hamburger, nothing happens, she washes everything thoroughly and stays well. Or she has a touch of food poisoning, recovers. Or she dies of a new modern virulent form of E. coli. Or—

She excuses herself from the line, mumbling something about a forgotten item. But she forgot nothing. On the contrary, she remembers too much. She heads for another line, stops in her tracks. Who's to say the customer three or four places ahead of her, already in the parking lot, didn't leave the cashier's hands and the conveyor belt already contaminated?

She decides to go back to the produce department for plastic bags for her fruit. Then she spots a cashier spritzing her station with disinfectant, wiping everything down, switching on the light that says the lane is open. Katherine scurries over, stepping in front of a slow old man with a package of pork chops. She smiles apologetically; he nods and his eyes twinkle. She puts the mango and pineapple onto a conveyor belt, which still glistens with disinfectant. She will wash them before cutting them up, before closing her mouth around their incomparable sweetness. But she feels confident that even if the washing is not perfect, the fruit will not sicken her in this universe she has chosen/created.

If she gets sick, it will not be her fault. She has done what she can.

creating the secure universe: the aspiration of the mortally anxious

their ritual objects: plastic bags, helmets, antibacterial sprays, locks, alarms, sensors, diagnostic tests, seatbelts, organic foods, insurance policies

limits on creation of the "safe" universe:
    —ability to choose universes by taking precautions is limited to hazards which can be foreseen and prevented
    —for unforeseen/unforeseeable events, the only chance to choose lies in catching that moment, the fulcrum moment
    —but *how* to access other universes through that moment?

A REAL TEST

The phone rings. Katherine puts down the fork with mango still skewered upon it, reaches for the phone, pauses with her hand extended. She senses her mother at the other end of the line, tries to picture her face: relieved? devastated? worried but hopeful? This is it, the moment, she feels it, she *knows* it. How does she turn it aside? By never answering the phone? By answering in this moment rather than the next, by waiting another ring? By closing her eyes and taking some inward turn in her mind? By clicking her heels, turning left three times, saying "abracadabra"?

She sweats, she fights tears, but she cannot move her mind/self/reality into position to leap/fall/dissolve from this universe into another. She feels herself toppling into the well of anxiety, but rallies and lifts the phone. Hello.

Hello. Her mother's voice is strained. She wastes no time. "It" is malignant. She will have surgery right away. The doctor is hopeful. But—

Katherine watches the moment recede in her rear-view mental mirror, feels herself sitting at the bifurcation of universes—they split and split again into a great cauliflower-like fractal of possibilities, of realities—innumerable universes exploding from the moment and mushrooming up and out (those organic metaphors again) in great clouds.

In which universe does her mother die soon, die later, respond to treatment, not respond, go into remission, experience a complete cure?

Katherine hangs onto the phone, the tips of her fingers whiten. She wishes she could reach out and grab onto the "good" universes, let them pull her along and her mother with her, into a place where squirrels still frolic and beagles play and, if she cannot avoid all pain, at least she can exercise some choice about which pain to experience and which to let go.

But the universes slip from her hands like so many silken cords. She clings to the one that remains, praying, with all that is within her, that this is the right one, the one where she belongs, and that the pain will not be more than she—than I—can bear.

THE CHAPTER OF THE HAWK OF GOLD

Noreen Doyle

Two hundred years have peeled paint, broken shingles, and cracked the granite step of the shed that houses the Healy Tompkins Museum. The beams are sound, the floor solid, and most of the glass original. Everything in the museum is in this same state: whole inside, broken only outside.

Periodically the Ladies of the Pithom Historical Society make these outsides someone's business. Jenny Alcock feared that it would happen to her someday. Her mother doesn't attend the Historical Society; her father drives for an out-of-town vending company owned by an old French family. Who else at Pithom Independent High School is better suited for the task? Everyone else has their excuses: camp, job, summer school, parents with influence. It is a long, solitary task, and she protests. But even her own mother insists. It will keep Jenny out of trouble.

Askew on the wall hang amber-colored panoramics of uniformed men, with names scrawled in what looks like white ink. In one cabinet, a Down East sailor's ropework valentine beds down beside a carved lacquer cup stand from China. A thin, balding rug from Ghiordes carpets the floor in faded Turkish red and yellow. A Spanish silver candlestick, supplied with a beeswax candle, occupies a George I burl walnut side table. (So the labels say.) The silver is tarnished, and alternating seasons of damp summer heat and dry winter cold have split the walnut veneer.

To Jenny such decay is at once opulent and familiar. At home, linoleum peels away from the floorboards, hard water has pitted and stained the stainless-steel sink, pink sheets are mended with blue thread. Thumbtacks hold sun-faded Polaroids to a wall. They have no names written on them. No one in Jenny's home (except maybe Jenny, now and then) ever cares about these things. The Ladies of the Pithom Historical Society, however, do worry about dust and tarnish, at least now and then. It is the only tolerable thing about them. Jenny just wishes that they would care for someone other than Healy Tompkins, at least now and then.

Healy Tompkins was a paper-mill baron and traveler almost a hundred years ago. He went often to Egypt on business and made pilgrimages to most of the Christian shrines in Jerusalem, of which she finds old photographs in a steamer trunk. One cabinet is devoted to such things as "Sliver of the True Cross" and "Saint Peter's Tympanum." But of all Healy Tompkins's Egyptian travels, this museum holds only one souvenir.

The label, pounded out on an old Underwood that cut out all the o's, reads: Hawk Mummy. Late Period. Purchased Cairo, 1889.

Covered in dust as thick as gray felt, it feels light, like the paper-mâché parrot she made in seventh grade. Light as a bird.

A wooden mask, once gilded but now mostly bare, encases the head. Jenny pities it, wings all linen-bound, and she always dusts it twice each week.

Why had Healy Tompkins returned to Pithom, Maine, of all the places in the world he could have gone? Jenny thinks about this while she wipes the bull's-eye window panes and soon decides that his mill and his bank accounts and his big house must have been enough for him. Those days, however, are long past. The paper mill is a ruin.

Why did any Alcock—once millwrights, now painters and carpenters and truckers—ever stay?

Jenny envies her father and the company truck, his road trips to Portland's shopping centers, its airport, all its people. Each time he went out, she thinks as she props a stereoview of the Wailing Wall on a shelf, it was a little like Healy Tompkins's pilgrimages.

Her father has spent a lot of time away lately, although Portland is scarcely an hour's drive from Pithom, and last night her parents fought about that. This morning her mother, still in pink curlers and white feathered slippers, followed him out into the dooryard. Was he coming home tonight? Of course, he said, he always came home (although he had not been home the night before last). He was sorry, he was so very sorry, Ellen, Ellen, it was nothing, nothing at all, just one night. Then they kissed, memory of their harsh words swept away by promises and I'm-sorries.

Jenny, whom no one balms with promises or I'm-sorries, does not, cannot, forget. Memory of what has happened coats her like dirt.

She dusts the hawk—poor thing—for the third time this week, wishing that someone, just someone, would do as much for her someday.

As the ceiling fan vibrates the overhead light, the hawk winks its black glass eyes.

The Ladies of the Pithom Historical Society usually arrive at four.

Someone from the Maine State Museum will be visiting, they say and run a white glove across the glass display cases, put a cotton wad on a yardstick and thrust it down behind shelves. This won't be like your parents' trailer, they say. It's to be cleaned and polished, the panoramics of Union soldiers will hang so evenly that Mrs. Egars will be able to balance a pea on top. The same grade of paper will be used for each label, all t's crossed, i's dotted, and p's and q's properly tidy, that's how it's to be you little snot.

One of these inspections dislodges a sheet of brown paper behind the mummy.

Which leaps from its shelf.

Mrs. Egars jumps two feet straight. Madame President Wallace shrieks and throws herself to the floor, but the hawk follows. It is five minutes before everyone has calmed down enough to see that Mrs. Egars knocked it over with the yardstick.

For all its hard fall, the hawk mummy's glass eyes stare as brightly as ever, looking proud of its first flight in more than two thousand years.

The Ladies of the Pithom Historical Society leave early that day.

The paper, written by Healy Tompkins, is headed: Book of the Dead, Chapter LXXVII. Transforming to Hawk of Gold. Am I, it goes in English beneath Egyptian hieroglyphs, rise I from secret place like hawk of gold coming from egg his. Fly I like hawk of cubits seven across back his. Be glorious I.

The English is fractured, as if he'd written drunk (wouldn't that shock the Ladies of the Pithom Historical Society!), but the writing is businesslike. The hieroglyphs marching between the lines of English are neat and tidy and precisely drawn.

She likes it. More than two thousand years ago some ancient Egyptian had felt exactly the way she feels. Unlike her mother (who again this morning went out to the dooryard in pink curlers, the feathers of her slippers now tattered and brown), Jenny Alcock is going to leave behind this town and make something of herself. She will be free and with her she will take no dusty excuses, no filthy I'm-sorries.

Having dusted the hawk again, she turns to the panoramics. She sees typically Egars noses, the broad hands of Mackees. In all these years they have not changed. The new Wallaces look like the old Wallaces. Even in some Great-Great-Great-Uncle Somebody Alcock she can see a reflection of herself and she shivers. But there are no Tompkinses in Pithom. Not anymore.

Soon perhaps there will be no new Alcocks in Pithom, either. Because, unlike her father (who again this morning said he was sorry, Ellen, and promised that of course he would be home tonight), when Jenny leaves, she will never come back.

On an old Underwood she types new labels, hitting the o gently, so as not to cut out the letters. She tends to the photographs first, then to the sailor's valentine. Lastly she taps out a new label for Hawk Mummy. Late Period. Purchased Cairo, 1889.

But what, then, about the paper written out by Healy Tompkins? The poem should be written better, and she will, and play a trick on the Ladies of the Pithom Historical Society.

With pen and ink and old brown paper from Healy Tompkins's writing desk, she meticulously practices his handwriting. For an entire week, twenty minutes each day, she practices the long loops of his g's, the firm dots of his i's, the miserly crosses of his t's. Satisfied at last by her progress, she buries these papers in Mr. Mackee's pile of leaves, knowing that they will be ashes before noon.

Today she will rewrite Healy Tompkins's poem.

"A Translation, in His Own Hand," a label will say. "Found by Mrs. Charles Egars."

The Ladies of the Pithom Historical Society will look foolish when someone from the State Museum notices that the ink is fresh. Jenny's mother will punish her for making trouble, but Jenny doesn't care. As soon as she is finished, she will fly away from Pithom and this museum and her parents' fights and everything. She is ready. Knapsack, one-way bus ticket to Portland, woolen jacket, and extra pair of sneakers wait by the door.

The hawk mummy winks at her with black glass eyes, although by now it is late October and the ceiling fan isn't on and the light hangs perfectly still.

It is not much of a poem, but she likes it anyway. Shabby outside, its strength lies within its words.

Jenny knows the power of words. She has heard her father work them upon her mother: I'm sorry, Ellen, I didn't mean it, she doesn't mean anything to me, it won't happen again, I'll come home tonight. Words make what he says true, even when it happens again.

But no one offers Jenny apologies to brush away the gray mat of lies that mantle her shoulders. They don't care about the filth. Do they even see it? No matter. If no one will remove it, she will escape it. She will escape it and never look back to Pithom and will never need to look back because before her will lie the entire rest of the world. Someone, somewhere, will care.

She writes in her best Healy Tompkins hand:

> I AM!
> May I rise from this tomb
> like a hawk of gold
> coming forth from his egg,
> May I fly on wings seven cubits wide
> and I will be GLORIOUS!

Before she can complete the exclamation point, the pen shoots across the shed as a spasm tears through her wrist. The inkwell tips and brown-black ink streams off the burl walnut desk onto the Ghiordes rug, which drinks it in.

It is nearly four o'clock.

Fear knots her stomach and arms and legs, which cramp with terror because soon the Ladies will be here; but no, it is something deeper than fear. It is something that knots up her bones and her skin and her arteries and her hair and reweaves them from the inside.

Legs shorten and twist, fingers lengthen, toes extend, a feather sprouts from each follicle.

She has wings to spread!

They are fast against her side, but she has wings and will fly. Far below will Pithom be, she will come forth from this tomb. Away from the Ladies of the Pithom Historical Society and away from her parents, Jenny Alcock will become glorious.

The shed is too small for her wings; they remain fast. The spell says seven cubits, which Jenny suddenly realizes must be very large. How big is a cubit? Outside there would be room for seven cubits, and more. Jenny takes a step forward toward the window and the wide world beyond. And cannot.

She is linen-bound.

To one side of her sits a fragment of wood and above it a label: Sliver of the True Cross. At her feet is another label, its o's gently typed: Hawk Mummy. Late Period. Purchased Cairo, 1889.

Jenny finds herself stared upon by herself. But this other girl who has Jenny's face and Jenny's shoes and Jenny's hair has eyes that are too shiny, too black, like polished glass.

This glass-eyed-thing with Jenny's face speaks in a language thick and throaty with age. Jenny cannot understand it, but she recognizes the words. Hieroglyphs have sound in them, and this is that sound.

The thing with Jenny's face throws open a window with bull's-eye panes. Wind flashes through the shed, tearing gently typed labels from their pins, shattering cabinet doors, snowing dust over shelves and tumbling precious, ancient relics: the tympanum of Saint Peter, the sailor's valentine, the hawk mummy.

As Jenny falls she shrieks, or would shriek, if her beak were not bound up like her wings.

The thing with Jenny's face replaces hawk-mummy Jenny carefully upon the shelf, dusts the linen wrappings and the wooden mask, and winks.

And flies out the window on wings seven cubits wide.

THE BUNG-HOLE CAPER

Thomas A. Easton

The aliens came to Earth the same spring that Cyrus Holmes found the old barrel. It was buried under a stack of old lumber in a dark corner of the barn, and it would have stayed buried if Cyrus hadn't been looking for his grandfather's tool chest. Grandpa had been a cooper all his life, and when he was gone, the tools had been stored away. They included a cooper's adze, which Cyrus thought might be just the thing for roughing out a new plow handle.

He found the adze. Once sharpened, it worked as well as he had hoped. He also found the barrel, and that was in rather worse shape. It had been drying for half a century, forgotten in the shadows, and its staves now fitted as badly as fence pickets. But a month or two in the pond would fix that, he told Allie, his wife. Then he could replace the hoops and have a decent vessel to harden his cider in.

All through that summer, Cyrus tended the barrel. He soaked the wood in pond water, watching the wood swell and tighten. He replaced the hoops with cobblings from his workbench. He stood the thing in the yard, filled it from the hose, and watched as the last leaks slowed and stopped. Finally, it was as tight as it would ever be, and the apples in his small orchard weren't quite ready.

In the meantime, there were the aliens. Cyrus knew all about them. He didn't have a tractor or a chain saw or an electric milker. He worked his fields with a yoke of oxen, cut his firewood with an axe, and milked his dozen cows by hand. Still, he was up-to-date enough. He had a car, for getting to church of a Sunday and so Allie could drive to her job in town. He had a radio or two. He even had a teevee set, and he never missed the six-thirty news.

He knew all about the aliens. He'd seen pictures of them, all smothered in pastel-patterned coal-scuttle helmets, like something out of a movie about the Great War. He'd heard they were refugees from some foreign disaster or war, and he knew they were asking for a place to settle in the ocean shallows, promising not to interfere with navigation or fishing—they farmed their food on land—and offering to trade. They had science beyond anything Earth knew, they had technology, and they had a price list. The space for a small colony, a little place to call their own, for instance, was worth the plans for a space drive. Help in settling in was worth a map to worlds that men could live on. Other things were worth money, credits that could be exchanged for travel tickets, for lesser goods, even for alien encyclopedias, suitably translated. Earth was drooling.

Cyrus thought it all interesting enough, but he was a farmer, a raw-boned, weathered outcropping of Maine's coastal hills. The aliens scarcely touched his life, and they never would, any more than the rest of modern life did. Too, he'd never seen an alien. Not many people had, for though they traveled plenty, they did it in closed black limousines, chauffered by UN flunkies.

Cyrus—he hated being called "Cy" so much that anyone who dared be so familiar might get day-old eggs or half-soured milk—Cyrus put the aliens on a par with Florida hurricanes and California floods and Detroit strikes. They were all interesting. They all made the news. And he thought about them only when they crossed the flickering screen of his teevee set.

But the day came, it did. His apples ripened, and he gathered up the falls and picked the rest. He set a basket of the best down cellar for winter eating, helped Allie put up two dozen jars of applesauce, and filled the trailer with the bags and boxes that remained. Then he visited the cider mill.

The mill was Bob Witham's. An ancient rig of flapping belts and groaning gears, powered by a gasoline engine, it was nearly as decrepit as its toothless, flatulent owner. But it made good cider.

Cyrus binned his apples and watched the endless belt haul them up the chute to the grinder. As old Bob paddled the pulp into the burlapped flats for the press, Cyrus said, "Got a barrel now." He had to roar to be heard above the machinery.

Bob glanced up from his work. "Good for you."

"Ayuh. Old one. Found it out in the barn."

"Hope it's tight," Bob held up a hand to examine a gob of apple pulp sticking to a thumb. He licked it off. "Good apples this year, Cyrus."

"Should hope so. M'nured the bejeezus out of 'em. Soaked the barrel, too."

"Oughta do it. Stand back now." Bob threw a switch, and the grinder overhead groaned into silence. He flipped the last fold of burlap into place, laid a flat on top, and leaned into the pile of neatly wrapped squares of pulp. They rolled into the press on their dolly and jolted to a stop. He hauled on the lever that lowered the immense plate of the press into position. He flipped the lever that fed power to the belt that drove the press's screw. The screw turned. The plate mashed down. Juice spurted from the flats, collected in the gutters, and was pumped to the holding tank on the wall above their heads.

"Where's that cup?" asked Cyrus. Bob turned to point at the wall. There hung, just as it did every fall, a battered dipper. Once it had been enameled gray and blue. Now it was mostly rust, but Cyrus didn't mind. He took it off its nail and held it to catch the dripping cider. He drank deeply, and then he offered it to Bob. "It's good."

"Ayuh. Barrel'll do it more good'n them plastic jugs of yours, too."

"Hope so." The juice was sweet and tart, yet not too tart. Once hardened and settled, it would have a decent kick to it.

When the last drop of juice had left the press, Cyrus fetched his jugs from the car. They were the five-gallon inflatable things the hardware store sold to campers. Cyrus had found them good for cider, for maple sap at sugaring-off time, even for hauling water in dry spells. Now he puffed them open and held them under the hose from the holding tank. They filled slowly, since the hose was none too big, but he was in no great hurry. The cows would need milking when he got home, but they could wait for half an hour. Sixty gallons of cider was well worth a little patience.

He didn't unload the trailer till after supper. Between milking the cows in the pasture and the other chores, he had no time, and even then he didn't have enough. The barrel was in the barn, resting on its side, the bung-hole neatly plugged, its filling port on top and open. He ranged his jugs beside it. Then he selected one and took it into the house. "Fresh cider," he said to Allie. "Want a glass?" She did. They drank. They filled a pitcher for the fridge and put the rest in smaller jugs for the freezer. It would keep there, and they would have it for their grandchildren, for nieces and nephews, for themselves whenever they didn't care for hard cider. "I'll put the rest in the barrel tomorrow," he told his wife, "That's soon enough."

They refilled their glasses then, took them into their small living room, and turned on the news. And there were the aliens again, big as life. It seemed the French had sent them a case of wine. They liked it, asked for more, and paid, generously. "Our guests," said the teevee announcer, "have said they will pay for whatever they want. And we want their money, for only with it can we buy the wonders they have to sell. The trick has been finding things they want. We are very different creatures, with different tastes and different needs, and they are far ahead of us in technology. Too many of the things we make, they can make better, and they have less desire for our handicrafts than we have for Indian pots and blankets. After all, we aren't related." The announcer smiled, showing well-kept teeth.

Cyrus grunted. Allie said, "Maybe they would like your cider."

Cyrus grunted again. "Doubt it. 'Tain't wine, is it?" She agreed. Cider was a country thing that rarely appealed even to most humans, living as they did in cities. Most folks preferred wine and beer. Why should the super-civilized aliens be any different?

First thing next morning, as soon as the milking was done, Cyrus headed for the barn. He wanted to get his cider into his barrel, get it working with a touch of baker's yeast, get it started toward his favorite brew. But when he entered the barn, the barrel was not as he had left it. The bung hole was no longer plugged, and the barrel itself had rolled a bit.

He scratched his head. Had someone come last night to steal some cider? No. All the jugs were there, just as full as he had left them. He swore.

When the barrel twitched, he swore again. When he saw a movement behind the unplugged bung-hole, he did it once more. Damn! His cider barrel, that he was counting on to give him better drink, was occupied. A rat? A mouse? It was late in the year for snakes, and birds would never enter such a place.

There was a sound, like a watery voice. The movement repeated, and a ropy thing, a tentacle, emerged from the bung-hole. With difficulty, he realized what he had. An alien. Of all things. What was it doing here? Where was its chauffeur? Where was its shell? He traded his puzzlement for a growing anger. What right did it have to take over his barrel, to deny him proper cider?

The tentacle wriggled. "Please, excuse," the voice burbled, echoing within the barrel. "Shell, too-small. Abandoned, vehicle. Seek, other."

Cyrus hunkered down. He peered into the bung-hole, trying to make out a detail or two. It was too dark in there, but he glimpsed what might have been an eye, a damp hide, a lobsterish mouth. By all accounts, the things were harmless enough. He didn't fear, and his anger was fading, already giving way to fascination.

The tentacle writhed. It tapped the end of the barrel above the bung-hole. It tapped twice, once to either side. "Make," the voice burbled again. "Holes. Eyes." It tapped below, along the barrel's curving flank. "Legs."

There was a pause while Cyrus thought it over. The creature didn't speak the language well, but it could get its wishes across well enough. Cyrus knew what it wanted, all right. But he knew, too, that boring all those holes would ruin the barrel. He'd be stuck with plastic cider for another year, and maybe longer. Finally, the voice spoke again. "Will, pay," it said.

That was another matter. "All right," said Cyrus. "Though I want to know why you chose my barrel." He stood and headed for his workbench. He found his electric drill and the hole saw. He added over his shoulder, "How big you want the holes?"

When the voice said, "This," he turned to watch the tentacle sketch a two-inch circle. Fine, he thought. The saw could handle that. He plugged in the extension cord and fetched his equipment back to the barrel. "Back off, now," he said. The tentacle withdrew, and he pulled the trigger. The saw bit and whined, once, twice, and the alien had eye holes. As he sat back on his heels, the eyes appeared. They were on stalks, and they were extended a good six inches out the holes. "Thank," the alien said. "See, now." The voice still burbled, but it echoed less. The new holes made a difference.

"Now," said Cyrus. The barrel wasn't really ruined yet. He could always fit a new top to it. But now. . . . "Where do you want those leg holes?"

Once more the tentacle emerged. It lengthened, more than he would have guessed possible, and it pointed. The saw whined again, six times, and the job was done. Or was it? Cyrus thought a moment and said, "You want more room around that arm of yours?" When the tentacle quickly sketched an oblong around the bung-hole, he obliged.

He rose, put his tools away, and returned. The head of his barrel now reminded him of nothing more than a Halloween pumpkin, all eyes and mouth, though no pumpkin ever had stalked eyes and a mouthful of wormy tentacles. No pumpkin had legs, either, shiny and lobsterish, emerging from holes in its bottom. And no pumpkins walked, with a lurching, rocking gait, sideways across the barn floor. It struck him then, that the aliens resembled hermit crabs, wearing borrowed shells and moving into larger ones as they grew. He wondered if a real hermit crab might try a pumpkin.

He watched as the alien exercised its limbs. It crawled, it ran, it even capered as it grew used to its new shell, but it remained clumsy. A barrel just wasn't built to walk. Finally, it settled again, facing Cyrus, and burbled, "Thank."

Cyrus almost grinned. He prided himself on rarely going into a flap, no matter what the crisis. And he had a crisis here, for sure. An alien, away from its people, free of its human guides and chauffeurs. It would have to go back, of course. It would probably want to, unless it preferred a holiday among the natives. In the meantime, well. . . . "Mind if I call you Hermit?"

There was no answer. He added, "It's time to talk, you know. Why my barrel?"

The tentacles withdrew. In a moment they returned to scatter a handful of plastic strips on the floor before the man. The alien money. One tentacle retained a strip and held it up. "Pay. New, shell. Food?"

"Soon," said Cyrus. "But first, why?" Damn, he thought. It's got me doing it, too. Though it's not hard. We do talk that way here, a bit.

"Found, first." The alien's burble was somehow plaintive. "Hungry."
Cyrus said nothing. After a moment, the alien went on. "Grow, we.
Shells, change, always. Small, natural. Bigger, smarter, plastic. Change,
must. Too-weak, not. Too-soft."

Cyrus stared intently, thinking, beginning to see. . . . He was interrupted by a gasp. He turned, and there was Allie, a hand to her mouth, an
apron around her waist. "I wanted the eggs," she said. "What's that?"

He told her. She scooched beside him, staring, too. "They grow all
their lives," he said. "Move into bigger shells as they grow. It says they get
smarter, too. I guess the brain must get bigger as they grow."

She nodded. Her gray hair bobbed. Her thin lips pursed. She smelled
of the kitchen and soap. Her thigh was soft against his haunch, and he remembered. . . . The past, their past, was far from dead, but though he
still loved her, she wasn't the girl he had married, the girl who had left
him for college and then returned for a farmer's life. She said, murmuring, "I suppose it must have been learning how to build their own shells
that let them get smart enough for civilization, then."

"Skin," the alien burbled. "Wood. Metal. Plastic. Food?"

"What would you like?" asked Allie.

"Egg? Cheese? Potato, mash?"

"Right away." She rose to her feet, as graceful as ever, and headed toward the back of the barn and the door to the hen house. In a minute she
was back, an egg in her hand. She laid it down before the barrel. A tentacle enfolded it and hauled it within. There was a crunch and a sound of
sucking. "Thank."

"They aren't very big today, are they?" said Allie. She left again.
While she was gone, Cyrus peered through the widened bung-hole. Despite the holes, it was still dark in there, and he had to lean close to make
out the broken egg, cradled in a nest of tentacles beneath a writhing mass
of mouthparts. He leaned too close, in fact, for when the alien was done,
the discarded shell bounced off his brow. He rocked back on his haunches
with a muttered curse. "No manners," he said. "None at all."

"Whatever do you mean?" asked Allie. She was back, standing behind
him, her apron sagging with the weight of eight more eggs. "Maybe you
shouldn't have been prying. I imagine it likes its privacy as much as we
do."

"Then it should have stood at home."

"Enough of that, Cyrus!" She scooched beside the barrel and laid her eggs down on the floor. She held one out toward the bung-hole. "Would you like another?"

"Thank." A tentacle plucked the egg from her grasp. There was another crunching, sucking sound. She added, "It's a stranger, Cyrus. Away from home, and it probably doesn't know how it's going to get back. We should be nice to it."

"I suppose we should, Allie." They had always been as hospitable as they knew how, with friends and strangers alike. Every winter saw at least one stranded motorist warming himself before their stove and dining at their table, even passing the night in their guest-room bed. But never before had they hosted a stranger as strange as this one. "But I am curious."

"I know. I don't think anyone's seen them naked."

The alien had obviously been listening. "No," it burbled, discarding the second eggshell. "Fear. Eat, be. Call? Phone?"

"You want us to call your friends? At the UN?"

"Yes. Please. Thank."

As they stood, another egg disappeared into the bung-hole. "I'll just leave them all," said Allie. "The poor thing's probably hungry."

"Enough, now. Take."

"All right." Allie gathered up the remaining eggs, and they turned to leave, thinking the alien would stay put. But as Cyrus was holding the door to the kitchen for his wife, they heard a scrabbling behind them. They looked, and there was the barrel, lurching along on six shiny legs, stalked eyes waving as they took in the yard, the car, the oxen behind their rail fence.

"We haven't had a dog for years," said Cyrus. "Wish we could keep it."

"Cyrus!"

The word got out, of course. By the time the limousine arrived, the yard was choked with neighbors, townsfolk, and local reporters. There was even a wire-service helicopter in the pasture. Their alien was the center of attention, and it was loving it. It burbled happily away, posing for pictures, answering questions, and making comments. At one point, its gist seemed to be that its new shell reminded it acutely of a precious antique it had had to leave at home. "Hurry," it burbled sadly. "Danger. Fear. Leave, all. Now, new. Bigger!"

When the car pulled in, honking aside the crowd, the alien turned to watch, raising itself to the tips of its legs. It was silent as the driver, a young black man uniformed in powder blue, jumped out, saying, "What's been happening?" It remained silent as three of its fellows emerged from the back seat. They wore the coal-scuttle shells everyone knew from the teevee, and they were small, no larger than a bushel basket. When they saw the barrel, they sank on their legs, just as if they were bowing. They didn't speak, though it seemed natural to think they would have come armed with more than one choice phrase for their runaway.

The barrel lurched toward its smaller fellows. They flinched, retreating toward the car. "Up!" it burbled. "Home. Now!"

The others scurried. "Master!" they chorused. Their voices piped liquidly, and Cyrus thought their shells must have very different acoustics from his barrel. Their attitude puzzled him, too, until Allie jogged his elbow with her own and said, "It's so much bigger. That must be it."

"They think it's smarter!"

She nodded. She turned toward one of the reporters and told him what they had learned. "If size and intelligence go together, then the bigger ones must be the leaders."

The reporter, a fiftyish man with a bulbous nose and white hair, answered in a whiskey voice. "Then you must have the boss-bug of them all here. I've never seen a bigger one."

Cyrus said, "It's just the barrel." He noticed the patch on the reporter's sleeve. The symbol was the same as the one on the helicopter. "Though I suppose it gives it plenty of room to grow."

They turned their attention back to the aliens as the newcomers scrambled nimbly into the limousine. The barrel followed, just managing to squeeze through the door. It was a tight fit, and Cyrus was glad his barrel hadn't been any bigger. Or was he? He was sorry to see the alien go. He'd been counting on that barrel for his cider, and, besides, he rather liked the alien. It was such a peculiar little bugger.

The fuss died down soon enough. There was better local news, such as the flying saucers seen near the nuclear power plant in Wiscasset, and the aliens were drawing more attention with their request for a piece of the Florida Keys for their colony. The ocean was shallow enough there, they said; the islands would give them enough land for their needs, and the climate was much like that they had left. The locals, of course, wouldn't hear of it, but the rest of the world didn't think the spot a bad idea at all. At least, so said the teevee.

But the story didn't end there. The limousine was back before Thanksgiving, bearing a silk-suited diplomat and an alien whose wooden barrel was now smoothed and polished and covered with the pastel patterns that denoted rank or, perhaps, identity among its kind. It looked more like a dressed-up pumpkin than ever.

The diplomat introduced himself as Vince Barger, the Second Assistant Under-Secretary for Alien Relations. "A new department, you understand," he added with a smile that kept his teeth carefully covered. "We try to mediate between K-ssniskit's people and our own."

"Snickit?" asked Cyrus.

"K-ssniskit. Didn't she tell you her name before?"

Cyrus shook his head, wrinkling his nose at a strong whiff of Barger's cologne. "Can't say she did. Though she didn't seem to like what I called her much. Thought she was sorta like a hermit crab."

"So he called her Hermit," put in Allie.

All three watched the alien as she moved around the yard, stalked eyes peering into barn, pasture, and house, renewing her brief acquaintance with the place. She must have grown used to the weight of the barrel, for she no longer lurched. She must also, thought Cyrus, have grown a little.

Barger chuckled smoothly. "I can see why. But you probably irritated her. They're very sociable creatures, really.'

He stopped talking when the alien scuttled closer. She stopped at Cyrus's feet and cocked her eyes up at his lanky figure. "Greet," she burbled.

"Greet, yourself." Cyrus squatted to be nearer her level. "What're you after now?"

"Cyrus!" said Allie. She turned to the alien. "Don't you mind him, K-ssnickit," she said. "We are glad to see you, and if we can do anything to help, we will." She bent to lay a hand on the rim of the barrel, just above the eyes. She looked as if she were petting it.

"Greet," the alien repeated. "Shells, like." A tentacle stretched to stroke the barrel's flank. "More. Make?"

"I suppose I could," said Cyrus. "Grandpa's coopering tools are still in the barn, and he taught me a little when I was a boy."

"Thin. Light. Polish, too. Sizes, many. Two, thousand," K-ssniskit burbled.

Cyrus whistled. That was a lot of barrels. "Take time," he said. "What'll you pay?"

Barger held out a piece of paper. "Here's the order," he said. "Fifteen hundred dollars apiece, as long as you meet the specifications. We pay you, and they'll pay us."

Cyrus whistled again. He took the paper, unfolded it against its crisp resistance, and read. "Ayuh." He turned to look at Allie. She showed nothing but approval in her face. And they could surely use the money. "I suppose I might," he said. "But why me?"

"She insisted."

And that was that. Or almost that. Cyrus took the order, though at first he felt a little as he guessed a Navajo must feel, selling pots and blankets to jet-borne tourists. But he soon realized that it wasn't *his* heritage he was selling. He was more like a Hong Kong Chinaman making colonial trivets for Williamsburg shops.

Not that he minded, except for one thing. He was fast growing rich, he was honing long-forgotten skills, he was indulging a love for different woods and finishes, but he never seemed to have the time to make a barrel for himself. He still had to harden his cider in those damned plastic jugs.

DANCE BAND ON
THE *TITANIC*

Jack L. Chalker

The girl was committing suicide again on the lower afterdeck. They'd told me I'd get used to it, but after four times I could still only pretend to ignore it, pretend that I didn't hear the body go over, hear the splash, and the scream as she was sucked into the screws. It was all too brief and becoming all too familiar.

When the scream was cut short, as it always was, I continued walking forward, toward the bow. I would be needed there to guide the spotlight with which the captain would have to spot the buoys to get us all safely into Southport Harbor.

It was a clear night; once at the bow I could see the stars in all their glory, too numerous to count, or spot familiar constellations. It's a sight that's known and loved by all those who follow the sea, and it had a special meaning for we, who manned the *Orcas*, for the stars were immutable, the one unchanging part of our universe.

I checked the lines, the winch, and ties in the chained-off portion of the bow, then notified the captain by walkie-talkie that all was ready. He gave me "Very well," and told me that we'd be on the mark in five minutes. This gave me a few moments to relax, adjust my vision to the darkness, and look around.

The bow is an eerie place at night for all its beauty; there is an unreality about a large ferryboat in the dark. Between where I stood on station and the bridge superstructure towering above me there was a broad area always crowded with people in warm weather. The bridge—dominating the aft field of vision, a ghostly, unlit gray-white monolith, reflecting the moonlight with an almost unreal cast and glow. A silent, spinning radar mast on top, and the funnel, end-on, back of the bridge, with its wing supports and mast giving it a futuristic cast, only made the scene more alien, more awesome.

I glanced around at the people on the deck. Not as many as usual, but then it was very late, and there was a chill in the air. I saw a few familiar faces, and there was some lateral shift in focus on a number of them, indicating that I was seeing at least three levels of reality that night.

Now, that last is kind of hard to explain. I'm not sure whether I understand it, either, but I well remember when I applied for this job, and the explanations I got then.

Working deck on a ferryboat is a funny place for a former English teacher, anyway. But, while I'd been, I like to think, a good teacher, I was in constant fights with the administration over their lax discipline, stuffed-shirt attitudes toward teaching and teachers, and their general incompetence. The educational system isn't made for mavericks; it's designed to make everyone conform to bureaucratic ideals which the teacher is supposed to exemplify. One argument too many, I guess, and there I was, an unemployed teacher in a time when there are too many teachers. So I drifted. I'd lost my parents years before and there were no other close relatives, so I had no responsibilities. I'd always loved ferryboats—raised on them, loved them with the same passion some folks like trains and trolley cars and such—and when I discovered an unskilled job opening on the old Delaware ferry I took it. The fact that I was an ex-teacher actually helped; ferry companies like to hire people who relate well to the general public. After all, deck duty is hectic when the ferry's docking or docked, but for the rest of the time you just sort of stand there, and every tourist and traveler in the world wants to talk. If you aren't willing to talk back and enjoy it, forget ferryboats.

And I met Joanna. I'm not sure if we were in love—maybe *I* was, but I'm pretty sure Joanna wasn't capable of loving anyone. Like all the other men in her life, I was just convenient. For a while things went smoothly—I had a job I liked, and we shared the rent. She had a little daughter she doted on, father unknown, and little Harmony and I hit it off, too. We all gave each other what each needed.

It lasted a little more than a year.

In the space of three weeks my neat, comfortable, complacent world came apart: First she threw that damned party while I was working, and a cigarette or something was left, and the apartment burned. The fire department managed to get Joanna out—but little Harmony had been asleep in a far room and they never got to her through the smoke.

I tried to comfort her, tried to console her, but I guess I was too full of my own life, my own self-importance in her reality, that I just didn't see the signs. A couple of weeks after the fire she'd seemed to brighten up, act more like her normal self.

And, one evening, while I worked on the boat, she hanged herself.

Just a week later that damned bridge-tunnel put the ferry out of business, too. I'd known it was coming, of course, but I'd made few plans beyond the closing—I'd figured I could live off Joanna for a while and we'd make our decisions together.

Now here I was alone, friendless, jobless, and feeling guilty as hell. I seriously thought about ending it all myself about then, maybe going down to the old ferryboat and blowing it and me to hell in one symbolic act of togetherness. But then, just when I'd sunk to such depths, I got this nice, official-looking envelope in the mail from something called the Bluewater Corporation, Southport, Maine. Just a funny logo, some blue water with an odd, misty-looking shape of a ship in it.

"Dear Mr. Dalton," the letter read. "We have just learned of the closing of the Delaware service, and we are in need of some experienced ferry people. After reviewing your qualifications, we believe that you might fit nicely into our operation, which, we guarantee, will not be put out of business by bridge or tunnel. If this prospect interests you, please come to Southport terminal at your earliest convenience for a final interview. Looking forward to seeing you soon, I remain, sincerely yours, Herbert V. Penobscot, Personnel Manager, Bluewater Corp."

I just stood there staring at the thing for I don't know how long. A ferry job! That alone should have excited me, yet I wondered about it, particularly that line about "reviewing my qualifications" and "final interview." Funny terms. I could see why they'd look for experienced people, and all ferry folk knew when a line was closed and would naturally look for their own replacements there, but—why me? I hadn't applied to them, hadn't even heard of them or their line—or, for that matter, of Southport, Maine, either. Obviously they had some way of preselecting their people—very odd for this kind of a business.

I scrounged up an old atlas and tried to find it. The letterhead said

"Southport—St. Michael—The Island," but I could find nothing about any such place in the atlas or almanac. If the letterhead hadn't looked so convincing, I'd have sworn somebody was putting me on. As it was, I had nothing else to do, and it beat drinking myself to death, so I hitchhiked up.

It wasn't easy finding Southport, I'll tell you. Even people in nearby towns had never head of it. The whole town was about a dozen houses, a seedy ten-unit motel, a hot dog stand, and a very small ferry terminal with a standard but surprisingly large ferry ramp and parking area.

I couldn't believe the place warranted a ferry when I saw it; you had to go about sixty miles into the middle of nowhere on a road the highway department had deliberately engineered to miss some of the world's prettiest scenery, and had last paved sometime before World War II, just to get there.

There was a light on in the terminal, so I went in. A grayhaired man, about fifty, was in the ticket office, and I went over and introduced myself. He looked me over carefully, and I knew I didn't present a very good appearance.

"Sit down, Mr. Dalton," he offered in a tone that was friendly but businesslike. "My name's McNeil. I've been expecting you. This really won't take long, but the final interview includes a couple of strange questions. If you don't want to answer any of them, feel free, but I must ask them nonetheless. Will you go along with me?"

I nodded and he fired away. It was the damndest job interview I'd ever had. He barely touched on my knowledge of ferries except to ask whether it mattered to me that the *Orcas* was a single-bridge, twin-screw affair, not a double-ender like I'd been used to. It still loaded on one end and unloaded on the other, though, through a raisable bow, and a ferry was a ferry to me and I told him so.

Most of the questions were of a personal nature, my family and friends, my attitudes, and some were downright *too* personal.

"Have you ever contemplated or attempted suicide?" he asked me in the same tone he'd use to ask if you brushed your teeth in the morning.

I jumped. "What's *that* have to do with anything?" I snapped. After all this I was beginning to see why the job was still open.

"Just answer the question," he responded, sounding almost embarrassed. "I told you I had to ask them all."

Well, I couldn't figure out what this was all about, but I finally decided, what the hell, I had nothing to lose and it was a beautiful spot to work.

"Yes," I told him. "Thought about it, anyway." And I told him why. He just nodded thoughtfully, jotted something on a preprinted form, and continued. His next question was worse.

"Do you now believe in ghosts, devils, and/or demonic forces?" he asked in that same routine tone.

I couldn't suppress a chuckle. "You mean the ship's haunted?"

He didn't smile back. "Just answer the question, please."

"No," I responded. "I'm not very religious."

Now there was a wisp of a smile there. "And suppose, with your hardnosed rationalism, you ran into one? Or a whole bunch of them?" He leaned forward, smile gone. "Even an entire shipload of them?"

It was impossible to take this seriously. "What kind of ghosts?" I asked him. "Chain rattlers? White sheets? Foul fiends spouting hateful gibberish?"

He shook his head negatively. "No, ordinary people, for the most part. Dressed a little odd, perhaps, talking a little odd, perhaps, but not really very odd at all. Nice folks, typical passengers."

Cars were coming in now, and I glanced out the window at them. Ordinary-looking cars, ordinary-looking people—campers, a couple of tractor-trailer rigs, like that. Lining up. A U.S. Customs man came from the direction of the motel and started talking to some of them.

"They don't look like ghosts to me," I told McNeil.

He sighed. "Look, Mr. Dalton, I know you're an educated man. I have to go out and start selling fares now. She'll be in in about forty minutes, and we've only got a twenty-minute layover. When she's in and loading, go aboard. Look her over. You'll have free rein of the ship. Take the complete round trip, all stops. It's about four hours over, twenty minutes in, and a little slower back. Don't get off the ship, though. Keep an open mind. If you're the one for the *Orcas*, and I think you are, we'll finish our talk when you get back." He got up, took out a cash drawer and receipt load, and went to the door, then turned back to me. "I *hope* you're the one," he said wearily. "I've interviewed over three hundred people and I'm getting sick of it."

We shook hands on that cryptic remark and I wandered around while he manned his little booth and processed the cars, campers, and trucks. A young woman came over from one of the houses and handled the few people who didn't have cars, although how they ever got to Southport I was at a loss to know.

The amount of business was nothing short of incredible. St. Michael was in Nova Scotia, it seemed, and there were the big runs by CN from a couple of places and the Swedish one out of Portland to compete for any business. The fares were reasonable, but not cheap enough to drive this far out of the way for—and to get to Southport you *had* to drive far out of your way.

I found a general marine atlas of the Fundy region in McNeil's office and looked at it. Southport made it, but just barely. Nova Scotia—nor a St. Clement's Island, either—the midstop that the schedule said it made.

There were an *awful* lot of cars and trucks out there now—it looked like rush hour in Manhattan. Where *had* all those people come from?

And then there was the blast of a great air horn and I rushed out for my first view of the *Orcas*—and I was stunned.

That ship, I remembered thinking, *has no right to be here. Not here, not on this run.*

It was *huge*—all gleaming white, looking brand-new, more like a cruise ship than a ferryboat. I counted three upper decks, and, as I watched, a loud clanging bell sounded electrically on her and her enormous bow lifted, revealing a grooved raising ramp, something like the bow of an old LST. It docked with very little trouble, revealing space for well over a hundred cars and trucks, with small side ramps for a second level available if needed. I learned later that it was 396 feet long—longer than a football field by a third!—and could take more than two hundred major vehicles and twelve hundred passengers.

It was close to sundown on a weekday, but they loaded more than fifty vehicles, including a dozen campers and eight big trucks. Where had they all come from, I wondered again. And why?

I walked on with the passengers, still in something of a daze, and went up top. The lounges were spacious and comfortable, the seats all padded and reclining. There was a large cafeteria, a newsstand, and a very nice bar at the stern of passenger deck 2. The next deck had another lounge section and a number of staterooms up front, while the top level had the bridge, crew's quarters, and a solarium.

It was fancy; and, after it backed out, lowered its bow, and started pouring it on after clearing the harbor lights, the fastest damned thing I could remember, too. Except for the slight swaying and the rhythmic thrumming of the twin diesels, you hardly knew you were moving. It was obviously using enormous stabilizers

The sun was setting and I walked through the ship, just looking and relaxing. As darkness fell and the shoreline receded into nothingness, I started noticing some very odd things, as I'd been warned.

First of all, there seemed to be a whole lot more people on board than I'd remembered loading, and there certainly hadn't been any number staying on from the last run. They all looked real and solid enough, and very ordinary, but there was something decidedly weird about them, too.

Many seem to be totally unaware of each other's existence, for one thing. Some seemed to shimmer occasionally, others were a little blurred or indistinct to my eyes no matter how I rubbed them.

And, once in a while, they'd walk through each other.

Yes, I'm serious. One big fellow in a flowered aloha shirt and brown pants carrying a tray of soft drinks from the cafeteria to his wife and three kids in the lounge didn't seem to notice this woman in a white tee shirt and jeans walking right into him, nor did she seem aware of him, either.

And they met, and I braced for the collision and spilled drinks—and it didn't happen. They walked right *through* each other, just as if they didn't exist, and continued obliviously on. Not one drop of soda was spilled, not one spot of mustard was splotched.

There were other things, too. Most of the people were dressed normally for summer, but occasionally I'd see people in fairly heavy coats and jackets. Some of the fashions were different, too—some people were overdressed in old-fashioned styles, others wildly underdressed, a couple of the women frankly wearing nothing but the bottoms of string bikinis and a see-through short cape of some kind.

I know I couldn't take my eyes off them for a while, until I got the message that they knew they were being stared at and didn't particularly like it. But they were generally ignored by the others.

There were strange accents, too. Not just the expected Maine twang and Canadian accents, or even just the French Canadian accents—those were normal. But there were some really odd ones, ones where I picked out only a few words, which sounded like English, French, Spanish, and

Nordic languages all intermixed and often with weird results.

And men with pigtails and long, braided hair and women with shaved heads or, occasionally, beards.

It was weird.

Frankly, it scared me a little, and I found the purser and introduced myself.

The officer, a good-looking young man named Gifford Hanley, a Canadian from his speech, seemed delighted that I'd seen all this and was not the least bit disturbed.

"Well, well, well!" he almost beamed. "Maybe we've found our new man at last, eh? Not bloody soon enough, either! We've been working short-handed for too long and it's getting to the others."

He took me up to the bridge—one of the most modern I'd ever seen—and introduced me to the captain and the helmsman. They all asked me what I thought of the *Orcas* and how I liked the sea, and none of them would answer my questions on the unusual passengers.

Well, there *was* a St. Clement's Island. A big one, too, from the looks of it, and a fair amount of traffic getting off and wanting on. Some of the vehicles that got on were odd, too; many of the cars looked unfamiliar in design, the trucks also odd, and there were even several horse-drawn wagons!

The island had that same quality as some of the passengers, too. It never seemed to be quite in focus just beyond the ferry terminal, and lights seemed to shift, so that where I thought there were houses or a motel suddenly they were somewhere else, of a different intensity. I was willing to swear that the hotel had two stories; later it seemed over on the left, and four stories high, then farther back, still later, with a single story.

Even the lighthouse as we sped out of the harbor changed; one time it looked very tall with a house at its base; then, suddenly, it was short and tubby, then an automated light that seemed to be out in the water, with no sign of an island.

This continued for most of the trip. St. Michael looked like a carbon copy of Southport, the passengers and vehicles as bizarre—and numerous—and there seemed to be a lot of customs men in different uniforms dashing about, totally ignoring some vehicles while processing others.

The trip back was equally strange. The newsstand contained some books and magazines that were odd, to say the least, and papers with strange names and stranger headlines.

This time there were even Indians aboard, speaking odd tongues. Some looked straight out of *The Last of the Mohicans*, complete with wild haircut, others dressed from little to heavy, despite the fact that it was July and very warm and humid.

And, just before we were to make the red and green channel markers and turn into Southport, I saw the girl die for the first time.

She was dressed in red tee shirt, yellow shorts, and sandals; she had long brown hair, was rather short and stocky, and wore oversized granny glasses.

I wasn't paying much attention, really, just watching her looking over the side at the wake, when, before I could even cry out, she suddenly climbed up on the rail and plunged in, very near the stern.

I screamed, and heard her body hit the water and then heard her howl of terror as she dropped close enough so that the propwash caught her, sucker her under, and cut her to pieces.

Several people on the afterdeck looked at me quizzically, but only one or two seemed to realize that a woman had just died.

There was little I could do, but I ran back to Hanley, breathless.

He just nodded sadly.

"Take it easy, man," he said gently. "She's dead, and there's no use going back for the body. Believe me, we *know*. It won't be there."

I was shocked, badly upset. "How do you know that?" I snapped.

"Because we did it every time the last four times she killed herself and we never found the body then, either," he replied sadly.

I had my mouth open, ready to retort, to say *something*, but he got up, put on his officer's hat and coat, and said, "Excuse me. I have to supervise the unloading," and walked out.

As soon as I got off the ship it was like some sort of dreamy fog had lifted from me. Everything looked suddenly bright and clear, and the people and vehicles looked normal. I made my way to the small ferry terminal building.

When they'd loaded and the ship was gone again, I waited for McNeil to return to his office. It looked much the same really, but a few things seemed different. I couldn't quite put my finger on it, but there was something odd—like the paneling had been rosewood before, and was now walnut. Small things, but nagging ones.

McNeil came back after seeing the ship clear. It ran almost constantly, according to the schedule.

I glanced out the window as he approached and noticed uniformed customs men checking out the debarked vehicles. They seemed to have different uniforms than I'd remembered.

Then the ticket agent entered the office and I got another shock. He had a beard.

No, it was the same man, all right. No question about it. But the man I'd talked to less than nine hours before had been clean-shaven.

I turned to where the navigation atlas lay, just where I'd put it, still open to the Southport page.

It showed a ferry line from Southport to a rather substantial St. Clement's Island now. But nothing to Nova Scotia.

I turned to the bearded McNeil, who was watching me with mild amusement in his eyes.

"What the *hell* is going on here?" I demanded.

He went over and sat down in his swivel chair. "Want the job?" he asked. "It's yours if you do."

I couldn't believe his attitude. "I want an explanation, damn it!" I fumed.

He chuckled. "I told you I'd give you one if you wanted. Now you'll have to bear with me, since I'm only repeating what the company tells me, and I'm not sure I have it all clear myself."

I sat down in the other chair. "Go ahead," I told him.

He sighed. "Well, let's start this off by saying that there's been a Bluewater Corporation ferry on this run since the mid-1800s—steam packet at first, of course. The *Orcas* is the eleventh ship in the service, put on a year and a half ago."

He reached over, grabbed a cigarette, lit it, and continued.

"Well, anyway, it was a normal operation until about 1910 or so. That's when they started noticing that their counts were off, that there seemed to be more passengers than the manifests called for, different freight, and all that. As it continued, the crews started noticing more and more of the kind of stuff you saw, and things got crazy for them, too.

Southport was a big fishing and lobstering town then—nobody does that any more, the whole economy is the ferry.

"Well, anyway, one time this crewman goes crazy, says the woman in his house isn't his wife. A few days later another comes home to find that he has four kids—and he was only married a week before. And so on."

I felt my skin starting to crawl slightly.

"So, they send some big shots up. The men are absolutely nuts, but *they* believe what they claim. Soon everybody who works the ship is spooked, and this can't be dismissed. The experts go for a ride and can't find anything wrong, but now two of the crewmen claim that *is* their wife, or their kid, or somesuch. Got to be a pain, though, getting crewmen. We finally had to center on loners—people without family, friends, or close personal ties. It kept getting worse each trip. Had a hell of a time keeping men for a while, and that's why it's so hard to recruit new ones."

"You mean the trip drives them crazy?" I asked unbelievingly.

He chuckled. "Oh no. *You're* sane. It's the rest of 'em. That's the problem. And it gets worse and worse each season. But the trip's *extremely* profitable. So we try to match the crew to the ship and hope they'll accept it. If they do it's one of the best damned ferry jobs there is."

"But what causes it?" I managed. "I mean—I saw people dressed outlandishly. I saw other people walk *through* each other! I even saw a girl commit suicide, and nobody seemed to notice!"

McNeil's face turned grim. "So that's happened again. Too bad. Maybe someday there'll be a chance to save her."

"Look," I said, exasperated. "There must be some explanation for all this. There *has* to be!"

The ticket agent shrugged and stubbed out his cigarette.

"Well, some of the company experts studied it. They say nobody can tell for sure, but the best explanation is that there are a lot of different worlds—different Earths, you might say—all existing one on top of the other, but you can't see any one except the one you're in. Don't ask me how that's possible or how they came up with it, it just *is*, that's all. Well, they say that in some worlds folks don't exist at all, and in others they are different places or doing different things—like getting married to somebody else or somesuch. In some, Canada's still British, some she's a republic, in others she's a fragmented batch of countries, and in one or two she's part of the U.S. Each one of these places has a different history."

"And this one boat serves them all?" I responded, not accepting a word of that crazy story. "How is that possible?"

McNeil shrugged again. "Who knows? Hell, I don't even understand why that little light goes on in here when I flip the switch. Do most people? I just sell tickets and lower the ramp. I'll tell you the company's version, that's all. They say that there's a crack—maybe one of many, and this allows you to go between the worlds. Not one ship, of course—twenty or more, one for each world. But, as long as they keep the same schedule, they overlap—and can cross into one or more of the others. If you're on the ship in all those worlds, then you cross, too. Anyone coexisting with the ship in multiple worlds can see and hear not only the one he's in, but the ones nearest him, too. People-perception's a little harder the farther removed the world you're in is from theirs."

"And you believe this?" I asked him, still disbelieving.

"Who knows? Got to believe *something* or you'll go nuts," he replied pragmatically. "Look, did you get to St. Michael this trip?"

I nodded. "Yeah. Looked pretty much like this place."

He pointed to the navigation atlas. "Try and find it. You won't. Take a drive up through New Brunswick and around to the other side. It doesn't exist. In this world, the *Orcas* goes from here to St. Clement's Island and back again. I understand from some of the crew that sometimes Southport doesn't exist, sometimes the island doesn't, and so forth. And there are so many countries involved I don't even count."

I shook my head, refusing to accept all this. And yet, it made a crazy kind of sense. These people didn't see each other because they were in different worlds. The girl committed suicide five times because she did it in five different worlds—or was it five different girls? It also explained the outlandish dress, the strange mixture of vehicles, people, accents.

"But how come the crew sees people from many worlds and the passengers don't?" I asked him.

McNeil sighed. "That's the other problem. We have to find people who would be up here, working on the *Orcas*, in every world we service. More people's lives parallel than you'd think. The passengers—well, they generally don't exist on a particular run except once. The very few who do still don't take the trip in every world we service. I guess once or twice it's happened that we've had a passenger cross over, but, if so, we've never heard of it."

"And how come I'm here in so many worlds?" I asked him.

McNeil smiled. "You were recruited, of course. The corporation has a tremendous, intensive recruiting effort involving ferry lines and crew members. When they spot one, like you, in just the right circumstance in all worlds, they recruit you—all of you. An even worse job than you'd think, since every season one or two new Bluewater Corporations put identical ferries on this run, or shift routes and overlap with ours. Then we have to make sure the present crew can serve them, too, by recruiting your twin on those worlds."

Suddenly I reached over, grabbed his beard, and yanked.

"*Ouch!* Damn it!" he cried and shoved my hand away.

"I—I'm sorry—I—" I stammered.

He shook his head and grinned. "That's all right, son. You're about the seventh person to do that to me in the last five years. I guess there are a lot of varieties of *me*, too."

I thought about all that traffic. "Do others know of this?" I asked him. "I mean, is there some sort of hidden commerce between the worlds on this ferry?"

He grinned. "I'm not supposed to answer that one," he said carefully. "But what the hell. Yes, I think—no, I *know* there is. After all, the shift of people and ships is constant. You move one notch each trip if all of you take the voyage. Sometimes up, sometimes down. If that's true, and if they can recruit a crew that fits the requirements, why not truck drivers? A hell of a lot of truck traffic through here year 'round, you know. No reduced winter service. And some of the rigs are really kinda strange-looking." He sighed. "I only know this—in a couple of hours I'll start selling fares again, and I'll sell a half dozen or so to St. Michael—and *there is no St. Michael*. It isn't even listed on my schedule or maps. I doubt if the corporation's actually the trader, more the middleman in the deal. But they sure as hell don't make their millions off fares alone."

It was odd the way I was accepting it. Somehow, it seemed to make sense, crazy as it was.

"What's to keep me from using this knowledge somehow?" I asked him. "Maybe bring my own team of experts up?"

"Feel free," McNeil answered. "Unless they overlap they'll get a nice, normal ferry ride. And if you can make a profit, go ahead, as long as it doesn't interfere with Bluewater's cash flow. The *Orcas* cost the company more than twenty-four million *reals* and they want it back."

"Twenty-four million *what?*" I shot back.

"*Reals*," he replied, taking a bill from his wallet. I look at it. It was printed in red, and had a picture of someone very ugly labeled "Prince Juan XVI" and an official seal from the "Bank of New Lisboa." I handed it back.

"What country are we in?" I asked uneasily.

"Portugal." He replied casually. "Portuguese America, actually, although only nominally. So many of us Yankees have come in you don't even have to speak Portuguese any more. They even print the local bills in Anglish, now."

Yes, that's what he said. Anglish.

"It's the best ferryboat job in the world, though," McNeil continued. "For someone without ties, that is. You'll meet more different kinds of people from more cultures than you can ever imagine. Three runs on, three off—in as many as twenty-four different variations of these towns, all unique. And a month off in winter to see a little of a different world each time. Never mind whether you buy the explanation—you've seen the results, you know what I say is true. Want the job?"

"I'll give it a try," I told him, fascinated. I wasn't sure if I *did* buy the explanation, but I certainly had something strange and fascinating here.

"Okay, there's twenty *reals* advance," McNeil said, handing me a purple bill from the cash box. "Get some dinner if you didn't eat on the ship and get a good night's sleep at the motel—the company owns it so there's no charge—and be ready to go aboard at four tomorrow afternoon."

I got up to leave.

"Oh, and Mr. Dalton," he added, and I turned to face him.

"Yes?"

"If, while on shore, you fall for a pretty lass, decide to settle down, then do it—*but don't go back on that ship again!* Quit. If you don't, she's going to be greeted by a stranger, and you might never find her again."

"I'll remember," I assured him.

*   *   *

The job was everything McNeil promised and more. The scenery was spectacular, the people an ever-changing, fascinating group. Even the crew changed slightly—a little shorter sometimes, a little fatter or thinner, beards and mustaches came and went with astonishing rapidity, and accents varied enormously. It didn't matter; you soon adjusted to it as a matter of course, and all shipboard experiences were in common, anyway.

It was like a tight family after a while, really. And there were women in the crew, too, ranging from their twenties to their early fifties, not only in food and bar service but as deckhands and the like as well. Occasionally this was a little unsettling, since, in two or three cases out of 116, they were men in one world, women in another. You got used to even that. It was probably more unsettling for them; they were distinct people and *they* didn't change sex. The personalities and personal histories tended to parallel, regardless though, with only a few minor differences.

And the passengers! Some were really amazing. Even seasons were different for some of them, which explained the clothing variations. Certainly what constituted fashion and moral behavior was wildly different, as different as what they ate and the places they came from.

And yet, oddly, people were people. They laughed, and cried, and ate and drank and told jokes—some rather strange, I'll admit—and snapped pictures and all the other things people did. They came from places where the Vikings settled Nova Scotia (called Vinland, naturally), where Nova Scotia was French, or Spanish, or Portuguese, or very, very English. Even one in which Nova Scotia had been settled by Lord Baltimore and called Avalon.

Maine was as wild or wilder. There were two Indian nations running it, the U.S., Canada, Britain, France, Portugal, and lots of variations, some of which I never have gotten straight. There was also a temporal difference sometimes—some people were rather futuristic, with gadgets I couldn't even understand. One truck I loaded was powered by some sort of solar power and carried a cargo of food-service robots. Some others were behind—still mainly horses or oldtime cars and trucks. I am not certain even now if they were running at different speeds from us or whether some inventions had simply been made in some worlds and not in others.

And, McNeil was right. Every new summer season added at least one more. The boat was occasionally so crowded to our crew's eyes that we had trouble making our way from one end of the ship to the other. Watching staterooms unload was also wild—it looked occasionally like the circus clown act, where 50 clowns get out of a Volkswagen.

And there *was* some sort of trade between the worlds. It was quickly clear that Bluewater Corporation was behind most of it, and that this was what made the line so profitable.

And, just once, there was a horrible, searing pain that hit the entire crew, and a modern world we didn't meet any more after that, and a particular variation of the crew we never saw again. And the last newspapers from that world had told of a coming war.

There was also a small crew turnover, of course. Some went on vacation and never returned, some returned but would not reboard the ship. The company was understanding, and it usually meant some extra work for a few weeks until they found someone new and could arrange for them to come on.

The stars were fading a little now, and I shined the spot over to the red marker for the captain. He acknowledged seeing it, and made his turn in, the lights of Southport coming into view and masking the stars a bit.

I went through the motions mechanically, raising the bow when the Captain hit the mark, letting go the bow lines, checking the clearances, and the like. I was thinking about the girl.

We knew that people's lives in the main did parallel from world to world. Seven times now she'd come aboard, seven times she'd looked at the white wake, and seven times she'd jumped to her death.

Maybe it was the temporal dislocation, maybe she just reached the same point at different stages, but she was always there and she always jumped.

I'd been working the *Orcas* three years, had some strange experiences, and generally pleasurable ones. For the first time I had a job I liked, a family of sorts in the crew, and an ever-changing assortment of people and places for a three-point ferry run. In that time we'd lost one world and gained by our figures three others. That was 26 variants.

Did that girl exist in all 26? I wondered. Would we be subjected to that sadness 19 more times? Or more, as we picked up new worlds?

Oh, I'd tried to find her before she jumped in the past, yes. But she hadn't been consistent, except for the place she chose. We did three runs a day, two crews, so it was six a day, more or less. She did it at different seasons, in different years, dressed differently.

You couldn't cover them all.

Not even all the realities of the crew of all worlds, although I knew that we were essentially the same people on all of them and that I—the other me's—were also looking.

I don't know why I was so fixated, except that I'd been to that point once myself, and I'd discovered that you *could* go on, living with emotional scars, and find a new life.

I didn't even know what I'd say and do if I *did* see her early. I only knew that, if I did, she damned well wasn't going to go over the stern that trip.

In the meantime, my search for her when I could paid other dividends. I prevented a couple of children from going over through childish play, as well as a drunk, and spotted several health problems as I surveyed the people. One turned out to be a woman in advanced labor, and the first mate and I delivered our first child—our first, but *Orca's* nineteenth. We helped a lot of people, really, with a lot of different matters.

They were all just specters, of course; they got on the boat often without us seeing them, and they disembarked for all time the same way. There were some regulars, but they were few. And, for them, we were a ghost crew, there to help and to serve.

But, then, isn't that the way you think of anybody in a service occupation? Firemen are firemen, not individuals; so are waiters, cops, street sweepers, and all the rest. Categories, not people.

We sailed from Point A to Point C, stopped at B, and it was our whole life.

And then, one day in July of last year, I spotted her.

She was just coming on board at St. Clement's—that's possibly why I hadn't noticed her before. We backed into St. Clement's, and I was on the bow lines. But we were short, having just lost a deckhand to a nice-looking fellow in the English colony of Annapolis Royal, and it was my turn to do some double duty. So, there I was, routing traffic on the ship when I saw this little rounded station wagon go by and saw *her* in it.

I still almost missed her; I hadn't expected her to be with another person, another woman, and we were loading the Vinland existence, so in July they were more accurately in a state of undress than anything else, but I spotted her all the same. Jackie Carliner, one of the barmaids and a pretty good artist, had sketched her from the one time she'd seen the girl and we'd made copies for everyone.

Even so, I had my loading duties to finish first—there was no one else. But, as soon as we were underway and I'd raised the stern ramp, I made my way topside and to the lower stern deck. I took my walkie-talkie off the belt clip and called the captain.

"Sir, this is Dalton," I called. "I've seen our suicide girl."

"So what else is new?" grumbled the captain. "You know policy on that by now."

"But, sir!" I protested. "I mean still alive. Still on board. It's barely sundown, and we're a good half hour from the point yet."

He saw what I meant. "Very well," he said crisply. "But you know we're short-handed. I'll put Caldwell on the bow station this time, but you better get some results or I'll give you so much detail you won't have time to meddle in other people's affairs."

I sighed. Running a ship like this one hardened most people. I wondered if the captain, with twenty years on the run, every understood why I cared enough to try and stop this girl I didn't know from going in.

Did *I* know, for that matter?

As I looked around at the people going by, I thought about it. I'd thought about it a great deal before.

Why *did* I care about these faceless people? People from so many different worlds and cultures that they might as well have been from another planet. People who cared not at all about me, who saw me as an object, a cipher, a service, like those robots I mentioned. They didn't care about me. If *I* were perched on that rail and a crowd was around, most of them would probably yell "Jump!"

Most of the crew, too, cared only about each other, to a degree, and about the *Orcas*, our rock of sanity. I though of that world gone in some atomic fire. What was the measure of an anonymous human being's worth?

I thought of Joanna and Harmony. With pity, yes, but I realized now that Joanna, at least, had been a vampire. She'd needed me, needed a rock to steady herself, to unburden herself to, to brag to. Someone steady and understanding, someone whose manner and character suggested that solidity. She'd never really even considered that I might have my own problems, that her promiscuity and lifestyle might be hurting me. Not that she was trying to hurt me—she just never *considered* me.

Like those people going by now. If they stub their toe, or have a question, or slip, or the boat sinks, they need me. Until then, I'm just a faceless automaton to them.

Ready to serve them, to care about them, if *they* needed somebody.

And that was why I was out here in the surprising chill, out on the stern with my neck stuck out a mile, trying to prevent a suicide I *knew* would happen, knew because I'd seen it three times before.

I was needed.

That was the measure of a human being's true worth, I felt sure. Not how many people ministered to *your* needs, but how many people *you* could help.

That girl—she had been brutalized, somehow, by society. Now I was to provide some counterbalance.

It was the surety of this duty that had kept me from blowing myself up with the old Delaware ferry, or jumping off that stern rail myself.

I glanced uneasily around and looked ahead. There was Ship's Head Light, tall and proud this time in the darkness, the way I liked it. I thought I could almost make out the marker buoys already. I started to get nervous.

I was certain that she'd jump. It'd happened every time before that we'd known. Maybe, just maybe, I thought, in this existence she won't.

I had no more gotten the thought through my head when she came around the corner of the deck housing and stood in the starboard corner, looking down.

She certainly looked different this time. Her long hair was blond, not dark, and braided in large pigtails that dropped almost to her waist. She wore only the string bikini and transparent cape the Vinlanders liked in summer, and she had several gold rings on each arm, welded loosely there, I knew, and a marriage ring around her neck.

That was interesting, I thought. She looked so young, so despairing, that I'd never once thought of her as married.

Her friend, as thin and underdeveloped as she was stout, was with her. The friend had darker hair and had it twisted high atop her head. She wore no marriage ring.

I eased slowly over, but not sneakily. Like I said, nobody notices the crewman of a vessel; he's just part of it.

"Luok, are yo sooure yu don' vant to halve a drink or zumpin?" the friend asked in that curious accent the Vinlanders had developed through cultural pollution by the dominant English and French.

"Naye, I yust vant to smell da zee-spray," the girl replied. "Go on. I vill be alonk before ze ship iz docking."

The friend was hesitant; I could see it in her manner. But I could also see she would go, partly because she was chilly, partly because she felt she had to show some trust to her friend.

She walked off. I looked busy checking the stairway supports to the second deck, and she paid me no mind whatsoever.

There were few others on the deck, but most had gone forward to see us come in, and the couple dressed completely in black sitting there on the bench was invisible to the girl, as she was to them. She peered down at the black water and started to edge more to the starboard side engine wake, and then a little past, almost to the center. Her upper torso didn't move, but I saw a bare, dirty foot go up on the lower rail.

I walked casually over. She heard me, and turned slightly to see if it was anyone she needed to be bothered with.

I went up to her and stood beside her, looking at the water.

"Don't do it," I said softly, not looking directly at her. "It's too damned selfish a way to go."

She gave a small gasp and turned to look at me in wonder.

"How—how dit yu—?" she managed.

"I'm an old hand at suicides," I told her. That was no lie. Joanna, then almost me, then this woman seven other times.

"I wouldn't really haff—" she began, but I cut her off.

"Yes, you would. You know it and I know it. The only thing you know and I don't is why."

We were inside Ship's Head Light now. If I could keep her talking just a few more minutes we'd clear the channel markers and slow for the turn and docking. The turn and the slowdown would make it impossible for her to be caught in the propwash, and, I felt, the cycle would be broken, at least for her.

"Vy du yu care?" she asked, turning again to look at the dark sea, only slightly illuminated by the rapidly receding light.

"Well, partly because it's my ship and I don't like things like that to happen on my ship," I told her. "Partly because I've been there myself, and I know how brutal a suicide is."

She looked at me strangely. "Dat's a fonny t'ing tu zay," she responded. "Jost vun qvick jomp and *pszzt!* All offer."

"You're wrong," I said. "Besides, why would anyone so young want to end it?"

She had a dreamy quality to her face and voice. She was starting to blur, and I was worried that I might somehow translate into a different world-level as we neared shore.

"My 'usbahnd," she responded. "Goldier vas hiss name." She fingered the marriage ring around her neck. "Zo yong, so 'andzum." She turned her head quickly and looked up at me. "Do yu know vat it iz to be fat and ugly und 'alf bloind and haff ze best uv all men suddenly pay attenzion to yu, vant to *marry* yu?"

I admitted I didn't, but didn't mention my own experiences.

"What happened? He leave you?" I asked.

There were tears in her eyes. "Ya, in a vay, ya. Goldier he jumped out a tventy-story building, he did. Und itz my own fault, yu know. I shud haff been dere. Or, maybe I didn't giff him vat he needed. I dunno."

"Then you of all people know how brutal suicide really is," I retorted. "Look at what it did to you. You have friends, like your friend here. They care. It will hurt them as your husband's hurt you. This woman with you—she'll carry guilt for leaving you alone the whole rest of her life." She was shaking now, not really from the chill, and I put my arm around her. Where the hell were those marker lights?

"Do you see how cruel it is? What suicide does to others? It leaves a legacy of guilt, much of it false guilt, but no less real for that. And you might be needed by somebody else, sometime, to help them. Somebody else might die because you weren't there."

She looked at me, then seemed to dissolve, collapse into a crescendo of tears, and sat down on the deck. I looked up and saw the red and green markers astern, felt the engines slow, felt the *Orcas* turn.

"*Ghetta!*" The voice was a piercing scream in the night. I looked around and saw her friend running to us after coming down the stairway.

Anxiety and concern were on her stricken face, and there were tears in her eyes. She bent down to the still sobbing girl. "I shuld neffer haff left yu!" she sobbed, and hugged the girl tightly.

I sighed. The *Orcas* was making its dock approach now, the ringing of bells said that Caldwell had managed to raise the bow without crashing us into the dock.

"My Gott!" the friend swore, then looked up at me. "Yu stopped her? How can I etter? . . . "

But they both already had that ethereal, unnatural double image about them, both fading into a world different from mine.

"Just remember that there's a million Ghettas out there," I told them both softly. "And you can make them or break them."

I turned and walked away as I heard the satisfying thump and felt the slight jerk of the ferry fitting into the slip. I stopped and glanced back at the stern, but I could see no one. Nobody was there.

Who were the ghosts? I mused. Those women, or the crew of the *Orcas*? How many times did hundreds of people from different worlds coexist on this ship without ever knowing it?

"Mr. Dalton!" snapped a voice in my walkie-talkie.

"Sir?" I responded.

"Well?" the captain asked expectantly.

"No screams this time, Captain, I told him, satisfaction in my voice. "One young woman will live."

There was a long pause and, for a moment, I thought he might actually be human. Then he snapped, "There's eighty-six assorted vehicles still waiting to be off-loaded and might I remind you that we're shorthanded and on a strict schedule?"

I sighed and broke into a trot. Business was business, and I had a whole world to throw out of the car deck so I could run another one in.

WHEN THE ICE GOES OUT

Jessica Reisman

The summer she'd drowned, Rosetta woke hungry. She hungered for light and color, for small things that glittered, for warmth and life. Someone, anyone; the need was new to her. She had yet to learn discernment.

Isobel sniffed the air, chill and wet. The lake was just visible through tall pine and birch. Her boots tracked over the root-humped ground, in the silence among the trees. At the lake edge, the tall shadow of the woods brushed the water. From this little cove, the other summer places were invisible.

The lake conveyed its great size through the echo of its waves lapping beyond the inlet. The edges of the cove, shaggy and ice-rimmed, had half-swallowed and partly digested the wooden dock their father had built. A few more years of neglect and it would be gone.

Isobel stepped out onto it and sat down, hiding her hands inside the sleeves of her sweater, arms around her knees. A mourning dove called from the woods.

Her sister Rosetta surfaced. She looked at Isobel across the chill expanse, then sank back down; a moment later she resurfaced close to the rotting dock.

"Ross," Isobel greeted her. She examined her sister's face for changes. When she'd first seen Rosetta, two weeks after her drowning, there'd been changes. Her skin was a clear, pure thing, an essence. Her face, which had been fiercely expressive, now looked remote, beautiful. Expressions came into it like light through a pane of glass, vivid, but not integral to the glass itself.

Rosetta stared back, her eyes darker than Isobel remembered them, the color of the deepest parts of the lake. "Isobel," she said, having retrieved the name like a pearl: precious, cold, and streaming wet. She looked at Isobel with pleasure in the stillness of her face.

Rosetta had drowned the year before during a storm. She'd gone out in the canoe, despite a sullen sky. The violence of the storm had been like the Maine summer itself: promised but unexpected.

The lake had been dredged, but Rosetta's body had not been found.

That summer, first in a new life for Isobel, two dogs disappeared near the lake. Nobody dredged for dogs as they did for people. Syd Grainger's was a retriever, Beth Williams' a collie-Lab mix.

Several days after the second disappeared, Isobel had seen Rosetta. Apparently the swift, straightforward energies of two dogs had been enough to resurrect her.

Now Isobel had come to the neglected cabin after dreaming about it five nights in a row. Her father would not come to the cabin again, he said. He had begun to seem to her like a figure in a Chagall painting, floating somewhere above her, connected to his family by a few threads of color, and the suggestion of a shared context. Her mother had stopped coming many years before Rosetta drowned. When Isobel was eight and Rosetta nine, their mother had left the summers in Maine behind, much as she'd left her marriage behind, in search of warmer climes.

In the hardness of the end-of-April light and the barren darkness of the land, Isobel saw her sister's existence differently than she'd seen it last summer.

She watched Rosetta swim a lazy circle. "What did you do this winter?"

"Sleep," Rosetta spoke slowly, her inflections and intonations different, though her voice tugged familiarly at Isobel. "For three months, under the ice."

"I talked to Dad before I left; he's going to marry Grace." Isobel rubbed her finger over a rough spot in the worn wood. "Mom told him to sell the cabin." She was getting cold. Rosetta swam in lazy, small circles. Suddenly she dove. She surfaced a moment later with something glinting wetly in her fingers. She brought it to Isobel and set it on the dock before her. Isobel picked it up: a glass eye. It cut one sharp crescent of refracted light across her palm. She rolled it around in her fingers. The eye was blue, and heavier than she would have expected; it dripped icy lake water onto her hand.

Isobel had an old coffee can filled with the things Rosetta had brought her last summer, small things carried from far parts of the lake: three thumbnail-size carved jade beads; an antique pair of bent, gold-wire eyeglass frames with half of one cloudy lens still intact; a set of rusted camping utensils linked on a metal ring; a miniature train, also rusted; assorted marbles; a plastic doll's head with brilliant gold hair; buttons; matchless earrings; and about two sixty-eight in change, though some of the coins were so old that Isobel thought they might be worth more.

"Bring me the things?" Rosetta said, bobbing slightly. The water beaded on her dark blonde eyelashes and glazed her lips. "The pretty things."

She kept the coffee can in the cabin, on a shelf with the paperback murder mysteries her father had read over the summers. She went to get the can, poured its contents out, and watched her sister's face as she ran her fingers over them. Leaning up over the edge of the dock, she picked each one up and held it to the light. Her face had a slightly perplexed look of concentration. When she had gone through all the objects, her dark eyes turned up to Isobel. "It's not here," she said slowly. "What I need . . . it's not here."

Isobel narrowed her eyes, trying to understand. "What, Ross? Is something missing?"

"No. Yes . . . what I need." Rosetta stared up into Isobel's face, her eyes moving slowly. She touched Isobel's hand and poured her gaze into Isobel's until a faint droning filled Isobel's head. Isobel swayed.

Abruptly Rosetta removed her hand and drifted from the dock, watching Isobel. A tiny line creased the smooth skin between Rosetta's eyes.

The droning faded slowly and Isobel rubbed her ears, feeling like she'd been de-pressurized too quickly. She watched Rosetta drift farther away, wondering what had just happened.

Toby came to see her, as she did every summer. Isobel was getting split logs from what was left of last year's cord when the older woman came out of the woods, walking up from the cove. She wore an assortment of layers, among them long johns, two skirts, a wool sweater, and a flannel shirt. In one hand she gripped a pair of heavy leather gloves.

"Heard you were up," Toby said, kissing Isobel gently on the cheek. She smelled of tobacco, chill wind, and mint. "My nephew's here visiting me, thought you might like to meet him." She glanced behind her into the woods, called back, "Jay, where are you? Come on up."

"Cold for a canoe," Isobel said as she hefted the wood. She looked curiously towards the woods. She'd never met any of Toby's family.

"Nah," Toby said. "When the ice goes out, it's warm enough."

"How's the greenhouse?"

"Doing fine." She touched a pocket while holding the cabin door open for Isobel. "Brought you some mint leaves for tea; I'll bring you some other things next week. Wanted to make sure you were here." She cast a searching glance back over the trees. "Where is the boy?"

Toby lived on the far shore of the lake; she didn't own a car. The lake was her community. She kept three black goats and a coon cat and laid in supplies a few times a year, getting a ride into town with a neighbor up the road.

Jay appeared finally, out of the woods. Isobel wouldn't have called him a boy; he was in his mid-twenties, with ashy brown hair and the disheveled appearance of a graduate student. He looked back over his shoulder several times. When he reached them, Isobel saw he had a nice face and Toby's wryly turned mouth. He seemed distracted.

Toby waved a hand between them. "Jay, Isobel."

"I forgot how cold it would still be here," Isobel said as she knelt to add splits to the woodstove. "The cherry trees were blossoming when I left D.C." The kettle whistled and she made tea. While Toby inspected her father's paperbacks, Isobel and Jay sat by a window that looked down through the trees and over the lake.

Isobel blew on her tea before breathing in the hot steam. Mint, sweet and vivid, filled her nose and throat. She watched Jay's long fingers around the chipped mug.

"You're in grad school, yeah?"

"Yeah." He nodded, sipped his tea. "Madison; physics." He set his cup down and leaned forward over it. The steam loosened his hair and several strands fell over his eyes. "Aunt Toby told me about your sister. I'm sorry."

Isobel glanced at Toby. She had moved on to the can of Rosetta's treasures, peering into it, picking through them. The clink of metal, glass, and plastic filled a moment's silence.

Isobel's gaze drifted, then, out the window, to the surface of the lake, a scattering of burning light through the trees. She gripped the cup tighter. She felt caught between the sweetness of flirting with Jay and the chill dark of the lake where Ross had dreamed under the ice all winter.

Although Jay seemed about to say something more, he lowered his gaze to the table, tracing the wood grain with one finger. "It's a strange lake," he said after a moment, "isn't it?"

"What do you mean?" Isobel looked at him, at the lashes shading his eyes. He shrugged.

"All lakes are strange," Toby said, holding the glass eye up to her own, frowning.

The next morning, Isobel went down to the cove and waited. When the sun was slanted low over the trees and a thin mist skimmed several feet over the surface of the lake, Rosetta surfaced, far out. Her head gleamed as sleek as an otter's.

"Ross," Isobel called, softly, her voice carrying over the water. Rosetta came no closer, however. She bobbed there for a while, just outside the cove. Then she sank back down, disappearing. Isobel waited. She grew cold, waiting, straining her eyes to see her sister's head appear again.

A week later the ground began to thaw significantly.

"Mud season," Toby announced, as Jay set down a box of greenhouse produce: dark, bunched spinach, onions, new potatoes, a small cluster of radishes. Toby wore rubber fishing boots under her skirt and looked smaller: she'd shed a layer. The mineral smell of mud came with her and Jay into the cabin.

He smiled shyly at Isobel and she found herself smiling back.

"Rowboat floated in empty night before last," Toby said. "Boat from the old Bellows place down the south cove. Summer person staying there; he's gone missing." She stretched, cracking her back.

Isobel looked away. "Are they going to dredge?"

"Well; he's alone. Syd's getting in touch with the agent, see if they can't find some of the man's family."

Fresh, rooty smells clung to Isobel's hands as she put the produce away. She saw Jay peering into the coffee can, tilting it to the light, and the sight gave her a queer little lurch in her stomach.

It seemed like longer than a week ago since Toby and he had stopped by. She couldn't remember very well what she'd been doing the last week; sleeping a lot, sitting on the dock, reading her father's mystery novels . . . waiting for Rosetta to come.

"Would it be okay if I came back later, after we finish the deliveries?" Jay asked, studying one of the coins from the can.

"I told him you play chess," Toby said. "He'll drop me back home and come back in the canoe."

"Sure. Of course." She looked at the onion in her hand. Being alone was making her a little vague, she thought.

Toby was watching her shrewdly.

She walked them back down to the cove. The canoe held three other boxes of vegetables and rode low in the water. As they paddled smoothly from the shore, the slim boat broke and rolled the surface of the water away in a widening vee.

The day was so filled with light it crackled against Isobel's skin. When the canoe was gone around a curve of the land, Rosetta surfaced and swam to Isobel. She set something on the dock and turned to go.

"Ross, wait, please, wait!" But her sister kept going, disappearing under the surface. Isobel looked after her, then crouched down to see what she'd left.

It was a man's watch, the kind with a black rubber wristband, a large face, many functions. It seemed pretty new, like it hadn't been under too long; it was waterproof and still ticking.

The time and date it gave were current.

That little lurch in her gut came again, the tug of opposing forces.

Toby and Jay and the watch broke the bubble she'd been in for the last week. She thought of her life in D.C., of her father, her job at the museum, her mother; of Toby and all the people who lived on the lake, Ray, Syd, Beth Grainger; of Jay. She remembered the warm sting of attraction and desire, smiling into his eyes, the flicker of connection.

She'd forgotten him, and everything else, as if her life were no more than fragmentary scraps of dream.

The watch scared her awake.

She shivered, feeling cold, so cold she couldn't seem to get warm. She fed the woodstove and set it burning hot, then curled up on the couch, wrapped in a down comforter.

She woke in the late afternoon, sobbing. Her throat was tight. A raw, hollow feeling filled her chest, lodged like a structure of hard edges and empty spaces in her arms, back, groin, and thighs. Hiccupping over sobs, she got up slowly, wiping her face.

She touched the watch, which sat on the coffee table. Seeing the time, she wondered if Jay had come for his chess game and then gone without waking her.

She put on her boots and went down to the lake. The air dried and cooled her face. The sky was the color of early lilacs; the lake, very still beneath, gave back soft reflection. Insects swept and darted through the air and across the water.

Half-beached in the grasses at the cove edge sat Toby's canoe. Rosetta floated in the water a little way out, Jay in her arms. Together they looked like a strange starfish.

Isobel ran, splashing into the water, stopped at the shock of cold. "Ross, what are you doing?"

Rosetta looked up. She lifted one hand from stroking Jay's hair. They floated nine or ten feet away, past where the bottom dropped. Isobel took another step. The mud and sand sucked at her boots.

"This is what I need," her sister said slowly, softly. "In his eyes, in him."

Isobel dove out into the water. The coldness shocked her through her clothes a moment after the water closed over her head. Her boots filled quickly and weighed her down. She surfaced and stroked toward Rosetta, gasping. Even here in the little cove she felt how big the lake was as the bottom dropped away beneath her and she reached her sister and Jay.

Rosetta looked at her over Jay's head. Her face bore an incandescence, something gentle and pure in her expression that made Isobel think of a religious icon.

Paddling with one arm, she pulled Jay from her sister's grasp. Unresisting, only looking perplexed, Rosetta let him go.

Jay was barely conscious. He murmured, head lolling, limp weight in her arms. Isobel gripped him around the collarbone and chest and kicked, trying to get back to the shallows. The boots weighed her down. She went under a moment, the cold water closing over both their heads, came back up. Jay started coughing, struggling. He cracked his head back into Isobel's jaw and her grip on him loosened at the pain.

She got lake bottom under her finally and dragged him up into the grass. She breathed rawly, exhausted, fingers and toes numb, head pulsing. Jay groaned, choked on a breath, then rolled over to his knees, coughing water.

Isobel scanned the lake surface. "Ross?"

Rosetta resurfaced, closer. "I need him," she said softly.

"No, Ross, you can't."

Rosetta looked at her, into her. As before, Isobel heard a distant droning in her head; she ceased to feel the cold. Languor and warmth stole through her bones.

Then Rosetta shut her eyes and turned her face away. The droning hum died away, the cold snapped back through Isobel like a whip.

Rosetta looked back at Isobel, once. Then she sank below the surface, leaving a ripple.

Isobel watched the ripple for a moment, then felt a great shudder go through her. "No! Rosetta!" She glanced at Jay, torn for half a breath, but then she ran back out into the water, ran until it became too deep and then dove under, swimming out.

She opened her eyes on a foggy, secret land. Streamers of milfoil leaned over variegated pebbles, disappearing into dusk only a body-length away. She could barely see Rosetta in the waving weeds, her long hair floating around her like corn silk. Then Rosetta turned away and disappeared into the dim.

Isobel looked up; the wash of pale color that was the sky rippled. She heard her heart pushing her blood, heard her breath—and then she couldn't breathe. She choked as ice-cold water rushed inside of her.

Clamoring for the surface, she flailed out, trying to kick out of her boots. There was nothing to grab onto, nothing to get purchase against . . . time drifted, moments opening wide. She began to fall into this widening, into nothing.

That was okay, she realized. She would be with Ross.

A shadow crossed between her and the surface, a hand plunging in to take hold of her shirt and drag her upwards.

Up in the cabin, Toby stamped about, muttering under her breath as she fed the woodstove and made tea. Jay sat wrapped in the comforter, Isobel in a wool blanket.

Isobel fingered the sore spot on her jaw where Jay had bashed her. She had coughed water until her lungs and gut ached and now shivered continuously.

A small hardness, like a walnut, lodged inside her.

"What will happen to her?" Jay asked suddenly, his voice rough and low. Something in it, forlorn, touched the hard knot in Isobel.

"Hush, you," Toby said. She settled heavily beside Isobel, putting a mug of tea into her hands. "Did you tell her no?"

Isobel thought, nodded. "Yes." Then she understood what Toby had asked her. She looked at the can of things on the bookshelf, and then the watch, ticking on the coffee table. Then at Jay.

Toby rubbed her face. "Well. That may end it. She'll fade, go on."

Isobel stared at her. "Toby . . . you knew about Rosetta?"

Toby grunted. "This lake has always had a . . . spirit." She waved her hand, hmmphed, dissatisfied with the word. "One at a time. They might stay for a day, a week, an hour. Or years. Who's to say? But you, Isobel, not wanting to let go, needing Rosetta. That helped to keep her."

"Did . . . does she have to . . . " Isobel glanced at Jay, lifted her chin, "you know?"

"They always do."

"And I told her no, so she'll stop . . . and—fade?"

Toby took out her tobacco. She rolled a cigarette, licked it. "It depends," she said then. "Did you mean it?"

Isobel tucked her chin down, frowning.

She had a sudden memory of Rosetta's hand in hers, warm fingers strong and callused. In her mind she saw Rosetta's face as she'd held Jay, floating in the water.

Isobel looked away from Toby's nephew, away from his wet hair and his shivering, and whispered, "I don't know."

CREATION STORY

Steve Rasnic Tem

"So, what's *your* story?" the old Indian asked Morgan. Morgan knew he didn't mean it the rude way it sounded, as if he expected Morgan to lie. But Morgan didn't bother to answer—an answer wasn't really expected. It was like the fellow's version of "Hello, how are you doing?"

As soon as he'd asked the question he pressed one hand and the side of his face against the rough bark of the tree. The eye Morgan could see seemed to be peering directly into the bark, applied like a microscope to the ridges and valleys of wood. He doubted the fellow could see anything at such close range—surely everything must be a blur.

Morgan was contending with his own blur: too many trees, too many shades of green, brown, and blue, too many lakes, too many mountains. He'd lived in Maine most of his life, but he'd spent little time in this northern part. He'd been a town kid; he liked things orderly. Up here above Millinocket it looked like it hadn't been that long since the glaciers had passed through, leaving behind great ponds and broad fields of moraine, deep-clawed valleys like the tracks of giant cats, raw mountains of broken stone thrown down or dug out of the world by some curious deity. Every time they pushed through a wall of trees it seemed they were faced with some body of water, as if the land were rotting, exposing the great cold sea underneath, a confusing mix of trees standing or tumbled around its edges. The waters had names like Pemadumcook, Daicy, and Wassataquoik, but Morgan was convinced they were just different views into the same body.

There appeared to be an unlikely mix of trees: both deciduous and evergreen, hard and soft woods. He recognized the birch, maple, pine, spruce, didn't know most of the others, although his brother claimed to. Morgan didn't believe him.

He had no name for the tree the old Indian had been leaning up against, but the fellow had been like that for almost an hour now, absolutely still. Morgan was fascinated by the man's aged skin, especially his hands. As wrinkled as the bark they were pressed against, as complicated. They blended together until they were all of a piece. He could see something of what the old Indian had claimed. The trees were flesh; they simply hadn't been made aware of it yet.

He would have to stop thinking of him as the "old Indian," of course. It was disrespectful. Most of the time the guy lived in another world, but he did have lucid stretches. This was his grandfather, although he didn't know him from Adam. Morgan had never even met the man until yesterday, when Gary decided they should spring him from the nursing home in Lewiston. He wasn't sure about "Indian." Did they prefer "Native American" now? The fact that he didn't know embarrassed him.

The "old Indian" was what their mother, his daughter, had always called him, but he was in high school before he realized she was talking about their grandfather. He hadn't even realized he was part Passamaquoddy until that day.

Not that that made any real difference. He didn't look Indian, had never felt it. His dad had been white, a trucker from Denver, according to their mother. Gary's dad was Hispanic, from Bar Harbor.

Their grandfather had maintained pretty much the same posture—his face pressed against the passenger side window—in Gary's beat-up Dodge as they escaped Lewiston, talking to himself, talking to the window, it was hard to tell. Their granddad just talked.

"Glooskap, he was the one who set us free. So tall he always had leaves in his hair from scraping his head through the tree branches when he walked. Shot arrows into the ash tree—that's where we was hiding. Made holes in the bark so that we could climb out. We would still be trapped in there, Glooskap hadn't gotten us out."

He said all that with his lips pressed into the window, his tongue writing the words sloppily onto the glass. Morgan thought he might be drunk, drugged, or just addled, just old. They both talked about him as if he wasn't in the car. Gary thought their grandfather was having visions.

Gary said, "Stop thinking like a white man. You were always nervous around old people."

Morgan knew Gary was right. He wasn't proud of it, but he'd never been able to get over the way an old person just seemed to shrink up until their skin was too big for them, as if they'd been marinating all those years. He didn't know how to talk to somebody in their seventies or eighties. You knew they'd probably be dead in half a dozen years. With that in mind everything you tried to talk about seemed less than important.

But what he said to Gary was, "You don't know what you're talking about. I just try to show a certain amount of respect and reverence and *I listen*—I'm not trying to talk his ear off. Do you think his skin is okay? It's pretty dry and loose, and he keeps rubbing it up against things. Maybe he needs some lotion or something."

Then their granddad started telling stories again, and they listened. It was hard not to listen, although a lot of the stories were basically the same, with slight variations, and here and there he would introduce new elements into the narrative. "Glooskap got mad at Raccoon one day because Raccoon had gotten into his corn field and was eating all the ripe ears. So he came up behind Raccoon and grabbed him by the neck. But as everybody knows, Raccoon gots very loose skin so he twisted and twisted until he'd twisted right out of his skin and that's how he got away. But at least Glooskap got a fur coat for his lost corn. That's why you never know if a raccoon is really a raccoon, though—it might be another animal wearing his skin." Then he turned to Morgan and asked, "So what's your story?"

"I don't have a story, Granddad."

And his grandfather replied, "I'm sorry. That's too bad."

Their grandfather was doing something with his lips now. It looked as if he was compulsively trying to kiss the wood. "So, what do you think he's doing over there?" Morgan didn't try to lower his voice—half the time he didn't seem to know they were there.

Gary looked up from the can of pork and beans he'd been scooping out with two fingers. They had spoons, but his brother apparently felt using his fingers appeared more Indian. He looked the part, at least from his perspective: lumberjack shirt, jeans, hard-soled moccasins, beadwork belt, beaded leather strap holding back his long, straight jet-black hair. Gary had been dyeing his hair since high school, back when he'd been a Goth, so he hadn't far to go appearance-wise into Indian territory. He glanced over at their grandfather, nodded. "He's seeing if that's the tree he came from, as one of the original Indians. Or maybe he's talking to the Indians still inside. He told me this morning that some Indians were left inside, and that they've been waiting all these centuries to be set free. I think he intends to make a swap—he goes into the tree, somebody new comes out."

"Well, that tree can't be much over fifty years old. He's ninety-two next month. Old, but not centuries. I still can't quite get my head around how he thinks he's one of the original Indians. I don't want to say he's se-nile—he's been pretty coherent, so far. But I have to say, he gets weirder the longer he's away from the home."

"You're thinking like a white man again, brother."

"Cut the crap, Gary. I helped you sneak him out of the nursing home, risked a kidnapping offense, or whatever they might charge us with."

"He's our grandfather, it can't be kidnapping."

"We don't have custody. And he wasn't in there exactly voluntarily. They ruled him incompetent."

"Well, we got custody now. And you need to let go of this . . . linear way you were brought up to look at things. Grandfather says you can't tell by appearances. He says the old look young and the young look old. It's all happening *right now*. That's his truth, and that truth is our legacy."

"I'm just afraid . . . he's going to get sick and *die* on us. He's so *old*. Look at his skin—it looks like it could tear any second."

"He's already sick, he's already dying. He wanted to see Katahdin be-fore he died. I don't care what his mental state might be, a human being is entitled to do what they need when they're dying. It doesn't matter what the State of Maine has to say about it."

Morgan didn't disagree with that—it was a large part of why he went along with this in the first place. He hadn't seen Gary in more than two years, but when his brother came to him, said "We can't let our own grandfather die in a nursing home," he went with him. But it wasn't until they were loading their grandfather into the car, after Gary slipped out a back door with the old man and a pitiful laundry bag full of belongings, that Morgan realized how far over the line they had gone, and then he'd gotten scared. It had been Gary's deal all the way—he just hadn't been able to say no.

They'd abandoned the car well away from the south gate to Baxter State Park and hiked their way in, avoiding the established trails. They didn't want to answer any questions, and in any case the daily quota for day hikers would have already been filled (Gary said camping permits took months). The first time Morgan saw a bear not twenty yards away he knew he was in over his head. Gary led at first, but Granddad kept wandering off, so after awhile they just followed his lead. He appeared to know what he was doing; *they* just didn't know what he was doing. He kept heading up these vague, trampled paths over layers of windfall, but the branches along the edges appeared neatly clipped. Their grandfather caught him examining one, said, "Moose. You don't want to run into one, in the dark." Morgan wanted to tell him there was no way he was going to be hiking in the dark, but the old man was already well up the ill-defined path, Morgan struggling after, feeling desperate from mosquito bites.

Eventually their grandfather stopped his communing with the tree—apparently this wasn't the right one—and they headed northeast toward the serrated crest of the Knife Edge, rising high above the world into mist and rain. Although their grandfather had not shared his intention as to their final destination, Morgan assumed they wouldn't be going anywhere near there—none of them had the physical ability for such a climb. Morgan had never been to Mount Katahdin, in fact he had spent very little time in the northern part of the state. He knew the peak only as the background of the L.L. Bean logo.

"You know this is pretty much the forest primeval, what we have here," Gary stated importantly, stretching and filling his lungs. "The original paradise, kept in trust by the Indians, ruined by the white man."

Morgan was out of breath, his lungs working painfully, but still he couldn't let his brother's arrogant misinformation pass. "You know that's *pretty much* a myth. By the time Columbus arrived the Indians had cleared forests, made grasslands, massively destroyed wildlife, created significant erosion. It was a humanized landscape. The environment actually recovered in some areas as the Indians depopulated."

"'Depopulated'? What kind of mealy mouthed white man's word is that? You mean they died from disease the white man brought, the plagues they introduced into paradise!"

Suddenly their grandfather was between them, gazing up with milky cataract eyes. "You boys quarrel like jays," he said, and headed off at a smart pace through a thick wall of trees. His grandsons scrambled to catch up.

For a while that day, their grandfather seemed almost normal. He was friendlier, pointing out to Morgan a weasel, a raccoon, and once a bobcat, although try as he might Morgan couldn't distinguish it in the indicated tree. They'd passed through the remains of an old lumber camp, the undergrowth jeweled with rusted metal, and something about that amused the old man. He sang a little song as he picked up old forks and spoons, a bottomless coffee pot, examined them, threw them back into the brush. He turned his face toward Morgan and grinned. Encouraged by the contact, Morgan tried to talk to him like a regular person. "Was the nursing home that bad, Granddad? Didn't they take good care of you there?"

His grandfather looked into the distant sky over Mount Katahdin. Something he saw there made him smile more. "They treated me okay," he said, eyes still on something that obviously amused him. "They fed me well, and they talked to me, asked me how my day was going. A small thing, but it is something everybody should do. Do you ask people that, Morgan?"

He couldn't remember the last time. "Yes, yes I do," he lied.

"Then you should do it more often. It lets people know you understand that just trying to make it through a day can be hard for some people."

"Everybody needs a Glooskap, right?"

"That is right. Everybody needs a Glooskap. They were okay, at the nursing home. But you grow older, you become less like you were. Your skin is hard, your skin is soft. You put on Raccoon's coat and it swallows you." He laughed. "Your pants don't fit. Your insides don't fit. You wonder why you are on this earth. It is time to go back where I came from, give you young ones a chance.

"I have talked to Glooskap for many years. I have asked him many times, 'Were they all released?' He has never answered my question, until now. His answer is 'No.' This is what I have always believed—I was just waiting for him to say it. This is my story, Grandson. What is yours?"

Dark came early, and their grandfather led them for a time through that dark, much to Morgan's dismay, who kept his eye out for moose. Just as he decided he could not tolerate another branch slashed across his face, another step into barbed underbrush biting into calves and knees, his grandfather called a halt. They camped beside a pile of boulders, the wall of stone hiding the grandfather's modest fire. Morgan admired the way he corralled and controlled it, feeding it the way a sculptor might add clay to a new work. The way the fellow stared at the fire, regularly making adjustments to its fuel, whittling away at its boundaries, Morgan imagined he might be shaping it to fit his recollection of some previous fire, made when he was a younger man with no grandsons to drag around.

Of course that night by the fire their grandfather told them another story. It was essentially the same story he'd been telling them, with additions, reinterpretations of the more dramatic parts. Morgan thought he made it up as he went along, to fill the gaps in a failing memory. During one particularly loud and incoherent bit he whispered to his brother, "Did you hear that? He sees a firefly and that becomes a character in the story, he sees a squirrel and the squirrel suddenly walks on stage. Yesterday he saw that broken-down pickup and sure enough, it became a key feature in last night's version."

"Don't you see—the story goes on forever—it includes everything. No one could remember it all. So he tells us what he remembers, as he remembers it. The things he sees remind him of different parts. It's all one story, really, it just has a thousand parts, a thousand different versions."

Their grandfather's voice gradually became louder, as if trying to drown out their side-talk. "The giant Glooskap came walking into this land out of the sunrise. His head brushed the stars, while his feet scraped the ocean floor. There were no Indians here, only the Elves. Glooskap took his bow and arrows and shot into the basket-trees, the ash trees. The Indians lived inside there, hiding, sleeping. And wherever he shot the Indians woke up, and came out of that bark.

"Glooskap then made all the animals. He first made the animals huge, the moose, the squirrel, but since he loved the Indian the best he remade the animals smaller, so that the Indians could kill them. Only the mammoth refused, but Glooskap knew a great flood would come and drown him.

"We were like babies when we came out of the trees. We knew nothing. We cried and called for our mothers. Glooskap taught us how to build fires, how to make canoes, how to hunt the animals he had made for us.

"At the end of his days Glooskap left the earth for fairyland. He promised he would return, but he never has."

By dawn Morgan had just about had it. He couldn't sleep, finally passed out from exhaustion, woke up with sore spots up and down his torso from lying on uneven ground—rocks interspersed by mushy patches of damp ground, and half-eaten by the mosquitoes. He'd been so exhausted, and so cold, even under his fur-lined jacket, that he could not move enough even to get closer to the fire. He remembered worrying about his grandfather—he didn't even have a jacket!—but he'd been unable to think it through enough to do anything about it.

He gazed into the gray and pink-haloed light of morning, gasped as several deer wandered through with unexpected majesty, and saw his grandfather standing there, taking off all his clothes.

"What the hell? Granddad! Gary! Gary, do something!"

"Hey," Gary's voice issued from a pile of leaves on the other side of the dead fire. Morgan couldn't help admiring his brother's cleverness, and wished he'd built himself such a bed. "Hey, Grandpa. I don't think you really want to do that."

But their grandfather did not appear to hear them, his lips moving rapidly, almost inaudibly, in prayer or story. Both brothers scrambled to their feet, struggled to get their shoes on.

Before they could move to stop him, he had finished stripping off all his clothes, and was now passing through the trees, his arms outstretched, hands briefly caressing each tree as he passed. With each minute more light was exploding in the spaces between trunks and in the gaps of the branchy canopy overhead as daylight spread like an out-of-control fire. Morgan watched the aged legs as he stepped through low-growing bramble, winced as scratches appeared on his shins, blood mixing with wild blackberry stains over his flanks and wrinkled belly.

It seemed impossible, but whether because of his forest skills or some hidden reservoir of strength, he was faster than either one of them. They managed to barely keep him in sight (and that only, Morgan suspected, because he allowed it), but they could not catch him.

Finally he stopped before a stand of large trees and started dancing, gazing high up into the top branches as if he expected to see Glooskap's head nodding there. He was naked, bloody, and completely out of his mind. The distant Knife Edge was just visible above the trees, a glistening shard of sacrificial metal in the new sun.

Morgan and Gary stopped a couple of hundred feet away, and didn't even try to approach him. Morgan was doubled over, his head raised just enough to keep an eye on his grandfather, but he thought he was in serious danger of passing out. It gave him grim satisfaction that Gary, for all his Indian pride, looked no better.

"So that's . . ." He jerked his head to point. ". . . our legacy."

"Bro . . . you're not looking . . . at it . . . right."

"I see . . . a naked old man . . . exposed . . . to the elements . . . waltzing . . . through the woods . . . tearing . . . up his skin, trying to find . . . a particular tree . . . he's going to climb inside, because . . . that's where he originally came from. What else am I supposed to see?"

"He's doing something that *means* something to him. That's more than we can say for you. Or for me either, most of the time."

The brothers finally managed to straighten themselves up. They gazed at their grandfather, who'd stopped dancing. Now he just stood there, perfectly still, looking up into the tree.

"That's why he stopped," Gary said. "Just look at those trees, so close together they might as well be a solid wood wall. He's never going to get through them. You go over there and talk to him, try to calm him down. God, I hope he doesn't have a heart attack! I'll go get his clothes. He got to see the mountain, and all these trees. I think we can take him back now."

"Wait, I thought you said he had a right . . ."

"He does. But I didn't know . . . it would be like this. Did you?" Morgan shook his head. "But hey." Gary turned back down the trail. "At least now he's given us a helluva story to tell."

Morgan looked over at his grandfather, just as his grandfather walked into the trees.

"There's nothing to worry about," Gary said, walking beside him. "Just look at this, you can't move fast through here—I bet he's not more than half a dozen feet away, probably sitting on the ground, leaning against one of these trunks. You know he likes the feel of the bark."

"I know," Morgan said, straining his eyes, looking for a glimpse, any kind of indication their grandfather had been through here. Gary was right—it was slow going, almost impossible to move. The trunks were so close together, and the undergrowth so thick. A serious fire danger, he thought. He couldn't understand why the parks people had left it this way. And no signs of their grandfather's passage.

Gary said, "Really old people get like that, I've heard. They get . . . fixated . . . on a texture, a feeling, even a sound. They get compulsive like that."

Eventually they split up to cover more ground, calling back and forth so that they, too, did not lose each other. Here *was* the forest primeval, it seemed. It was difficult to conceive of human beings controlling this kind of growth. Here the forest was sky, and ground, and everything in between. Here it was the air you breathed.

"Hey . . ." Morgan called, and heard his brother's distant, responsive *hey*.

He struggled to raise his knees within a particularly dense tangle of limbs and vines, lifted his head, and saw the enormous tanned leg, its foot jammed into the ground, raising the forest floor around it, the top of the leg, approximately where the thigh must begin, hidden within the dense cover above.

He thought to turn and struggle his way out of there, but instead pushed forward, unable to turn away from this living bit of his grandfather's creation story. He felt silly when he got there—from a few feet away it was obviously bark, not skin, just the biggest tree he'd ever seen, personally. He got right up on it, and could not help reaching out, and touch, and found it to be as rough and textured as he'd expected, and yet meant, somehow, for his hand. He was weak from the search, and the bark seemed to move under his skin, and in the soft sigh of wood breath, he heard, "You tell your own story. You make it up as you go along."

He tilted his head to hear better. "This is my story—what is yours?"

And looking off the edge of the tree, saw that a face had appeared there, just around the edge: dark and smooth and untroubled, with little character reflecting the simple wear and tear of living. It was a baby's face, if that baby were six feet tall and in his twenties.

It disappeared, and Morgan scrambled around the perimeter of the tree, and saw the naked skin flashing through slits in the dense foliage, moving impossibly fast.

They made their way out and reported the disappearance, but when they led the parks people back to where they thought they had last seen their grandfather, there was no sign of the dense stand of trees, and nothing like the massive tree Morgan had encountered. Growth like that, they were told, did not exist here.

They were in a great deal of trouble, and both did jail time, and both were scared, but thought they deserved it. Gary's dad hired the lawyer, who told them they didn't need to go to jail. No one thought they'd done away with him. They'd just been reckless, and lost him. But they refused to speak in court of the experience, and that angered the judge. They had their story, they said, but it was a family tale they didn't want to share.

"His name was Joseph," Morgan told the judge. "I called him the old Indian because that's what my mother called him. But his name was Joseph, and he was Passamaquoddy."

"He was our grandfather," was all Gary would say.

Three weeks after their grandfather's disappearance, some hikers found a young Indian man, naked, up on the Knife Edge. He spoke mostly gibberish, grunts, and a few Passamaquoddy words, and apparently unable to hunt, had been surviving on berries and carrion. When asked where he'd come from, he pointed to the trees below, and repeated "*Nikuwoss! Nikuwoss!*" A local man translated it as "My mother! My mother!" The papers ran articles on feral children over the next several weeks, but as so often happens, news of this nameless Indian gradually faded away.

ABOUT THE
CONTRIBUTORS

KAREN JORDAN ALLEN grew up in Indiana and earned a master's degree from Yale Divinity School, but she has now spent half her life in Maine and expects never to live anywhere else. Her fiction and nonfiction have been published in a number of magazines and anthologies, including *Asimov's Science Fiction, Maine Times, Bates: The Alumni Magazine, A Nightmare's Dozen, The First Heroes: New Tales of the Bronze Age,* and *Interfictions: An Anthology of Interstitial Writing.* When not writing, she moonlights as a pianist and Spanish teacher.

LEE ALLRED's stories have appeared in publications ranging from *Asimov's Science Fiction* magazine to DC Comics, but he is perhaps best known for his Civil War stories, such as "East of Appomattox" (*Alternate Generals* III) and "For the Strength of the Hills" (*Writers of the Future* Volume 13). The latter was a finalist for the Sidewise Award for Alternate History. He served three tours of duty in Iraq and recalls that upon return from his first tour, his plane touched down in Portland where he was greeted warmly by a large group of Mainers.

JACK L. CHALKER (1944–2005) was born in Baltimore, Maryland, where he taught history for more than 10 years. Among his several awards is the New England Science Fiction Society's E. E. Smith Memorial Award. Best known for his novel *Midnight at the Well of Souls* and its sequels, he published more than 60 novels in addition to numerous works of short fiction and nonfiction. He founded the Baltimore Science Fiction Society, Mirage Press, and among his avocations was an abiding interest in ferryboats.

NOREEN DOYLE has lived most of her life in Maine. Publications featuring her fiction and nonfiction include *Realms of Fantasy, Weird Tales, The Mammoth Book of Egyptian Whodunnits, Dig, The Greenwood*

Encyclopedia of Science Fiction and Fantasy and *Fantasy: The Best of the Year, 2008 Edition*. With Harry Turtledove she edited the World Fantasy Award-nominated *The First Heroes: New Tales of the Bronze Age*. She earned a B.A. from the University of Maine (anthropology and art) and M.A.s from Texas A&M (nautical archaeology) and the University of Liverpool (Egyptology).

Author or editor of more than 80 books, GARDNER DOZOIS edited *Asimov's Science Fiction* for 20 years and has been compiling *The Year's Best Science Fiction* collections since 1984. During that time he has won the Hugo Award for Best Professional Editor 15 times. His short fiction has also earned two Nebula Awards. His most recent novel, co-written with George R. R. Martin and Daniel Abraham, is *Hunter's Run*. Born in Salem, Massachusetts, he now lives in Philadelphia.

TOM EASTON holds a doctorate in theoretical biology from the University of Chicago and teaches at Thomas College in Waterville, Maine. His recent nonfiction books include *Classic Editions Sources: Environmental Studies, Taking Sides: Clashing Views on Controversial Issues in Science, Technology, and Society*, and *Off the Main Sequence: Science Fiction and the Non-Mass Market*. His latest novels are *Firefight* and *The Great Flying Saucer Conspiracy*. He has been writing the book review column for the SF magazine *Analog* since 1979.

GREGORY FEELEY is the author of *The Oxygen Barons, Arabian Wine*, and many novellas, stories, and articles. His fiction, which has earned Nebula Award and Philip K. Dick Award nominations, can be found in *Asimov's Science Fiction, Interzone*, and many other magazines and anthologies, including several best-of-the-year volumes. He lives three small states away from Maine, which he visits whenever he can for its bookstores and hiking trails.

ELIZABETH HAND is the multiple-award-winning author of numerous novels, including the psychological thriller *Generation Loss* and the contemporary fantasies *Illyria, Mortal Love*, and three short fiction collections. She is a longtime contributor of book reviews and essays to many publications, including *Down East* magazine, the *Washington Post Book World*, and *Salon*. She moved to Maine in 1988, where she lives in

Lincolnville Center with her two teenage children and her partner, UK critic John Clute. "Echo" won a Nebula Award in 2007.

Now an editor with 30 years in journalism, DANIEL HATCH has been a reporter for, among other newspapers, *The New York Times*. He is also a veteran of the U.S. Coast Guard. Today he lives in Springfield, Massachusetts, though his ancestors moved to what later became Maine. He has resided in Lisbon Falls and spent time every summer on Tripp Lake in West Poland, where he has had occasion to go after that largemouth bass hiding in the reeds and the shallow water.

JEFF HECHT is a free-lance science and technology writer whose articles can be found in such periodicals as *Omni, Earth, Cosmos*, and *Bulletin of the Atomic Scientists*. His short fiction has appeared in *Analog, Asimov's, Interzone, Nature*, and other magazines and anthologies. His books include *Beam: the Race to Make the Laser, City of Light: The Story of Fiber Optics*, and *Understanding Fiber Optics*. He earned his B.S. electronic engineering from the California Institute of Technology and vacations regularly in Maine.

LUCY SUITOR HOLT was born in Knox, Maine, and earned a degree from Rivier College in Nashua, New Hampshire. Now living in New Hampshire, she has served as a board member of The Monadnock Writers' Group. She produced *Occasional Shadows*, an audio CD of her short stories, and her short fiction can also be found in *Whispers from the Shattered Forum* and the online *Moxie Magazine*.

EDWARD KENT (1802–1877) served twice as Maine's governor, 1838–1830 and 1841–1842. During his first term in office, the bloodless Aroostook War broke out and resulted in fixing the disputed boundary between Maine and Canada. Fort Kent was named in his honor. Not generally known as a fiction writer, Kent contributed "A Vision of Bangor in the Twentieth Century" to the so-called "Bangor Book," published in 1848 as *Voices from the Kenduskeag* to raise funds for a girls' orphanage.

One of the most important writers in America today, Maine native STEPHEN KING has published more than 50 novels, most recently

Duma Key. His body of work earned the Medal for Distinguished Contribution to American Letters from the National Book Foundation in 2003. He is an active philanthropist, providing scholarships for local students and supporting charities in Maine and beyond. Most of the year he lives in Bangor with his wife, writer Tabitha King.

JOHN P. O'GRADY was born in New Jersey, but escaped to the University of Maine to study forestry, believing this was a chance to dwell in deep groves and sequestered places. His environmentalist sensibilities were not encouraged in Nutting Hall, so he went on to pursue graduate studies in literature. He now works full-time as an astrologer in San Francisco. He has authored two books, *Pilgrims to the Wild* and *Grave Goods: Essays of a Peculiar Nature*, and co-edited an anthology, *Literature & the Environment*.

Born in New York to literary parents, EDGAR PANGBORN (1909–1976) made his literary debut pseudonymously, with a mystery novel in 1930 and short stories for the pulp detective and mystery magazines. In the early 1950s he began to write mysteries and science fiction under his own name. His work helped to firmly establish a new "humanist" school of science fiction. The post-apocalyptic *Davy* remains the most famous of his novels. In 2003 he was recognized with the Cordwainer Smith Rediscovery Award. He spent 1939–1942 farming in rural Maine.

JESSICA REISMAN grew up on the east coast of the U.S., was a teenager on the west coast, and now lives in Austin, Texas. She learned to swim in Maine lakes as a child, went to college, raked blueberries, and learned to be a film projectionist there, among other things. She is a writer, reader, and movie aficionado. Her fiction can be found in magazines and anthologies, including *Cross Plains Universe*, edited by Scott Cupp and Joe R. Lansdale, and *Sci Fiction*. Her first novel, *The Z Radiant*, was published in 2004.

MELANIE TEM is a novelist and playwright. The Rocky Mountain Women's Institute awarded her an associateship for 2001–2002. Her novel *Prodigal* won a Bram Stoker Award, as did *The Man on the Ceiling* (written with her husband, writer and editor Steve Rasnic Tem), which also went on to win International Horror Guide and World Fantasy awards. Among her 14 collaborative and solo novels are *Blood Moon, Wilding, Revenant,* and *Daughters.* Also a social worker, she lives in Denver with her husband.

Author of more than 300 published short stories, STEVE RASNIC TEM is a Denver-based writer whose fiction has been honored with the Bram Stoker Award, British Fantasy Award, International Horror Guild Award, and World Fantasy Award. His stories can be found in such annual anthologies as *Year's Best Fantasy and Horror, Best New Horror,* magazines including *The Magazine of Fantasy & Science Fiction,* and two collections, *City Fishing* and *The Far Side of the Lake.* His co-wrote his novel *The Man on the Ceiling* with his wife, Melanie Tem.

SCOTT THOMAS was born in Marlborough, Massachusetts. To escape urban sprawl, he moved to Maine in 2003 and settled Down East. He is the author of five short story collections, including *Westermead, Over the Darkening Fields,* and *Midnight in New England.* He co-authored the collection *Punktown: Shades of Grey* with his brother Jeffrey Thomas. His fiction has appeared also in the anthologies *The Year's Best Fantasy and Horror, Crypto-Critters* Volumes 1 and 2 and *Leviathan Three.*

Born in Concord, Massachusetts, American writer and philosopher HENRY DAVID THOREAU (1817–1862) is best known for *Walden; or Life in the Woods,* an account of his two-year stay at Walden Pond where he sought, in relative but not complete isolation, to examine human society. *Walden* and "On the Duty of Civil Disobedience" inspired later political and social activists from Martin Luther King, Jr. to Mahatma Ghandi. He made three trips to Maine, of which he wrote in the collected essays *The Maine Woods.*

TOM TOLNAY founded Birch Brook Press and is managing editor of the literary magazine *Pulpsmith.* His fiction has appeared in the *Saturday Evening Post, Woman's Day, Maine Guide, Ellery Queen's Mystery Magazine,* and other magazines. His short story "The Ghost of F. Scott

Fitzgerald," winner of *Literal Latte* Short Story Award, has been produced as a short film screened at the Toronto International and Hollywood film festivals. His most recent novel is *This is the Forest Primeval*, set in western Maine.

MARK TWAIN is the pen name of Samuel Clemens (1835–1910), one of the most important American writers. Born in Florida, Missouri, Clemens worked first as a printer, then as a Mississippi riverboat pilot. During the Civil War he became a reporter, and soon after his fiction followed, including *The Adventures of Tom Sawyer* and *The Adventures of Huckleberry Finn*, He visited Maine on his lecture tours and summered at York Harbor in 1902.

ACKNOWLEDGMENTS

"Alternate Anxieties," © 2007 by Karen Jordan Allen, first appeared in *Interfictions: An Anthology of Interstitial Writing*, edited by Delia Sherman and Theodora Goss; reprinted by permission of the author.

"And Dream Such Dreams," © 2008 by Lee Allred; printed by permission of the author.

"The Autumn of Sorrows," © 2008 by Scott Thomas; printed by permission of the author.

"Awskonomuk," © 2008 by Gregory Feeley; printed by permission of the author.

"Bass Fishing with the Enemy," © 2008 by Daniel Hatch; printed by permission of the author.

"The Bung-Hole Caper," © 1982 by Tom Easton; first appeared in *The Magazine of Fantasy & Science Fiction*; reprinted by permission of the author.

"By the Lake," © 2002 by Jeff Hecht; first appeared in *Analog*; reprinted by permission of the author.

"The Chapter of the Hawk of Gold," © 1997, 2008 by Noreen Doyle; first appeared in *Realms of Fantasy*; revised and reprinted by permission of the author.

"The County," © 2008 by Melanie Tem; printed by permission of the author.

"Creation Story," © 2008 by Steve Rasnic Tem; printed by permission of the author.

"Dance Band on the *Titanic*," © 1978 by Jack L. Chalker; first appeared in *Isaac Asimov's Science Fiction Magazine*; reprinted by permission of Eva Whitley.

"Dreams of Virginia Dare," © 2001 by John P. O'Grady; first appeared in *Grave Goods: Essays of a Peculiar Nature* by John P. O'Grady; reprinted by permission of the author.

NOREEN DOYLE writes fiction and articles for adults and children. She holds degrees in Anthropology and Art, Nautical Archeology, and Egyptology. Her fiction has appeared in *Fantasy: The Best of the Year 2008 Edition*, *The Mammoth Book of Egyptian Whodunits* and in *Realms of Fantasy*. She co-edited, with Harry Turtledove, *First Heroes: New Tales of the Bronze Age*, a book that was nominated for the World Fantasy Award. She resides in Gardiner, Maine.